# MIAMI
# MIDNIGHT

## A PETE FERNANDEZ MYSTERY

# MIAMI MIDNIGHT

## A PETE FERNANDEZ MYSTERY

# ALEX SEGURA

POLIS BOOKS

Copyright © 2019 by Alex Segura
Cover and jacket design by 2Faced Design

ISBN 978-1-947993-59-4
eISBN 978-1-947993-84-6
Library of Congress Control Number: 2019943438

First hardcover edition August 2019 by Polis Books, LLC
221 River St., 9th Fl., #9070

Hoboken, NJ 07030
www.PolisBooks.com

**POLIS BOOKS**

# ALSO BY
# ALEX SEGURA

"When you get a cat to catch the mice in your kitchen, you can't expect it to ignore the rats in the cellar."
-Philip Kerr, *March Violets*

"The past was worth remembering and knowing in its own right. It was not behind us, never truly behind us, but under us, holding us up, a foundation for all that was to come and everything that had ever been."
-Laura Lippman, *In a Strange City*

*For Eva, Guillermo, and Lucia. My heart.*

# PART I
# I LOST YOU

# BIG EXIT

*January 1, 1984*

**"Y**ou don't want to go in there, Osvaldito."
The deputy's words seemed to float in the air around the
entrance to the room, like fading smoke. As Detective Osvaldo
Valdez approached, the deputy backed away. Osvaldo knew he had
little choice in the matter. He had to walk into the dim, dank hotel
room that was already being cordoned off by yellow tape. The stuffy
hallway, reeking of cheap cologne and sweat, had been cramped with
uniforms and a forensics unit, but the room itself was empty—aside
from the body splayed out near the far window.

The woman—late thirties, skinny, brunette, hair cut short but not
boyish—lay on the floor at an odd angle. Her head was twisted up, as
if trying to look out the dirty, smudged window—the only source of
natural light in the dingy hotel room.

Osvaldo did his best to keep his footfalls light. He'd been on the
Miami Homicide team for a little over six months. His partner, Tino
Vigil, was catching another body downtown. That left Osvaldo here
in Overtown, feeling itchy and hot in the decrepit Hampton House
Hotel, checking on a body. The owner had called it in—complaining
that the man who'd rented the room had bailed, leaving him fifty

1

bucks short. He'd prattled on about the noise, too, the screaming. More than your usual Overtown kerfuffle. More than your usual New Year's Eve partying, too. Serious wailing. Thuds. *Boom-boom-crash*. Real loud, then dead quiet. Too quiet.

Osvaldo motioned over his shoulder for one of the uniformed officers, a kid named Mosher, to come in behind him.

"Don't touch anything yet, okay?" Osvaldo said. "I wanna get a feel for it first."

He stepped further into the room, his arms out a bit, palms open, as if trying to catch something, a sign of what had happened there. Static. Nothing.

But then, something, as he stepped closer, and a sliver of the New Year's Day sun fell on the woman's face, bruised and bloodied, illuminating the dark, purple marks around her neck, scratches streaking down toward her collarbone. Past the cuts and injuries, Osvaldo recognized something. A flicker of familiarity snapped at him.

"Fuck," he said, his eyes scanning the woman's face once more. Not just a woman. Not just a Jane Doe. Not anymore.

He wheeled around. He felt himself heat up, a sheen of sweat spread over him, prickling his back, then his face. *This can't be right*. But he knew it was true. Mosher, who had been shadowing his movements, jerked back, surprised by Osvaldo's quick pivot. The detective looked at the younger man, with his trimmed beard and eager eyes. *Those will fade soon*, Osvaldo thought. *You'll become a zombie, just like the rest of us.*

The ones who survive.

"Get everyone out of here except essential personnel," Osvaldo said, his tone flat, eyes locked on Mosher, who nodded. "And then get Carlos Broche on the phone. Fast."

*March 15, 2018*

Isleño Novo pulled his small suitcase from the overhead bin and waited for the people in front of him to disembark. The Newark-to-Miami flight had been pleasant enough. He'd even had an empty seat between him and the lady at the window. That was best, Novo thought. He didn't do well with small talk.

As the group filtered off the plane and through the gate into Miami International Airport, Novo veered right as the majority went left, toward Baggage Claim. He pulled a small black burner phone out of his coat pocket and dialed the number from memory. He already felt the tropical heat coating him, like a brush soaked in oil. He hated Miami.

"*Aquí estoy*," Novo said. *I'm here.*

The voice on the other line was flat and muted. Their exchange was brief. Numbers and a few words.

Novo closed the phone and tossed it into the first trash bin he passed on his way out of the airport. He'd memorized the address. The people who had paid for him to fly down to this festering hellhole would have a car waiting outside. The sign would read "Batista." He'd get in the forgettable black sedan and nod at the driver. On the way to meet his bosses—short-term bosses; Novo worked for himself, mostly—he'd get his uniform. His suit.

It was not a role Novo had sought, but he had to take it. His partner, Darien, back in Union City, was in awe when Novo told him. Impressed.

"They must really respect you, Isleño, to give you a job like this."

They'd equip him with a silencer and give him his marching orders. All those things were easy enough to transport. To get the job done, close-range. And Novo only worked up-close these days. His time as a long-range sniper, picking off Castro's goons in the mountains, and, later, from within Havana, trying to shoot his way back to freedom, was over. He was a legitimate businessman. Older, respected. Sometimes, when he laid his head down on his pillow and turned off the lights, he could see himself living a life purely financed by his "legitimate" earnings—the bodega on Central Avenue, the hardware store a few blocks north—but then he'd laugh, because he knew that day would never come. No matter how carefully Novo cleaned his money, or how much he scaled back his "real" work, he'd never be out of the game. A fighter too punch-drunk to know when to stop.

And this assignment was just too good to ignore. It was one he'd savor.

So, he'd do as he was told. He'd put on the long black coat and hat. He'd load the silencer. Then he'd make his way toward his target. He'd find the perfect time to sidle up next to the man. And, if he could, before the trigger was pulled, he'd whisper the words he'd been asked to say:

"The DeCalvacantes say hello."

Then he'd kill Pete Fernandez.

# CHAPTER ONE

**"W**hat are you working on now?" she asked, her tone relaxed, peaceful. "A new case?"

"I told you, I'm retired. I'm out of that game. For good this time."

Pete Fernandez squirmed on the long, leather couch as he faced his therapist, Allie Kaplan. Her posture was confident, present. Her demeanor was polished but casual as she sat across from Pete. Kaplan was in her mid-forties, with long black hair. She was well built with smooth features. She looked comfortable and relaxed, two things Pete hadn't experienced in what felt like centuries.

His body was in shambles. His left shin ached if the temperature dipped below seventy degrees—the spot where mafia captain Vincent Salerno had slammed his heel, before he left Pete for dead. Pete's jaw clicked if he yawned or laughed too hard—residual damage from too many punches to the chin. The pale white skin of his of his chest looked like it had been splattered with dark purple paint, a cornucopia of bruises and cuts healing at different speeds. That was the superficial stuff. Some nights, before sleep, Pete would feel the jolt—the first push from the first shot that entered his body. His back would tighten and his legs would spasm, as if bracing for another. Another shot to put him down for good.

Pete knew he was lucky to be alive. To have come *back* to life. For a minute or two, he'd been gone—the bullet holes in his chest had done him in, the bruises and cuts and broken bones combined with blood loss to write the final lines in Pete's story. But somehow, that wasn't enough. An FBI agent named Dave Sternbergh got to him. He'd been sitting in his unmarked car, waiting for his partner, Amanda Chopp, to return. He'd seen a suspicious figure follow Amanda into Pete's Spring Valley, New York office. Sternbergh pursued slowly. Faster, once he heard the gunshots. Even faster when he saw his partner of seven years dead on the floor and Pete Fernandez bleeding out a few feet away.

It'd been close. Pete would never fully recover. Months of physical therapy helped fix the external problems, fix them enough so he could live. But the flies buzzing around in his head were another matter. The white noise that coated every thought, every action. That's why he was here, in a small office buried in a nondescript building off Coral Way, sharing his deepest-darkest with a therapist who didn't really seem to buy Pete's stump speech: that he was fine. He was happy to be alive. He was retired. He was doing great.

*Because it wasn't true.*

"You keep saying that," she said. "But what does that mean?"

"It means, well, I'm out of the game," Pete said.

"Are you? You've done things that say you are out of the game," she said, a humorless, polite smile on her face. "But then you've done other things that say the opposite, I think."

"Like what?" Pete asked. "I mean, I'm barely a private investigator anymore—I don't even carry my gun. So what, then?"

"The self-defense training, for one."

"I think my ... my life experience has shown me it'd be good to know how to defend myself."

"I think that's valid."

"I was dead, clinically dead," Pete said, running a hand through his hair. "I survived. I had to figure out how to ... how to never be in that situation again. How to never find myself just relying on pure luck and my wits to survive."

"How do you feel now?"

"I feel stronger," Pete said. "I'm not scared. The aikido and gym time have been a good release, I guess. A good way to get my mind off of things."

"But wouldn't you think—and I'm just raising the question—that training in this way suggests you're ... preparing for something?"

"No, not at all," Pete said. "I'm just working at the bookstore, and that gets me enough to live. It's not the most exciting thing, but—"

"But it's enough?" she asked. "Would you say that?"

"Yes," Pete said. "It's peaceful. I've survived enough. I saw ... I was—"

"When you got shot?" she asked. "What did you see?"

"I saw a blackness," Pete said. "A void. An endless nothing .... Then I was back, like I'd been jarred awake from a deep, dark dream that was spreading out in all directions, like some kind of fast-moving oil spill. Then I was awake, and there were faces around me and I was ... It hurt so much. I was hurting everywhere, like I'd never felt—"

"But you've made so much progress," she said, leaning forward. "I mean, look at you. I wouldn't be able to tell—"

Pete winced. He knew she was lying. He had a thick beard now, to hide the scrapes and bruising on his face as best he could. If he walked too fast, he limped slightly. He had trouble lifting his arms above his head. And he would never be able to try out for the Dolphins. But, yes. He was alive. He had to remind himself of that.

"You don't have to tell me," Pete said. "I'm grateful to be alive."

"It's okay if you're not."

Pete looked up at Allie. Her expression was blank, waiting.

"What?"

"It's okay to resent being alive, is what I'm saying. Maybe part of you wanted to die that day."

Pete shook his head. "That's insane."

"Is it?" she said. "Your life—at least the last five years—has involved people gunning for you, friends dying, extreme physical and mental trauma, and lots of tragedy and infamy. You've done a lot of good, but I imagine that was as exhausting as life can get, right? To what end? You're working at a bookstore, your body is a mess, you're single, and you have no real family or friends to speak of."

"Wow, doc," Pete said, a dry laugh escaping his mouth. "And here I thought therapy was supposed to make me feel better."

"It is, eventually. But first, we need to look at things as they are, not just pretend it's great. And I think you're doing the latter. Pretending. Resigning yourself. But I think—and look, you can tell me to go to hell if you want—I think you must have learned something over the last few years, right? Realized you were good at some part of what was going on?"

"So?" Pete asked. "That little flicker of hope should keep me on the same track?"

"No," Allie said. "But it's something. It's more than just being stuck in a self-inflicted purgatory. You seemed to—on some level— like what you were doing. But for whatever reason, you chose not to fully embrace it. You just bumbled through it, barely surviving. It had consequences. But now it feels like you're preparing for something, while also denying that anything's coming."

Pete crossed his arms and looked away, not responding.

Allie pressed on. "Pete, you're a good man, a good person. I know that much from just sitting here and talking to you every week for the last few months. You've made mistakes. Who hasn't? Maybe the answer to the pain, the plan moving forward, isn't to shelter yourself from the stuff that's gone wrong, but to push forward with a clearer idea of what you want. Does that make sense? You're acting out of fear—and that's understandable. You almost died. But maybe the answer is to embrace who you are, to get better at that, rather than run from it, you know?"

Pete stood up abruptly.

"I think I have to go," he said.

"Pete, listen," Allie said.

"Can you just bill my card?"

"Pete," she said, grabbing his arm—the contact feeling electric and out of place, like a priest reaching across the confessional. "I know you're processing a lot. It's fine if you walk out. Just know I'm around if you need anything, okay? I'm here."

Pete nodded and moved toward the door, not waiting for Kaplan to continue, his footsteps growing fainter on the faded linoleum floor.

Pete mouthed a silent prayer as he stepped into the restaurant's foyer. Le Chic, a cozy eatery in the trendy Wynwood area, specialized in gussied-up comfort food. He could already feel the vibrations from the music blasting inside—Black Eyed Peas' obnoxious earworm, "Let's Get It Started"—as he reached for the door.

*Just make an appearance.*

The place was packed, the space felt hot and electric. The small dance floor spilled out into the restaurant's main dining area, a wave of swerving and gyrating bodes. They'd cleared the tables for the event, but the extra space was barely noticeable. The party felt chaotic, wild—as if it were building to some unknown crescendo, Pete thought. The restaurant was dimly lit, with most of the light coming from around the long, oak bar at the far end of the place and from the multiple TVs perched above the crowd playing the local news.

This might be easier than he'd anticipated. He might just be able to pop in, say hi, and slither out. Then he felt a tug at his arm.

"Thought you were gonna ghost this thing."

Pete turned around to see Robert Harras, ex-FBI spook with at least half a heart. They'd been through the fire together a few times. Pete considered him a friend. One of the few he still had.

"I told Kathy I'd be here," Pete said with a weary smile. "Good to see you."

"Good to see you, too," the older man said. "You're looking almost back to normal."

Pete nodded. They both knew Pete was far from "back to normal"—whatever that meant. Less than a year ago, he was being pushed into a New York emergency room on a gurney, his life signs flat and his blood loss heavy, the victim of a gunshot to the chest from a rogue mobster named Vinnie Salerno. It'd capped off a flurry of events that had left Pete destroyed—literally and figuratively. He'd just returned to New York, his makeshift home at the time, to collect his life and head back to Miami, energized and reinvigorated and, most importantly, eager to carve out a new place for himself in his hometown, surrounded by friends like his investigative partner Kathy Bentley and Harras.

Instead, he died. For a few seconds, at least.

"How's business?" Harras said, cutting through the silence between them. The DJ had taken a break, allowing the revelers to migrate toward the bar and reload their glasses.

Pete scanned the crowd. He caught a glimpse of Kathy, near a makeshift stage. She was smiling, her face pink and gleaming from dancing and drinking. Behind her was a banner—CONGRATULATIONS MARCO AND KATHY!—written in blocky, neon letters.

"Bookstore is fine," Pete said, not looking at Harras. "Quiet."

"Nice change of pace, eh?" Harras said. "Enjoying retirement?"

Pete shrugged. He looked at his watch.

"Bored already? Can't remember the last time I saw you. You're not hiding out again, are you?"

*You're not isolating and drinking again, are you?*

*You're not avoiding your friends, are you?*

That's what Harras meant, whether he knew it or not. Pete was an alcoholic. Always would be. But at the moment, for today, he was sober. Had been for a few years now. It had not been an easy road, and it was the kind of thing that required constant upkeep—meetings, prayer, and conversations with other alcoholics—just to make it through the day. But the upside was impossible to quantify. It meant Pete had a chance to live a life. That was something he hadn't even fully realized until recently, as he felt his life slipping away.

"I've been busy," Pete said, meeting his friend's stare. Pete knew what he looked like—weary, sad, worn out.

*You've lost weight.*

*Are you doing okay?*

*You should come out more.*

*What was it like?*

*Did you see a light?*

He knew he'd touched death. That his life had ended, for a moment. Yet now, a year later—Pete could not recall a time he'd ever felt more alive. But it was coated with a sadness he'd had trouble even beginning to shake. There was a sense of dread and finality that he couldn't figure out or remove. He shook his head with a slight jerk, as if to shrug off the feeling and touch the real world, the real things in front of him now. Like Harras. Like this party, and the reason he was here.

"I'm working a lot.... Trying to keep the bookstore going takes up most of my time. But I'm glad to see you. You're right—it's been too long."

Harras started to respond, but Pete felt himself being pushed forward, an arm wrapping around his shoulder.

"Well, look who decided to show their face?"

*Kathy.*

"Wouldn't miss it," Pete said, leaning into her, welcoming the embrace. She was glowing—her smile natural and warm, her flowing sundress almost radiant with its own light. Kathy's movements seemed sludgy but content—she was working a good buzz, no doubt, Pete thought.

She pulled back, leaning toward the restaurant's jammed dance floor, her hand tugging at Pete.

"Well, come on then," she said, her voice rising to be heard over the DJ's latest song—Taylor Swift's "Gorgeous." "You owe me at least one dance before you disappear without saying goodbye."

He looked at Harras, who responded with a noncommittal smirk. Pete let Kathy drag him into the crowd, bodies moving and sliding over each other, the temperature jumping up at least five degrees. The restaurant seemed to sway with each rhythmic change of the song, as Swift's ode to a perfect, unattainable lover hit its chorus crescendo. They reached the center of the dance floor and Kathy leaned into him, her breath tinged with the smell of red wine and something minty, her cheek warm against his.

"Where have you been, Pete?"

"I'm here," he said, his body close to hers, their posture stiff but electric, one hand on her lower back, his other hand gripping hers.

"You're late." The words poured out, like a pout, but Pete knew it was frustration. She wanted him to be happy about this. If he could be happy about one thing, it should be this.

"I'm sorry," he said. "But I'm here. I know it was important for you."

He knew the words were wrong when he finished the sentence, even if the sentiment was genuine. She pulled back, her face in front of his, her eyes clear and probing.

"It should be important for you to be here, period," she said, her tone sharp, but not fully combative, perhaps lulled a bit by the drink and celebratory evening.

Still, a warning to tread carefully. Kathy was his partner when it came to his now-paused investigative work, when she wasn't working full-time for a local culture site, *The New Tropic*. She was also his closest friend. But both of those relationships lived under a cloud of something else—a spark between them that was more than friendship and certainly more than professional. A spark that had

11

brought them together in ways he was still trying to untangle. If you'd asked Pete almost a year ago what was most important to him, as he boarded a plane to New York to gather his belongings and return to Miami, he wouldn't have hesitated. Kathy. She was it. His last, best hope at something. But after looking into a void he could have never imagined, he'd come out of the whole ordeal broken and wary. By the time he'd recovered and scraped some kind of life together, Kathy had moved on.

*Moved on* wasn't exactly true. She'd been clear with Pete, even before he boarded that fateful flight, that their prospects were dim. She valued his friendship over any kind of romance—a road she'd been down already and found wanting. From the moment they'd wheeled him into Spring Valley General, she'd been there. Waiting for him to wake up. Holding his hand through physical therapy, cheering him on. Pete vowed this would be the last time. He was done with danger. Done with drug gangs and explosions and murder. Kathy took him at his word. Helped him get situated with the bookstore and applauded his other efforts, too. They'd become closer than ever, Pete thought. But at the same time, she'd met Marco Lopez, a Miami real estate developer she'd interviewed for a piece on the burgeoning market as a freelance assignment for *The New Tropic*. Marco ended the interview with the offer of dinner. Kathy passed, but he persisted. Six months later, they were celebrating their engagement and Pete was just a guest who showed up late. Story of his life.

"You're right," Pete said, as they moved to the music, her cheek on his. "I'm happy for you. This is great."

"That's better," she said. "Even if you don't really mean it."

She draped her arms over his shoulders as the song shifted from T-Swift to "Just One of the Guys" by Jenny Lewis. The song's dreamy guitar intro wove around them as Lewis sang about friends getting on and girls staying young.

"Talk to me, Pete," she said. "I never see you. You look good, if slightly under your fighting weight. But definitely better. How are you?"

The music seemed to grow louder, enveloping him in a cloud of noise, adding a buffer between him and Kathy, even though she was close enough to kiss now. He could feel her breath on his face.

"I'm fine," Pete said, the words coming out in a stammer, unrehearsed. He wasn't fine, really. He wanted to scream. He'd debated whether to come here at all, whether he was really up for the torture of seeing Kathy celebrate being engaged to another man. But he'd shown up. Wasn't that something his AA friend Jack often said? *Most of life is about showing up.*

So, here he was. Being a good friend, feeling his insides churn, and hoping for a quick, painless exit.

"May I have this dance?"

They both turned to see a slightly younger man, tan, his black hair finely gelled, in a sharp gray suit. His smile was wide, but stopped short of his eyes. Marco Lopez had seemed puzzled by Pete since they met. Not because Pete was particularly mysterious. Marco seemed mostly curious about Pete's dynamic with his soon-to-be wife. He wanted to figure out what kept Pete and Kathy together—why they remained close after so much loss and violence. At least that was Pete's take. He might just not like Pete, which would put him in pretty esteemed company. Still, Pete understood the etiquette, and even if he wasn't fully on Team Marco, he was Kathy's friend, and he'd respect the process.

"Of course," Pete said, stepping back and motioning for Marco to join his fiancée. "It's your night."

"Pete," Kathy said, as Marco led her deeper into the crowd of dancers, her face resting on Marco's shoulder. "Don't you leave before we get to talk, okay? I will kill you myself."

Pete tapped the unlock button on the car key and heard the familiar beep as he approached his black Toyota Camry. He waited for the footsteps behind him to stop before he turned around to see Robert Harras.

"Leaving so soon?"

"I'm not much of a party guy," Pete said. "Not anymore."

Harras reached into his jacket and pulled out a can of Amstel Light, which he'd presumably swiped from the party. He popped it open and took a swig.

"If this bothers you, I can—"

Pete waved him off. "It's fine."

"Been hearing some weird rumbling."

"Oh?"

"Yeah, stuff simmering for a while," Harras said, looking out into the sludgy-hot Miami night. "You really upset the apple cart with Los Enfermos and that cult."

"We did that together," Pete said. "You were part of it."

"Don't get all defensive yet. I'm not finished," Harras said.

Los Enfermos, a Castro-fueled drug gang, had been presumed dead a few years back. But the remnants of the gun-happy gangsters had gone after Pete and Kathy a year ago, while the duo investigated the Miami cult known as La Iglesia de la Luz. Strange bedfellows and all that. It had seemingly ended with the gang's leader, Lionel Oliva, dead, his head splayed on the road that connected Miami to Key West.

"Are Los Enfermos back?"

"No, not exactly," Harras said. "But my contacts at the Bureau think people are trying to pick up those pieces—namely, the cocaine trade. Los Enfermos still exist, in some way, but they're not big enough to make much noise. Yet. In the meantime, it's looking like other people are stepping in and trying to make a go of running drugs through Miami."

"New boss, same as the old boss," Pete said. "What can I do to help?"

"Not sure yet. My info is spotty. I'm the definition of 'out of the loop' these days," Harras said. "What else are you working on? Gimme something interesting to talk about, at least. I've been leaning against a wall, slowly going deaf in there. My deepest conversation was with the waiter, who is somehow a Seattle Mariners fan in Miami."

Pete cracked a smile. Harras and Kathy were right. He hadn't seen them much over the last few months. Once he'd healed enough to be released from the hospital, Kathy fell into her relationship with Marco, checking in with Pete by phone or email every week or so. Harras wasn't much for phone chats, texts, or email, so Pete heard from him even less. After the events of the last year—the death of Jackie Cruz, the battles with the cult, and Pete's near-death encounter—he couldn't blame them for wanting to take a break.

"It's been quiet. Calm, for once," Pete said. "Can't complain."

The store was The Book Bin, a used bookstore on Bird Road that was now under Pete's watch. Its previous owner, Dave Mendoza, had signed control over before disappearing a little less than a year ago, in the wake of the revelations that he and his family were part of the deadly cult that had tried to eliminate Pete and Kathy.

Pete found the work soothing, in stark contrast to the high-octane chaos of his previous exploits as a PI. It was easy to lose himself in the minutiae of the job—ordering and organizing books, dealing with his regular cast of customers, and managing his sole part-time employee, Isabel Levitz, a retired librarian who couldn't retire her passion for books. She was quirky but well read, and had saved Pete's ass many a time when a customer came in asking for books Pete had never heard of. It also made the hours sitting at the front desk a little less solitary. Financially, the store made just enough to stay open and to float Pete his rent and expenses, meaning he could turn down any occasional investigative jobs that cropped up. Fernandez Investigations lived on in name only, intentionally stuck in neutral. The days of car explosions and dead friends were over. Pete Fernandez, semi-retired never-was.

The bookstore and the life he'd built around it kept him afloat, but it was the AA meetings he tried to attend—and the fellowship surrounding the recovery program—that kept him alive.

*Alive.*

The concept still seemed foreign to him, especially after the months of recovery, pain, and stretching to reach a modicum of normal. He'd found himself basking in the banality of things: a cup of coffee in the morning. Driving to work. A quiet meal.

"Nice to see you out of that hospital gown."

"Tell me about it. But, hell, I was happy to be around to wear it."

"I can imagine," Harras said. "You cut it pretty close."

"Too close."

"They ever get a line on Salerno? Or what his deal was?"

"Chopp's partner, Sternbergh, the guy who was waiting in the car—"

"The guy that rushed in when he heard the shots?"

"Yeah, saved my life," Pete said. "He said they lost Salerno after that. Heard a few things, a sighting in Baltimore, but nothing else. Guy's in the wind."

Harras's stare became distant as he mulled the info over. After a moment, he shifted gears.

"Heard anything from Dave?"

Pete shook his head. Pete hadn't seen Dave since he put a bullet in the head of Gary Sallis, the up-to-that-point secret leader of a dormant, murderous Miami cult. Shamed and blacklisted, Dave went into hiding, speaking only through his attorney as he battled charges and tried to stay out of prison for his part in the murder of Miami teen Patty Morales a decade before.

"My contacts on the force tell me he's not doing so hot," Harras said. "They've been keeping tabs on him."

"What do you mean?"

"Dave was on their radar long before the stuff with La Iglesia. Once the church scandal hit, it got a lot of people in my line of work interested. They say he's living on the street these days, drinking and using, spending whatever money he and his family have left," Harras said, taking another pull from the beer. "The Iglesia stuff last year sent him reeling. We put a bright light on his deepest, darkest secret and then he ran. You'd know better than me, but it feels like he's self-destructing."

The idea that Dave, one of his closest friends, one of the few people who stuck by Pete when he was at the lowest bottom of his own alcoholism, was now in the throes of addiction hit Pete hard. The guilt stabbed and turned inside Pete's stomach. How had he let it go on this long? he wondered. He should have sought Dave out sooner. Tried to help him. If anyone knew what it was like to want to dive headlong into the darkness of drink and drugs, it was Pete.

"Got a bead on him?"

"Actually, I do." Harras dug into his back pocket and handed Pete a slip of paper. "Just the basics—last seen, KAs, the usual. Keep me posted."

"You got it," Pete said as he turned toward his car.

Before he could finish the pivot, Harras cleared his throat. Pete wheeled back around.

"Hey, gotta ask—how're you feeling?" Harras said, motioning toward the restaurant. Pete could hear the droning beats of New Order's "Regret"—clearly a Kathy choice—coming from the space. "About all this?"

"Fine," Pete said, not hesitating. "I think it's good. I'm glad they're happy."

"But are you happy?"

"I'm happy for Kathy."

16

"That's not the same thing."

Pete ran a hand over his face.

"She deserves to be with someone like Marco," he said. "She wouldn't be happy with me. Not me six months ago or me today. Plus, she turned me down. So, this is just the way it goes. I can't blame her."

"That's pretty mature of you," Harras said. "Hell, I'm surprised I even got invited."

"Yeah, I wondered how you finagled that."

They shared a quick, staccato laugh. They both turned their heads at the sound of the restaurant's front door swinging open.

"How charming, two boys sitting outside and whining about girls," Kathy said with a smirk. "I mean, I'm assuming that's what's happening. I'm usually right."

"We're just catching up," Harras said as Kathy joined them. She motioned for Harras's beer and took a swig before handing it back.

"Is that all?" she said. "Quite the after-party you guys have going out here. I'm not even going to get into the fact that it looks like you're fucking leaving, Pete Fernandez."

"Harras was telling me what he'd heard about Dave," Pete said. "I'm going to try and track him down."

"Like, right now? Well, good luck with that," Kathy said. "I've tried. He doesn't want to be found. He's strung out."

"We'll see about that."

Pete heard the car pulling into the strip mall parking lot as he yanked his keys out of his pocket. He reached for the front door of The Book Bin and waited a moment. It was close to one in the morning and, aside from Pete's own car, the lot had been empty. A black Oldsmobile flashed its lights at Pete, beckoning him. Pete ignored it and slid the key into the lock. Pete heard the car door open and slam shut in quick succession. He pulled the key back and turned around. A wiry man with sparse brown hair was making his way toward Pete.

"Can I help you?" Pete asked.

"Pete Fernandez?"

"That's me."

"I'm Edward Rosen. I'm an art dealer and attorney, but I also ... represent important people. One in particular," the man said, close now, extending his nicely manicured hand. "And my client would like to discuss something with you."

"That's nice," Pete said. "But seeing as how it's one in the morning and I'm exhausted, I'm going to have to—what's the right term? Put a pin in this one for a bit."

"I apologize for disturbing you," Rosen said. "But it's of great urgency that my client speak to you. He guarantees that the meeting will be mutually beneficial. He would consider your speedy response a personal favor."

"Mr. Rosen," Pete said. "You seem nice enough. Well-mannered, that sort of thing, so I won't be rude—but, first off—why would you expect me to get in a car with you and go somewhere at this time of night? Second, I'm retired. I'm not taking new cases."

"I'm aware of your status, so I won't beat around the bush, Mr. Fernandez," Rosen said, absentmindedly cracking the knuckles on his left hand. "I represent Alvaro Mujica. Perhaps you've heard of him?"

Pete had. Mujica was an old school *bolitero*—a numbers guy who ran illegal lotteries around Miami, plus who knows what other illicit activities. Though the landscape of Miami's underworld was an ever-changing beast, Mujica had managed to carve out a constant place for himself. The former Bay of Pigs infantryman claimed to the press that he was just a humble, retired mamey fruit farmer. But the truth was very different.

Pete sighed and let his keys drop back into his pocket.

"I know your boss," Pete said, his voice flat. "If that was your trump card, then I'm gonna ask you to leave. It's late. I'm tired. And I've spent too much of my time working for bad men. It usually ends up with me beaten or shot. Kind of done with that for a long while. Nice to meet you, though."

"Dismissing me would be unwise," Rosen said. "Like I said, Mr. Mujica is looking for some help with a very delicate—and personal—matter."

With that, Pete turned around and started to open the door again. As it closed behind him, he could still see Rosen standing there, watching him through the smudged front door glass.

Pete knew something was off the second he walked in. For one, a light was on—near the back, where the bookstore office was. The space Pete sometimes used for clients and his investigative work. "Used" being the key word. It was late and he knew he'd turned the light off. He heard noises, too. Thumping. A muttered curse word.

*Gonna be one of those nights*, he thought. He wasn't carrying his gun. He didn't do that anymore. And for the first time since he'd decided to permanently tuck his father's old firearm in a lockbox, he felt regret.

Pete walked slowly through the darkened bookstore, the layout of the small space imprinted in his brain, trying to keep his footfalls silent. As he got closer to the noise—and the person causing the ruckus—he was able to make out a few words.

"This is unbelievable," said the voice, sounding tired and put-upon. "There's no end in sight."

A few more paces and Pete let out a short sigh of relief. He was glad he didn't have his gun after all.

He found Isabel Levitz in the SCI-FI/FANTASY aisle, sitting on the floor, surrounded by mass market paperbacks from every decade—Star Trek and Star Wars novels, Asimov, Herbert, Tolkien, and more—moving one book onto another pile and then moving it back, hypnotized by a mission only she seemed to be aware of.

"Isabel?" Pete asked.

She jerked, and her glasses rattled to the floor. She glanced up at Pete, squinting as she tried to grab for her fallen bifocals. She put them back on her face before responding.

"Pete? Oh, hi," she said. "I didn't expect to see you this late."

"I could say the same to you," Pete said. "Is something wrong?"

"Oh, well, no," she said, her shoulders slumping slightly as she looked around at the various piles of books, placed in an order only she could comprehend. "I was lying in bed and realized our organizational system for this aisle is a mess, so I figured I'd come by and fix it before we opened tomorrow, and, well, that became its own mess...."

Pete laughed. A genuine laugh—not laced with sarcasm or snark. It felt nice.

"Are you sure this has to happen now?" He knew the answer. Isabel was retired. Books had been her working life and now, alone with no children and little family, books were all she had. He was lucky to have an employee who was this committed to the store.

She chuckled. "I guess not, but here I am."

"Well, don't stay too late, all right?" Pete said. "I just came by because I needed to pick something up from the office."

She waved at him as he made his way to the back of the store. He walked past the shelves of books and related paraphernalia with no shortage of nostalgia. It was in this store that he'd gotten his footing after the bottom fell out. His friend, Dave Mendoza, had offered Pete a lifeline of sorts: part-time work with full-time pay, and a place to call home that wasn't dimly lit, playing bad classic rock, and reeking of gin. That felt like a long time ago. Pete had a few years under his belt. Plenty of bad decisions. He hadn't envisioned himself walking through these doors again, much less running the place. But skating past death tends to change your perspective.

Now Dave was gone. Harras was retired. Kathy was spending more time writing about crimes than helping to solve them—not to mention her life with Marco. Pete had almost lost his life trying to atone for the years he'd misspent. Time spent drinking. Doing the wrong things. He felt that he'd atoned for that. It was time to simplify.

Pete turned down the MYSTERY/THRILLER aisle. He grabbed a copy of William Boyle's *The Lonely Witness* before making a left at the far wall, and entered a tiny office. He set the book down on his desk, which took up most of the room, along with a small cot that nearly blocked the door. It was in this space that he'd barricaded himself, a few years previous, as a serial killer tore through the city. It was here that he reached for a vodka bottle and embraced the demons that had been scratching at the walls of his mind. It was here that he let them back in.

He heard Isabel's light footsteps and the click and clack of the front door lock, followed by the jangle of the chime hanging off the knob. She wasn't big on goodbyes, he thought, and smiled.

Pete, like most alcoholics, had come into the rooms when he'd hit his bottom—the lowest point of his life that also created a moment of clarity, a break in the dark clouds that allowed him to see, for once, that he needed to make a change. He never thought he could sink lower, but he did on that day. His ex-fiancée, Emily, had just been abducted by a bloodthirsty madman named Julian Finch, and he felt completely helpless—and guilty—for the darkness swirling around them. He'd opted out. He chose to dive into the abyss and let go rather than face reality and try to help. Emily survived. She never forgave him.

*Emily.*

Their relationship had been fraught long before, though. Years ago, she'd left him, his drinking souring a relationship they thought fast-tracked to happiness. Then she'd married, settled into a photogenic, suburban life. When her husband started fucking his assistant, her annual holiday postcard life had been flipped.

Emily lived in Europe, last Pete heard. It'd taken a while, but the parallels between his relationship with Emily and his off-and-on romance with Kathy had not been lost on him. He was trying to course-correct. But often, the heart does what it wants.

He sat in front of his laptop and waited for it to boot up. The idea that Alvaro Mujica wanted anything to do with him could not be good. His gut told him to call Kathy, but he doubted the party was over—or that she'd be interested in talking shop tonight. He gave his email a quick glance. He flagged a query from an investigator he knew in L.A., Juniper Song, and promised to deal with it later. Then he closed the browser and tapped a few keys to load a familiar file. His eyes scanned the text: dates, locations, some grainy surveillance camera stills.

These five pages were all the information Pete had on Vincent Salerno, the man who had nearly killed him. The document was a garbled puzzle of bits of intel—sightings, tips, rumors—cobbled together from Pete working the phones, trying to figure out the "why" behind what Salerno did. The only active case on Pete's docket.

The lead-in to Vincent Salerno's appearance in Pete's Spring Valley, New York, office was fuzzy, but Pete could make out shapes and movement. At the time, Pete had been seeing a woman named Jen Ferris. She worked as a stripper at a club a short drive from Pete's business. As with Emily and Kathy, the romance had not been healthy, and it imploded due in large part to Pete's inability to deal with the realities of adult relationships. He wanted something. He knew that. But he wasn't ready to open himself up to the price of intimacy. Jen sussed him out fast, and was quick to cut him loose.

Jen's father had been a two-bit mob associate, working on the fringes of the DeCalvacante crime family, the New Jersey satellite to one of the larger Five Families of New York. Something Doug

Ferris did got the attention of Salerno, who decided to approach Pete about the man, with a mob pal along for the ride. Pete managed to overpower and shame the two gangsters. Soon after the incident, he was on his way back to Miami, pulled away by a case involving a missing state senator's son. Upon his return to New York, a trip Pete had taken just to load up his belongings and head back south, Pete was approached by an FBI agent named Amanda Chopp. The agent didn't mince words—Doug Ferris and his daughter were dead. What did Pete know about it? Nothing. That was the truth. Nothing at the time. Enter Salerno. RIP Chopp, bullet to the head. Pete was close to meeting the same fate, had Chopp's partner not arrived when he did. Even then, it had been close.

The file had become a totem of sorts for Pete. The thing he thought about when his head hit the pillow, or when he was stuck in traffic. It filled the empty spaces between the life he'd scraped together in the wake of the attack. What would drive a mid-level mobster like Vinnie Salerno, who was probably making a decent if illicit living for himself, go rogue and murder three people and gravely injure a fourth? Every time Pete got a bit of info, a photo, a tip, or a whiff of what might tie it all together, it disappeared as soon as it popped up, leaving conflicting ideas and jagged, confusing strands of thoughts in its wake. Pete had no idea where to go from here.

He got up with a start at the sound. He'd been so immersed in the file that he hadn't recognized the familiar front door buzzer. Had Isabel lost her keys or forgotten something? He walked back toward the door and saw a figure standing outside, backlit by streetlights on Bird Road. *Rosen again?*

As Pete got closer, he realized he did not know the man—older, gruff-looking, and overdressed—wearing layers of clothing that didn't fit the perpetually humid Miami weather. A man out of place.

*Frightened.*

Pete opened the door.

"We're closed."

The man looked up to meet Pete's eyes, as if being awoken from a deep sleep.

"Pete Fernandez?" he said, his voice a hoarse croak. "What do you know about your mother?"

# MY MOTHER THE WAR

*June 12, 1983*

"**H**e did it. Un-fucking-believable," she said, dragging the large trash bag packed with clothes, toiletries, and who knows what else behind her as she approached the door to D's apartment. "He finally did it."

She jammed her finger into the doorbell and let it ring for much longer than she should have. Even that little bit of release felt good. Her head spun. She leaned on the wall adjacent to the door and waited. It was early. D was probably asleep. Jesus, she hoped she was asleep. Which at least meant D was at home. She had nowhere else to go.

The door creaked open and D's head popped out into the hallway, dark purple circles under her eyes. She scanned in both directions until her gaze fell on her friend and the bag of belongings she'd brought with her.

"He finally did it, huh?" D asked with a frown.

D ushered her into the small apartment, which was tidy and well decorated despite the crappy neighborhood and deteriorating building. D took care of what she had. It was one of her most admirable traits.

*I guess she has me now*, she thought, taking a seat across from D on the tiny couch. *Can she take care of me?*

"What happened?" D asked. "Do you want a drink?"

"Yes, oh yes," she said. "Maybe twelve."

D wandered a few feet away to the apartment's small kitchen. She heard D preparing what she hoped would be a strong, tangy screwdriver. D returned with a giant glass that was more yellow than orange.

*D never goes light on the vodka, thank God.*

"Tell me everything," D said.

"I should have seen it coming," she said, her voice clear. But that strength wavered almost immediately, as the details rushed into her mind's eye, pulling her back to the confrontation, the nightmare her life had become in less than a few hours. "I got home—it was around two in the morning, I guess. I don't know for sure. He'd packed all my stuff in this garbage bag. The only reason I saw him was that he'd gotten up because the kid was crying. Awkward way to run into your husband."

"Oh, honey," D said, patting her hand gently. "It was bound to happen, you know?"

She ignored her friend. She didn't want the judgment. She pressed on, wiping the tears from her face with a rough motion.

"Well, it was a surprise to me, okay? I mean, I usually manage to sneak into bed, all clear, right? At least crash," she said. "Doesn't dodge the passive-aggressive attitude in the morning, or the doe-eyed, concerned looks—but it lets me sleep off the worst of it. Some nights I just need to let off some steam, you know? I can't just sneak sips from the bottle all week, pretend to be June Cleaver, hiding in plain sight. I'd go insane, D."

"I know," D said, nodding, waiting for her friend to continue. "I know."

"Anyway, so he busts out with the usual shit. He said I had a problem. That I knew it. Even the kid could tell—which, is bullshit, okay?" she said, her voice rising. Was it too early to be making this kind of noise? She wasn't sure what time it was. "Look, that baby—toddler, whatever—just wants to eat, shit, crawl around a little, and sleep. More power to him, I say. Kid is after my own heart. I love that boy. He knows that, too. So, he's trying to get to me. He's hitting me where it hurts."

"Okay," D said.

"What was I going to do? I took my stuff and left. Used my last twenty to hop into a cab and come here, D," she said, her head shaking, the dust beginning to settle around her new world. "This is insane."

"You just need to rest," D said, standing up. "You know you always have a place here. Take the couch. Sleep it off. You still smell like weed and cheap rum, okay? Just being honest."

She let out a wet laugh as D hugged her.

"Fuck him," she said. "Right, D? I'm not a mess."

"Of course not, sweetie," D said, giving her forehead a slow peck. "Just rest, all right?"

"He's not going to take that boy from me," she said, lying down on the couch, resting her body and mind for what felt like the first time in years. "I packed my bags, but I'm not gone. He knows that."

D walked toward her own bedroom, nodding her head in agreement.

"Just rest," D said. "We'll talk more later. We can get lunch at that Cuban place you like, all right? But you need to sleep."

D closed her bedroom door.

She heard the click of the lock and wondered what D was scared of. Her head felt heavy and soaking wet, like she'd almost drowned but managed to survive at the last possible moment. She started to doze off, embracing the blackout she knew was waiting for her.

"I'll see my son. I'm an adult. People split up all the time," she said, her voice jagged and choked. "I'm a good mother. I love my son."

# CHAPTER TWO

Pete handed the older man a glass of water, then sat down behind his desk. The man's hands shook as he took a long sip.

"You really know how to make an entrance," Pete said. "Though people popping in on me unannounced is starting to get annoying, Mr.—?"

"Osvaldo," the man said. "Osvaldo Valdez."

The name felt familiar, but the face was not. Pete waited a beat.

"I worked with your father," Valdez said. "Not directly, but we were both in Homicide together."

Pete cleared his throat. "So you knew Carlos Broche, my dad's old partner?"

"Yes, yes," Valdez said. "I know he died ... not long ago."

Broche had been like an uncle to Pete, and partnered with his father for most of Pedro Fernandez's time on the Miami Homicide team. But it had ended badly for Carlos. On Pete's first case, trying to find a missing woman named Kathy Bentley, he'd uncovered the truth about Broche: that he, like many cops on the force, was corrupt—on the payroll of the Silent Death, a mob killer of killers who had his sights set on Pete.

26

"Varela, Posada, Smith, Vigil, I knew them all," Valdez said. "Some were good, most weren't that good. Your father, though, was a good man. An honest man. That's why this shames me."

"You mentioned my mother," Pete said, leaning back. "What about her?"

"What do you know of your mother?"

"Nothing, really," Pete said, not hesitating.

It was true. His mother had died while giving birth to him—leaving his father to raise him alone and deal with not only the death of his wife, but the murder of Pete's grandfather, Diego, a few months prior.

"She died in childbirth," Pete continued. "My dad had a few pictures around, and he talked about her. But she was an only child. Her parents were gone. I didn't know that side of my family too well."

Valdez grimaced. He didn't want to be having this discussion. It made Pete uneasy.

"This isn't the place," Valdez said. "Or the time. But soon. We have to talk. I have things I need to show you … to prove what I know is true."

Valdez stood up abruptly, as if just realizing he had somewhere else to be, and was running very, very late.

"That's all I can say now," he said, his gravel-fueled voice wavering. "I made a promise to an old friend a long time ago, but I've grappled with that for too long. He is dead now. You deserve to know this truth. I just need some time to organize it."

The rush of memory came then—a barrage of images and pieces of his life that Pete couldn't remember experiencing before. A hand wrapped around his tiny fingers as he crossed the street. A warm kiss on his forehead as he slipped to the floor. The sweet smell of tart sweat and the feel of her skin. Then screaming, muffled by walls. Arguing. Slammed doors. Darkness and tears. Her face was a blur, a shape that was familiar but incomplete—like a figure under muddy water. He knew what she looked like, of course. He knew of her, from stories and pictures and things he assumed must have happened—how she fell in love with his father, how she lived, how she died.

What were these flashes? Why was he imagining these things now? Had he really pushed away any thought of his mother that far down into himself? He'd never known her. Never spent time with her. So what were these dreams? Projections, hopes—or something more?

*Memories?*

Pete shook his head. "You can't just barge in here, say something vague about my mom and how she died, and expect me to let you leave."

"You have no choice—and don't put words in my mouth. I'll tell my story when I'm ready. Now is not the time. You're not truly alone, it seems like."

"What do you mean?"

"I need your full attention to discuss this. Now, I know you're a good man," Valdez said. "I've kept up with your exploits. I know you're trying to live a good life. Your father would be proud. Your mother, too. Let's talk tomorrow night. Here is my address—"

Valdez jotted down a Little Havana address on a legal pad near the edge of the desk.

"Come by around seven," he said. "Be patient, *hijo*. It will be worth it. Thank you for humoring a sick old man."

"Sick? What's the—"

But before Pete could finish his thought, Osvaldo Valdez was gone.

# CHAPTER THREE

**P**ete slept fitfully that night and awoke around six, his head pounding in a way that was familiar, but had nothing to do with one too many shots the night before. He rolled out of bed and walked into the living room of his tiny house in the quiet Westchester neighborhood of Miami. He'd been raised in the area, and his father's house had been a few streets away before it was burned down a few years back, in an attempt on Pete's and Kathy's lives. This house reminded Pete a lot of the home he grew up in, so he didn't regret the expense and relished the sense of home.

He made his way toward the narrow kitchen and flicked on the coffeemaker. A sliver of sunlight peeked through the blinds. Pete poured himself a large glass of water and palmed a few Aleve. He'd spent the remainder of the night pacing his small office before calling it around three in the morning, exhausted and angry. At himself for not chasing after Valdez. At the old man for coming into his office and derailing his day; hell, his life—a life he had tried to keep simple and focused over the last year.

He was left with questions about everything. What did Valdez know about his mother? Was there more to her death than what he'd been told since he could remember? And what of those visions—*memories*?—that seemed to explode in his mind as Valdez spoke? The images and flashes of action felt so real—like a sudden dream, his senses on fire, awakening for the first time. It all led to one bigger question that Pete, drunkenly scrambling for his life for the last few years, hadn't had time to process: What did he really know about Graciela Fernandez?

Pete pondered as he poured himself a large mug of black coffee and scanned the notifications on his phone. One missed call: Kathy.

He'd left her a long, rambling message last night—touching on the Valdez news, but also wishing her well.

"Look, Kathy, I'm sorry if I seemed distant and weird tonight," he'd said, stammering, but unburdened by the release the voicemail brought. "You know how I feel. How I've felt. Things got so derailed when that…when I got hurt. I can't expect you or anyone to sit around and wait for me to act, or that it even matters. What I'm trying to say, I think, is that I am happy. I'm happy for you—happy that my friend has found someone like Marco. I wish you guys the best, and I hope that I am at least in the running for maid of honor…."

Pete snapped back. His phone buzzed. He checked the display and picked up.

"Good morning," he said.

"Open your door, loser."

He walked over to the front door and followed instructions. Kathy was on the other side, looking like she hadn't slept at all. A fading black T-shirt, jeans, and last night's mascara. She walked in before Pete could say anything.

"We need to talk."

"Again, good morning."

She stopped in his living room and turned around, forcing Pete to hit the brakes to avoid crashing into her. Their faces were inches apart.

"What are you doing?"

"Having coffee?"

"No, not literally, like, this instant," she said, her face crinkling in frustration. "I mean, in general—to me."

"I—have no idea what you're talking about."

"Pete-fucking-Fernandez, of course you do. I thought we put all this to bed when you left for New York?"

"Kathy, help me out here—"

*Spell it out.*

She let out a sigh, turning away from him, hands on her hips.

"I'm glad you're alive. I'm glad you're healthy," she said. "I'm happy to be friends, but this sad-eyed puppy dog thing you're doing ... it's not sustainable. It's actually pretty fucking annoying."

Pete didn't respond. He waited a beat as she paced around his house.

"Here's the thing. We're friends," Kathy said, gripping her hands together, as if she was pleading with Pete. "We can't be anything else. We tried it. It did not work. I moved on. Then you left, got shot, got better, and here we are. Just because you want things to be different doesn't mean they will be, okay?"

"You're right."

She looked up at him, as if he'd interrupted her during a speech on the Senate floor.

"What?"

"You're right," Pete said. "I need to give up the ghost. It's not fair to behave that way—to you, or to me. Like I said on the phone, I—ah, shit. Look, I just need to give it some time. But me acting this way just makes it toxic."

"Well, I was not ... expecting that. Are you sure you're okay?"

"I'm fine," Pete said. "Coffee?"

"God, yes."

She followed him into the kitchen and leaned on the counter as he poured her a fresh cup.

"It sounds like you had an eventful evening."

"Despite my best efforts," Pete said, handing her the mug. He took a spot next to her on the counter. "Do you know Alvaro Mujica?"

"Ex-Bay-of-Pigs war hero turned Miami illegal-gambling don," she said. "Broad strokes, yeah. But last I heard he was retired."

"That's what I thought. And he might still be, but why would his attorney-slash-art dealer reach out to me?"

"Who can say, my dear? You didn't hop into his car in the middle of the night to find out."

"Can you blame me?"

"On my list of things I blame you for, that does not make the top ten. Twenty, even," she leaned into him playfully.

"Did you really just come here to yell at me about last night?"

"Yes, isn't it obvious?" she said, motioning over her attire. "I'm wearing whatever I found on the floor, unshowered, and probably still drunk."

He moved toward her. Slowly. Giving her time to step back, to decline the advance. She didn't.

Pete caressed her face, a light touch, brief and instinctual. She responded, hesitant at first, but then moved her face toward his hand, kissed his fingertips as they slid past her lips. He moved his hand to the back of her neck, cupping her head as she leaned over, his face close to hers, her hand sliding over his face.

"Pete …"

They shared a slow, exploratory kiss, their lips connecting and disconnecting, their mouths hesitant but hungry for more. Kathy pulled back, her hand still on Pete's face. Then she moved in for another kiss, longer, more thoughtful and slow, before pulling away and locking her eyes on his.

"You are unbelievable," she said, kissing him again, her breathing growing heavy. "Fuck."

"I'm sorry," Pete said, his body now leaning into hers, his hands sliding up the back of her shirt. "I —"

"Jesus, shut up for once," she said, and kissed him again. "Just stop talking."

They'd barely made it into the bedroom before they were kissing again, this time with more purpose, their hands tugging and sliding over each other, their mouths open and lingering, searching on instinct and a need to feel something. By the time they wrestled each other onto Pete's bed, his shirt was lost on the hallway floor along with Kathy's top and jeans.

He slid his hands behind her back, unlatching her bra and felt her smile as he kissed her.

"Not your first time, huh?" she said, her voice husky and hungry.

She helped Pete yank his pants off and toss them to the floor. She ran her fingers over his boxers and lingered on him before she started inching the shorts down, pulling him toward her as she lay back on the bed.

Her hand still on him, she scooted her underwear off with a swift motion of her free hand, lifting her ass up and pushing them down fast, her eyes still on Pete, her hand still on him.

And then he felt her soft gasp, his mouth on her neck, her lips next to his ear, sounds of pleasure and surprise spilling out, mixing together, quiet at first but getting louder.

Pete tried to say something, but she shushed him with a slow finger over his lips and he felt himself start to move with her. They leaned into each other, and he was overcome by instinct. Her noises seemed to be speeding up with each move their bodies made together, until she clamped her hands on his shoulders and he felt her tighten around him. Then he was gone, too, feeling the familiar wave of surprise. She pulled him closer, her mouth on his, desperate to stretch the moment out.

As Pete collapsed next to her, shaking with feeling, they wove together and settled, their arms and legs tangled. He kissed her forehead, sliding a hand over her cheek as she let her arms wrap around him, and allowed sleep to take them away.

Pete awoke and rolled over to check his phone. It was ten in the morning. The bed was empty, but he heard Kathy making noise in the kitchen. He cursed under his breath. He slid into his boxer shorts and T-shirt and made his way toward the sounds. He found her looking through a cabinet over the sink. She was already back in the clothes she'd worn when she arrived.

"Do you not have sugar in this house?" she asked.

"Next to the coffeemaker."

She swiveled around, not looking at him. She grabbed the sugar and poured an unhealthy amount into her cold coffee mug from a few hours before.

"Call me later," she said, taking a long swig from the mug before setting it down in the sink. "I think we have a lot to talk about. Just not right now."

She turned around and looked at him. Her eyes seemed tired but not angry, which brought Pete some relief.

"If this is happening, like really happening, it can't be this way forever, okay?" Kathy said. "I hope that makes sense."

Pete nodded.

Kathy turned around and walked out.

Pete looked up at the clock hanging over the door to the living room. He had some time to kill before his meeting with Valdez. He took a quick shower and considered how complicated his life had become in less than a day.

He got dressed and made sure to grab the paper he'd stuffed into his suit jacket pocket the night before. He had to find an old friend. But first he needed to clear his head.

The Miami Aikikai was the oldest aikido dojo in Miami—open for more than forty years. Pete had been coming a few times a week for months, ever since he'd been given clearance from his doctors to resume activities that were more strenuous than getting out of bed or pouring a glass of water.

Allie had been right, to some degree, Pete thought as he changed into his *gi*—or uniform—in the gym's expansive locker room. He was preparing for something. Bracing for something, really. As simple as his life had gotten—by design and by force—at any point, something could blow up. A shadow could crawl through the cracks and find its way to him. He was a magnet for harm, and he wasn't going to cross his fingers and hope he could skate by. Not anymore.

But he wanted to do it his way. If he'd come out of his near-death experience with anything, it was a sense of how valuable life was, and how careless he'd been with it. He'd killed people. He'd shot people. He'd hit people with cars. Okay, he wasn't a mass murderer, but he'd also been forced to use extreme measures to make up for his relative inexperience. No longer. If he was going to use violence—as a means to an end or to defend himself—he was going to be smart about it. Aikido fit the bill perfectly.

Aikido was a fairly modern Japanese martial art, one that synthesized spirituality and self-defense. The idea was to focus on defending yourself while also not inflicting excessive harm on your attacker. The spiritual side focused on energy—and the idea that by choosing this kind of self-defense, you were unifying, rather than dividing, your life energy. Heady stuff. But Pete had come to look forward to these weekly practice sessions that in a way that felt akin to an AA meeting. He felt lighter when he was done—physically spent and also mentally clear.

He needed clear right now.

The reunion with Kathy had been good, Pete thought, but his life would soon get much more complicated. And it was his own fault. He replayed it in his head as he practiced a few *tenkan* movements in front of the sparring floor's wall-to-wall mirrors. It was still relatively early—too late for the before-work crowd, too early for the midday rush—so the place was empty. Which is what Pete wanted. Room to breathe. Time to think.

He loved her, he knew that. Before Salerno almost murdered him, he had told her as much. But even then, Kathy had been clear—she wanted his friendship and partnership. She wasn't sold on the idea of Pete as Boyfriend. When he returned to Miami, bruised and battered, she was a constant presence—but kept him at arm's length when she felt he was getting too attached. Eventually, Pete took the hint. Eventually, Marco showed up and swept Kathy off her feet. It should've been a done deal.

Pete turned to face the mirrored walls and practiced a few variations of *irimi*, or entering—taking steps toward an attacker. He felt the sweat start to coat his body. Felt his blood pumping. Adrenaline. He welcomed it. He needed it.

*"Where have you been, Pete?"*

He couldn't shake the vision of Kathy from the night before, half-drunk, face beautiful and glowing as she caught a glimpse of Pete. *This is how she really feels*, he'd thought then. But he'd buried it. Pushed it aside. He knew it'd be wrong to even try to engage with her on that level, but when she came into his apartment, he'd stopped caring. But momentary pleasures can have lasting consequences.

He tossed his towel on the floor and did a top-speed run-through of the moves. It wasn't clicking. The physical was there, but his head wasn't in it. He cursed under his breath as he walked back toward the locker room. He tried to shake the feeling that his easy life was careening toward something darker, like a car spinning off a bridge into a foggy, black river.

# CHAPTER FOUR

**P**ete was a tracker. It was part of being a PI. You found people. Oftentimes, that was the bulk of your business. Even now, "retired," Pete could call upon the tools of his trade to locate even the most slippery individual. And, with Harras's help, he had to tap into those tools to find this particular person.

Pete's search had brought him to the streets of Overtown, a neighborhood that had seen it all. Once pulsing with music and life, the Overtown city limits were now an expanse of vacant lots, the distant honking of horns replacing the lively jazz brass that dominated the area.

Known as the "Harlem of the South," Overtown was a historically black neighborhood in Northwest Miami, and stands as one of the oldest in Miami, founded in 1896. At the beginning of the twentieth century, Overtown had been carved out for the black workers building the city's nascent infrastructure—railroads, streets, buildings. Like many of the country's biggest and best cities, Miami survived on the back of black and marginalized labor, who made up the bulk of the city's workforce.

# MIAMI MIDNIGHT

In the twenties, the neighborhood was a segregated area, or "Colored Town." Overtown still managed to be a hotbed for the arts, and Northwest Second and Third Avenues were loaded with jazz clubs hosting legends like Lena Horne and Cab Calloway, as the stars did pop-up gigs while touring through South Florida. Then I-95 bulldozed the neighborhood, closing businesses and forcing families to abandon their homes.

Despite the setbacks, segregation, and poverty that marred large stretches of Overtown's history, the neighborhood found a way to thrive as a hub of business, arts, and culture. But even the area's best efforts were often derailed by the country's perpetually unstable and toxic racial climate. Over the years, Overtown had been the scene of various violent clashes   most notably the McDuffie riots of 1980. These days, the streets remained in a constant state of flux, faded storefronts mingled with new, shinier businesses. An ever-changing swath of streets and a community constantly striving to pull out of a decades-long tailspin.

Pete parked his car on Northwest 14th Street. He got out and tried to keep pace with the man, who was looking around nervously, his hands buried deep in his overcoat pockets. The coat was another sign that the man was out of sorts, seeing as how the temperature was creeping toward 90 degrees on this typical Miami day. Pete already felt his shirt sticking to his body and the atmosphere around him getting thicker, the humid air creating an invisible fog of heat.

Overtown, like many working class or impoverished areas, was being eaten alive by the opioid epidemic. Junkies wandered the streets, burnt spoons and needles littered the ground. Harras had pointed Pete here, but he was pretty sure he would've made his way here first anyway. If you wanted to score, this was the place to go.

The man turned around, catching Pete off guard. A glint of recognition appeared in the pair of glazed, hazy eyes before he pivoted down into an alley.

Pete sprinted behind him. "Dave!" he called. "I just want to talk!"

Dave Mendoza was thinner. The beer belly and healthy cheeks were gone. His face was marked and scarred by scratches and festering scabs, with dark bags under his eyes. He wobbled a bit, and it was clear that the run had ruined whatever high he'd been riding. He looked half-dead.

"Dave."

"Go," Dave said, his voice ragged, as if these were the first words he'd spoken aloud in days. "Go away, Pete."

"You have to let me help you," Pete said, taking a step toward his friend. "You're in trouble. I've been there."

Dave was no stranger to the wrong side of the law. He'd run drugs and been a part-time thug and gangster through most of his twenties, only reforming recently, when he'd retired from the street to run The Book Bin—and where he met Pete, who was spinning out of control from late-stage alcoholism and desperate for a lifeline.

Now the roles had been reversed, and Pete knew he had to reach out his hand to Dave, even if his friend saw it as a menacing claw, grasping for what remained of his life.

"Just leave me be," Dave said, backing up. "Just let me do what I need to do. What I deserve."

Pete took a step toward him, stopping when he saw Dave reach into his coat. Dave's shaky hand appeared again, this time holding a small Smith and Wesson, the barrel pointed down as if to say, "I have this, but I don't want to use it."

"Put the gun down—"

Dave took a step in Pete's direction, this time pointing the gun squarely at Pete's chest.

"This bring back memories?" Dave asked. "You cut it close last time, huh? You really want to push it again? Just leave—"

Pete didn't wait. He stepped and turned forward, his training kicking in. He grabbed Dave's gun hand and yanked him forward, moving his body toward Dave and chopping at his arm in one smooth motion. The gun clattered to the floor as Pete yanked Dave's hand behind his back, grimacing as his friend yelled in pain. Pete shoved Dave down to the floor and picked up the gun.

"Aughh! Dammit—dammit," Dave said, still on the floor, holding his bruised arm. "What the hell was that?"

"Aikido," Pete said. "You were right. I did cut it close last time. That won't happen again."

Pete slid the gun into his waistband and walked over to his fallen friend, who was moaning softly to himself.

"You need help," Pete said as he crouched down. He slid his hands under Dave's arms and hoisted him up, grunting as he propped him against the alley wall. Dave didn't respond, but didn't fall, either. He sagged against the grimy brickwork and refused to make eye contact with Pete.

"I'm here when you want to come back, okay?" Pete said. "Like you were there for me. I know what you're going through. You have to want it. You have to see what you've become. Push through that hate you have for yourself, man. Because you can. I can't force you to want to live. I can't make you want to scrape together a life. But I'm here."

Pete pulled out a business card and stuffed it in Dave's shirt pocket. He patted it tenderly before stepping back and turning toward his car, hoping he hadn't seen the last of the man who'd once been his friend.

Osvaldo Valdez lived in a battered house in Little Havana, a few blocks off of Calle Ocho. As Pete parked, he noticed the lights in the house were off. Osvaldo was either sitting in the dark, asleep, or not home. There was a faded blue Pontiac in the driveway. The Miami sky was turning a purple gray as the sun set, giving the street a quiet, pensive feeling.

Pete walked up to the front door and buzzed. The ring echoed through the house. Pete didn't hear any sounds coming from inside. He gave it a few minutes and rang again. Nothing. The door was slightly ajar. He pushed it with his fist and stepped inside.

"Hello? Osvaldo?"

Past the entrance was a small foyer, with a door to the left and a bigger living room at the end of the hallway. Pete flicked on his cell phone flashlight and took a few cautious steps forward.

That's when he saw a hand, splayed out on the floor of the living room, as he looked around the doorframe that divided the hallway from the rest of the house.

"Fuck," Pete said, and rushed into the room.

Osvaldo Valdez lay sprawled on the ground, mouth agape, with a single bullet hole in his temple. The stream of blood had run over his forehead and over his nose. His eyes were open, a look of surprise still on his face. The retired cop had been blindsided.

Pete stooped down. He pulled a handkerchief out of his back pocket and wrapped it around his left hand, which he placed on Valdez's neck. He knew the man was dead, so checking for a pulse was pointless. But he wanted a sense of when Osvaldo Valdez had been shot down—which would help him get to the why of it all.

Valdez was cold, but rigor had not set in, meaning he'd been killed fairly recently. Pete stood up and looked around the dark living room. He saw no signs of a struggle, beyond a nearby chair that had been knocked over, ostensibly while Osvaldo Valdez was taking his last drop.

Pete retraced his steps, wiping the door handles and anything he remembered touching. This was a crime scene, and he wasn't very popular with the Miami PD. He pondered how much time he had and figured it wasn't a lot.

He paced around the room, looking for anything that might serve as a clue about Valdez and his demise, but nothing jumped out at him. The house was musty, the shelves loaded with books—legal texts, Cuban history books, pulp novels—and framed photographs, some of a younger Valdez in Cuba, with a woman who Pete guessed was his wife. There were more-recent pictures, probably from around the time Pete's mother died, of Valdez and his daughter, one of him in uniform with a few other cops.

Pete gave this photo a second look. One of the men with Valdez was Carlos Broche, his father's partner. The man, who had been overweight and graying when Pete last saw him, slumped over and dying, looked vibrant in the photo. A man at the top of his game. Full head of hair, strong jaw, and a knowing look. Time forgives nothing, Pete thought.

He heard a siren then and knew he wouldn't be able to leave through the front door. Pete started to make his way to the back of the house, hoping the rear entrance would give him some cover. He found it off the kitchen, using his covered hand to push the door open slowly, making sure to lock it as he closed it again. He cut through the backyard, sticking close to the fence, his body hunched low. Soon, he was walking up Southwest 19th Avenue toward Calle Ocho, the sirens growing louder in tandem with the thrumming in his head.

# CHAPTER
# FIVE

"**D**ead? That's not good." Kathy took a long swig from her glass of red wine before continuing. "Who else knew you were meeting him?"

"I have no idea," Pete said, his eyes hovering over the wineglass. "No one."

He looked up at Kathy. She'd made no move to discuss what'd happened between them, aside from a low chill to her mood that made it pretty clear to Pete the encounter would not go beyond an isolated affair. She was wearing a turquoise blouse and black skirt. Business casual. She'd met Pete for lunch. Sugarcane was a moderately fancy sushi place in Wynwood, near Kathy's—and Marco's—apartment. She wanted to sit outside, she said. So here they were.

"You look nice."

"Thanks," she said dryly, not meeting his eyes. "Let's focus. What do we know about the murder?"

She wasn't being completely frigid, not yet. But if Pete had expected things to remain warm and affectionate like they had been at his house, he'd been wrong. She'd greeted him with a peck on the cheek and a stiff hug.

"He was shot point-blank. Not a lot of mess left behind, from what I could see. The *Times* did a small online piece that just went up, but it was light on details."

"Shocking, considering the bastion of journalism the *Miami Times* has been and always shall be," Kathy said, popping another spicy tuna piece in her mouth.

Both Pete and Kathy had spent time at the paper, though they hadn't known each other well then. Pete was well into his metamorphosis from functioning alcoholic to unemployed deadbeat, while Kathy was climbing out of her reporter dad's shadow to make a name for herself. If her father, Chaz Bentley, hadn't hired Pete to find her—well, things would've been different.

"Why did you call me?" Kathy asked, looking at Pete for what felt like the first time. "Today, I mean?"

"Who else would I call?"

"Hm. You're still really good at compartmentalizing," Kathy said, rolling her eyes slightly. "Did you forget the part where we had sex, Pete? Or do I need to remind you that I'm engaged to Marco, thus complicating things like us having sex?"

"I didn't forget," Pete said, leaning back in his chair, taken aback by Kathy's sudden offensive. "I just—I don't know. I didn't think you wanted to talk about it."

"Oh, I want to talk about it," she said, nodding. "On my terms. So, when you called me, I thought you had, oh, I dunno, decided you wanted to have an adult discussion about the adult things we did to each other, and the ramifications of it all. Instead, we're talking dead cops and robbers again."

Pete hesitated, struggling for a response.

She reached across the table and grabbed his hand briefly. "We messed up, okay?" Kathy said. "It was a moment of weakness for both of us. That's all I know right now. I need some time to think about everything else. Just … stop with the puppy dog stuff. The, 'you look nice'-slash-'please love me' stuff, all right? That's what got us into this mess."

Pete opened his mouth to respond, but she cut him off.

"That sounded much meaner live than it did when I practiced this morning," she said. "Sorry."

"No, it's fine, I get it."

Pete noticed her eyes drifting away from him and focusing on something behind his seat.

"Do you know that guy?" Kathy said, motioning toward the entrance to the restaurant's outside seating area.

Pete turned around to see Eddie Rosen approaching, a creepy grin on his long face.

"Mr. Fernandez," Rosen said as he approached the table. "Ms. Bentley, I presume?"

"Yes, how very Victorian of you," she said. "Who might you be?"

"Eddie Rosen. I represent someone who would like to speak with Pete here."

"Ah, right," Kathy said. "Alvaro Mujica."

Rosen nodded, as if surprised Kathy would utter his client's name aloud.

"Look, I told you I'm not talking to your boss, okay?" Pete said. "So let us be."

Rosen dropped a folder on the table. "I wouldn't be so quick to usher me out," he said.

Pete opened the folder. Inside were a stack of large, glossy photos that featured Pete entering Osvaldo Valdez's house, and a few of him exiting via the back door. The pictures in between included shots of Pete wiping down the front and back doors for fingerprints. Pete closed the folder quickly and slid it over to Kathy, a blank expression on his face. She scanned the photos fast, realizing immediately that a shakedown was happening.

"What do you want?"

"Oh, just some answers," Rosen said, his expression smug. "Would be bad if these photos got into the hands of law enforcement, wouldn't it?"

Rosen was right. Pete had made a name for himself by shining a light on the department's worst practices—whether it involved rooting out corruption, past indiscretions, or ties to organized crime. Though his dad had been a detective, the Miami PD was not fond of Pete. This would be manna from heaven for them. A chance to take out a pesky fly with a blowtorch.

"Again, what do you want?" Pete asked.

"I want you—and your partner here, if that's how you want to play it," Rosen said, nodding toward Kathy, "to meet my client. I want you to consider taking on the case he wants you to look into.

I want you to do that with the knowledge that I am in possession of these photos, and I can forward them along to the right—or wrong—people with the click of a mouse."

"Lawyers, huh?" Kathy said, grabbing another avocado piece. "They get you over a barrel and suddenly you owe them your firstborn. Look, we'll meet with you. It's fine. But we don't respond well to blackmail. So promise to dump those photos and we'll come to the meeting in good faith."

Rosen seemed momentarily surprised. He pursed his lips.

"I'm sure we could come to some kind of arrangement," he said, his attention on Kathy now. "But—"

"We'll consider the case, okay?" Pete said. "What more do you want? You win. We'll meet. Just tell us when."

Rosen shrugged. "No, it doesn't work that way," he said. "You'll meet Mr. Mujica, and—unless there's some extreme, extenuating circumstance—you will take this case. A car will pick you up outside your house tonight at eight. Be ready. Dinner will be served, too, so come with an appetite and dressed like you give a damn."

Rosen grabbed the folder and left.

Pete watched as the tall man entered a dark luxury car and drove out of sight.

"Guess we know what our next case will be," Kathy said.

"You don't seem worried."

"I'm not the one in those pictures leaving a murder scene. But, as usual, I will help you."

"Let's see what he says. How bad could it be?"


Pete and Kathy sat on Pete's small front porch a few minutes before eight. He was wearing a suit, unsure what attire was expected when you were meeting a reputed mob boss. Kathy was wearing a sleeveless, slinky black dress, with a gray sweater on reserve.

Pete looked at his watch. "What could this guy want with us?"

"With you, you mean," she said, checking her reflection on her phone. "I'm just coming along for the ride. I'd like to ensure you live, even if you're going back on your promise to retire. But yeah, it does seem a little strange he'd go to such lengths to get us on a case."

"Maybe I shouldn't have brushed Rosen off so quickly."

"Regrets, you've had a few."

"How's Marco?" Pete asked, trying to change the subject.

Kathy looked up at him with cold eyes.

"He's ... fine, I guess," she said. "Let's avoid the topic for now, all right? I still need to work some things out before we can talk. I need to talk to Marco, too. Moment of weakness or not, I made a mistake. If I want to salvage anything with him, he needs to know."

"Fair enough," Pete said.

"And for future reference, I am not the type to ever want to have a major discussion about 'us' as we wait to get put in a car driven by gangsters. Sorry if that doesn't jibe with your schedule."

"That's fine," Pete said, his defenses up.

With that, they saw the black town car pull into Pete's driveway. A man in a crisp black tuxedo stepped out and opened the back door. He motioned for them to slide inside. They walked down the porch steps and got in the car, which was empty.

Eddie Rosen was in the front passenger seat. He looked back and smiled as they clicked their seatbelts in place.

"Glad reason won out," he said. "This'll be good for all of us. And, I should add, financially rewarding, too."

"I can't wait to swim in a pool of dirty money," Kathy said.

"The checks will clear, don't worry," Rosen said.

"I don't think that's what we're worried about," Pete said.

"Mr. Mujica is a very busy man. Even in retirement," Rosen said, as if reading from a prepared script. "We'll meet with him, have dinner, and then Cunningham will drive you back. You should be home before the eleven o'clock news."

"Can't miss Fallon," Kathy said.

Rosen nodded at the driver, who flipped a switch on the dashboard. A tinted mirror slid up, closing the gap between the front and back seats.

"We'll be there soon," Rosen said, his voice muted by the glass separating them.

The Redlands was a long, wide swath of unincorporated Miami–Dade County, southwest of downtown. It was littered with sprawling farms and long, rolling patches of green. The Redlands was named for the large stretches of red clay common to the area. Also common? Peacocks. The large, obtrusive birds were all over. As the dark car sped through the vacant, poorly lit streets, Pete wondered just what he'd gotten himself into.

They pulled into a winding gravel driveway and stopped in front of a tall black wrought-iron gate. The driver touched a few numbers on a phone keypad stationed near the doors. The doors slowly creaked open and the car drove through.

From what Pete could tell, they were off of 167th Avenue, in the high 200s, street-wise. A circular path around a fountain served as an entryway to the estate at the end of a long road. The house driveway was massive—gray and off-white brick, with a central, looming edifice with smaller, similar house-like structures stacked around it. The stars were easier to make out here, but it also made it hard to see much beyond the sheer size of the house. Calling it a mansion was an understatement.

"Our client is not starving," Kathy said as the car pulled up near the front door.

She had been mostly silent during the forty-or-so minutes the drive had taken. Pete wasn't sure if she was still stewing over his poorly timed Marco question or merely trying to figure out a plan. Either option left him in the dark.

Cunningham stopped the car and came around to open the door for Kathy. Pete slid out after her and they followed Rosen through the front door, which was being held open by a tan Hispanic man with gray hair and a wispy moustache, in a light-blue guayabera. He nodded at Pete and Kathy as they entered.

Once they were all inside, the man closed the door and walked in front of the group, his hands clasped together.

"Don Mujica will see you in the dining room," the man said. "He is not a man to be kept waiting."

The man, whom Rosen called Eugenio, guided them through the house's cavernous and twisty hallways. The walls were loaded with original art and photos of a younger Mujica and his family.

"All of the art hanging on the walls is Cuban," Rosen said in a hushed, reverential tone. "All before the revolution. As you probably know, Don Mujica was part of the invading army at the Bay of Pigs."

"He must have been very young," Kathy said.

"He was barely sixteen," Rosen said. He pointed to a picture of a teenage Mujica standing near a group of older men. "He lied about his age to get into the training program in Guatemala, and by the time they realized he wasn't even eighteen, it was too late. When he was captured, the Castro regime treated him like anyone else."

"That'll make you grow up fast," Pete said.

Rosen nodded.

Eugenio bowed slightly and opened two oak doors that revealed a wide, expansive dining room. A long, dark wood table stretched through the middle of the room. Seated at the far head was an older man in a dark suit and navy blue tie, with closely cropped gray hair and a full, well-trimmed beard. The man was sturdy, but not chubby—he had the look of a former baseball slugger who'd managed to stay in shape despite the temptations of retirement. He nodded in their direction.

Rosen stepped into the dining room and sidestepped to face Mujica and Pete. "Kathy Bentley and Pete Fernandez, this is Don Alvaro Mujica," Rosen said, waving a hand toward the older man, who did not move.

Pete walked toward Mujica, his hand extended.

The older man didn't stand up to meet Pete. He took Pete's hand, his grip strong but not forced. He brought his face close to Pete's, his voice soft and low.

"Welcome to my home," Mujica said to Pete before shifting toward Kathy. He took her proffered hand and kissed it gently. "We have much to discuss, I am told. Please, sit down."

Pete and Kathy sat across from Rosen, with Mujica at the head of the table. They waited as the older man situated his silverware, positioning the cutlery in a formation only he seemed to know. After a few moments, he cleared his throat.

"My colleague, Mr. Rosen, tells me it was quite difficult to bring you here, to my home," Mujica said, his words rolling out languidly and soaked with regret, his accent strong but not indecipherable. "That's unfortunate. But I am happy to see you, regardless."

Pete fought back the urge to push the conversation. Alvaro Mujica didn't seem like the type who was pressed into talking when he didn't want to.

"I just ask that you take whatever preconceived notions you have about me and put them on the shelf," Mujica said before taking a sip of water. "What you read in the papers is not always the truth."

"Don Mujica has heard great things about you," Rosen said, looking at Pete and Kathy. "And we need help from people who can be discreet but effective."

"Your names are always around," Mujica said, waving his hand over his plate. "That cop, Varela, owes his life to you. The nasty business with that cult, too. You have a reputation. I respect that."

"The suspense is killing me," Kathy said.

Mujica shot Kathy a look—a motion that felt out-of-place, so quick and in contrast to the thoughtful, sedate demeanor he'd presented thus far. The viper could snap.

Eugenio walked in, a tray in his hand. He placed plates of food in front of Pete, Rosen, and Kathy—*arroz con pollo* and a small side salad. Before leaving, he filled Kathy's wine and Pete's water. As the butler bowed and exited, Rosen spoke.

"Don Mujica's son, Javier, was murdered a few weeks ago," Rosen said, his expression solemn. "Gunned down outside of a jazz club downtown. The police have no suspects. No motive. And, because of my client's reputation, no desire to pursue the case beyond the basics."

"My son was a good boy—a good man," Mujica said, clearing his throat. "We had our disagreements, like all children and parents do. But there was a strong love between us. I had high hopes for him and his life. Now those hopes are gone forever. To think he was taken out like some kind of street animal … it brings me great pain."

"I'm sorry for your loss," Pete said. "And while I'd love to be of help, doing a private investigation of an open murder—whether the police are working it or not—is going to be very hard. The Miami police don't like me much, and I doubt they'd be open to me riding along with them."

"Be patient," Mujica said, raising a hand slightly. "There is more to this story."

"To put it gently, Javier and his father had some issues," Rosen said, folding his napkin onto his lap. "Javier had no interest in carrying on his father's business. He wasn't suited for that kind of thing, he thought. He wanted to pursue music. He was a fairly accomplished jazz pianist. I don't know how familiar you are with jazz, but if I had to describe his style, it'd be a mix of Bill Evans and Lennie Tristano, with a Latin flair. He was a rising star on the scene, for what it's worth."

Mujica continued: "The problem with me and my son is a common one, I believe. Javier wanted to run off and play his music and I wanted him to work, to make a living, to be a man. Start a family. But he had problems, too. Drugs. Drink. And that woman. That woman is why you're here."

"*Cherchez la femme*?" Kathy asked.

"Excuse me?" Mujica said, squinting at her.

"Look for the woman," she said.

"Yes, he was married," Mujica said. "His wife is the one who interests me in this."

"Javier got married a month or so ago to a woman we know very little about, beyond her name," Rosen said, forming a steeple with his fingers over his now cold food. "We don't even have a photo of her. But we know she exists, and we know she's on the run. We need to find her."

"Allow me to ask a dumb question, but … why?" Pete asked. "Javier is dead. I mean, aside from a desire to get to know the daughter-in-law you've never met, why track her down?"

"She has something that belongs to me," Mujica said, his voice growing hoarse and gravelly. "Something she should not have. Something that has been in this family for some time."

"What does she have?" Pete asked. "Money?"

"Javier had no will, but he was wealthy, thanks to his father," Rosen said. "So all of that now goes to his wife—even if she is only just recently his wife. Are you familiar with the painter, Armando Garcia Menocal?"

"Cuban painter, yes?" Pete asked. "I've seen some of his work."

"*Si, ese es*. He was a freedom fighter in my country—against Spain, before Castro was even a thought in our minds." Mujica said. "'Death of Maceo' is one of his most famous pieces. But what many people do not understand is that Menocal also did variations on this piece. One of which was complete—and in my possession. My son was very fond of this painting. He would sit and stare at it for hours as a child. He wanted to hang it in his home, he said. Promised to keep it safe. So, I agreed. Who am I to refuse my only son? I thought the responsibility might even help him. But now he is dead, the painting is missing, and this woman has disappeared in a cloud of smoke. You see what my problem is?"

"I get it," Kathy said. "You want the painting back. But let's not dance around this. The press makes it pretty clear that you're someone who is not scared of—how do I say this?—putting people down if they defy you. And by 'down,' I mean 'dead.' So, if we find this woman, what can you guarantee in terms of her safety?"

"Right," Pete said. "We aren't going to be party to murder."

Mujica's eyes flared. He turned to Rosen, an imperceptible exchange happening between them.

"My client is a very successful mamey farmer," Rosen said, a wry grin on his face. "There will be no repercussions beyond getting the painting—and Javier's money—back. Because they rightfully belong to my client."

"Not according to the law," Pete said. "They belong to his wife."

"She is a wife on paper only," Mujica said, his tone still serene and glacial. The older man's demeanor sent a chill through Pete. "What kind of wife is a stranger to her husband's family? What kind of wife doesn't attend her own husband's funeral?"

Mujica took a slow sip from his wineglass and turned to Rosen.

"I'm glad you brought these people here, Eddie, I think they'll do a fine job. They're smart. They'll know what to do next," Mujica said, nodding to himself. "Please show them to the car and explain the terms before Cunningham takes them home."

With that, Mujica returned his attention to his meal, as if he were the only person in the room.

They didn't get to finish dinner.

Rosen, following a skittish Eugenio, led them out of the dining room. Their goodbyes with Mujica were brief and perfunctory. He was done with them.

By the time Pete and Kathy piled back into the car, Cunningham was behind the wheel, and Rosen was ready to speak, leaning over the roof and peering into the car's dark back seat.

"Javier's wife was named Beatriz de Armas," Rosen said. "That's all I know. A name. No social, no picture, no birthdate. Just the name on the marriage license."

"Do you have any info on Javier?" Pete asked. "The clubs he played in, people he knew, photos, anything? I didn't get much time with the big man in there."

"Don Mujica does not like to waste time. He does not like to debate things he feels are defined in his mind," Rosen said.

"You really know how to make these things easy, Eddie," Pete said.

"You're the detective, right?" Rosen said, tapping on the hood. "Earn your money."

"We'll send you our billing info and rates, don't you worry," Kathy said.

"And we'll send you the proof that the photos are gone when you find Beatriz," Rosen said. "No sooner. Cunningham, see that these two get home safely. We need them fresh and ready to work."

"You got it, boss," Cunningham said.

"Before we go," Pete said. "One question."

"Sure," Rosen said, waving at Cunningham to hold off.

"Why us? Mujica doesn't strike me as down on his luck. He could afford any kind of investigator. And, well, I haven't exactly been active in the field since I got hurt—"

"Died," Kathy said. "Like, was literally dead for a short while."

"You have a way of getting entangled in these kind of cases," Rosen said with a smirk. "Figured it made sense to come to you first, this time."

"One more question, Eddie," Pete said. "What was your relationship with Javier like?"

Rosen stiffened.

"Relationship?" Rosen said. "I've worked for Don Mujica for almost twenty-five years. I saw Javi grow up. I took him to baseball games and soccer practice. He was like a son to me. I helped raise him, basically."

Pete was surprised by the emotion in Rosen's voice. The man's jaw was clenched, as if trying to stave off tears.

"I could care less about that stupid painting—and art is my business. But I work for Don Mujica, and he wants it back," Rosen said, his teeth gritted. "What I do care about is finding out who took Javi away. If that means sending you on a wild hunt for a piece of art, in the hopes that finding his mysterious wife will lead us to his killer, then I'm all for it. Does that answer your question?"

"Sure does," Kathy said.

"Then get to work," Rosen said, as he backed up. Rosen waved at them as they pulled away from the house and down the winding driveway.

Pete's sense of dread increased with every mile of distance between them and the gigantic, solitary house, like a fading vision that still managed to haunt him.

# CHAPTER SIX

Kathy and Pete parted ways after Cunningham dropped them off in front of Pete's house. Her look was distant and preoccupied, as if she had somewhere to be, but wasn't sure where. They agreed to circle back to Javier Mujica's favorite haunts to get a sense of the man before diving into things in earnest. Kathy said she'd do a few basic record searches to see if she picked anything up on Javier—and, more importantly, on the mystery woman known as Beatriz de Armas.

But Pete hadn't been able to sleep, and he was even less adept at being patient. He didn't want to wait until Rosen sent over a list of venues where Javier Mujica had played. He could figure that out for himself.

The rest of the night—at least until dawn—was spent scouring the web for any kernel of video or audio involving Javier Mujica. Pete had started simply: with the music. He dug around and downloaded a few of Mujica's records—one solo, the rest with his band, the Javier Mujica Quintet, a tight, traditional jazz unit that resembled the first Miles Davis Quintet with a healthy dose of Latin flair. The horns were hot, the piano grooved, and the drums propelled the songs.

Pete wasn't a jazz person. At least not until the last year or so. Even then, he was still just intermediate when it came to jazz knowledge. But he knew enough to know what he liked—Coltrane, pre-fusion Miles, Dexter Gordon, Bill Evans, Charlie Parker, Ahmad Jamal. From what he'd heard of Javier Mujica, Pete felt like he'd like his music, too.

Mujica's piano was silky-smooth, his mastery of the keys fluid and nuanced, like a polished painter laying down the foundation for a beautiful landscape. He managed to strike the rare balance of impressive instrumental proficiency with a swing that often eluded jazz players who dabbled in the classics. Javier Mujica couldn't just play—he could play hot, the keys coming alive at the right moments to inject life into his solos and kick the songs up to another level.

The Mujica clips on YouTube were scant and of poor quality, shaky phone cameras drunkenly recording Mujica solo sets in and around Miami. Mujica himself seemed to vary from clip to clip—sometimes looking buttoned-up and professional, other times more ragged and gaunt. But the playing remained consistent. Whatever his vices, Mujica was a top-flight piano man. Pete knew that probably hurt more than helped. Addicts often rationalized their problems based on how they survived or worked—and if the work was still getting done, and getting done well, what was the problem? Mixed in with the Miami footage were a few long-distance concert shots from down the East Coast and a few clips from Europe. The one spot that kept cropping up was Le Chat Noir. It seemed like a good enough place to start.

Before picking up Kathy and visiting the bar, Pete needed to make a pit stop. One that he hoped would shed some light on not just Javier Mujica, but on his father—and on the painting in question.

Alina Caldera was retired, living in a quaint if cluttered bungalow in Miami's chic Coconut Grove neighborhood. She lived her life out of the spotlight: donating to worthy causes anonymously, shopping for antiques and, when the mood struck, buying art. It was the latter that interested Pete.

Before selling her world-renowned Cuban art gallery, Caldera was one of a handful of noted experts on the topic. Since then, she'd stepped back into the shadows, hoping to retire quietly from a bustling, active life lived in the spotlight. From the '60s until very recently, Caldera had been one of the most vocal and visible advocates for Cuban art in exile—promoting the much-admired *vanguardia* artists, such as Carlos Enriquez, José Mijares, Daniel Serra Badue, and many more. She, along with other equally passionate gallery owners and connoisseurs, had made it their mission to establish a beachhead for Cuban artists creating works on U.S. soil, away from their homeland, as they waited for its inevitable liberation. Or so they thought—and hoped—at the time.

Pete had reached out to her manager via email, on the off chance that she'd see him. Her rep had been quick to reply and very frank—if he hadn't been specific about what he wanted to discuss, she would have declined. But her curiosity was high, and she wanted to hear more. She would see him right away. And could he bring some *pastelitos de guayaba*? She didn't get out much, and she missed the tasty Cuban pastries.

Pete was happy to oblige.

Before he could knock, the door swung open. On the other side of the doorway was a woman well into her seventies, but looking more like she was on the long side of fifty. Alina Caldera was not one for vices, or so Pete had learned while researching her life and work. She didn't drink, she didn't do drugs, she rarely had coffee, and couldn't fathom a day without exercise. No, the only addiction she had was to Cuban art—the images created by fellow Cubans in exile, specifically. Over the years, she'd become a noted speaker and writer on the topic of art created on the island prior to Castro's takeover.

"You're Pete Fernandez?"

"That's me."

"Come in," she said. "Susana will get you coffee or whatever you'd like to drink. Let's meet in my office. I don't have a lot of time today."

Pete nodded and followed Caldera into the main foyer and down a winding hallway. The aforementioned Susana intercepted them. Pete declined a drink and entered Caldera's spacious office, which would have been a bit more spacious if it hadn't been cluttered by every kind of canvas in every size—some stacked against a wall, some hanging around the large window that looked out onto the bustling neighborhood of Coconut Grove. Books, notepads, and sketch pages took up the rest of the office's surface area.

"Not a computer person?" Pete asked, taking a seat across from Caldera.

"Not anymore," she said with a limp smile. "My vision's basically shot, so I just dictate by phone or record myself, if I ever think of anything worth repeating."

Pete laughed. He liked this lady.

"Like I said, I don't chat with reporters or investigators often— I'm retired, I'm done working," she said, waving a hand toward the clutter in her space. "Or so I say. But you mentioned something that I couldn't ignore."

"The lost Menocal painting?"

"Yes," Caldera said, her sharp features tightening a bit at the thought, like a lost idea she desperately wanted to remember. "Yes, I just can't wrap my head around that."

"That it exists?"

"Well, first off—it doesn't exist," Caldera said. "At least not to my knowledge. Menocal was one of Cuba's most beloved painters and had a lush, vibrant style that lent itself to many things, like landscapes and historical scenes—but, I don't believe he ever did ... different versions of his work. Which is to say, the idea that there is another, alternative take on 'Death of Maceo'—that I find completely baffling. And I'd love to know more."

"What can you tell me about Menocal?" Pete asked.

"He came from a well-known family," she said. "He studied art from some of the best Cuban artists at the time, including Miguel Melero. After a time, he went to Spain and studied under another great painter, Francisco Jover. He also became part of the culture there—hobnobbing with major players in the arts in Spain. He exhibited his work and was generating a great buzz, if that was even a word back then. After a while, he returned to his homeland and joined Cuba's battle for independence from Spain. Once the war ended, he went back to painting, and to teaching art. His work is well known—he's not some obscure nobody, mind you. His art can be seen in the Presidential Palace, Havana's Municipal Building, and more places that I can't recall off the top of my head. Suffice to say, he left his mark."

"Do you think the painting might be a fake?"

Caldera laughed. "First, I want to know who owns this painting," she said. "Then I'd like to see it. Then I'll decide whether it's real or not."

"My client would prefer to remain anonymous," Pete said, not without a bit of shame. "So, I don't think I can be helpful there."

Caldera's eyes squinted slightly, the smile remaining on her face long after the laugh ended. She didn't need Pete to tell her anything. "It's Mujica, isn't it?"

"I can't say," Pete said, his tone soft enough that he might as well have exclaimed "Bingo!"

"You know, I'm surprised, because usually Eddie doesn't get fooled," Caldera said. "He's smart. He has a few galleries. I ran into him from time to time over my few decades in the business."

"What was he like as an art dealer?"

"The worst kind," she said, no malice in her voice. Stating a fact. "He knew what he liked, and he didn't care about the market or building up an artist's career. If he liked something, he'd gobble them all up."

"Isn't that a good thing?"

"Not if you want to build a name for yourself," Caldera said. "Not if you want people to talk about your work and bid on it and create a sense of a movement. It'd be like someone buying every Sinatra record and locking them away so no one could hear them—only, maybe, hear *about* them."

"Why would he do that?"

"Eddie didn't care about the business, or about ethics, or about helping artists," she said. "He cared about himself, and if a painting was worth ten thousand and he could flip it by neutering the rest of the artist's work, he'd do it. He'd bury someone to make a buck. It's part of the reason he's not as active in the art world anymore. He's got a bad rep."

Caldera looked at her slim watch. "I think it's time I took a nap," she said. "But if you do decide to let someone look at this painting, if and when you get it back, I'd love to discover a 'lost' Menocal. At least long enough to know it's a fraud."

Pete started to get up, but hesitated. "Is there anyone else I should speak to about this? Who might be able to help?"

"Well, I guess I should be humble and note that I am not the be-all, end-all on Cuban art," she said, looking out the large window, letting the hot Miami sun coat her aging face. "Susana can give you a few contacts—just some gallery owners that might be able to assess the veracity of this claim. And, honestly, we may all be wrong. Stranger things have happened. But call me dubious and wary."

Pete shook the woman's hand. "Thanks for your time," he said. "I'll keep you posted."

"Be careful with Mujica," Caldera said. "He's a shark. He plays the part of the mamey farmer very well, and Eddie is adept at giving him great cloud cover—he's often the bad cop in these situations. But make no mistake—Mujica's in charge. Every move Eddie makes comes from his boss. Eddie's just along for the ride, wherever Mujica's going."

Le Chat Noir was a cramped, two-level jazz club in downtown Miami. Its black and red exterior seemed out of place in the blazing Miami sun, but Pete soon found himself grateful for the dim lighting, blasting air conditioning and soothing sounds that embraced them as he and Kathy stepped inside. Aside from the bartender, the place was empty.

The main area of Le Chat Noir was like many restaurants in the area trying to maximize their space. The big difference was a small, compact stage at the far corner of the first floor, surrounded by floor-to-ceiling shelves loaded with wine bottles, giving the place a claustrophobic, musky vibe.

"Do you think they play jazz here?" Kathy said, wiping at her brow.

"Safe bet," Pete said. He didn't let his arms rest on the bar. Didn't let his body lean into it, or his eyes wander the far wall, which boasted every kind of vodka, gin, and scotch. The obsession had, in some form, been lifted. But you don't poke the bear.

"Help you?" the bartender asked. The dark-haired woman's skin was eerily pale, with no makeup to speak of and a wary, defensive look. She probably wasn't used to seeing patrons this early.

"I'm Pete, this is my partner Kathy. We wanted to know if we could talk to someone about Javier Mujica?"

The bartender paused, her eyes scanning Pete again before she shook his hand. "Annie," she said. "And, uh, our owner's not here. So I'm not sure what I can say."

"We're not reporters," Kathy said, moving closer to the bar. 'We're private investigators."

"I recognize you both," Annie said. "You were caught up in that cult thing last year. Thought you were dead."

"He was," Kathy said.

"I got better."

"Well, nice, but I still don't know what you want from me."

"We're trying to find someone," Pete said. "They were close to Javier."

"Javi was a sweet guy," Annie said. "I liked him a lot. We were all torn up when he died. But I dunno if I can say more. I'm not, like, an official spokesperson for the club."

"No one wants to quote you," Pete said. "We just need to talk to people who knew Javi. To get a sense of him, you know? We can meet you later, too."

Pete took out his card and slid it over the bar. The eggshell white cardboard was plain and direct: *Pete Fernandez, Bookseller: 305-226-6851.*

"You sell books, too?" Annie said.

"He's a man of many talents," Kathy said, her delivery flat.

"My friend and I are going to grab a bite at …" Pete turned to Kathy.

"Balans is good," she said. "I can drink there, too."

"At Balans, on Brickell," Pete said. "Swing by. We'll be there for a few hours. We just want to chat."

Annie looked around the empty bar. "Let's just talk here," she said. "I can't leave my post, or whatever. Want a drink?"

"Yes, please," Kathy said. "Vodka tonic with a lime."

Annie looked at Pete, eyebrows raised.

"Club soda."

She poured seltzer into a large glass from the bar's beverage gun and slid it over to Pete. She started mixing Kathy's drink and motioned for them to take the two seats facing her.

"This way, if my boss does decide to show, I'm just serving two lushes."

"Why would he care if you were talking about Javier?" Pete asked.

"My boss, Larry, he was getting a lot of flak," Annie said, sliding a small straw into Kathy's drink and handing it to her. "Over Javi, you know? Letting him play here."

"Why?" Kathy asked. "From whom?"

"He wouldn't say," Annie said. "Just that someone wanted him off the bill. Which would've sucked, because Javi was really, really good—when he wanted to be."

"What do you mean?" Pete asked.

"Javi had problems," Annie said. "He partied too hard. Drank too much. Had some major drama with his partner, wife, whatever she is. If he showed up halfway sober, the set would be amazing. If he was fucked up, it'd still be okay, but if you knew his music—if you were a fan—you'd be bummed. You came to see Oscar Peterson and ended up getting Oscar the Grouch. People would be asking for refunds. There was only one bad, really bad night—the only time he fell apart while playing. He just zonked out, fell asleep at the piano. It was sad."

"Any journalists come out?" Pete asked. "You know, to review the sets?"

Annie paused for a second. "Not really, no," she said. "There was one guy, Albert or Angel, older. Cuban. Was a big fan. Did radio, I think?"

"Menendez?" Pete asked.

"Yeah, that's him. Javi was excited when he'd show up. It meant some good buzz. He'd get so excited. It was cute."

"You cared about him," Pete said.

"Yeah, of course," she said. "He was my friend. I mean, not like, extremely close or anything, but a lot of times it was just me and him sitting at the bar, talking about life, after closing."

"Were you together?" Kathy said after a long pull from her drink.

"What? No way."

"Why no way?" Kathy said. "He was a handsome guy, talented. You're pretty and smart. You obviously had time and opportunity."

"It wasn't like that," Annie said, wiping down the bar, not meeting their eyes. "I mean, whatever, I understand he was with someone else. But we helped each other. I wasn't expecting anything else. It was complicated, I guess."

"Complicated is my middle name," Kathy said with a warm smile. "So, was it just something where you'd hook up after he played? Or were there sleepovers? Did his wife find out?"

Annie leaned on the bar, her shoulders hunching over, giving her the look of someone trying to excise something deeply buried.

"I don't know, I don't care," she said. "He didn't want to be with her anymore. She was driving him nuts. I don't think he wanted to be with me, you know, like in the end. But he wanted a change. He felt really confined. He wanted to work on his music, move to New York or somewhere else, with a better jazz scene. Away from his father."

"What did he say about his dad?" Pete asked.

"He hated him," Annie said, looking up at Pete. "His dad's a gangster. He pulls this BS where he's some kind of mamey farmer, but the guy's a killer. One of the OG Cocaine Cowboys, you know? *Bolitero*, whatever. He didn't want Javi to play music. Hated that he was a drunk and a junkie, a flawed person. Wanted to keep him under his roof and watch. Javi didn't want that. So he married this woman, moved out here, started playing in the club as often as he could, and kept living off daddy's money. It was his form of protest, maybe."

"What about this woman?" Pete asked. "What can you tell us about his wife?"

"Ah, the mysterious Beatriz," Annie said, a frown forming on her thin face. "I met her once. She hardly ever came to hear him play. Didn't seem Hispanic, honestly. I don't know how PC that is, but fuck it. I didn't really even know it was her until Javi pointed her out. I mean, look, everyone here knew we had a thing going, so I could sidle up to him, be affectionate. Not all couple-y, but more than strangers. So, my point, he came up to me first thing and introduced her—kind of winking, like, hey, turn it down, Annie, be cool."

"What was she like?" Kathy asked.

"A frigid bitch, if I'm being honest," Annie said. "Barely said hi."

"What did she look like?" Pete asked, trying to steer things away from Annie's jealousy.

"She was attractive, in a cliché, *Pretty Little Liars* way," Annie said. "Thin, blond hair, nice lips, good body. She was older, like your age—"

"How old are you?" Kathy asked.

"Twenty-seven."

"So she was in her mid-to-late thirties?" Pete asked, trying to keep things going.

"Yeah, she looked good for her age, like you do," she said, nodding at Kathy. "No offense."

"Plenty taken," Kathy said before finishing off her drink. "You owe me one."

Annie nodded and started prepping Kathy's refill.

"Anyway, that was the one time I met her," she said. "Beatriz just sat near the stage, listened to Javi's set, and left on her own after the first part. Which, honestly, was a huge fucking relief because fuck that bitch. She treated him badly, and I don't think he even wanted to marry her."

"It is pretty weird how that stuff is forced on men these days," Kathy said, accepting the next round.

Kathy's joke flew over Annie's head.

"Any idea where Javi lived?" Pete asked. "Anything else that stands out that might be helpful to us?" Pete stood up.

Kathy downed the rest of her drink.

"Nah, I never went to his place. It never got to that point, honestly. I'm trying to think of anything—I mean, this is probably nothing, but it sticks with me for some reason," Annie said. "It was a few nights before he—before he died. We were in the back, he was taking a break before his next set, and ... we were just messing around, you know? He was fucked up. High, definitely. Drunk, too. We're back there, kissing and stuff, and he stops, like he was struck by lightning, and looks at me—eyes all wide—and says, 'They got to her, Annie, they got to her and she's gone now, all gone.'"

**Y**ou didn't tell me this case would require us entering the hellmouth," Kathy said as Pete pulled into the large parking lot in Doral.

Think of a nondescript, generic corporate headquarters and you're probably imagining an area that resembles Doral, a municipality that's bookended by the Florida Turnpike and Palmetto Expressway. Cookie-cutter housing projects pepper the landscape, crowding around parks and bland-looking business centers. This was where journalism had come to die. *The Miami Times* was not the place Kathy and Pete had left behind years before. The original building, nestled in downtown and overlooking Miami Beach, was gone—sold off to real estate developers a few years back. Now, the paper did most of its editing—the actual page design was outsourced to the *Times*'s parent company in Baltimore—in a compact, three-story building that looked more like a medical office than a grizzled haven of enterprising journalism. But life, like the newspaper landscape, was ever changing, and the *Times* had hit on some hard, well, times. Dropping ad revenues, competing online outlets, and buyouts had left the staff depleted, inexperienced, and overworked. If you asked Pete, the newspaper wasn't on life support *per se*, but closer to hospice care.

They got out of the car and walked toward the peach building, the parking lot half-empty. Over the entrance hung a massive sign—THE MIAMI TIMES MEDIA COMPANY.

"Even they don't want to claim to be a newspaper anymore," Kathy said.

Pete chuckled, but he wasn't in a good mood. He didn't want to be here either. Despite his acrimonious end with the *Times*—his boss, Steve Vance, had let him go after a final bit of insubordination—he still held the place in some regard. Journalism mattered. It pained him to see the paper in exile like this, and he knew it was still staffed by some good, talented people. He figured Kathy was going through the same speed cycle of grief.

"Why are we here again?" Kathy asked. "It's late. I'd like to get some food and wine in me."

"The *Times* also owns a public radio station, WLRZ," Pete said as they reached the door. "One of their shows focuses on jazz—'Late Night Jazz.' The host is an old friend of mine."

"So you want to pick their brain about our friend Javi?"

Before Pete could continue, they were intercepted by a slim, clean-shaven older man, his gray hair slicked back to reveal a smooth and unblemished face. He was wearing a light blue polo and khakis.

"Pete Fernandez," the man said. "Never thought I'd see you here again." Steve Vance extended his hand.

Pete shook it, the man's grip limp and brief. Vance, if Pete's info was up-to-date, was the paper's managing editor of special projects. A fancy title that could mean anything. He was also the man who had fired Pete a little over five years ago, a final move made after Pete's excessive tardiness, mistakes, and general inability to handle his duties. He'd had been drinking heavily around the time Vance fired him, spinning out before crashing hard and reaching his bottom. At the time, Pete had come to hate Vance. Now, even though the man was probably just as obnoxious as he'd been back then, Pete understood why he'd pulled the plug on Pete's journalism career.

"Steve, hey," Pete said. "How's it going?"

"Not too bad," Vance said, looking over Pete's shoulder. A glimmer of recognition in his eyes. "Well, I guess it's old home week here. Kathy?"

"Hi, Steve," Kathy said, a dry smile on her face.

"I hear you're doing some good work for the *New Tropic* these days," Vance said, sliding his hands into his pockets and leaning back. "Would love to see if we could get you back here. Your dad, despite how things ended, left a pretty big legacy."

"I'm not sure I could suppress the clutching nausea I feel each time I get close to this office enough to do it every day, Steve," she said with a straight face. "But thank you for the offer."

Vance nodded, the smug smile still on his face. "Well, I gotta run," he said, shaking Pete's hand again. "But it was good to see you. Glad you landed on your feet."

Pete held on to Vance's hand for a second longer than the man expected. "Steve, I'm actually glad to see you."

"Oh?"

"Yeah, this may sound ... strange," Pete said. "But I wanted to thank you, for what you did."

"For letting you go?" Vance said, a look of bafflement on his face. "Son, don't think I did that with any gusto—"

"No, no, it's not that. I just needed the wake-up call. I was angry with you for a long time. But now I know it was the right thing."

Vance, still perplexed, nodded to himself. "Well, okay," he said, looking as if he expected a surprise or gag of some kind to kick in. "I'm glad you got your life together. It seems like we're all doing well."

"This was not totally painful, but let's move on before things get too awkward," Kathy said. "Plus, I would really like to be inside, where the air conditioning is working and my blouse isn't sticking to my skin."

Vance nodded again.

They exchanged pleasantries and moved inside.

"Did you check him off your little resentment list?" Kathy said as they approached the security desk. She knew Pete worked the program, and part of that program involved making amends to people you'd wronged while drinking—or even sober, when not acting soberly. Though Pete wasn't sure he'd directly wronged Vance, he knew that the man had been affected by Pete's irresponsible behavior.

"Yeah, I guess," Pete said. "Never thought I'd see him again."

"I prayed I'd never see him again," Kathy said. "He was my dad's boss on the city desk when he was a reporter. They were buddies. I remember him coming over for dinners at our house a few times a week, when my parents were still married and pretending to like each other. Nice enough, forgettable guy, if a bit power-mad, but he always gave me a creepy vibe, too. Like a car salesman desperate to close out the month."

They showed the security guard their IDs and explained why they were there. He ushered them toward the elevators and told them to go up to the third floor.

Kathy leaned on the far elevator wall as it creaked up the three flights.

"So, who is this we're seeing?"

"My old boss, Angel Menendez," Pete said. "He was the sports editor at the paper when I moved back to Miami. Gave me the job on the copy desk. He probably wouldn't have fired me."

"Why did Vance get the shot?"

"Angel was sick, cancer," Pete said. "He beat it, thankfully, but came back to nothing. His old job had been filled and they treated him poorly. So, they shifted him to a gig with their public radio station. Same pay, benefits, similar work, plus a radio show every night."

"Could be worse."

The doors slid open and they walked into the newsroom.

The WLRZ studio was on the far end of the third floor, tucked into a corner, past the advertising and finance departments—a dead zone where most journalists feared to tread. You knew you weren't near any newspaper-making because the halls were quiet, painfully so. You could hear a phone vibrating if you tried hard enough.

They reached a door labeled WLRZ Studio. Above it, a red sign that read RECORDING was off. Pete rapped on the door.

"Did your grandfather ever bring you to his radio station?"

"Don't remember, but maybe he did," Pete said. His memories of his grandfather Diego Fernandez were blurry. Diego, a Cuban exile and Miami radio magnate, had been gunned down by Castro agents—the early members of what would become Los Enfermos—when Pete was very young.

The door opened and a stocky man in his late fifties stood in the doorway. He was tan, a salt-and-pepper beard paired with thinning wisps of hair on his head. His initial reaction to the knock was one of annoyance, but that faded as soon as he realized it was Pete on the other side of the door.

"Well, damn, I thought you were just blowing smoke when you said you needed to talk," the man said, stepping toward Pete and yanking him into a strong hug. "Good to see you."

"You too, Angel," Pete said, pulling back. "This is my partner, Kathy Bentley."

"Nice to meet you," she said as they shook hands.

"Likewise," Menendez said, nodding. "Heard a lot about you."

"My reputation precedes me, I guess," she said.

"You guys are in the paper a lot," he said. "Serial killers, drug gangs, that cult thing—almost feel like we've kept in touch all these years."

It was a veiled jab, and an understandable one. Angel Menendez had given Pete his job at the *Miami Times* when Pete was forced to rush back to Miami from New Jersey in the wake of his father's death. What he'd first thought would be a few weeks of mourning and organizing his father's affairs had turned into a move, with his fiancée Emily in tow. Upon realizing the relocation would be permanent, Pete reached out to Menendez, looking for something less exhausting than the investigative sports reporting he'd done—at diminishing quality in correlation to his alcohol intake—for the *Bergen Light*. Menendez, an old friend of Pete's editor at the Light, had seen untapped potential in Pete—a talent he could groom and hopefully revive.

Things didn't work out that way. Soon after Pete took the job on the *Miami Times* sports copy desk, Menendez went out on an extended sick leave. By the time he returned to the paper, Pete had been fired and had stumbled into a new, more dangerous calling. They'd spoken off and on over the years, but this was the first time they'd seen each other.

"Pete manages to find trouble on a regular basis," Kathy said, smiling. "I just ride along."

Menendez nodded, a signal he was done with pleasantries. The man was glad to see them, but that didn't change his usual demeanor: no-nonsense, blunt, and to-the-point. They had come and diverted his workday, and he wanted to get on with it.

"I need some information on a jazz pianist, guy by the name of Javier Mujica," Pete said.

"Investigating his murder?"

"Not exactly," Pete said.

"Step into my office, let's talk," Menendez said.

They followed him down the hall.

Menendez's office was a tiny space at the other end of the floor, just enough room for a small desk and two chairs. It was sparsely decorated; an Ornette Coleman poster hanging on the far wall was the only sign that this room was actually assigned to a particular person.

Pete and Kathy took their seats.

"So, if you're not looking into the kid's murder, what else is there?" Menendez asked, popping a piece of Nicorette gum in his mouth. "I mean, he was a good player. I saw him live a few times. Kid had a lot of baggage, that's for sure, beyond just playing music."

"You know his dad, right?" Kathy asked.

"Mujica? The *bolitero*?" Menendez asked. "Yeah, of course. Ask people around Miami and he's either a patriot for trying to topple Castro, or a drug-running scumbag. I'm thinking it's somewhere in the middle, but what do I know? I just do radio now."

"What about Eddie Rosen?" Pete asked.

"He's harder to pin down," Menendez said. "Been Mujica's right-hand guy—*consigliere*, basically—since it all started. Runs a pretty successful art dealership, too. One of those Art Basel bigwigs. Doesn't do many interviews or stuff like that, keeps his profile low. But he's basically another limb for Mujica and his organization."

"Were you on the news desk when he was coming up?" Pete asked. He knew Menendez when he got to the sports section, but the journalist had hopped around the *Miami Times* newsroom earlier in his career.

"For a bit, yeah, I was an ACE," Menendez said.

ACE stood for Assistant City Editor, a slot reserved for capable local news reporters who wanted to run around less, work with copy more. It was also the first step up the ladder to management, if that's what you wanted. It'd apparently worked for a while with Menendez. Then life happened.

"Mujica was a big fish. It was him, Los Enfermos, and the various other ethnic gangs—Colombians, Albanians, Italians ... but mostly

Mujica and Los Enfermos. But Mujica focused on *bolita*, he came from Cuba via Union City, in Jersey. So, they left each other alone. Los Enfermos ran drugs, a lot of drugs, and Mujica played the numbers. The peace was fragile, but lasted."

"So what changed? Why would someone take out his kid?" Kathy asked.

"Not sure, really. But that's assuming this was gang-related," Menendez said. "And I thought you weren't investigating his death?"

"We're not," Pete said. "We're trying to locate his wife."

"Wife?"

"Yeah, he was married," Kathy said. "To a woman named Beatriz de Armas. Except, the only women who exist in Miami with that name—and it's a long list—don't fit the bill. We've spent the last few days going through public records trying to pinpoint who she might be."

"Assuming she had a Florida driver's license with a Miami address," Menendez said, not missing a beat. Pete appreciated the man's quick brain and knowledge of how investigations work. "Which isn't a lock. Millions of people filter through the city, with papers, without papers—whether our esteemed *presidente* wants them to, or not."

"So we've hit a dead end," Pete said.

"You've hit them before, you'll hit them again," Menendez said. "I'd just retrace Mujica's steps in the months before he was killed. You said he married this woman recently? What does she have that's of interest to your client?"

"Can't get into that," Pete said. "Just know it's something of great monetary and personal value."

"More valuable than the truth about his son?" Menendez said, scratching his chin. "Color me curious."

"You said you saw him play a few times," Kathy said. "What was that like?"

"I go down to the club—Le Chat Noir—a few times a month," Menendez said. "It's nice. Very un-Miami. Cool, dark, good music. They mix it up, too, not just Latin jazz fusion. Mujica was old school—you could pinpoint his influences in a second. Bill Evans, a little Dave Brubeck, some Ahmad Jamal, and a dash of Bud Powell and Lennie Tristano, too. Does that mean anything to you?"

"Just names to me," Kathy said.

"Right, right," Menendez said. "Well, the kid had chops. He could play well with others—he'd make his solos count, and he also knew how to defer to his bandmates. He could also carry the load with his keys if he had to. Very versatile. He could do classy, pinkie-in-the-air stuff but also get down and dirty with the keys. I'd never seen anything like him, really. He was a talent."

"How did he rate with other players on the scene?" Pete asked. "How did he fit in?"

Menendez sighed and leaned back in his chair.

"He was in demand. Other players respected him, other instrumentalists wanted to play with him. That's the top line. There's no time to give you a more extensive jazz piano tutorial, but maybe pick up a few records and get a sense of what this guy dedicated his life to," he said. "I know Mujica had a Soundcloud account and posted his records there, too."

"I checked out a few clips," Pete said. "But I'll dig into that later."

"There are worse forms of research," Menendez quipped.

"No record deal?" Kathy asked.

Menendez shook his head. "The days of artists—well, new and unknown artists—getting a big label deal are done," he said. "At least when it comes to jazz. Most try to scrape together a living playing live and selling music directly. From what I could tell, Mujica was doing that—regular residency at the club, some decent-selling albums put out on his own label, and a few bigger tours to fill out the gaps. Packages, mostly."

"Packages?" Pete asked.

"Yeah, a bunch of artists pool together and create a bill, and that's what the tour organizers shop internationally," Menendez said. "They put together package tours of Europe and places where jazz musicians actually make money, and there's an audience beyond hardcore fans."

"What can you tell me about his group?" Pete asked. "Was he still playing with them at the end?"

"For a while, yes," Menendez said. "Until recently, when he decided to fly solo at Le Chat Noir. He was the lead of the Javier Mujica Quintet—with a bassist, sax, trumpet, and drummer."

Menendez pulled out his phone and started scrolling.

"I don't have the drummer's info, guy named Jamie Cacace," Menendez said. "He's pretty good, if a bit overpowering. But good.

The bassist I know. A veteran of the scene, if there is such a thing. I just texted you his info. Name of Rugova. Matt Rugova."

"Is that Spanish?" Pete asked.

"Mattias Rugova," Menendez said, putting the phone away. "Cuban-Albanian, if you believe it. Helluva bassist. Plays trumpet, too. It was hot gossip when Javier disbanded the trio and went solo."

"Do you know if he had a manager?" Kathy asked. "Someone handling gigs and stuff like that?"

Menendez rubbed his chin, then began rifling through a desk drawer. He pulled out a business card that had seen better days. He tossed it at Pete.

"This guy," Menendez said. "At least for a few years. He got the boot not long ago, which makes me think Mujica's new wife took over the business side for the rest of the kid's life. Lots of change for musicians who tend to like consistency—new manager, no band. A stark breaking point."

Pete looked at the card. Devon Owens—Artist Management. He slipped it into his pocket.

"Anything else?" Pete asked.

"Haven't seen you in years and that's how it is?" Menendez asked.

Pete could tell he was joking. The man knew what it was like to chase a story, for print or not.

"When our boy Pete has a bone in his mouth," Kathy said, getting up, "it's hard to distract him for too long."

"Let me know what Devon has to say," Menendez said as Pete and Kathy made for the door. "He was pushing really hard for me to interview Javier on the show, up until he got fired. Desperate, I would say."

"What do you mean?" Pete asked, his hand on the doorknob.

"He was begging me to do it," Menendez said. "Emotional. Pleading. He said it just might save Javier's life."

"To get on a public radio station?" Kathy said, incredulous.

"To get him away from the pills, from the needle," Menendez said. "For a second. To remind him of why he got into the music to begin with. He was worried the kid had forgotten, and that he would never pull himself out of the darkness."

# NIGHT STILL COMES

*May 5, 1983*

She knew she was laughing too loud. Swaying too far. But she didn't care. She was free. She felt good. The coke had kicked in. Formed a chemical reaction with the four whiskey sours. She was good. Not too high, not too low. Just right. Fairy tale time. She felt it pumping through her—like a turbocharge. An electric burst in her mind and body. The bar's dim lights made it all feel off somehow, like a dream.

She reached over to him, this man, and palmed his neck. She pulled him close. He seemed surprised at first, but that faded fast. The kiss was quick, dirty, not romantic but sexy. That's what she thought, at least. He seemed into it, too. They kissed for a while. She fell forward, almost collapsing onto his barstool. The jukebox was playing Dylan. "Tombstone Blues."

God, she hated Dylan.

The bells jangled and she heard footsteps behind them. The bar was empty aside from them, the bartender—a middle-aged *Marielito* named Juan, and an older man passed out in his beer at a booth near the bathroom. The place smelled of cigarette ash and wet clothes. It was close to midnight and they were on the fringes of suburbia on a weeknight. Most of the world around them was asleep. This man, this person she met and conned into giving her a few bumps in the bathroom, he'd probably be at home with his wife right about now. He was handsome, she guessed. Not ugly. She couldn't really tell, she admitted to herself, as her tongue slipped into his mouth, tasting the cheap beer and pretzels that made up the man's diet.

She felt something on her shoulder. It took her a second to pull back and away from—Steve? Stan?—this guy, through the haze of the cocaine and the drinks, and figure out what the hell was happening. A hand. Then she saw *him*.

She saw her husband, his hand on her shoulder, and eyes as black as any hole she could ever imagine. A burning anger she'd never seen on his face before. A look of pure rage that made her feel shame and disgust all at once.

"This is how you're living your life now?' he asked, his voice monotone, like a phone operator asking you to please wait on the line. "This is how things are for you?"

Stan or Steve or Stew stirred, turning his attention from the broken kiss to the man who interrupted him. He started to get up, but her husband raised a hand.

"What the fuck is going—"

He raised a hand with a Miami Police badge in it.

Stan or Stew sat down. Then slid off the chair, shrugged his shoulders and went to take a piss. Not worth the fight. She didn't think less of him for it. She couldn't really think less of him, anyway.

"What are you doing here?" he asked. "You should be home. With your son. Not out on the street, drunk, high, doing who knows what with anybody you find—"

"You're just a high and mighty asshole," she said, her voice loud and hoarse. She heard the bartender backing away behind them. "Who the fuck do you think you are? What, are you following me now? Trying to make sure I never see our kid again? *Hijo de puta.* That's what you are."

He didn't rise to the bait. Remained calm. The seething anger a faded memory.

"You never call me," she said, her voice still loud, but less confident. She sounded like she was trying to convince herself of something. "You kick me out of the house and the only time I hear about you or our son is when I call you. I'm living on a fucking sofabed, man.

I don't have a job. I don't have any money. Is that what you want for me? Your wife? Do you even give a shit? Doesn't seem like you do."

"When you're ready, you can come home."

"Fuck you," she spat.

She could see the veneer crack. See the stoic cop exterior go brittle. Was she ashamed? Sure. But fuck him. She'd made him mad. She'd won. And yeah, fuck him. She needed some time. Time to herself. To have some fun for once. To relax and breathe, *coño*.

Did his eyes burn red when he saw the man's hand on her leg, sliding up past her skirt, his other arm draped over the chair—like an animal claiming ownership. Well, fuck them both, she thought. Neither of them had a stake in her. They just thought they did.

He wiped at his face, then looked at her. She saw the wetness in his eyes, the defeat in his expression, and whatever victory dance she was doing in her head shriveled and died like a plant left on the side of the road.

Her husband didn't respond. Didn't say anything. He turned around and walked out. She thought she saw his head shake—a small move, a small sign of displeasure—but she couldn't be sure. The drinks and drugs flowed back to her brain, like a dam breaking inside her skull, and she felt light-headed and awash in disgust and fear.

"I guess this is how things are now," she said to herself. She saw Stan or whatever his name was walk out of the bar, waiting just long enough to ensure her husband wouldn't catch him on the way out.

"I'm sorry, I'm sorry, I'm sorry," she said, first softly, then louder, trying to push down the tears and keep herself together. Then she realized she was curled into herself, her head on her knees, her body balanced precariously on the rickety stool in this shitty bar in Kendall with nowhere to go that even resembled a home. "You have to understand, you have to forgive me, Pete."

She would fix this. She would make it right. She just needed a minute. A chance to breathe. Maybe another drink.

# CHAPTER SEVEN

It was too late to pay Devon Owens a visit, and Kathy didn't seem interested in discussing the status of their affairs beyond a quick peck on the cheek and a promise to check in tomorrow. Pete looked at his watch: 7:00 p.m. He had enough time to make it back to Westchester.

The drive was quick and uneventful, Miami's streets sedate in the sky's fading sunlight. He pulled into the St. Brendan's parking lot, which was mostly empty, and stepped out of the car. He noticed the cluster of people right away—the cloud of cigarette smoke wafting above them as they paced and chatted outside the entrance to the church's basement. Pete nodded at a few familiar faces and made his way inside.

The chairs had been set up and the coffee was brewing. The signs—familiar slogans Pete had been reading for years—were hanging on the walls, and the room's spastic fan was sputtering. "One Week Away Makes One Weak." "One Day At A Time." "Easy Does It." "Let Go And Let God."

The slogans felt comfortable, even if they bordered on the cheesy. They worked, he thought.

Pete felt a hand on his shoulder.

"Hey, Pete, good to see you."

It was Jack. Pete's old sponsor and an ex–Miami cop. They'd lost touch when Pete moved to New York briefly, but reconnected over the last few months. He was a good man, and had basically saved Pete's life in one way or another a few times.

"Jack," Pete said. "How's it going?"

"Not bad," he said, smiling. "Your timing is impeccable."

"Oh?"

"Yeah, Duane can't make it tonight, so I'm looking for a speaker," Jack said. "You game to share?"

Pete winced. He loved Alcoholics Anonymous. The program and its 12 steps had helped him survive not only sobriety, but the tragedies and pitfalls life had thrown at him over the last five years. But he hadn't been as connected as he usually was over the last few months. Part of it was because he was recovering—physically and mentally—from his brush with death. The bullets Salerno sent into his chest missed his heart by an inch and did plenty of damage. As Kathy liked to bring up routinely, Pete had died. It was a miracle he was still standing, much less working on another case. When he thought about it that way, it made him feel more guilty about not being more diligent with the program. But he wasn't in the mood to share. Not tonight.

"Ah, I'd love to, but I don't think I can," Pete said. "Just not ready."

Jack frowned.

"No one's ever ready," he said. "You know that. Plus, what happened to what I taught you? Never say no if you can say yes to someone in the program. You don't get anything if you're not giving back."

Pete knew he was right, but he also knew he couldn't hack it. Not tonight.

"Maybe next time," Pete said. "I'm not up for it."

Jack was a mellow man—laid back, quick with a joke, low key—but Pete could tell he'd hit a nerve.

"You gotta start living, son," Jack said, moving over to the central table that was covered by flyers and AA literature. "You didn't just get a second chance to do the same things you were doing. Don't think I don't know how you were up in New York. Hiding from your life down here, going through the motions. Don't fall back into that routine."

"I'm not that person anymore," Pete said, trying to keep his tone neutral.

Jack started organizing the stacks of books, making the display seem more appealing.

"No, you're not," Jack said, nodding to himself. "You tell me you're fine and I should believe you. But I don't, really. Answer me this, Pete—do you have a sponsor? Are you sponsoring anyone? How many meetings you hitting a week? It's about putting the stuff that's eating us up inside out there, so we're free of it, and I know you're dealing with it in your own way ... but that hasn't worked, has it?"

Pete didn't make a response. He had none.

"Right, okay," Jack said, clearing his throat. "Here's another thought, Pete—one that I've hesitated to bring up because, well, it's a foundational thing. It isn't just about drinking. But it is about living. You got this second chance. This shot at life, at happiness. Did you ever consider that, I dunno, maybe ... this life you've chosen is hurting as much as it's helping?"

"What?"

Jack raised his hands. "Don't get defensive, not yet," he said, his kind eyes focused on Pete. "Hear me out. This thing, this injury you suffered—it taught you something. But you still seem to be processing it. You've told me before—it's like a new lease on life. Like you're awakened for the first time. But you still have to look back. You have to keep your side of the street clean. Take an inventory of your past. Where have you been harmful? Are the things that worked for you then—do they still work for you now?"

"**H**i, my name's Pete and I'm an alcoholic."

He cleared his throat and pushed his water bottle away slightly. He was at a small table, facing a group of about twelve other alcoholics seated in stiff, uncomfortable folding chairs. The group varied from weekly visitors to the wounded faces of those new to the rooms, still reeling from their own bottom, raw and uncertain. These were the most important people in the rooms—the ones who needed to hear his message most. Jack had been right. He owed it to them to do this. And, who knew? It might end up helping him, too.

His story started in the typical way—with some kind of disclaimer about drinking in his family. Every story was different. Some alcoholics had alcoholic parents. Some didn't drink until they were adults. Some landed in the middle. Pete's father had not been a drinker, but every now and again, Pete remembered seeing his dad crack open a beer or have a glass of wine. For him it never became a thing. A scene. A memorable drunk.

*"My first drink was in a car, with an older friend, it was a Corona and I chugged it ..."*

The memories cut through Pete's mind as he spoke, and he felt each word as if it were happening for the first time. The sip of the golden liquid, the repulsive taste and the sense of pressure, of wanting to fit in with the older kids, to be someone who was ready to drink. Like a man. Like an adult.

*"It wasn't until college, though, that I started drinking for real ..."*

The dirty, burning taste of the cigarette in his mouth for the first time, the wind slapping his face as he and his friends drove down to the Grove. The spectrum of flavors, each beer tasting so different at first, then blending into a sludgy, neutralizing sameness. The exhilarating dizziness of being drunk for the first time. The best time. The laughter that bubbled to the top with no filter, no hesitation. The jokes that landed perfectly.

*"But I never drank to have just one ..."*

The 12-pack he drank over a few hours, sitting with his friends in the college newspaper office. The back-to-back to back White Russians that "tasted like a milkshake" at a party later that night. The hazy drive home. The morning after—a brutal, throbbing pain in his skull that seemed to seep down to his toes. The pool of vomit on the floor beside his bed, and an aching, confusing desire to die.

*"I'd cover one eye while driving just so I could see straight ..."*

Nods of understanding. A few mumbled words of agreement from the small crowd. Pete's story echoing around the church basement.

*"I was waking up in strange places, with people I barely knew. I was behaving badly. Treating people badly, people I was supposed to care about ..."*

Eyes opening with a jolt, body covered in a cold sweat, looking around, trying to piece together the night before through the haze of morning light. An unfamiliar place, an unfamiliar shape next to him. The dry, coppery taste in his mouth. Cuts. Bruises. Shame.

*"I hit my bottom on a dirty bathroom floor in a Miami Beach hotel karaoke club ..."*

Hands on the cold, dirty tile floor. Saliva dripping from his mouth. Vision blurred as he tried to wipe vomit from his shirt. An aching pain in his face. People walking, looking down, moving on. Bad scenery.

*"My relapse proved to me that you pick up right where you left off when you go back. It was like nothing had changed. Except it got worse, much worse."*

The first sip, lukewarm vodka in the back room of The Book Bin. The familiar burning in his throat. The sad, empty release as he fell forward into the familiar abyss.

*"It was hard to even get drunk anymore. I holed myself up in a motel room with every intention to die there."*

Pete moved to look at his watch but felt his hands shaking. He looked into the eyes of the crowd, trained on him, waiting for the rest of his story. He hadn't wanted this to turn into a drunkalogue, where he just listed every bad thing he did while drinking—but it had, and that was fine. That was what he needed to share.

Pete tapped the brakes on his story a bit, easing into his life now. His job. His friendships. His routines and habits to help avoid another relapse. It wasn't perfect. He could go to more meetings. He could work the program better. He could be better. But the process was ongoing, and, as the book said—it was progress, not perfection. He had to keep reminding himself.

*"That's all I've got. Thanks for letting me share."*

The applause came, and it felt right—genuine and heartfelt. Pete was grateful for that. He took a long sip from his water bottle and then asked if anyone else wanted to share. A few hands popped up.

**"H**ow do you feel?"

Jack's question caught Pete off guard, as he folded one of the chairs and stacked it near the basement's far wall. The meeting had cleared out and a handful of group members were tidying up. He hadn't stopped to consider how he felt.

"Good, good, I think."

"You tapped the vein there. Felt like I was hearing you for the first time."

"Yeah, it felt ... different," Pete said. "Cathartic, I guess. I don't want to get all emotional about it, but it was good to clear out that headspace."

"You working a case now?" Jack asked.

"Sort of. Trying to locate a woman tied to a murder," Pete said. "And wondering about another dead body."

"Oh yeah?"

"So much for retiring to run a bookstore," Pete said with a dry laugh.

"Sounds nice, huh?" Jack said. "Hope you enjoy the good feeling from the meeting for a bit."

Pete nodded. He did feel lighter. Like he'd just run a few miles and was still riding an adrenaline high, minus the sweat and ache that came with exercise. But he needed time to himself. As much as he liked Jack, he didn't want to do a postgame analysis of his deepest, darkest secrets yet.

"Gotta run," Pete said. "But if you're open to it, I know a PI who could use a sponsor."

"Thought you'd never ask," Jack said with a smile as they shook hands.

"Catch you later," Pete said as he walked toward the door. He felt the soft vibration of his phone in his pocket as he stepped out of the basement and back into an area where he got reception. He checked his iPhone display: "Call me. ASAP."

Harras.

Pete jogged up to the first floor and stepped out into the muggy Miami night, the cloud of humidity slapping him in the face as he made his way to his car. He pushed the phone icon by Harras's name.

"Hey."

"Was trying to call you," Harras said, his voice sounding more hoarse and tired than usual. Something was wrong. "Kept going straight to voicemail. You in hiding?"

"Was at a meeting. What's up?"

"Got a call from one of my contacts on the PD," Harras said. "Like you asked, I'd been sending feelers out about Salerno."

Salerno. Pete had done everything he could—once he was able—to try and figure out what the man had wanted. But since then, nothing. He'd disappeared, despite Pete's best efforts.

"Yeah, and?"

"He's dead," Harras said. "They found him last night with two bullets in his skull."

# CHAPTER EIGHT

"**Y**ou didn't see these," Harras said as he slid the folder across the table.

They were seated at Pete's dining room table. Harras had already been on his way to Pete's when he called him.

Pete opened the folder and winced at the first photo on the stack. From what was left of the large man's face, Pete could tell it was Salerno, but it was not a pretty sight. The bullet holes made a gaping cavern on his forehead, above his still-open eyes. His mouth was curled into a confused, disappointed grimace.

"Where'd they find him?"

"Somewhere on Ocean Drive," Harras said. "My contact said there was some kind of verbal altercation, according to a few wits. Salerno got into it, other guy drew a gun, dropped him, and then hopped into a dark sedan. No prints, no leads."

"Mob hit?"

"Seems sloppy for a hit," Harras said. "Almost like whoever took Salerno out knew the guy personally—and knew he was here, in Miami."

81

"Why the hell was he here?" Pete said, letting the folder drop back onto the table. "After me?"

"Doubt it," Harras said, running a hand over his tired face. "When he came to you in New York, he wanted to find out if you had any info on a deal Doug Ferris had scored. He killed the guy's daughter, right? What's her name …?"

"Jen," Pete said.

Saying it out loud took him back to those cold months in New York and the time he'd spent with her. He'd been a chore—an older guy who had no sense of what he wanted out of life, sleeping with a twentysomething stripper who was more together than he'd ever hope to be. Vinnie Salerno had tortured her for info and then put two in her chest, leaving her to bleed out on her kitchen floor. Her only mistake was taking the day off to work on her thesis.

"Right, he couldn't get any leads, and he thought you were gone, so he moved on. Ended up here."

"We don't know what happened in between," Pete said. "Maybe the deal went down."

"From what I could dig up, Ferris got a line on a big drug score—a connect with a group of Colombians looking to offload a lot of cocaine somewhere—regularly," Harras said. "It was a life-changing find, which is the only reason why a made guy like Salerno would risk his mob life to get in on it."

"So, let's assume Salerno digs up the intel on the score," Pete said. "Then what?"

"Odds are, the drugs are coming from here, or—" Harras said. "Or, better put—*through* here."

Pete leaned back. He felt himself getting tugged at. Something reaching for him and trying to yank him into a familiar problem. His life was rarely simple, but after a few months of calm, the problems seemed to be sprouting problems of their own: Kathy, Osvaldo Valdez, the Mujica case, and now the return—although he was dead—of Salerno. Pete had just kicked over a hornet's nest, and he couldn't find a path that led him to safety.

"Any drugs that come through Miami used to go through Los Enfermos," Pete said. "But they're gone, basically."

"That we know of."

"Right, right. But assuming they're still, at best, fragmented, who was playing hall monitor and getting a slice before the drugs went to

Salerno?" Pete asked. "And then who was Salerno selling the drugs to? He didn't have the manpower to distribute—he was on the run."

"No clue," Harras said. "But I do know one thing. If Salerno, via Ferris, got his mitts on a ton of drugs, you can guarantee they were meant to go to someone else."

"And whoever that may be," Pete said, looking at his old friend, "they're probably very, very upset."

"You have a gift for understatement."

Pete stood up and started pacing from the dining area to his small living room.

"I'm getting too old for this shit," Pete said, staring out the living room's main windows, which overlooked the empty residential street that intersected with 87th Avenue.

Harras turned in his chair to respond. "We all are," he said. "Believe me."

"Get anything else on Valdez?" Pete asked, changing the subject, trying to clear his mind.

"A few more crime scene photos," he said. "I sent them over email. Nothing really out of the ordinary."

The doorbell rang.

Pete looked at his watch. It was close to eleven. He wasn't expecting anyone.

"I'll get it," Harras said, standing up and moving toward the door.

"Wait," Pete said, stepping toward the door.

Before he could say anything else, the door swung back, a kick sending it almost off its hinges. They saw the barrel of the silencer before they caught a glimpse of the man wielding it, but once Pete did, he knew they were in trouble.

The black mask, the flowing coat and hat were like something out of a pulp novel—but they were also a memory ripped out of Pete's most haunted moments: *The Silent Death*. An urban legend responsible for the deaths of many gangland figures, dating back from before Pete was even toying with the idea of being a detective. A mask Pete had removed to uncover his own, long-lost friend—Javier Reyes. Most important, a man Pete had seen die years ago.

It was impossible.

The masked man wheeled around, the gun pointed at Pete.

He didn't hesitate. Pete dove to his right, rolling onto the floor and hitting the far wall hard. It was a sloppy fall, but he was spared a direct hit, though he felt some of the shrapnel burning into his arm and right leg. He caught a glimpse of Harras grabbing the man from behind, his arm wrapped around his neck and pulling him backward.

Before Pete could think on it too long, the man moved the gun up, as if to shoot his own arm. Instead, the blast went over him, hitting Harras in the neck and shoulder. His friend's scream rang in his ears for what felt like a century. Pete watched as Harras stumbled back, hands clutching at his bleeding neck, the surprised yell now a droning moan.

"No," Pete said, standing up.

The man in the mask stepped toward Pete, the silencer trained on him as Harras fell to the ground, no longer moving.

Pete swung a wide kick in the man's direction, knocking the gun out of his hand. The masked man swung at Pete, a wide, sloppy arc. Pete dodged and grabbed the man's wrist. He pulled and twisted. The man dropped to his knees, the scream coming through the dark mask clearly. Harras wasn't making any noise.

*He's dead.*

Pete grabbed the man's head, his fingers digging into the mask, and felt his left hand form into a fist and crash into the man's face, making him go limp. He wanted to hit him again—over and over, but he stopped, took a deep breath, and let the masked man drop to the floor, unconscious. He rushed to Harras.

His friend, or what remained of him, was shaking violently, metal shards peppering his face and a hole in his neck revealing blood, bone, and more than Pete ever wanted to see of the inside of someone's body. He was dying.

"Hold on, okay?" Pete said. He reached inside his pocket and pulled out his cell phone. He started to dial 911.

But there was no holding on. In the second it took Pete to glance at the display of his phone and ring the police, Harras went limp. Pete felt an aching in his chest that threatened to burst through him. He didn't hear the hurried, stumbling footsteps as the masked man darted out of the house. Pete couldn't bring himself to care.

# PART II
# 'ROUND MIDNIGHT

# CHAPTER NINE

*Three months later*

"This is your office?"

Eddie Rosen seemed perplexed and a bit disgusted, like a princess walking into a janitorial closet. He scrunched up his long nose and tried to plaster a grin on his lupine face. He was here to deliver some bad news, Pete could tell.

"It's a bookstore first," Pete said, locking the door behind Rosen. "My office is in the back. But I meet clients here after hours. Well, when I used to have them. Like this."

Rosen nodded and continued to look around the packed and dusty shelves of The Book Bin. The store resembled a hoarder's garage more than a Barnes & Noble, but Pete felt that was part of the charm. For some book buyers, the journey was the experience—looking for just the right book. Or twenty.

"You wanted to meet?"

"My boss is not happy."

"I'm sad to hear that," Pete said, taking the seat behind the register. He was not sad.

"You're lucky he's a forgiving man."

"Guess it's my lucky day."

"Cut the crap, Fernandez," Rosen said, his words suddenly sharp and agitated. "I don't want to be here any more than you want me here. But you've produced nothing since we hired you and your girlfriend to find this woman."

"Beatriz de Armas is gone," Pete said. "If she ever existed."

Rosen stepped closer to the desk where the store's register sat and planted his hands facedown in front of Pete, his eyes open so wide Pete half-expected a vessel to burst from the strain.

"Mujica wants you gone. You're fired."

"I'll send you my last bill, or I can prepare it for you now," Pete said. "Got a printer in the back and everything."

"Are you insane?" Rosen said. "You're lucky Don Mujica is an understanding man. If this were fifteen years ago, you'd be dead. But he gets it. Your friend is gone, your lady friend stayed with her man ... you've hit a rough patch."

"It's not a rough patch if your life is always this way."

Rosen let out a protracted sigh, like a balloon deflating. "Send me the bill if it's reasonable," he said. "I'll make sure we're settled up, all right? But don't expect me to recommend you to any of my friends. You can rest easy about the photos, too. The books are cleared. Just leave us alone."

"I wouldn't dream of bothering you, Eddie."

Rosen shook his head before making his way out the door. The chimes signaled his exit, clanging heralds cutting through the quiet that usually enveloped the small bookstore.

Pete waited a few moments, for the sound of Rosen's car starting and turning out of the strip mall that surrounded The Book Bin. Then he got up, put his battered Marlins cap on, and walked out.

The car ride was brief, the streets empty in the wake of another painful Miami rush hour. It was September, so the swamp-like summer was beginning to ease into a less turgid fall, if there was such a thing in this town. He'd gotten the text a few minutes before Rosen's unwanted pop-in, and he was running late. Liz Phair sang about fucking and running, and Pete felt bad he was too distracted to sing along.

Rosen had a right to be disappointed, but Pete couldn't bring himself to care. He'd worked the Mujica case—he and Kathy had, for the most part—as best they could. Aside from a few rumors and innuendo, nothing pointed to a suspect in the murder of Javier Mujica, much less to the whereabouts of his wife, Beatriz de Armas. On top of that, Pete had been distracted by much bigger, more disturbing developments.

Robert Harras had survived the Silent Death's attack—but barely. At least that was the belief Pete clung to. But the reality was, he could be dead for all Pete knew. The ex–FBI agent had been whisked away into government protection almost immediately after multiple emergency surgeries to save his life. The narrative, as far as anyone else was concerned, was simple: Former FBI agent Robert Harras was dead, gunned down in Pete's own home by a man dressed up like the Silent Death, the mob killer of killers. He'd worn the same uniform as the man who'd menaced Miami for years and had ended up bringing Pete and Kathy together during Pete's first—albeit unlicensed and unofficial—case.

But who was wearing the mask now? And why had he been gunning for Pete? Pete's efforts to get any kind of answer about Harras from the Bureau—or the hospital—had hit a wall. Robert Harras was dead, as far as they were concerned; why did he keep asking?

The thought of Harras made his chest ache, a dull, burning feeling that Pete knew was grief and confusion. He didn't have time to mourn. His friend, wherever he was, would want him to push forward, to solve this thing. But the deeper he got into it, the less he came back with, like a man shoving his hands into burning sand, trying to find a missing coin.

Pete had spent the better part of the last few months trying to regain some level of control—over his life, his world—in the wake of Harras's encounter with the Silent Death. He hadn't come close to succeeding. But with the Mujica case stalled, Pete had thrown himself headlong into trying to figure out what happened to his friend—why someone had donned the mask and gear of the Silent Death and attacked Pete, only to escape with Harras barely breathing. Had Pete not been the target? If not, why had Harras been in the Death's sights?

The results had been almost nil. He'd chased down every contact, every informant he'd cultivated over the years—nothing. No one had anything to share. Some refused to talk. The fear was evident. They were scared of someone—or something—else more than they'd ever be afraid of Pete.

And he was doing it alone. Kathy had changed her mind, or at least had stepped back from the edge when it came to Pete. Probably a smart idea. Dave had been in the throes of early recovery. But Pete pressed on. Worked his old cop contacts. Tried to make new ones. He'd heard rumblings in the underworld of a general unrest—an imbalance in how the gangs and families and cartels played with each other. Something was disrupting the regular business of things. Someone was making a play. But that could be anything. It didn't point directly to Harras or the Silent Death.

His focus on Harras had helped the Mujica case wilt, Pete knew. But he didn't care. He didn't care about some retired gangster's dead kid, or his wife, or the painting she stole. His friend was gone. His mentor, Pete could admit that now. When they first met, he and Harras had been at odds—a decorated FBI agent and a two-bit private eye. But over time, he'd come to admire the old man. He'd learned from him—about being an investigator, about following clues and tracking down leads. But none of that had helped him. Harras was gone, and Pete was nowhere closer today to finding out where he was or who pulled the trigger than he had been when he saw his friend's body being loaded onto an ambulance.

Pete found a spot a half a block away from the Conde Contemporary Art Gallery and walked in. The place was empty, aside from a thin young woman with sunglasses near the front; a couple ogling a particularly confusing, colorful work at the far end; and the man he was there to meet. Pete nodded at the woman as he walked past her.

Dave Mendoza turned as the sound of Pete's approaching footsteps echoed through the gallery. "Thanks for coming."

"You call, I answer, that's the deal," Pete said, shaking his old friend's hand. "How're you holding up?"

"Fits and starts, man. But I'm sober today. Have been for about a week," Dave said with a genuine grin. His face looked fuller, more color spreading across his cheeks than the Dave Pete had encountered a few months back. It would have been a much starker change if he hadn't been meeting with Dave a few times a week over the last few months.

"That's great," Pete said, gripping Dave's shoulder. "Keep it up. Did you find a sponsor yet?"

"Yeah, I think so," Dave said, looking at his feet. "Guy at my home group seems to be on my wavelength. Gonna ask him next week."

"Ask him tonight," Pete said. "You know I can't be your sponsor."

Dave nodded. Though the mechanics of Alcoholics Anonymous and Narcotics Anonymous were similar, it wasn't the kind of thing where you could cross-pollinate the message. Though many drunks were also addicts and vice versa, the idea was you stuck with your program for official guidance. But Pete wanted to help Dave, so he'd agreed to guide him along until he found a real sponsor. It had taken his friend a while to even start considering it.

"Everything else okay? Your text seemed urgent."

"Yeah, I'm fine, I'm good, actually," Dave said, nodding a bit too fast. "Just trying to figure out what's left of myself, you know? The lawyers disentangled enough of our finances to get me a place around here and I'm doing some investing ... still have a few properties and now I'm trying to build up what I burned through after ... what, well, you know. Trying to get my shit together."

"Won't happen overnight," Pete said. "Be patient."

"Right. How're you?"

"Fine," Pete said. "Lost the Mujica case. Officially."

"Yeah?"

"Rosen fired me," Pete said. "Came by just as I was coming to meet you. Wasn't surprised. Hard to care, you know? Not with everything going on."

Dave grimaced. The loss of Harras had sent Pete reeling, but it'd also had a powerful, destructive effect on Dave. Though he and Harras had never been particularly close, the loss managed to disrupt the fragile balance of his sobriety. But despite the relapses and mistakes, Dave managed to hold on. For now.

"So, if it's not about your program, what is it?"

"Might be nothing, honestly."

"Didn't sound like a nothing," Pete said.

"You ever been to Lagniappe?"

"The jazz club?"

"Yeah, it's a cool spot," Dave said. "I went in there—met up with some friends—a few nights ago."

"Uh-huh."

"Anyway, we're in there, and I remembered the Mujica thing you've been working on," Dave said, his eyes darting around the gallery. No one else had entered since Pete arrived. "Y'know, just asking around to see if anything would shake loose."

"Dave," Pete said, a sprinkle of impatience in his voice. "Get to it. I'm not gonna give you shit for going to a bar. I trust you didn't drink or shoot up in the bathroom, okay? You know better, anyway. So just tell me what you texted me to say that couldn't be in the text you sent, all right?"

"That woman, de Armas?" Dave said. "She'd been there. A few weeks before."

"What? How do you know?"

"The guy playing—well, one of the guys in the house band, the drummer, forget his name," Dave said, hands shaking a bit. "He said she'd come by to listen to them perform. She was gushing over their set, I guess—offered to manage them. Gave them her card."

"Do you have it?"

Dave reached into his back pocket and pulled out a dark business card, with white letters on one side. BEATRIZ DE ARMAS—ARTIST MANAGEMENT. Under the name was a yellow star and the words "WE WILL FIND YOU" in smaller letters.

"Just when I thought I was chasing a ghost," Pete said, mostly to himself. "Can I hold on to this?"

"All yours," Dave said. "Not sure you can do much with it—no number."

Pete took a step toward the door.

"It's a start. Keep doing what you're doing, okay?" Pete said. "And get a sponsor. I want to hear what he's making you do the next time we talk."

Dave nodded in agreement. He rubbed at his eyes. "It's hard, man," he said. "Nothing has ever been this hard. I never thought I'd be—I mean ..."

"An addict?" Pete said, stopping in his tracks.

"Yeah, it sounds terrible, but yeah," Dave said. "You never think it'd happen to you."

"Denial is a hell of a drug," Pete said, placing a hand on his friend's shoulder. "But you're aware of it now, which is a huge step."

"Yeah," Dave said. He looked around the gallery. "How's Kathy?"

"Not really sure," Pete said. "With Marco, planning a wedding. With the Mujica case frozen, we haven't talked much."

Pete had given Dave the bare minimum of info. The truth was, Kathy had made it clear she wanted to fix things with Marco, and part of that meant minimizing her contact with Pete. He'd pushed back, but to no avail.

"Well," Dave said. "Now you have an excuse to talk to her, I guess."

Pete nodded to himself before turning back toward the gallery exit.

He pressed the buzzer again, letting it ring—a long screeching sound that Pete could hear through the apartment front door. After a few moments, a voice.

"Who is it?"

"Me."

"You realize what time it is, right?" Kathy said, her voice getting louder as she unlatched the locks and swung the door open. She was wearing a black T-shirt and boxers, her hair rumpled and chaotic. Pete tried not to stare. "Why didn't you call or text first, like a normal person?"

"Yeah, sorry," Pete said. "Di—did I wake you? You guys?"

Kathy flinched at Pete's stutter, but let it go with a shrug. "What's up?"

"Got a lead on de Armas."

"Pete ..." Kathy said, her voice dispirited with a slight tinge of frustration. "Can we talk about this later? I actually have work in the morning, okay? This is not acceptable. Especially after I told you—"

The door was still half-closed, Kathy blocking the way. Her words came out in hushed whispers. He was home.

"Marco here?"

"Let's talk tomorrow, okay?" she said, shaking her head. "I'll try to stop by the store."

She didn't wait for Pete to respond. The door shut with a loud *thunk* and Pete was left in a dark, empty hallway, his eyes boring into the thick, brown door—as if by staring at it he could will it to open again.

Pete heard the footsteps trailing him once he reached the parking lot to Kathy's building. He didn't need to be a private investigator to know who they belonged to.

He turned around to face Marco before reaching his car.

Marco was wearing a black hoodie and sweats. He did not look particularly happy, either. "I think we need to talk," he said, stopping a few feet from Pete. His demeanor was calm, not threatening. "Look, man, I really think you need to stop bothering us—stop bothering Kathy. I don't want to go all aggro, either. Let's just have a civil conversation about this, okay? You seem like a reasonable guy."

"Hey, I'm genuinely sorry for bothering you," Pete said. He meant it, but also realized he wasn't living up to his words by showing up at their apartment after midnight. "For what it's worth, I shouldn't have come here."

Marco shook his head, a humorless smile on his face. "It's not worth a whole lot, to be frank with you, man," he said. "You're not exactly my favorite person in the world. You've caused Kathy a lot of grief, and—"

"Look, Marco, I barely know you," Pete said. "And I realize what happened—well, wasn't ideal, but we're both consenting adults and I—"

Marco took an imbalanced, hesitant step back. His expression one of confusion, followed by hesitant realization.

"What the hell are you talking about?" Marco asked. "What happened?"

*Shit.*

# CHAPTER TEN

**S**hit.

The confrontation with Marco had ended with Kathy's fiancé turning on his heels and heading back toward their apartment. Pete had tried to call Kathy on his way home, to give her a heads up— *Marco might know*—but she didn't pick up. She hadn't responded to his subsequent calls or texts, either.

There would be little sleep tonight. Pete's brain was revved, and he needed to work a few things out before he'd have a shot at any kind of rest.

He reached The Book Bin and plopped himself down in the tiny back office. He flipped open his laptop and clicked on a familiar file. The bundle of images opened up fast, and Pete was once again transported to Osvaldo Valdez's living room. The images had been sent to him via email by Harras before their meeting in Pete's house. Before they were attacked by the Silent Death.

Over the last few months, Pete had pored over the photos— trying to find some kind of clue that would explain why the aging ex-cop had been put down so violently just hours after tipping Pete off to something, and moments before Pete was supposed to show up and meet with him. But he'd continued to draw a blank. Looking over the images had become almost ceremonial, like an arcane ritual meant to conjure up some evidence that would help him solve the case.

Pete understood what it really was: a desperate attempt to commune with Valdez and Harras. *Always chasing dead men.* The Miami police had let it go cold, unable to figure out who would have murderous eyes for the frail Valdez. Plus, there were bigger, more salacious cases to worry about. This was a blip on the evening news. Pete shook his head.

He was about to quit the program when his eye caught something in the last photo, a zoomed-in shot of Valdez's fallen body, a pool of blood forming around the man, his arms splayed out in an awkward position. A small piece of cloth near his left hand. No, not cloth—cardboard. A business card.

Pete used the program's zoom tool to get a closer look. It was a white card, but Pete could only make out the last few letters—"ENT." Under that line a few more letters—"OU." Underneath the text, a sliver of black and yellow. He pulled Beatriz de Armas's business card from his pocket and held it up to the screen.

"Huh."

He leaned back in his chair. Normally, he'd call Kathy. Or Harras. Or Dave. But it'd all gotten muddy of late. His romantic reunion with Kathy had soured faster than the first time, and Pete was sure he could have handled it better. The run-in with Marco was the most egregious example. His feelings for her hadn't changed. But Kathy, ever the smart one, wasn't into throwing caution to the wind anymore. In Marco, she'd found a stable, honest man who loved her, as opposed to an erratic, unemployed, and seriously injury-prone private investigator. He couldn't fault her. But he missed her. And now he'd have to grapple with the fact that he had potentially ruined whatever happiness she'd made for herself.

Harras was gone, and there was only so much baggage Pete could toss on Dave's fragile shoulders. Dave was in the tense, uncertain days of early recovery, where a small frustration that one brushed off normally could have seismic effects—and lead to a drink or a drug. No, he couldn't call him. Even if he'd been the one to give him de Armas's card.

But it was a bigger question that hit Pete like a sucker punch to the jaw: what was Beatriz de Armas doing in Osvaldo Valdez's apartment the night he died? The more complicated question could be, why would someone want Pete to believe that? It wasn't a coincidence that Dave got the same kind of card. Pete had looked over the image a number of times and had paid no mind to the piece of paper on the floor. He'd needed the actual card, fresh in his mind, to make him notice.

He stood up and slid the card back into his pocket. He closed his laptop and walked out, the horns and screeches of Miami traffic echoing through the night.

Lagniappe was a cozy, smoky bar-slash-restaurant on Second Avenue. The smell of tobacco and red wine mixed smoothly with the charcuterie that made up a large part of the menu. The lights were dim and the crowd was relaxed, lulled by the polished, tight band playing on a small stage at the far end of the space, near a set of doors that lead to a patio area. The entire venue gave off a buzzed, sated vibe—like the one Pete remembered having after a good meal, when you could savor a sip of wine. Except Pete had never sipped wine and didn't drink one glass after dinner. No, most times he chose to drink over dinner, and it rarely happened in a restaurant as nice as this.

Pete got to hear the band's last song—a faithful cover of the Miles Davis Quintet's "It Never Entered My Mind." The somber, plaintive number struck Pete as an odd choice to close out the set, but he was more used to rock shows, with their second encores and crowd-sung anthems. The crowd seemed into it, swaying to the moody trumpet lead, the tickle-touch piano providing a subtle dressing to the tune. As the number wound down, the bar erupted in applause—not raucous, but not stuffy, either. Jazz fans could get excited, too, Pete mused.

He started his approach just as the band was shutting down, packing their stuff up in the routine, automatic way gigging musicians make second nature. Pete made a beeline for the drummer, a solidly-built man with wispy hair and horn-rimmed glasses. He was Pete's age, but looked to have a decade on him just based on how he dressed.

"Excuse me," Pete said.

"All done for the night, sorry," the man said, loosening one of the notes on his snare drum, his back to Pete. "But we'll be here tomorrow night, I think."

"Thanks, but I was wondering if I could ask you a few questions."

The man turned around, his face wary. "About what?" he said. "You a cop?"

"Private," Pete said, extending his hand. "Pete Fernandez."

The man shook it, a knowing look on his face. "Huh, okay," he said. "Am I in trouble?"

"I don't think so, Mr. ...?"

"Lovallo," the man said. "Stu Lovallo."

The other musicians—a chubby piano player with a bald pate; a bearded, lanky trumpet player; a clearly loaded sax player; and a tall, stocky man wheeling a large bass guitar toward the bar—were moving away, as if understanding they didn't want to be part of this discussion.

"Stu, I'm trying to locate a woman, by the name of Beatriz," Pete said, pulling out the business card. "A friend of mine, Dave Mendoza, said he spoke to you a few nights ago about her and you gave him this."

Stu looked at the card and nodded to himself. "Yeah, yeah. She was by here a lot. Said she dug our sound. Thought we had some potential."

"When was this?"

"She in trouble?" Stu asked, standing up, the task of putting his drums away forgotten. "Because, look, this industry is tiny, tiny. I don't want to ruffle any feathers. We're just trying to make a—"

"No, she's not in trouble," Pete said. "I just need to get in touch with her."

"It's usually not good when a PI is looking for you."

Pete chuckled. "Never good when anyone's looking for you, huh?"

"Got that right," Stu said, rubbing his neck. "Man, I gotta tell you, I was smitten with this lady. But her card doesn't even have a number. How the hell am I supposed to find her?"

"Welcome to the club."

"What a knockout," Stu said, looking out into the empty bar. "Though, the hair was a clear dye job. But those eyes. Man. Killer body, too."

"Relax, Stu. We're only just getting to know each other."

Stu chuckled and went back to unpacking his kit.

"Buy you a drink?"

"Sure, yeah," Stu said, not looking at Pete, focused on yanking out his snare drum. "Whiskey, neat. Whatever they have in the well. I won't drink you dry."

"Price isn't too steep—just wanna pick your brain about this de Armas lady."

"Not much to talk about," Stu said. "Though, I'm really selling myself short here. You know most of it. Wish I'd gotten her number ..."

"I hear you, pal," Pete said, pulling out his wallet and handing Stu a twenty. "Anything else come to mind? This should cover a round. Consider it a tip for a good set."

"Did you really like it?"

"I like all kinds of creative things," Pete said. "Music, paintings, you name it."

Stu shrugged. "Money's money. So, okay—here's the rub, and you'll probably judge me for this."

"We're in a judgment-free zone, my friend."

"I followed her."

"Like, for days, or what?" Pete asked. "Because your creep factor grows exponentially the longer you do."

"No, no, not like that," Stu said, shaking his head. "I mean, kind of like that, but ... well, just to her apartment."

"She walked home?"

"Yeah, she lives nearby," Stu said. "Down the block."

"That's pretty damn creepy, Stu."


The 2 Midtown building was indeed a few blocks away from Lagniappe—a massive fortress-like condo that didn't really scream "pop in" when Pete reached the main entrance. Not surprisingly, Stu didn't want to tag along with Pete, despite his disturbingly intimate knowledge of Beatriz's life. He'd have to circle back to him at some point, Pete thought. He entered the lobby and stopped at the front desk, where a drowsy security guard looked up from his copy of the *Miami Times* sports page.

"Can I help you?"

"Here to see Beatriz de Armas," Pete said, his tone flat.

"No one here by that name."

"Black hair, around my age, pretty mysterious?" Pete said. "Works nights? Music industry type?"

"Jazz lady? Yeah, I know who you're talking about. Place is under another name, though. Burgos."

"Yeah, Burgos is her married name. My mistake."

"She expecting you?"

"Of course. But you know how she is, probably forgot to put me on the list."

The guard shrugged, unimpressed with Pete's banter. He picked up a phone at his desk and dialed a three digit code. Pete watched his fingers move. 419.

A few moments passed, then the guard hung up. His nametag said Humberto.

"No response," he said, palms up. "Sorry."

"Can you try again?"

Humberto cleared his throat and met Pete's eyes. "She ain't here," he said. "Haven't seen her come down in a while. I won't waste your time if you don't waste mine, okay?"

"No offense, Humberto, but it doesn't look like you're working all that hard. I mean, that's yesterday's newspaper, for God's sake."

"Turn around and leave, sir."

Pete pulled out his wallet and placed five twenties on the desk in front of Humberto.

"I think there's a hole in my wallet," Pete said. "And Beatriz has my sewing kit."

Humberto slid the money into his pocket, then gave Pete a frustrated look.

"These cameras pick up audio?"

"Nah, just video," Humberto said, motioning his head toward the camera monitor next to his computer screen. "And there isn't one pointed right at my desk."

"Figured," Pete said. "So call that hundy a tip and maybe you can look away while I take the elevator up to Beatriz's apartment?"

Humberto nodded. "Do your thing, bro. Just don't murder her."

"Gotta say, it's weirding me out you're so cool with a strange dude going up to this lady's place," Pete said, backing away. "Maybe consider another career? Something that doesn't involve people's privacy?"

Humberto looked away.

Pete walked toward the elevator and pushed the UP button.

419 was to the left of the elevator bank and around a corner. Pete rapped on the door. After a few moments he did it again. He waited. He leaned in, his ear close to the door. No sound. No rustling or "Gimme a minute!"-style exclamation. He wrapped his hand around the knob. Locked.

Pete started to reach into his pocket when he heard a noise. Faint, at first. A scurry of footsteps across a tile floor. He stepped back. The door swung open, a small figure—female—draped in a long black coat stepped out. A pair of large, dark shades covered a pale, stricken face, which was in stark contrast to the jet-black hair, cut in a short bob. But even with the eyewear and hair dye, Pete recognized her immediately, and he felt a sledgehammer hit him squarely in the face.

"Emily?"

# CHAPTER ELEVEN

"**S**tep back," she said, her eyes ice cold, even through the sunglasses. She'd pulled a gun out of her coat and had it pointed squarely at Pete's chest.

Pete did. His hands up. His mind was screaming. This couldn't be right. Things like this didn't just overlap. He felt his legs start to shake slightly.

"Emily—"

"Be quiet," she said. "Back off. I don't know you."

But Pete wasn't fooled. He saw the recognition in her expression. He knew the curves and details of that face too well to be misled by designer shades, a fancy haircut, and a dye job. He took a step forward.

"Emily, come on. It's me, Pete—"

"You have to leave all of this alone," she said. "You're not as lucky as you think you are."

"What are you—"

She moved the gun barrel closer to him. Her hands steady. Her vibe cool, collected—she'd handled guns before. Old hat. No worries. She motioned with her chin for Pete to step off.

"Don't make me hurt you," she said, her voice dry, no emotion, like a kid reading their homework aloud. She stepped away from the door and took a few quick paces toward the elevator before turning around. "Do not follow me. I'll hear you. I'm not coming back here."

And she was gone.

Pete heard the ding of the elevator and waited a few moments. He walked to the elevator bank and pulled out his cell phone. He dialed the number that he knew from memory. The voice answered on the first ring.

"Yeah?"

"You're not going to believe who I just saw."

"Not on the phone. We've got a situation."

"What?" Pete asked. "What now?"

"I'm texting you an address. Meet me there ASAP," Dave said.

The line went dead.

Dave would have to wait, Pete thought as he stepped into the open door of Beatriz de Armas's apartment. *Emily's apartment.* He took a few slow breaths. There'd be time to process what he'd just seen. For now, he had to gather as much evidence as he could before anyone else showed up.

The apartment was barren—a space barely used. Either she'd just moved in or was moving out. He flicked on a light in the tiny living room to get a better look, using his sleeve to avoid touching anything. There was a futon taking up most of the front space and little else. A cheap-looking coffee table next to it, covered with a handful of receipts, spare change, and some takeout menus. The kitchen, which was on the right as he entered, was equally spartan—a few glasses in the cabinets and a fridge that only featured a few restaurant containers and a half-empty carton of soy milk. The small coffeemaker was cold, half a pot still inside.

The apartment's sole bedroom was another story. The room empty aside from a twin-size mattress on the floor near the far corner, which was opposite a flimsy IKEA desk. Clothes and a stack of paperbacks—Chandler's *The Little Sister*, Margaret Millar's *The Fiend*, and Patricia Highsmith's *Deep Water* jumped out at Pete. Emily had gotten a taste for mysteries. He'd have chuckled if the circumstances had been different. There was no dresser or nightstand, just piles of neatly folded clothes near the end of the bed and a few toiletries in the bathroom. Emily had not been here long.

As he reached the desk, Pete felt his phone vibrating. *Dave.* Something was going on. But this would be his only chance to piece together why Emily Sprague-Blanco was back, masquerading as someone else.

The desk drawers were empty—and the top was barren aside from two notepads and a small, bound memo book. Both Post-It pads were blank, but as Pete ran a finger over one, he noticed someone had written on a page recently—leaving the indent of whatever was written on the following page. Pete grabbed a pencil from the Dolphins mug resting on the desk and yanked a page from the other yellow pad. Carefully, he shaded over the page, trying to capture the text that someone—presumably Emily—had hastily written on a page before taking it with her.

*~~Emily Blanco~~*
*Beatriz de Armas?? SWITCH OUT!!*
*Daniela Burgos—maybe*
*-*

*~~Bogota~~*
*Havana??*
*~~Mexico City~~*
*US? Not viable*

Beyond the first two names, the rest meant nothing to Pete. But that could change. He pocketed the sheet and rummaged through the rest of the desk. Nothing. He turned his head toward the door. He thought he'd heard footsteps. It was time to go.

In the car, Pete's mind spun out. *Emily.* He'd lost touch with her before she'd left Miami for Europe, where she'd planned to spend her dead husband's money and try to escape Los Enfermos. The final coda to their relationship, when she'd asked Pete to find out who'd killed her husband, fizzled as soon as she boarded that plane, two years ago.

But she was back. And she was somehow entangled in a case that Pete had put on the back burner when Harras disappeared. Was Emily Sprague, Pete's ex-fiancée, also Beatriz de Armas, widow to Javier Mujica? It was possible, sure. There were no photos of Beatriz anywhere—which was a minor miracle in an age where even people's pets had Instagram and Twitter accounts. It made little sense. He didn't have enough information. But he had a lot of questions. And that was a start.

The D Towers in Hallandale Beach.

Pete pulled into the visitors lot and walked past the security desk, nodding at the guard, an older, heavyset woman reading a copy of *Entertainment Weekly*. Pete took the stairs up to the fifth floor, feeling winded by the time he reached apartment 547. The door swung open before he could knock. A hand waved for him to step into the darkness.

"What the hell's going on?" Pete asked, grabbing Dave by the arm. "What's up with the cloak-and-dagger shit?"

Dave's face, illuminated briefly in the moonlight, looked haggard and pale. For a second, Pete worried his friend had slipped—and called Pete out of shame and remorse. But his eyes looked clear. He just seemed shaken to his core.

"There's someone you need to talk to," Dave said, the words coming out flat and detached, like a prayer repeated before bed. "Turn on the light."

Dave's words seemed directed to someone else. That's when Pete heard a voice he never thought he'd experience again.

"What—no hello, or how are you?" the voice said.

The living room lights flickered on. Pete turned toward Dave to see that his friend was not alone. He was being shadowed by a dead man.

"The fuck is this?" Pete said.

"I can explain," Harras said, moving toward Pete, his hands out, palms up.

Pete took a few quick steps back. He felt in his belt for his gun, but remembered he wasn't carrying it anymore. His head was spinning. First Emily, now Harras. It was too much. He felt off-balance. He felt Dave's hands on his arm, trying to hold him up.

"Everyone said you were dead," Pete said. "I saw you dying. I figured you were as good as dead, or you were never coming back."

"I didn't die, but I wasn't planning on coming back, either," Harras said. "Let me explain."

"How is this ..." Pete said. He moved his eyes to Dave, who was still trying to keep Pete from falling over. "You ... you knew about this? Why?"

Dave could only muster a nod.

The visions came back. Holding Harras's limp body, blood gushing from his neck. The smell of gunpowder and smoke in the air as the Silent Death slipped away. The sirens and questions as Harras was rushed off. The funeral. The driving obsession he'd embraced to dull the pain of another lost friend. All for what? He didn't know whether to cheer or scream.

"I know you're still processing this," Harras said. "Come with me."

Pete, with Dave a few paces behind, followed Harras into the living room. Pete got a closer look at the older man's face, now dusted with shrapnel wounds that would never heal right. It gave the already rough-and-tumble looking man a deeper edge. He'd seen some shit.

"You look pretty good for a dead guy," Pete said, his voice wavering.

"Sit," Harras said, taking the love seat across from the couch. The place was lightly furnished and looked like it'd been decorated via Amazon and IKEA online. When you move in a hurry, you don't have time for mementos.

"I know you have questions."

"You're goddamn right I do," Pete said, refusing Harras's offer of a seat. Choosing to loom over his friend instead. "Why would you do this? To me? To Kathy? To your life? No one even gave me the time of day— I knew you could be alive, but everyone acted like you'd died on the operating table. Eventually, I started to wonder if I'd lost my mind."

"It couldn't be helped," Harras said, genuine regret flashing over his face. "Now sit the fuck down and let me explain."

Pete sat. He couldn't bring himself to look at Dave. Not yet.

"The Bureau saw an opportunity when I got wheeled into that operating room," Harras said. "A chance to figure out what the hell is going on."

"An opportunity?"

"Once they realized they could save me, but no one really knew I was being saved … they acted," Harras said. "Put me into deep cover, short-term. They have systems for this. I was given the works—death certificate, obit, funeral … you saw it."

"But for what?" Pete asked. His head was buzzing, white noise behind his eyes. Emily was back, pretending to be someone else.

Harras was alive, hiding in plain sight. Pete felt himself being stretched in a million directions, with no sense of when it'd stop.

"There's a war coming," Harras said. "And someone in Miami is the spark plug. Someone is sowing the seeds for a big gang war. Unlike anything we've seen. I'm not just talking Los Enfermos shooting up a street corner. I mean, mob families sending hired guns down here to throw down with someone just as big, just as bad."

"I don't understand," Pete said, head in his hands. He should be happy—Harras was back, sitting right in front of him. Why did he feel like everything was falling apart?

"Let me simplify it first," Harras said, rubbing his chin. "The guy who attacked you? The new Silent Death? He didn't want you dead."

"What do you mean?"

"He was gunning for me," Harras said. "Because I figured him out before he wanted to be seen."

"The new Silent Death?" Pete repeated to himself. "Why am I even saying that sentence?"

"Just let him finish, Pete," Dave said, placing a hand on Pete's shoulder. "He's got an—"

"Fuck you, man," Pete said, pulling away from his friend's grip. "You're complicit in this—after all I've done to help you? How could you two just keep this under wraps for months?"

"In Dave's defense, he found out a few hours ago," Harras said. "My operation's over, but—believe it or not—it isn't easy to come back from the dead."

Pete felt a pang of guilt but buried it. He didn't want to feel bad for Dave. Didn't want to be arguing with Harras. He had to figure out why his ex-fiancée was back in Miami sporting a dye job and using another name. He had to figure out what she had to do with the death of Osvaldo Valdez, the man who claimed to know something about Pete's mother. Instead, he was talking to a ghost.

"Harras updated me on what he was working on, or had been working on," Dave said. "I set him up here, until he gets his life in order."

"I guess I'll just sit here patiently until you explain what it is you were working on, then," Pete said. "If you get around to it, that is."

"You have a bounty on your head," Harras said. "Or had. A big one. Seems the DeCalvacante family is not a big fan of Pete Fernandez."

"You mean Vincent Salerno's crew?" Pete asked. "That's not surprising."

"It should be," Harras said. "This wasn't your typical 'kill 'em next time you spot him,' deal. They wanted you gone, as quickly as possible and in the worst way possible."

"Why?"

"Not sure yet," Harras said. "But it was enough to motivate the DeCalvacantes to dust off the Silent Death motif. The Death has always been a rented gun any gang of note could use to solve a problem. They hadn't thought of it in years, but suddenly the crime families and gangs felt they needed a new Silent Death, so they put word out on it, and this guy—well, he stepped up. Had a flair for the theatrical already, so he relished the chance to be this kind of urban legend, a killer of killers. And he's built a good rep for himself, mostly in New York and New Jersey, doing freelance work for different drug gangs when things get heated between organizations."

"Got a name?"

"Isleño Novo," Harras said. "Cuban. Older. Based in Union City in New Jersey, but came down here with his sights on you. That backfired. No idea where he is now."

"So much for the Silent Death being shrouded in mystery."

"Novo's a killer, tons of bodies to his credit—but he's not young," Harras said. "My gut says he was looking at this as a final gig. A retirement fund."

"You said he was gunning for you, though," Pete said. "That doesn't line up."

"I was onto him," Harras said. "Well, not exactly—but I'd turned up enough rocks for him to think I was onto him before he wanted to be seen. I'd been working with the Bureau freelance—trying to figure out what had all the gangs and crime organizations rattled. Why they were spinning around. Why things felt so off-kilter. Novo came up. He'd done so much work for so many different people, it made sense to check him out. And he was on the move. I noticed he'd come down to Miami recently, so I flagged it to the Bureau. I didn't connect it to you, didn't tab him as the new Silent Death, didn't think it'd blow back to me. But it did. He'd followed me to your house. Saw an opportunity to get me and the Bureau off his back and get that nice bounty on your head, all at once."

"But why me?"

"I'm sorry, have you not scanned your CV lately?" Harras said, scoffing. "You've pissed off the mob, Los Enfermos, and pretty much everyone that was using the Silent Death years ago."

"Right, but Reyes went down years ago," Pete said. "Before we even met. Why take so long to come at me?"

"That's a good question," Harras said. "I'm getting the sense that while offing you was definitely on his to-do list, Novo also had other stuff to take care of."

"Like Salerno?" Pete asked. "But Salerno's a DeCalvacante made guy. They don't just off their own people, do they?"

"Not often, no," Dave said. "But they can make exceptions."

"Salerno went rogue, remember," Harras said. "Word on the street was he had a lead on something big."

Pete nodded.

"That jibes," Pete said. "Salerno was hungry to get in on Ferris's deal—whatever it was, so much so that he killed him, then his daughter, and tried to kill me to try and get the info. Could it be he got what he wanted?"

"Maybe?" Harras said with a shrug. "But whatever that was, and whatever that did to piss people off isn't clear. Drugs, is my guess. The mob frowns upon their made guys dealing in drugs, though everyone does it. So, if Salerno had a lead on a big score, it must have been huge enough to push him to risk everything."

"So, Novo comes after you, you fake your death to find out more—What did you get?" Pete asked. "And why'd you come back? Not that I'm unhappy to see you, but—"

"Novo's off the grid, gone under—maybe dead," Harras said. "The DeCalvacantes aren't fond of people failing on their contracts. The mafia doesn't use outside killers often. When they do, they don't want to be found out. My guess is he's going underground until he can regroup or make good on his note. Not an auspicious start to the new Silent Death. But the moves—one of the Five Families using a hired gun, Novo gunning for me—were enough for the Bureau to pull me in and put me to work."

"So," Pete said, looking from Dave to Harras. "What'd you find out?"

A strange silence draped the room for a few beats. Dave cleared his throat.

"You didn't get anything, did you?" Pete asked.

Harras hesitated. His friend looked broken, battered. Better than the last time he'd seen him, but not by much. Had Harras awoken from his near-death experience to learn his life had been ended for him, with a new, covert mission dropped onto his lap? How must that have felt?

"I failed," Harras said. He looked away, unable to meet Pete or Dave's gaze. "I couldn't crack it. There are too many threads. Too many strands that don't fit. The Italians are going wild, the cartels are buzzing—talking, making moves—like never before and things here in Miami are too quiet. After a few months of this, tapping phones, watching surveillance footage, trying to work every contact and informant I had … I stopped. I pulled the pin."

"I'm sure that went really smoothly," Pete said.

Harras responded with a gruff laugh.

"They were not pleased," Harras said. "But they had little choice. Either they figured out a way to make my transition back to the land of the living smooth, or I'd be creating a lot of problems for parts of our surveillance state that people didn't even know exist. That was a few weeks ago. Spent the rest of the time just … recovering. The blood, the shot. All that was real."

"So where does that leave us?" Pete said. "What are we walking into?"

"Into the crossfire of something big," Harras said. "Something that we can't begin to brace ourselves for."


**A**re you sure it was her?"

Dave's question was delivered softly, probably to not stoke the fires of Pete's lingering anger toward him and Harras and partially because he couldn't believe it. But tonight was the night for the unbelievable, it seemed.

"It was her," Pete said.

Once the dust had settled from Harras's abrupt return, Pete decided it was time to get back to work. He was glad his friend was back, fuzzy on the how, but also facing a number of other, more confusing and dangerous situations. The murder of Osvaldo Valdez. The Javier Mujica case. And, last but not least, the return of Emily Sprague-Blanco, in the guise of Beatriz de Armas.

"Why would she be pretending to be someone else?" Dave asked.

"She left Miami on bad terms, if I remember correctly," Harras said.

"Ran, is more like it," Pete said. "Her husband had been cleaning money for Los Enfermos. Then they found out he'd been skimming, so they killed him. He left her everything, so she took it and ran to Europe."

"How do you feel about all this?" Harras asked. "Emily? Your mom? Where's your head at?"

"Honestly? I think if you'd asked me this a year ago, I'd have pretended everything was fine, that I could power through it all," Pete said. "But I'm done with shielding myself from what's going on. I feel like everything's coming apart, and I'm tied to a chair, forced to watch it. Emily being back, bounties on my head, this black cloud you're hinting at—all of that is insane. But I also need to find out what this cop wanted to tell me. He died before he could get it to me, but I can't believe he died with that info. That he didn't share it."

"Valdez?" Harras said. "When Dave mentioned what was going on, I made some more calls on Valdez. Not a lot there. No idea why he'd have that de Armas lady's card. Or why he'd be trying to contact you. I mean, he knew your dad. But so did everyone on the force then."

"He mentioned my mom, specifically."

"Right," Harras said, scratching his beard. "Well, I don't have any intel on that. But I do have a name."

Harras dug into his back pocket and produced a slip of notebook paper. Written in clear handwriting was a name: Nisha Hudson.

"She's good police, believe it or not," Harras said, aware of Pete's opinion of the Miami PD. "Been around a long time. If anyone knows anything about your mom, it's her. She's survived every shake-up and scandal that's come down on the PD. She's a few steps from retirement, but I imagine she'd see you."

Pete pocketed the piece of paper and looked up at his friend. "You're leaving."

"How'd you figure that?"

"If you weren't, you'd have chased this lead down yourself," Pete said, a wry smile on his face. "But you didn't. You're passing it on to me. You're going into the wind, aren't you?"

"Can you blame me?" Harras said. "I'm spent, Pete. This case took the last bit of my reserves, and I failed. Not great for my ego and—well—maybe a sign that it's time to ride off into the sunset. Enjoy a few years without guns pointed at my head, you know? Don't think that's too much to ask."

"No, I guess not," Pete said. "There's no better time to disappear than when you're already believed dead."

"Exactly."

Harras extended his hand. "I'd say keep in touch, but where I'm going ... it's all about, well, not doing that."

"So this is it?"

"This is it."

They hugged. Awkwardly at first, their bodies stiff and unsure of the embrace, two men who had maybe shared a half-dozen handshakes in their years working together. But that soon melted away, and Pete found his eyes watering as he buried his face in his old friend's shoulder. They parted slowly.

"You've done well," Harras said, his voice catching a bit. "You don't need me around anyway. Send Kathy my best."

"Not gonna swing by on your way out of town?"

"I don't think I'm one of her favorites," Harras said with a smirk. "But I've never been the best judge of character."

"I'm not exactly on her phone favorites, either."

"You'll find your way back to each other," he said. "You always do."

Pete thought back to Harras and Kathy's brief dalliance. It felt like a lifetime ago, but had actually been only a few years back.

Pete gripped his friend's shoulder and squeezed. "I'll see you again."

"If you do," Harras said, "something's probably gone very, very wrong."

# CHAPTER TWELVE

"**R**obert sent you? Now that's a story I need to hear."

The stocky black woman leaned back in her chair and sized Pete up. Nisha Hudson had kept him waiting for almost twenty minutes and didn't seem mildly apologetic. She nodded toward the sole seat in front of her small, overloaded desk inside the Miami PD offices on the Northwest side of Second Avenue.

Pete didn't like coming here. Hadn't since as far back as he could remember. When he was a kid, it was because it meant long hours of sitting at his father's desk, waiting for him to finish work. In his adult years, it usually meant some kind of trouble—a detective berating him for interfering in their case or, now and again, an arrest. His old lawyer friend, Jackie Cruz, had been masterful at getting him out of those kinds of binds. But she was dead, and Pete hadn't felt this alone in a long time.

He took a seat. The nameplate in front of her desk read: Nisha Hudson – Homicide. Pete could tell it'd been in that spot for some time.

"Thanks for seeing me."

"Don't thank me yet," she said with a dry laugh. "I'm just doing a favor for an old friend. And for another old friend's kid."

"You knew my dad?"

"I knew your father very well. Good man," she said. "We have a lot of mutual friends, like they do on Facebook—Carlos Broche, Gaspar Varela, Orlando Posada, Paul Brownstein, Graydon Smith, Tino Vigil. All cops, some good, some pretty good, some very bad. I knew them all. They came in, came out, I stayed. Now I'm on my last lap and, lo and behold, you show up at my desk. Can't be good, I think. But I can spare five minutes if Harras asks me to."

"He's dead ... did you hear?"

"Pretty chatty for a dead guy," she said, a sly grin on her lips. "But yeah, he's dead. I get it. I'll miss the guy. He was always quick with that FBI corporate card at the bar. Now we'll all have to fend for ourselves, overtime or no overtime."

Pete waited for Hudson to slow down the banter. But she just sat there, clicking on her mouse as if Pete were just another flagged email she could deal with later. After a few minutes, her eyes darted to him, the only part of her body that seemed to move or recognize he was still there.

"You just gonna sit there?"

"No, no," Pete said, stammering. "Did you know Osvaldo Valdez?"

"Ozzie? Yeah, I knew him. Good man. Like, good-good, not just a good cop, okay?" she said. "What about him? Now, he's definitely dead."

"He came to me a few months ago," Pete said. "He told me he had information about my mother."

"Pedro's wife?"

"Yes, Graciela."

"Right, she's dead, too, huh?" Hudson said, pushing her chair back a bit and wheeling to face Pete directly. "What about her?"

"That's the problem. I don't know. He died that night."

"Wait a minute," she said, her eyes narrowing. "He comes to you, says, 'Hey man, I got some info on your mom,' then you hear he's dead? Same day?"

"Same day."

Hudson let out a long sigh.

"Did you think it might make a little bit of sense to bring this to us?" she said, her eyes wide with frustration. "Or is that too lowbrow for Mr. Big-Time Private Eye, Pete Fernandez?"

"I'm here now."

"Yes, you are, but I don't need to give you a tutorial on the art of murder police, right?" she said. "I know you must watch 'The First 48' or shows like that. Well, we're long past the first 48, son, and this case is frozen solid. Anything else you've been keeping under wraps while you wonder about your mommy?"

"Nope," Pete said. He'd keep Beatriz de Armas's—or Emily Sprague's—business card to himself. For now.

"Let's hope so," Hudson said. "Okay, your mom. Graciela Fernandez. How old were you when she died?"

"Less than a few hours," Pete said. "She died during childbirth. My birth, I mean."

The memories hit again. The wave of textures, sights, smells— from a long time ago, from moments Pete hadn't thought of ... ever. Were they images and experiences created by his subconscious? Or was he remembering something more important? *Someone?*

A frown formed on Hudson's face. A mix of concern, regret, and hesitation.

"What year were you born?" she asked.

"1981," Pete said. "Why?"

She stood up, dusting her blouse and jacket off.

"Follow me."

Hudson led Pete down a series of twisting halls to an elevator. She pushed the DOWN button and looked at him for the first time since they left her office.

"Tell Harras I said to go fuck himself."

Pete started to respond.

"No, in fact, let me tell him," she said, stepping into the elevator. Pete followed. "Because he has put me in a shitty position on a day that was already shitty. He knows the drill, too, so he should've done this his own damn self."

"Are you going to tell me what's going on?"

"Eventually," she said. "I have no choice."

They reached the bottom floor and Hudson stepped out first. Pete noticed the sign on the doorway near the swipe-pad where Hudson touched her ID card. COLD CASE UNIT.

They stepped into what Pete would consider, if he was being generous, a cramped closet. There was a tiny desk in the corner, surrounded by a phalanx of file cabinets. Seated at the solitary desk was a woman about Pete's age, late thirties—long, unkempt dark brown hair, a clean but worn business suit, and sharp green eyes behind black-framed glasses. She looked up as they entered.

"Hudson," the woman said, her voice husky and tired-sounding. "This is a surprise."

"Pete Fernandez, meet Rachel Alter," Hudson said, waving at the woman. "She's the head of—and only member of—the Miami Cold Case Unit. Well, this branch, at least."

"Nice to meet you," Pete said.

Alter kept her eyes on Hudson, ignoring Pete.

"What's this about, Hudson?" she said. "In case you missed it, I'm backed up until I retire, which is still a few decades away."

Hudson, who had already started to make her way toward the exit, wheeled around and looked at Pete.

"Pete Fernandez, your mother didn't die giving birth to you," she said, her tone slow and methodical, as if trying to ensure Pete understood every word. "She was murdered on New Year's Eve 1984, a few months after she abandoned you and your father."

# FEAR THE FUTURE

*August 11, 1983*

Graciela's eyes creaked open, the thrum and pounding in her skull making every movement slow, sluggish, and painful.

*It happened again.*

She waited a second before sitting up. She put her head in her hands once she did, exhausted and spent after such a minimal action. *It happened again,* she thought, *but not "again" as in "for the second time." More like "one more time this month."*

She was in bed. Well, the couch in D's apartment. That wasn't the problem. That's where she'd been sleeping since Pedro sent her packing. It had started to feel even more permanent after her run-in with him a few weeks back. No, the part that wasn't normal—though, it had become a bit more common—was that she had no idea how she got back. Or when the night had ended.

She checked herself, patting her clothes and feeling around her face and arms. She was wearing the dress she *did* remember putting on before she left the apartment, raring to get a good drunk on and enjoy herself. She remembered getting into the car with D. She remembered the bars they went to—up to a point.

116

The last thing she remembered—the last image that seemed to pop up in her mind as she slowly, painfully stood and walked toward D's war zone of a kitchen—was the shot. A massive, almost-full glass shot of Popov, which was cheap vodka that everyone knew was basically gasoline. She remembered feeling the clear liquid sliding through her, activating her insides and then ... blackness.

What had happened after? How had she gotten home?

She scanned her body. Bruises—purple and yellow marks on her legs, knees, and arms. Her mouth dry—feeling like it could crack and shatter at any moment.

*How did I get back here?*

She felt her body run cold. The shivers came strong, and she had to lean on the wall in D's small kitchen to stifle them a bit. She stepped out and looked toward the apartment's sole bedroom. The door was closed, a sign that D was inside and probably asleep. She could ask her when she woke up. She could get a sense, an idea of what happened, and then all the pieces would click together. D had probably gotten her home. Of course she had. She would fill in the gaps and the story would be complete.

*But that wouldn't make you feel any better*, a voice in her head hissed.

No, because the pieces didn't belong to her. She didn't know what happened. What she did. Who she went with. She'd just know someone else's version. The blackouts were happening more often now. She felt a whooshing in her skull, as if her head was about to explode but couldn't.

She poured herself another big glass from the tap and guzzled it down. The reflex triggered another memory. Clinking glasses. Pulling her neck back, opening her throat as the amber liquid poured into her. The smiles and sloppy high fives after, the dizzy euphoria of the buzz that quickly turned to sadness and disorientation.

"You can't be a mother if this is how you're going to act."

Pedro's words had boomed in her ears then and they came back to haunt her now, like a dark, terrifying *déjà vu*.

He hadn't told her this when he asked her to leave. That'd been simpler, cleaner almost. But the refrain had come up often in the days and weeks leading up to her exit. Like the night she'd jumped into oncoming traffic—screaming, arms flailing, completely whacked out on cokes, pills, wine—daring him to chase after her, Pete in the backseat of their car, looking out—his toddler eyes wide and confused, afraid.

Or the night she'd stormed out of a restaurant—a German place in Kendall—mid-meal, because she could have sworn Pedro, who had never so much as looked at another woman while they were married, was making eyes at the waitress. Or maybe it'd been the time Graciela had crashed the family car into ... a parked car in a strip mall, when she'd told Pedro she was running out to pick up a movie but instead decided to stock up on gin and score some coke. All the nights blurred together. The days seemed foggy and slow-motion.

Graciela felt herself collapse. Her knees hit the floor hard. Her hands were in her hair, pulling, tugging. She could feel the hot tears streaming down her face. This was not normal. This wasn't right.

But it was an easy fix, right? Had to be. She just needed a break. A day or two of rest. Then she could figure out what to do.

*I'm just tired.* She needed time in bed, some real food, and no partying. No drugs. No drinks. She needed to relax for a bit. The rest would work out.

It had to.

# CHAPTER THIRTEEN

**"W**ait, is she seriously leaving?"

Pete started toward the door, his head in a thick gray cloud. He felt his hand shake as he reached for the doorknob. He knew Hudson would be on the elevator by now. But he could catch her. He had to catch her.

"You won't reach her in time," Alter said as she stood up, her voice coming through loud. "She's gone. This is what she does. She's like a tornado."

Pete turned around, eyes wide. He didn't know what was happening.

"We can talk tomorrow, when I'm back in the office," she said, trying to sidestep him. Pete blocked her path. "I've got to be somewhere."

"Listen, Rachel, I'm sorry—but we need to talk now," Pete asked. "You and Hudson just dropped a bombshell on me and I'm not sure I can just sit at home and wait."

"I have somewhere I need to be, so I'm sorry," Alter said. Pete could tell she felt bad, but wasn't going to budge.

119

Pete rubbed his temples. For a moment, he let his thoughts drift back, to a time not so long ago when his biggest problem was how many copies of the latest James Patterson to order. Those days had been brief, glorious, and were very much gone.

"I'm going with you."

"No—"

"Look, you're a detective," Pete said. "This is major. I'm Graciela's only son. I have some information that might help you. I mean, no one ever contacted me about this case—even though you were working on it as a cold-case detective. Maybe we can solve this together."

"I need to pick up my daughter from her sitter," Alter said, shutting off the lights and opening the office door. "You can ride with me, but I'm not bringing you back here. Please don't make me regret this."

"I'll take a Lyft back, no sweat," Pete said, relief coating his voice. "But if you've been working this case, I need all the info you have, as fast as you can share it."

Alter slung her purse over her shoulder. She opened a nearby cabinet and grabbed a stack of heavy-looking file folders. "Fine, come with me."

"What are those?" Pete asked, following her out of the office.

"Work," she said. "I usually take four or five files home with me each night. This is light, considering."

Rachel Alter led Pete to her car, a red Toyota Camry that was a few years old. The backseat featured a car seat and was littered with toys, books, and what looked like tiny food pouches and a roll of paper towels.

"Mom life, huh?" Pete said as he slid into the front passenger seat.

"What?"

"Nothing, just trying to make small talk."

"The sitter isn't far, so maximize your time," she said, not looking at him as she started the car engine and backed out of the parking lot. Her manner was stern and distant, but Pete sensed there was more to the woman than she let on.

"How long have you been working in the Cold Case Unit?"

"That question implies we're a unit," she said, pulling onto the 836. "It's just me in this office. And I'm so backed up I barely get to work on anything. If we get a DNA hit, the case goes to the top of the pile. If there's a new true-crime Netflix documentary or book, same. We go with the evidence or the buzz. The rest of the files, the ones that aren't talked about on Reddit or saved by DNA, those stay in the cabinets."

"Like my mom."

She turned to meet his eyes, a flicker of life in hers. "Yes," she said. "Like your mom."

"What can you tell me about it?"

"What do you remember about your mother?"

"Nothing," Pete said. "Nothing, really. My dad said she was a caring woman, she died of complications during my birth—it was sudden and tragic. He raised me from there."

"You never thought to ask?"

"I did, here and there," Pete said. "But there was little to ask about. I saw some pictures. She didn't have any family, so I never met that side of my life, and my father never seemed really to want to talk about it. He'd mention her, sometimes, over the years. But as time went on—well, it sounds terrible, but we moved on, too. Her memory faded. I just went on living."

"It happens," Alter said. "We're built to compartmentalize and cope. It's how we survive."

"But this—this info, this suggestion—"

"It's not a suggestion," Alter said. "It's a fact. Graciela Fernandez was murdered. The question I have is: Why didn't your father tell you? Why didn't anyone from the Miami Police Department tell you?"

"I ... I have no idea."

"I'd hate to think it was a clerical error, but that's probably part of it. Graciela Fernandez was her married name," Alter said. "Her maiden name was Nuñez. She'd reverted to that name during the last year or so of her life. The murder book is under that name."

"Why was she using Nuñez?"

"Why do you think women revert to their maiden names?" Alter said, flatly. "Your parents were in the final stages of a divorce. Graciela had left your father—and you, a few years old, presumably—months before she died."

Pete shook his head. It felt like an unwritten chapter in his own history was being presented to him, complete and unabridged. He wanted to dig back, deeper into his own thoughts and memories, but he knew he'd find nothing. The story Alter was telling him resided in a void no one could reach—the blank, formative days of a newborn and toddler. But what of those visions? The memories that seemed to materialize when he'd talked to Valdez and then Hudson?

"I am sorry to be the one giving you all this information," Alter said. "It's not fair ... to either of us. Hudson likes to pass the buck, and she was downright gleeful in there. Dumping this on my desk like some kind of eviction form." She frowned. "No, that's not fair," she said. "This is your life. Whether you remember it or not."

She pulled the car into the driveway of a tiny house in West Kendall.

"Look," she said unbuckling her seat belt. "Let's keep talking. I just need to grab Ella and get her ready for dinner, then bed. Then we can keep going. All right?"

"What about your husband?" Pete asked, immediately regretting it.

"He doesn't exist," Alter said with a humorless chuckle. "Ella's actually my niece. I adopted her a few months back."

Pete started to talk, but Alter continued.

"My sister died in a car accident. She was older. Had the baby on her own—she wanted a kid, but didn't want to keep shopping for Mr. Right. Ella was less than a year old when a drunk driver mowed my sister down," Alter said. "I was the only person Ella had left. So I adopted her, basically. I'm her mom now, for better or worse."

"It seems like you're getting by."

"It's all I can do," Alter said, staring out at the house. She blinked and turned to Pete. "Stay here. I'll be right back."

She got out of the car and walked toward the front door.

Pete pulled out his cell phone and dialed Kathy's number. His hand was shaking. It rang a few times and went to voicemail. He hung up and tried again. No response. He tried once more, this time waiting for the message tone.

"It's me. Call me back. I need your help. It's important."

As he hung up, he felt the rear passenger side door open. He turned to see Rachel sliding a tiny, light-haired toddler into the car seat. She did it with the calm and expertise of someone who did this regularly, her hands moving over the small chair's belts like a musician plucking at an acoustic guitar. All the while, baby Ella slept, her head tilted to her left, mouth open, breathing slowly.

Rachel closed the door gently and sped to the driver's side. She got in and started the car, then looked at Pete. "This is bad."

"What happened?"

"She shouldn't be napping now," Rachel said, looking into her rearview and backing out of the house's driveway. "It's going to ruin her sleep tonight."

"I'm sure it'll be fine."

Rachel scoffed. "Said the man with no children."

"That I know of."

"I didn't think you could get any less charming," Rachel said. "Who were you calling?"

"I was trying to get in touch with my partner," Pete said. "Was hoping she'd be able to swing by and help us talk over the case."

"Is she coming?"

"No response," Pete said. "She didn't pick up."

"Huh," Rachel said, putting her turn signal on before making a right. "Sounds like you don't have a partner."


"**S**he's down," Rachel said, plopping down onto her tiny two-seater couch. "For now."

Pete was seated across from her, the living room of her three-bedroom townhouse littered with toys, a baby-gate enclosure, and stacks of parenting books—most of which were read, from what Pete could tell.

Rachel was clutching a small remote-like device, which was making a buzzing sound. The light from the monitor's display shone on Rachel's face, revealing her tired eyes and weary expression.

"How long does she sleep?"

"Four or five hours, if I'm lucky. Usually three or four before she needs to be fed. She slept through the night once and I woke up in a panic, thinking she'd died in her sleep."

"Jesus."

"Welcome to parenthood, pal," Rachel said, reaching for the glass of white wine she'd poured herself after her first attempt at putting Ella down went up in flames. "There is no normal."

"Seems like it."

"You ever get close to settling down?" she asked after taking a long swig. "Close to having kids?"

"A long time ago," Pete said. "I was engaged. Figured that was it. But who knows."

"You make it sound so romantic. 'That was it.' Like a death sentence."

"I just felt like the window had—maybe has—closed," Pete said, looking around the apartment. "What about you? No time for someone else? Something else?"

"Life happened," Rachel said. "And I ran out of time for hobbies. I used to love music. Going to shows. But these days, the only music I listen to is the kind that pops onto the radio when I'm in the car."

"I guess life is about sacrifice," Pete said. "If you're doing it right."

"Or just powering through the bad to get to the good, hopefully."

"I'm sorry about your sister," Pete said. "I know it can be hard. To lose someone you're close to, I mean."

Alter nodded. "Thanks," she said. "Yeah, we were close. I still see bits of her in Ella, and it guts me, but it also makes me happy— because it's like a part of my sister will live on."

"My dad died a few years ago," Pete said, rubbing his lap. "I was a mess when he died—it was sudden. He was healthy. Just retired. A legendary cop. I was, well, I was something else, I guess. A drunk. Not there, you know? Not present. I missed a lot of time with him because I was destroying myself. Maybe if I'd been more clearheaded, more of a son—he'd have told me about ..."

Pete trailed off, shaking his head.

Alter got up and placed her glass on the small brown coffee table separating their two seats. She walked briskly up the stairs, into one of the rooms. Pete could hear doors opening and closing, albeit gently.

When she returned, she was carrying a large folder, held together by a few rubber bands. She placed it down on the table next to the wine with care and removed the bands, setting them aside to be reused later.

"I wasn't sure if you were ready for this. It's not something ... well, we're not allowed to do this. But I keep copies of certain case files, and I brought this one with me, just in case," Alter said as she knelt in front of the thick collection of documents and looked up at Pete, who was sitting at the edge of a small love seat, watching.

"What?" Pete asked.

"This is a copy of your mother's file," she said. "Her murder book. This is all we have on her death. Now it's yours."

**"V**ictim died of manual strangulation. Manner of death: homicide."
Rachel Alter's voice stayed with him, haunted him. The words from the murder book rolling out of her mouth likes lines from a phone book—methodical, on beat—each word a new shock to his system.

"She was found partially dressed on the hotel room floor," Alter had read. "Victim was wearing a black cocktail dress, black heels, and a gold necklace with a cross. Time of death, 1:55 a.m."

Pete left her house in a daze. His hands were coated with sweat as he slipped into the backseat of his Lyft, which would take him back to his car. The Miami sky was a cold, dark black, the West Kendall street lights illuminating the back seat at intervals that were few and far between. Pete's mind whirled—he felt displaced, disconnected, on the tail end of a bad high that was soon going to get worse.

*"Autopsy showed broken bones in the victim's throat—including the larynx and hyoid bone—and burst blood vessels in her eyes, likely caused by a struggle."*

He'd left the house in a hurry, avoiding Rachel's attempts to go into more detail about what was in the file. That could—and would have to—come later. For now, Pete needed to be alone. He needed a chance to dive into what awaited him in the pages he held on his lap. He needed to process the fact that his father—the man he'd basically canonized—had crafted an elaborate lie to mask the truth about the mother he'd never known. Who was Graciela Fernandez? What had she been like? What drove her? And, most importantly to Pete: Who killed her?

*"Victim also had bruises throughout her body—arms, legs, back, and face, suggesting a violent struggle before the final—"*

Pete cleared his throat and motioned for the driver.

"Hey, change of plans. New address."

The driver grumbled about company policies and the app, but Pete wasn't having it. He tossed three twenties into the front seat and watched as the driver's demeanor went from irked to cooperative. Pete didn't want to be alone now, he realized. But if the person he was hoping to see shut him out, he'd have nowhere else to go.

"**P**ete, it's not a good time."

It was past midnight. The door to Kathy Bentley's apartment door was open a crack and Pete could make out a sliver that included Kathy's eyes—weary-looking and glazed over. The hallway was dim, but the apartment inside looked even darker. Pete knew Kathy was a night owl, so he rarely worried about waking her. But he was worried now. Of what, he wasn't sure.

"Let me in, Kathy," Pete said, gripping the door frame gently, to show he wanted to help. "We need to talk. I've been trying to call you since—"

The door gave way with surprising ease. Kathy stepped back into the room, the darkness enveloping her as Pete followed, the door slamming shut behind him. He tried to get a better look at her, but it was impossible. The apartment was quiet—the only sound the groaning of the building's central air and the horns and engines of the cars outside. Even Kathy's footsteps as she backtracked were silent.

"Kathy?" Pete asked. "What is—"

"He's gone," she said, her voice vacant, ethereal, like a distant chime. "Marco's gone."

"What? What happened?"

Pete reached for the wall and found the light switch. He flicked it on. He wished he hadn't.

"He left," Kathy said, her face worn and red. Her clothes looked wrinkled and tossed-on, not Kathy's usual put-together attire. Her hair was matted and loosely tied back. "Why do you think?"

Pete took a step forward.

"Stay there, okay?" Kathy said. "I don't want ... I don't need a sympathy card here. He had every right to leave. I fucked up. We both did."

"You told him?"

"Of course I told him," she said, spittle flying out of her mouth. "How could I not? You basically told him yourself. So, when he came back home, barging in and asking about it, I couldn't lie. I don't want to lie. I was going to marry him and I couldn't go into that knowing I'd fucked around on him, moment of weakness or not. But I wanted to tell him on my own terms, in my own way. It was a mistake, not who I am, and I wanted to explain that to him. I know you're fine with that, but—"

"I'm not—"

"Shut the fuck up for one second," Kathy said, her voice flat, emotionless. "Let me talk. This is my house. You barged in here, remember? My rules."

Pete nodded.

Kathy cleared her throat.

"I'm not Emily, okay?" Kathy said. "I'm not going to just fall into bed with you and wreck my entire life, then run away. I'm not going to let your indecisiveness mushroom into something that hurts me, okay?"

She leaned on the wall of the short hallway that lead to her living room, not looking at Pete, facing a PIXIES poster she'd picked up at one of their recent reunion shows.

"You never learn, that's your problem," she said, her voice wavering. "You just think the world is your playpen and that you can barge into anything. That's cool when you're a fucking private eye, but not in life, okay? Not in life. You're a problem. You break things ... You break people. I can't let this happen to me."

"Where's Marco?" Pete asked, trying to steer the anger he felt simmering in her, about to spill over and burn them both. "Where did he go?"

"That ... that's not the point here, Pete," she said, looking at him. "This is over. This has to be over. I care for you. You know that. You don't need me to spell it out for you. But I can't love you. Or be with you. I refuse to turn into a shrill, unbearable witch with you. What happened before ... that was a mistake. Not fully your fault ... I did my part. But it was a mistake. I made a promise to this man—to Marco—and I fucked that up and I need to fix that. I need to fix myself. I've been pushing and pulling at myself for years—since before I even met you. Bouncing from bad relationship to worse, and finally, finally, I thought I'd found a guy who not only treated me well—but seemed to give a shit about me. Then I wake up and realize that guy can't even figure himself out. That's you, Pete. You can't decide. You can't pick a lane. You want to keep all your options open. That's not how life works. That's a fairy tale. Marco is a good man. I need to fix this."

Pete reached out a hand, but Kathy didn't respond beyond a quick shake of her head.

"I need to talk to—"

"We are talking!" she said, her voice cracking, her eyes redder than Pete had ever seen them. "Except I'm talking to you now, instead of just waiting. Listen to me, closely, okay? I don't want anything to do with this. This ... whatever it is you're bringing to my door. I have to deal with my life. And it can't involve drugs, guns, dead bodies, or whatever is coming down your way. Okay? Please, understand that."

She motioned for the door, flailing her arm toward the exit, before walking into the living room and shutting the door behind her. Pete didn't follow.

# CHAPTER FOURTEEN

He made it back home close to midnight.

He dropped the heavy file on the dining room table. The furniture, he realized, was set up exactly the same way his father had situated it in his house. Before he died. Before the house was destroyed in a deadly explosion. That day, filled with screams and smoke and pain, felt so long ago.

But Kathy had been there then. She'd been with him after. Pete assumed she'd always be there. But maybe he'd been wrong. He was alone. The darkness surrounded him. He hadn't bothered to flick on the lights. He felt lightheaded, a growing dizziness making his movements slow and lethargic. He hadn't eaten anything since breakfast. Hungry, angry, lonely, tired ... those were the red flags. The moods the program knew could trigger a dangerous relapse, or a step toward one.

*Here I am again,* he thought. *Guess the simple life wasn't for me.* He pulled out his cell phone and dialed the contact.

"Hey," the voice said, tired but not surprised.

"Did I wake you?"

"Pete, I'm closer to 65 than 55," his sponsor, Jack, said with a brief laugh. "Of course you did. But I picked up. What's going on?"

"I ... I don't know, I just feel like I ..." His voice trailed off.

"I'll be there in thirty. Just sit tight."

When Jack arrived, five minutes early thanks to an unexpectedly quiet 826 Expressway, Pete was seated at the dining room table, staring at the file folder, unopened. Jack walked over and scanned the text on the folder's tab. He didn't need to know more.

"Don't move," Jack said and walked into Pete's kitchen. After a few minutes, he came back with a turkey sandwich and big glass of water.

"When was the last time you ate?"

"What day is it?"

"That's what I figured," Jack said, taking a seat next to Pete. "Eat. Drink some water. This folder can wait a few minutes, don't you think?"

Pete nodded and took a tentative bite. In a few minutes, the sandwich was gone. He'd been hungrier than he thought.

"How long were you staring at this before you called?"

"Not sure," Pete said, rubbing his eyes.

"You don't have to look at it until you feel ready, you know?" Jack said. "But knowing you, I'm assuming you've at least cracked it open."

"You could say that," Pete said, motioning for Jack to take a seat.

Pete opened the folder and handed Jack the top sheet—a point-by-point recap written by Rachel Alter summing up the murder of Graciela Fernandez, and any findings she had dug up.

"Well," Jack said. "You were right to call me. Where's Kathy?"

"Gone," Pete said.

Jack shoved Pete's shoulder. It wasn't a playful tap. Pete got the message: snap out of this funk and talk to me.

"Marco left, because of—well, what happened. But she wants to fix it. To be with him," Pete said. "She made a mistake."

Jack nodded. "*Hmm*, a discussion for another time." He passed the sheet back to Pete. "How're you taking this? From what you'd told me ... your mom died when you were a baby. Of an illness?"

"That's what I thought," Pete said, looking at his hands. "That's what my dad told me."

"But how did this stay under wraps for so long?" Jack asked, skimming a few other pages. An autopsy report. Photos from the crime scene.

"The cold case detective working the case, she said my dad made every effort to bury it," Pete said, no flicker of humor in his voice. "No pun intended, obviously. He didn't want the truth out there. He was fine with the murder going unsolved ... I guess?"

"I get that," Jack said, eyes locked on Pete. "But how do you feel about that? Your dad ... your father was like a god, or something, to you."

"But he wasn't one, was he?"

"I don't know."

"But to do this," Pete said, waving his hand toward the papers and photos littering the table. "To lie to your only child ... to the world ... about a woman you loved. That's not normal."

Jack shrugged slightly.

"You don't know what was going on in his life," he said, his tone flat, neutral. "And he's not here to talk to. Neither is your mother."

Pete rubbed his eyes. Jack was right. But Pete wanted something— someone—to be mad at. And his father was the easiest target.

Pete had always idolized Pedro Fernandez. At least in death. As a kid, his father had been a burden—a micromanaging parent who, after Pete got busted for a petty theft in high school, clamped down on his son so hard Pete couldn't even go to school without a police escort. It'd created a deep resentment between the two of them, one that only healed after Pete left Miami for college and began a career in New Jersey as a rising-star journalist. A few years later, his father was dead, much too soon. Pete and Emily, his fiancée at the time, rushed down to handle the funeral arrangements and to sort through Pedro's life. They never made it back to their comfortable three-bedroom apartment in Jersey. They never made it back to their relationship.

*Emily.*

"You worked Vice, right?" Pete asked, breaking the lingering silence. "You knew my dad."

"Not well," Jack said. "We'd have to talk now and again, but we ran on different tracks. I dealt with drug dealers, *boliteros*, thugs ... he got the bodies and caught the killers."

"You knew Alvaro Mujica?"

"Yeah, he's still around," Jack said. "He was smart. We could never pin him down on anything. He ran his operation well ... sharp. No recordings, no phone calls, violence only when extremely necessary. Slippery guy."

"Were you on the Mujica case?"

"Not directly," Jack said. "I was on a lot of things, though—we were short-staffed, and half the department was on the take, so the cops that were mostly clean got most of the work. I was all over the place. But the Mujica case was big. We were building it for a long time."

Pete grabbed a stack of photos from the table and started to look them over.

"She was strangled to death in an Overtown hotel room," Pete said, his voice raspy and strained. "Last person to have seen her was a friend—Diane Atkins. Or so the police report says. But I couldn't find her interview transcript here."

"You sure you're up for sifting through this now?" Jack asked. "When did you hit a meeting last?"

Pete waved him off. He didn't want to answer. The truth was, he hadn't been to a meeting in weeks, months. Not since before Harras was shot and seemingly killed. It'd started as a mistake—he'd been busy working the Javier Mujica case. Then the lack of meetings built momentum. Next thing he knew, it'd been over a month and he had no plans to go back. The thought crystallized in his mind, and it frightened him.

"Not in a while."

"Figured," Jack said. "Let's go. There's a midnight meeting that should be going late in South Miami. I'll drive. We can circle back to this later. You need some coffee and fellowship."

Jack was right. As Pete entered the tiny room—a small storefront that had once probably housed an insurance firm, but now served as a meeting space for AA and related programs—he felt a surge of relief. Of belonging. Suddenly the things that had been buzzing and jangling in his brain quieted, if just a bit. He felt at peace for the first time in a long while.

"Should've done this a while ago," Pete said as he took a seat near the back with Jack.

His sponsor nodded. They settled in just as the speaker, an older woman with curly red hair, took a seat at the wide table in front of the room.

The space smelled of coffee and dust, a musky, familiar odor that added to Pete's calm. He was home. Nothing else mattered outside of these doors. Nothing would matter if he didn't maintain his sobriety. If he didn't take each step he could to prevent himself from taking a drink.

The woman, who introduced herself as Connie, started talking. It was a story like many others but also unique. Early on, Jack had instilled in Pete the understanding that he was not special. People become drunks all the time. Their behavior and missteps are not special, because the solution is not special either. Don't drink, go to meetings—the words continued to resonate in Pete's brain, years after his last drink and years after first walking into a meeting of Alcoholics Anonymous. But like anything else, he needed to be reminded about it. He needed the repetition.

When Connie finished her share, she was met with applause. A few people got up to refill their coffees. Hands were raised, and members of the group took turns sharing their own experiences—thanking Connie for her service and relating to her story. Pete sat back and listened. As the clock ticked closer to one in the morning, he felt a slight jab in his side. He turned. Jack met his eyes and raised an eyebrow.

"Well?"

"What?" Pete asked.

"I didn't bring you here just to listen, buddy."

Pete raised his hand. Connie noticed and pointed at him.

"Hi, uh, my name's Pete, and I'm an alcoholic," he said. "Thanks for your story. I could relate to it. I needed to hear it. I needed to be reminded of why I'm here, and why I should be here."

Pete cleared his throat. He only had a few minutes to speak, but it felt like he was staring into a vast expanse.

"I've been in and out of these rooms ... more in than out," he continued. "I've seen friends die. I've lost jobs. Lost relationships. I've moved to escape my own past. I've done everything you're not supposed to do. But I didn't drink. I tried my best not to drink. That saved my life. These rooms continue to save my life."

He felt his hands begin to shake. He placed them in his lap. Held them together as he made eye contact with the speaker.

"I found something out today," Pete said. "Something bad. Something ... I don't even know. Something that changes my entire perspective on not only my life, but how I see my father—a man I always respected. Well, at least after he died I came to understand and appreciate him. And I regretted missing out on time with him. But this ... this news changes a lot. It makes me wonder what else he was hiding. Makes me wonder what else I've missed. I feel like life is all about moving forward, doing what we can ... but when you get something that comes out at you, that changes how you see everything else, that's the kind of stuff that makes you wonder. Makes you think that maybe it is smart to reach for that drink. To blow it all up because, damn, that one thing you thought was good ... that one man or person you thought was an example ... maybe they weren't what you thought."

Pete paused and looked at Jack, who gripped his shoulder briefly.

"But I didn't drink today," Pete said. "I don't need to drink. I know what that was like. I don't need to drink for any reason. I have a friend ... a friend who—I don't know how to explain it—who I'm tangled up with. We have feelings for each other. And we made some mistakes. She doesn't want to be my friend anymore. And I understand that. She's not the only person. I'm feeling really alone and without a tether or anchor. But that's what this disease wants. It wants you alone. Sitting in the dark and looking out, with the doors and windows closed, so it can sneak up and grab you ... seduce you. Pull you back into the darkness. But I can't do that. I have too much to live for. I've seen that darkness. I've looked at death and I know what that is. I'm not ready yet. Thank you."

A smattering of applause followed as the meeting attendees stood up and formed a loose circle, their hands clenched with each other's. Pete closed his eyes and felt them coated with tears.

# CHAPTER FIFTEEN

**P**ete gripped the steering wheel. He felt his knuckles crack. Felt the faux leather tighten under his fingers. Felt something. He needed to feel something. To push back on the numbness that had dominated his senses for the last twenty-four hours.

What had Graciela Fernandez felt, as the life was choked from her? What did she see in the waning minutes of her life? *His mother's life.*

Pete let out a long, shaky breath. He never knew his mother. Would never know her. Even here, sitting outside the house of someone he hoped would shed light on what happened, Pete felt no closer to closing the gap between his deep, unreachable past and present. His mother was dead. That hadn't changed over the last day. It would never change. Solving her murder wouldn't unlock a magical box within him, allowing him to be a better man. Immersing himself in the details of her brutal demise wouldn't solve his problems. But he didn't want her to exist as a mirage—a spectral figure, impervious and virginal. He wanted to see her, to know her—flaws, bruises, and all.

He stepped out of the car and walked up to the front door of the expansive Coral Gables home. The waterfront home's tropical landscaping adding a touch of claustrophobia to the wide chunk of property. He rang the doorbell and waited. He heard a faint voice on the other side.

"Give me a second," the woman said. The locks were shifted and the door swung inward, revealing a thin, well-dressed woman with short, graying hair. Diane Atkins, now Diane Crowther, looked well put together and at ease. She seemed slightly confused, probably expecting a delivery or perhaps a neighbor. Pete was neither.

"Can I help you?"

"Diane? I'm Pete Fernandez. I'm a private investigator."

"Oh, well," she said, hesitating. "How can I help? I don't practice law anymore, I've retired—"

"I want to talk to you about my mother," Pete said. "Graciela Fernandez."

Her face steeled and her eyes regained clarity. She nodded almost imperceptibly.

"Come in," she said, motioning for him to follow her. "Come in, please."

He followed her down a winding hallway, walls covered in framed black-and-white photos from decades past, pictures of what Pete assumed were family and friends long gone. The hallway looped around and ended in a large foyer or waiting room, dark wood paneling collecting the Miami heat and giving the space an oppressive, sauna-like feeling. She motioned for him to sit on a well-built, expensive chair. Pete did. She positioned herself across from him on another, equally high-end perch.

"How did you find me?"

Pete shrugged. "It's what I do," he said. "Find people. You changed your last name, moved around a bit, but you stayed."

"I'm from here," Diane Crowther said. "Why would I leave?"

"Just speculating," Pete said. "Your name appears on the police report—the file that outlines the details of my mother's death. But I couldn't find anything about you until about a decade later, when you got married. Then you became a lawyer. Then you retired. It was almost as if you went dormant for a—"

"What can I help you with, son? I'm starting to regret letting you in."

136

"You were friends with her—with Graciela," Pete said, trying to soften his tone, not lose the thread. "I'm trying to figure out what happened to her."

She sighed, straightening her dark slacks, delaying the words that she'd been bottling up for decades, Pete thought.

"Your mother was my best friend," she said. "We were like sisters. Since high school. We both went to school together—first Miami Dade, then Barry, then ... well, then she got married. And we stayed in touch, for the most part, but it was different. Less, I dunno, less fun."

"What do you mean?"

"Well, look, you're not a baby," Diane said. "Your dad was a cop. A cop's cop. Most cops back then were on the take or directly working for one drug gang or another. Your dad was one of the exceptions, or so I was told. He was a stickler for the rules. Once they got together— well, Gracie had to change. Had to behave, basically."

"What was she like?"

Pete felt his voice tremble as he asked the question and it took him by surprise. His mother was an enigma to him, an empty space that had never been filled—so feeling anything, a rush of pain, seemed bizarre. Yet it felt right.

Diane seemed to recognize this, gripping his hand for a moment.

"She was the best," she said. "Fun, funny, smart, beautiful—a great dancer. Loved to dance. She had this long, glowing black hair and was just a stunner. Amazing. We'd walk into a bar and every eye would be on her. She could keep up with everyone. She was tougher than the guys and sexier than the girls. She was a powerful woman."

"But you lost touch with her when she married my dad?"

"No, I wouldn't say that. We just saw each other less. She got married. That takes up some time, as you may know. Then she had you, and she was gone, basically. Not really, but I just assumed I wouldn't see her much."

"What were you doing?" Pete asked, trying to keep the question casual, not pointed. "While Graciela was settling into this life?"

"I was partying," Diane said. "I can say that because I'm a different person now, but I was a mess. I was drinking, doing a lot of coke, sleeping with anyone that bought me a drink, dancing all night and passing out all day. I loved it at the time, until it stopped being fun. Then I stopped. I didn't even have to hit a rehab. It had to stop, and I stopped. But when your mom was off playing house, I was partying as if every night was my last on earth."

"Where did she meet my father?"

"A bar, of course, some dive in Little Havana—Oso de Oro," Diane said, her Spanish precise if not authentic. "Your dad went in to talk to the manager about something, I dunno, maybe a break-in? And he saw your mom there. They hit it off and she gave him her number, thinking 'no way this stiff is gonna call me,' but he did, and he pursued her, let me tell you. Couldn't stop. Eventually, they fell in love and the rest is—well, you get it."

Pete straightened up in his seat, trying to focus. The dark room and the heat were lulling him a bit, but he had to focus. He had to see this interview through, and ask the question he'd come to get answered.

"When did my mom ... when did she come back?" Pete asked. "Back to you? When she left my father?"

Diane stammered for a second, confused, as if she'd just seen a car driving on the wrong side of the road.

"Leave your father?" she said. "No, no. Gracie didn't leave. You father kicked her out. He asked her to go."

"What? Why?"

"Pete, your mother was a drunk," Diane said, her eyes burying themselves in Pete's brain, an expression on her face he would never forget. "She was an alcoholic, the worst kind. Day drinking, hiding bottles, bringing you—her toddler—to bars with her, riding in strangers' cars, disappearing for days. She was spiraling out of control and your father couldn't leave her alone with you."

Pete felt the floor disappear, his body fuzz out of focus. He let the words replay in his mind: *Pete, your mother was a drunk.*

The mother he'd never really known, who lived in his brain as a cross-cut of buried memories and stories his father had told him, had been so much more. She'd struggled with the same problem that had dragged Pete to the edge of death more times than he cared to think about. Pete shook his head. Felt the tears welling up. The kind you can't control. He looked down, hoping to hide his face from Diane and failing.

Had she sought help? Did she find peace? What had his father done to support her? Had it played a part in her death? He needed these questions answered, he realized. More than anything else in the world.

He looked up, eyes red, and spoke.

"When did she come to live with you?" Pete asked, his voice sounding like the final cracks and scrapes of a car crash. "What happened?"

"It was a Sunday, I remember that," Diane continued, the light from the window dimming from a sharp white to a muted gray. "I was in my apartment, a small studio in South Miami, near my job, which I think I'd just lost—just a stupid waitressing job. But I hear a knock and my first thought is, who the hell is coming to my place at this hour? And it was your mom. She was dragging a bag, a Hefty bag or something, loaded with clothes. She looked terrible—dark streaks under her eyes, lipstick smeared, and just ... dirty. Like she needed a shower. She needed a place to stay, is what she needed. Pedro had kicked her out, told her she was a mess—made threats that he'd take the kid—well, you—away, and Gracie needed a place to be for a day or two.

"I mean, I hadn't seen her in months, the last time was at a friend's wedding, this guy—jeez, what was his name?—some guy we both dated at one point, totally blanking on his name. Handsome, I remember that. Anyway, it'd been a while. She'd even come to that wedding alone. Pedro was already getting sick of her. So, anyway, I bring her in and we talk for a while, she showers, she naps, then it's like she'd never been gone. We're back partying that very night—all about 'Fuck him!' and 'I do what I fucking want! Who the hell is he?' You know what I mean?"

Pete nodded, nothing to add—he wanted to hear her story, not guide it. He wanted to feel like he was there, experiencing this woman, this person who was his mother, for what felt like the first time.

"And, look, it was a blast. Your mom—she was, like I said, amazing," Diane said, a smile cracking through her lawyerly veneer. "We drank, we smoked, I think we both brought guys home—I'm sorry, is this weird? Well, whatever. She was single again, or on her way to it, and she knew she had a few days before she'd have to come back and figure out the logistics of what was happening, so she wanted to have fun, to blow off some steam. So we did. I introduced her to a lot of my friends, we stayed up late. It was beautiful. Until it wasn't."

"She was killed soon after, right?"

"It was a few months later," Diane said. "By then, Gracie had moved in with me. She'd gotten a job tending bar at this jazz club, Terraza. I think it's still open? She was working the bar, dating the owner, or one of them. Blanking on the guy's name. He was connected, though."

"They were a couple?"

"I mean, yes and no," Diane said. "They were sleeping together and they spent a lot of time in the same place because she worked for him, but I think he was married, too, so it was complicated. But I don't think Gracie was particularly concerned with marriage and monogamy at that point. She was cutting loose, too, drinking all the time. I remember a lot of nights where I'd had enough—I'd hit this wall, just couldn't, and she'd want to keep going. I had to leave her a few times, get a cab or try to drive. That ... that night ... was one of those. One of those nights I couldn't keep up with her anymore."

Pete nodded for her to continue.

"It was New Year's Eve. We were at Terraza, I think, or a bar around there," Diane said. "The owner ... Dammit, why am I blanking on his name? Anyway, he'd closed the place down, private party. Big deal. VIPs only, invite-only. We were all having a blast. Open bar, great music ... then the coke arrives and the party got really good. Just one of those crazy nights that had become routine for us. Do you know what I mean?"

"I—yeah, I think so," Pete said.

He knew exactly what she meant. Drinking wasn't all about painful falls, blackouts, and regrets. Most alcoholics will readily admit there was a time when drinking was fun. Vibrant. Lively. Most of your drinking life is spent chasing the high that comes from that first drink—the sense of completion and power that had previously eluded you. But that moment is a mirage, Pete knew. Another drink didn't take you back to the beginning. It shunted you right back where you left off, in the darkness, alone, desperate and craving. Pete relived some form of those final moments as a drinker every day. He had to, if he wanted to avoid going back down that path.

"Anyway, it was a crazy, crazy night," Diane said. "I can't remember much of it, but one thing sticks with me—there's one thing I'll never forget."

"What?"

"Just, and this is going to sound weird, but just the look on Gracie's—your mom's—face, as I was walking away, as I was leaving her with her boyfriend and the party, this look of complete fear. She didn't say anything, but it seemed that, even in the haze of whatever was in her body—drugs, alcohol, whatever—something cut through. Something sliced through the fog and she felt it. She felt very afraid. And I will always regret not staying with her that night."

Pete lost track of himself then, for a moment, but it was enough time—when he returned to himself, his head was in his hands and all he could see was blackness, even with his eyes straining to open wider, desperate for any glimmer of light.

# CHAPTER SIXTEEN

The black limo was parked in front of Pete's house when he arrived. It was late in the afternoon, almost evening, and Pete knew whoever was waiting for him wasn't paying a social call.

He walked up the steps, still reeling from his conversation with Diane Crowther. His mother had been a drunk. Like him. They'd walked the same field, tried to dodge the same land mines. Pete survived, for now. His mother hadn't been as lucky. What lessons could she have passed on to him if she'd lived? What bullets could he have dodged with her insight? Even after spending hours talking to Diane Crowther, Pete felt no closer to knowing this woman than when he first learned of her murder. He intended to rectify that.

He reached for the front door and noticed it was unlocked. He was only half surprised. As he stepped in, he announced himself.

"Whoever you are, you'd better have a really good reason for breaking into my house."

"Hello, Pete."

Pete saw Eddie Rosen and Alvaro Mujica, the latter flanked by two large bodyguards not bothering to hide their handguns. The men were burly, dressed in matching khaki pants and black polos, and wearing sunglasses, having mastered the art of looking tough and menacing. Pete wasn't impressed.

"Hey gents," he said. "What brings you to Westchester? It can't be the beaches. The pizza's no good here, either."

"My client wants to speak with you," Rosen said, a strained smile on his face. "It's urgent, which is why we made the trip out here, and waited patiently for you to come back."

"I check my phone pretty regularly, Eddie, and I don't have a missed call from you," Pete said. "Maybe it didn't go through? Verizon can really suck sometimes."

"We didn't call you, Fernandez, all right?" Rosen said, stepping around Pete's dining room table. "Let's talk."

"I'm off the case," Pete said. "I shouldn't have accepted it to begin with. I was retired. Now I'm working on something else—something more important."

"We made a deal," Mujica said, his voice a dark, low baritone. "I honor my promises, Mr. Fernandez. I was led to believe you did, too."

"Your man Rosen fired me."

"So I'm told," Mujica said, nodding slowly. His demeanor was thoughtful, but not casual—a professional hunter waiting for the right time to shoot. "But my argument stands. You owe me your time and effort. I have neither."

"This isn't about a painting, is it?" Pete asked.

"What do you mean?" Rosen said.

"I did a little digging after the trail went cold," Pete said. "And while your story of a lost Garcia Menocal painting was intriguing, it made no sense. I talked to a few experts—Cuban history, art history, you name it. There's no evidence this painting ever existed, much less that you even had it in your possession. Which makes me wonder— what did this woman, this Beatriz de Armas, steal from Javier?"

Rosen fidgeted and Mujica shook his head. They'd expected Pete to roll over.

"Mr. Fernandez, you insult me with your intimations, your insults," Mujica said, placing his hands on Pete's dinner table, palms down. "I came to you with a clear request. You accepted it. Now we are at an impasse. That frustrates me."

Mujica licked his lips slowly, as if preparing himself for a long, thoughtful speech. But Pete knew the man enough to know he chose his words carefully—for maximum impact.

"*Déjame hablar claramente*, Fernandez. Mr. Rosen tells me he offered to destroy something relating to you, something potentially damaging to your reputation," Mujica said, switching from Spanish to English with ease. "That was kind of him. Eddie is a trusting sort. I'm more direct—because my time is precious: Do as we ask, and I will personally clear up your problem. Ignore my request, and I can't guarantee what happens next will be to your liking. *¿Me entiendes, mijo?*"

He motioned to his bodyguards and they led the older man out Pete's front door.

Rosen lingered behind. "That didn't go as well as it could have," he said, his eyes on the door, waiting for his boss and his lackeys to be out of earshot.

"I'm not doing this," Pete said. "I have no reason to."

"Well, now it sounds like you do," Rosen said. "Doesn't it?"

"You lied about those photos being destroyed."

"I may have forgotten that I had an extra set," Rosen said with a shrug. "Old age, it gets to you."

"You're a piece of shit, Eddie," Pete said.

"You saw her, didn't you?" Rosen asked, changing the subject. "Why didn't you tell Alvaro?"

"Who?"

"Beatriz."

"Yes," Pete said. "For a minute. But then I lost her."

"You lost her?" Rosen said, shaking his head. "I'm going to forget to tell my boss that, too. Beatriz has become an obsession for him, understandably."

"If that's what you want to call her."

Pete turned away from Rosen. He didn't care. He wanted the men out of his house. Out of his life.

"What did you mean by that?" Rosen said, grabbing Pete's shoulder.

Pete shook Rosen's grip off. "Nothing," he said. "You can leave now, unless there's something else?"

Rosen looked out Pete's doorway, watched as Mujica's bodyguards shepherded the man into the back seat. Making sure they were able to talk freely.

"Your instincts were right," Rosen said. "There is no painting."

"Thanks, but it's not instinct," Pete said, before Rosen cut him off.

"Whatever you want to call it," Rosen said. "It's more complicated than that. Beatriz has something that belongs to my boss. Something that's ... how do I put it? Jeopardizing his business interests."

Pete turned to face Rosen, who upon closer inspection, looked weary and tired.

"That's a shame," Pete said. "Best of luck. Like I said, I've got other things I need to work on."

Rosen sighed and stepped closer to Pete. He could smell the art dealer's musky aftershave, could see the creases around his eyes and the dark rings under them.

"I don't want to put this woman—Beatriz, or whatever you know her as—at risk, all right?" Rosen said, eyebrows raised. "I can guarantee her safety. I want her to be safe. I don't care about her. But she has something we need. And it's directly tied to you."

Pete didn't respond.

"You almost died, months ago," Rosen said. "That gangster, Vincent Salerno, was after something. Information, you thought. Now he's dead. We don't know why. But the Italians want blood. Salerno was going rogue on them, but he was still a made guy. Someone took him out. The Italians—the DeCalvacantes—think Alvaro clipped their guy, and they don't like that."

"Wait, so Salerno wasn't killed by the DeCalvacantes?"

Rosen's eyes narrowed. "Where'd you get that idea?" he asked. "Why would they kill their own guy?"

"Who else would want him gone?" Pete asked. "The mob tends to self-regulate."

Images of that moment flooded Pete's mind. Walking into his empty Spring Valley office. The FBI agent, Chopp. Salerno appearing. Everything going dark. The beeping sounds. The shuffling. The pain. What had brought the gangster back there? What had he been after? And why was it coming back up again now, with Eddie Rosen?

"What does any of this have to do with, uh, Beatriz?" Pete asked. "What did Salerno want?"

Rosen looked over his shoulder, then back at Pete. "I gotta go, now's a bad time," he said. "But let's meet up. I'll call you, all right?"

He didn't wait for a response.

Pete watched as the man walked out of his house and slipped into a waiting limo.

# JEZEBEL

*August 16, 1983*

**G**raciela locked the front door to Terraza, a trendy jazz club downtown. The area was getting better, safer, but it was still not a good idea to be alone in an empty bar this time of night. She leaned on the door and sighed. It'd been a long night. The tips had been good, the crowd had been mostly well-behaved, and the band—a quartet that was really cooking toward the end of their Latin jazz set—had brought in more people than usual.

So this was what it was like to be part of the workforce, Graciela thought. Diane had finally drawn the line a week back. *Get a job.* Graciela understood. She'd been surfing on D's couch for months, not paying rent, eating her food. It made sense. Graciela hadn't waited tables in years, though. Not since before Pedro. But the tricks of the trade came back quick. Like muscle memory.

It felt good to work, she had to admit. To have some kind of purpose. A place to be. The tips were good, and she had to actually dress up for the gig. She felt like she had some momentum for the first time in a long while.

When she'd gotten the job—when D had come bounding into the apartment to tell her they'd hire Graciela—she'd told herself she'd grow up now. Drink only on the weekends. Go to bed at a normal time. She'd even called Pedro and asked to see Pete.

Graciela thought back to that humid afternoon, the drive—she'd borrowed D's car—out to Westchester, the pull of regret as she walked up those familiar porch steps. Pete had gotten so big. She'd cried when she saw him, cried harder as she pulled him close, as the familiar touch and smell of him invaded her senses, his little, chubby body warm on her chest.

*This is my baby,* she remembered thinking. *Where the fuck have I been?*

She had been ill-equipped in the moment, and found herself shaking with tears. Pete was crying, too. She remembered Pedro gently pulling their son back. Graciela got upset. Started screaming. Cursing. Stomping her feet like a toddler.

"How dare you keep him from me?" she'd screamed. "I can watch him. I can love him. I don't need your cop bullshit telling me I'm some kind of monster—some drunk. Just because you hate me."

Then she was spent, on her knees, panting, drenched in tears. She saw Pedro's dad, Diego, sitting in a corner, trying to ignore them all, reading his book, keeping some level of decorum. He'd never liked her, Graciela knew. The guy had escaped Castro, evaded gangsters—yet here he sat, looking at her like she was the worst kind of devil he'd ever seen.

Then she'd left. She'd run out. She couldn't see them again. She hadn't been ready. But Pete was fine. That was all Graciela needed. Now it was on her. She needed to get her life in order. Find her way back to her son.

She wiped down the bar. She wanted to keep things on the level. But it hadn't been easy. D wanted to go out every night, no matter what time Terraza closed. If it was too late, they'd end up drinking here, making sure not to skim too much off the top. They'd get a good buzz on the work supply, do a few bumps in the bathroom, and then jump in the car. Then they were off—to the beach, to that shithole bar near D's place, anywhere really. Sometimes they'd find themselves at a random house party and wake up in a spare bedroom or on a couch. It felt fucking great in the moment. When everyone was laughing, drinking, touching, moving ... but the mornings were something else. Something darker. Empty. It left Graciela feeling raw, inhuman. Like a piece of garbage.

Sometimes, in the morning, feeling the remnants of a buzz and beginnings of a headache, feeling like an alien in her own skin, Graciela would call people. Friends. Family. Usually Pedro. It'd always end in a fight. He'd be calm and patient at first, but she could feel the anger—the shame. Before it got too bad, she'd ask him to give Pete a kiss and hang up. She'd promise things. Too many things. She'd promise to come by for dinner. She'd ask to see their son. She'd promise this was just something she had to work through. That she'd be better soon.

"But will I?" she said, on the tips of her toes, trying to slide a bottle of vodka onto the bar's top shelf.

She finished restocking the bar and turned to see the door open. She was sure she'd locked it, so it could only mean one person was coming in. She felt a mixture of excitement and anxiety.

He walked in, looking like he'd just spent the day at the spa. His hair perfect, his suit impeccable, and his smile gleaming— something out of a catalogue. He locked the door behind him with his free hand, the other toting a large bottle of what looked like very expensive champagne.

He leaned over the bar and they kissed. A long, familiar kiss.

"I've been thinking about you all day," he said, a sly smile on his handsome face.

Graciela had become a cliché, and she wasn't sure she cared. It was one of the few bright stops she could find, when her head was clear and she could truly—soberly—assess her situation. He was smart, charming, and treated her well. He was probably married, too.

She was dating her boss and not sure she felt guilty about it.

# CHAPTER SEVENTEEN

Pete let the phone clatter onto the table. He'd left Kathy a third voicemail, this one more pleading than the last. He felt tangled up—threads weaving around him and pulling him in different directions. Why was Emily—his former fiancée— masquerading as someone else? What did Salerno have to do with Alvaro Mujica? Who was the mysterious man his mother was with on the night she was murdered? Who killed Osvaldo Valdez hours before he could talk to Pete about the death of his mother?

He didn't know where to go from here, or if there was a clear path. But he knew what he didn't want to do: work for Alvaro Mujica. Get ensnared by another powerful, corrupt man. *Fuck the photos*, he thought. He'd gotten out of worse jam-ups with police. He'd have to do it again. He wasn't going to be held hostage.

He grabbed his laptop and went to his most reliable search tools and databases—the first step to any investigation. Even now, "retired" as he was, he kept all his memberships and paperwork active. Well, he just hadn't taken the time to deactivate them, he thought. In the transition from shambling sometimes-PI to almost-dead ex-PI, Pete figured the best thing to do was just stop. Stop the work. Stop the flow of cases. He'd get to the details as needed.

For a moment, he was happy he hadn't. His past was reaching out to him—trying to pull him down into a darkness he couldn't make out. He had to dive into the work and find some footing, or risk drowning.

He typed the name into the search field: Emily Sprague. The information unspooled on the screen—much of it familiar to Pete. Banyan Elementary. West Miami Middle School. Coral Park High. Rutgers. The addresses. The one they shared in New Jersey. Her apartment on South Beach, the one she'd scurried to after leaving him, the cab loaded with luggage. The house in Homestead with her husband, Rick Blanco. Then ... nothing.

Rick Blanco was your typical Cuban alpha male—old-fashioned and family-oriented on the surface, up for a party and bending the rules underneath. He'd been nice enough, but he had a temper. And, Pete realized over time, he'd also dabbled on the wrong side of the law. After Rick's death and the conclusion of the Los Enfermos case, Harras said Emily had ended up in Europe, but Pete never followed up. Never expected to see her again. She was in the wind.

But everyone leaves a trail. Pete had learned this over the years. Every purchase, every move, every relationship, left a fingerprint. Emily was no exception. Shortly after the last time he'd seen her—a heated exchange that was more bitter dismissal than emotional goodbye—she'd flown to Barcelona. According to her credit card, she'd rented an Airbnb near Las Ramblas, a gothic maze in the heart of the city. She'd apparently stayed there for a few months before moving into an apartment nearby.

He pulled up another tab and scrolled through his recent bookmarks. Javier Mujica had a website for his group, The Javier Mujica Quintet. He clicked on "EVENTS" and scrolled back—almost two years back, syncing up with when Emily had left the country and settled in Spain. The Javier Mujica Quintet had embarked on a European tour a month before, and spent time in Spain around the same time Emily was getting settled. They'd played in a medium-sized venue, JazzSi Club Taller de Musics, which was relatively close to the apartment where Emily settled. Pete didn't believe in coincidences.

He went back to the Emily file and wasn't surprised to notice that her electronic footprint had become harder to make out, fading over time. Fewer purchases. No forwarding address.

Pete slid the laptop away and pulled out a small notebook. He began to write. Emily Sprague-Blanco. She'd left Miami in fear and shame—afraid her dead husband's former bosses, the bloodthirsty drug gang known as Los Enfermos, would come after her for absconding with money Rick had skimmed from them. Javier Mujica was the son of a gambling boss with ties to drugs and all things underworld, who'd left the long shadow of his father to become his own man, his own artist. It sounded almost romantic that these two people—on the run from their own pasts—could find love on another continent and start anew.

But life never worked out that way. And as much as he wanted to think Emily did find something special in the dark, winding streets of Barcelona, Pete was also sure she'd found something else. Pete felt his phone vibrating in his pocket and picked up.

"Hello?"

"Pete, it's Rachel Alter," the cold case detective said. "We've got a problem."

"What's up?"

"It's your partner," Alter said, her voice hushed. "She's in trouble. Bentley. The reporter."

"What?" Pete asked. "Where is she?"

"Downtown, here at the precinct," Alter said. "Hudson just asked me to give you a ring. Bentley's been arrested, for battery."

"Battery?" Pete said. He waited for a moment to hear Alter's response, but the line had gone dead.

Kathy walked outside the police station, wrapped in a jacket that was clearly two sizes too big, Rachel Alter a few steps behind her. When she noticed Pete, she shook her head slightly, letting it hang forward in defeat. She barely looked up at him when they stepped off the sidewalk onto the parking lot asphalt.

"Thanks for bailing me out, I guess," Kathy said, looking around the vacant lot.

"Marco's dropping the charges," Alter said, her voice flat. "Which is a good thing."

"Need a lift?" Pete asked.

Kathy shrugged and followed Pete, who nodded at Alter. The detective waved and walked back toward the precinct, a "this is your problem now" look in her eyes.

Pete and Kathy got into the car and backed out of the parking lot. They were silent for the first ten minutes of the ride back to Kathy's Wynwood apartment, the only sound coming from the radio—Cat Power plaintively asking Aretha to sing one for her.

"I'm pregnant."

Pete tapped the brakes and slid the car off the road, pulling into a residential street. He flicked the blinkers on and turned to face Kathy.

"What?"

"You heard me," Kathy said, still not looking at him. Her eyes were red from crying, whatever makeup she'd put on that day wiped away roughly over the last few hours.

"Is that what the fight was about? Marco was upset?"

"You could say that, yes."

Pete let out a dry laugh. "Not an ideal way to respond to the news that you're having a kid."

"I'd say it was pretty normal."

Pete turned his body toward Kathy.

"How is that normal?" Pete asked. "I'd think he'd be happy he was going to be a father."

"Pete," Kathy said, an annoyed frown on her face as she met his look for the first time since walking out of police headquarters. "The baby is yours. You're the father."

# PART III
# MOTION SICKNESS

# CHAPTER EIGHTEEN

He set Kathy up in his bedroom and took the couch. It was close to two in the morning by the time she was asleep. The suburban quiet of Westchester belied the internal scream Pete had felt since Kathy broke the news to him. *Pregnant*. He was going to be a father. The idea had been something he hadn't entertained in years.

He wasn't ready. He was certain of that. But he didn't have much of a choice now. That was life, Pete had discovered, over the last few years. Things happened and you reacted in the best way possible. That was all you could control.

They'd talked more freely after Kathy let him know, the walls they'd built up between each other temporarily taken down in the wake of the revelation. She wanted to keep the baby. It was hers. She wanted to be a mother. She didn't care if Pete wanted to be involved. Didn't care that Marco knew. Didn't care that her personal life was in tatters. She wanted the baby. She'd already lost one before.

Pete nodded. He wanted it, too. He realized it as he said the words aloud. He wanted this.

But what was "this," and what did it entail? Marriage? No, friendship was what he could offer now. Anything else ... well, that would come on its own. He tried to stretch out on his cramped couch, his bare feet leaning over the side.

Kathy had been matter-of-fact on the ride to Pete's house. She was glad Pete knew now. She wasn't sure how long she could have kept it from him. But she wasn't going to make the same mistake she made before, with Harras—the secrets and the anger and the regret. With the baby she'd lost. She was going to protect the child. She was going to focus on whatever she could do to ensure its survival. Whether that was with Pete or not, she didn't care.

Pete thought of his own father. The man he'd hated as a child—not because of any abuse or misbehavior, but because of the rules he'd imposed. The structure. All things that came to serve him well as an adult. Had his perception of the old man changed now, after Pete learned the truth about his mother? That she'd been murdered and had been an addict, like Pete? Why had Pedro Fernandez kept the truth from him? What could he do to dig deeper into the case? Was it even worth doing?

Pete sat up and ran a hand through his sweat-soaked hair. He reached for his laptop and did a cursory search for the bar, the jazz club his mother had worked at in her final days. Terraza still existed, he discovered, though it was an upscale eatery that sometimes featured music—ranging from live jazz fusion to Spanish hip-hop. He did a basic records search. He couldn't find anything that synced up with the time Graciela Fernandez worked there, but he did find a trail that led him to the current owner.

*I shouldn't be surprised,* he thought. *It was always one case. One thread.*

He stood up and hastily scribbled a note, his hand shaking as he let Kathy know where he was headed. He slid the sheet under his bedroom door and got into his car. He backed out and headed toward the 836 East. He didn't notice the dark sedan pulling out after him.

# CHAPTER NINETEEN

**P**ete rapped his knuckles on the door again. Hard. He knew it was late. He didn't care.

Eddie Rosen, Alvaro Mujica's art dealer-slash-fixer-slash-lawyer, lived on the fringe of Coral Gables, in a large house that could comfortably be called a mansion, or was maybe a small step below that rank. The front lawn was more foliage than grass—plants tangling together like some kind of miniature forest, hiding the large Mission revival–style home from passersby. He waited another minute. Rosen's black Lexus was in the driveway, but he wasn't responding to Pete's repeated calls. He'd promised to reach out to Pete with some hush-hush information about his boss, but Pete had gotten nothing. That meant that Eddie either changed his mind, or had his mind changed. Both roads interested Pete.

It was late in the evening, and Rosen didn't strike Pete as the partying type. No, he was home. But he was screening his visitors. Just as Pete started to turn back to his car, he heard the door creak open. He wheeled around, but didn't find Rosen waiting for him.

"Emily?"

"Pete," she said, a confused look on her face, followed by a nervous clarity. "Come in, hurry up."

Pete walked into the large foyer, Emily closing the door quickly behind him—her back leaning on the large oak entrance, her hands in her now jet-black hair.

"What are you doing here?"

"I could ask you the same thing, Em."

"Pete," she said, rolling the word around her mouth, unfamiliar yet comfortable. Like a childhood prayer. "No, no. You shouldn't be here. I thought it was ... someone ... someone else ... "

"Who? Eddie?" Pete asked. "What are you doing here?"

"You need to go, Pete," she said. "I'm in a lot of trouble. You are, too. But you can still get out. Stop chasing this."

"Chasing what?" Pete asked. "Let me help you. We can figure this out together."

"No, we really can't," Emily said, shaking her head. "Not yet. I tried to warn you, but you're as stubborn as ever. Back off from this. It's going to get a lot worse."

Pete grabbed her shoulders, a slight shake on contact.

She looked up at him, her eyes wide, as if noticing him for the first time.

"Emily," Pete said. "What the fuck is going on? Why have you gotten yourself invol—"

The sentence was drowned out by gunfire, the staccato beat of a machine gun shattering the large bay windows and shaking the house's front door.

Pete reacted instinctively, lunging into the foyer, his arm stretched out, dragging Emily down. They landed hard, his head thumping on the white Calcutta marble tile. He groaned as he rolled onto his back, just in time to see the door swing inward. He heard Emily's frightened intake of breath as a dark figure stepped into his view. He felt her roll to her feet and run. The masked man didn't flinch, his gaze locked on Pete.

He knew, in his head and heart, that the man beneath the large dark scarf, under the sharp black hat, was not the same man he'd grappled with years before. Yet, here he was—Isleño Novo, if Robert Harras's intel was right—the same figure that had stormed into his house months before and had almost murdered Harras. A figure that had leapt out of Pete's own nightmares and into this dark, musty room.

"No," Pete said, reaching for his back—for the place where he normally kept his father's gun. The gun \wasn't there.

But this man, this Silent Death, didn't know that. He drew a silencer-equipped pistol and spoke, a gravel-laced voice seeming to waft out from the dark house's very walls.

Pete had a moment, maybe two, to act. To not only avoid being gunned down by this killer, but also protect Emily. He mouthed a silent prayer before lifting his hands in surrender.

The move seemed to surprise the masked man momentarily.

"So, you're the new Silent Death?" Pete asked, turning into a sitting position. "Didn't realize it was a legacy thing, like James Bond or the Tonight Show."

The man stepped toward Pete, gun trained on his head.

The sound of the gunshot was deafening, echoing around the room and sending Pete reeling. He watched as the Silent Death crumpled to the floor, a mist of blood spurting out of the back of his head and onto the door and wall behind him. His face hit the tile with a soft *schlop* sound, blood pooling around it almost immediately.

Emily was standing, the gun still pointed at the space where the man once stood. Her hands were shaking, tears streaming down her face. She didn't fight when she felt Pete's hand wrap around hers, gently pulling the gun from her grasp. He put the gun in his back pocket and pulled her in to him. He felt her body shake as the wracking sobs overtook her, the low, wailing moan growing louder with each heaving breath.

# CHAPTER TWENTY

Nisha Hudson handed Pete a Styrofoam cup half-filled with a light brown liquid that had once been coffee. He took a hungry slurp. They'd been outside Eddie Rosen's house for what felt like days, but had only been a few hours.

Emily had been taken to the hospital for observation. The body of the man dressed as the Silent Death was identified as Isleño Novo, as Harras had guessed  a mob assassin with ties to the Five Families, the Albanian crime syndicates, and various other cartels. So, while not the Silent Death Pete remembered, Novo had been a Silent Death of sorts.

The bigger question was: Why had he been gunning for them?

"You all right?" Hudson asked, her stern features softening briefly as Pete finished his lukewarm drink.

"I'll be okay," Pete said. "Not sure how Emily will end up."

"Beatriz de Armas, you mean?"

"Formerly known as."

"She was barely speaking when they took her in the ambulance," Hudson said, looking down the street, littered with onlookers and

Miami-Dade Police green-and-whites, their lights flashing in the Miami evening. "Any idea why she was in the house?"

Pete shook his head.

"You gonna tell me why you were in Eddie Rosen's house? Without him there?"

"Not unless you really want to push it."

Hudson smirked. "You're a pain in the ass," she said. "Normally, I'd like that. But not tonight."

Pete started to respond, but Hudson persisted.

"I'm not asking as your dad's old pal," Hudson said. "I'm asking as a Homicide detective who's looking at a warm body in the house of a very well-known part of the community. And I'm asking you as a witness. What were you doing in Eddie Rosen's house, without Eddie Rosen in there? And what the fuck else happened?"

"I went there to see Eddie, but—"

Before he could continue, Pete heard footsteps behind him. He turned to see Kathy, speeding down the sidewalk, wrapped in one of Pete's FIU sweaters and black yoga pants. They embraced, a short hug, her face hot on his. Pete held onto her.

"What the hell happened?" she hissed into his ear.

"I'm fine."

She pulled away with a quick shove. She was mad, Pete could tell. But also relieved. The latter meant more to him. It gave him hope.

"Hudson, this is Kathy—"

"I know Ms. Bentley," Hudson said, extending her hand. "By reputation."

Kathy shook the detective's hand and nodded. "I get that a lot," she said. "I'll take this one as a compliment, I guess."

"It's good you're here, actually," Hudson said. "And, Pete, don't think I forgot about our little chat. You're a person of interest here. So either we talk now, tomorrow, or very soon. I'm not the type that likes to be ignored."

Hudson pulled out her phone and pushed a few buttons. She turned away from Pete and Kathy and muttered a few words into the phone.

"What was that about?" Pete asked as Hudson swiveled back to them.

"Turn around," Hudson said.

Pete and Kathy did.

"Miss me?" Robert Harras asked.

Pete's expression remain unchanged, if a bit bemused. Kathy's was a mix of anger, surprise, and happiness—which summed up her general feelings for Robert Harras, dead or alive.

"The gang's all here, I guess," she said.

"I thought you were dead," Kathy said.

"I told Pete to clue you in."

"He did, in his way, but we're not exactly on the best terms," she said. "And, you're technically dead. The world thinks you're dead."

"I'm not," Harras said.

"You shaved," Pete said. "That's like death."

They were in the backseat of a large police van, the tinted windows giving them some sense of privacy. The van was weaving down Le Jeune Road, heading toward the 836. Hudson was headed to the hospital to interview Emily, and Pete wanted to be there.

"Cut the stand-up routine for once," Harras said, his more familiar, curmudgeonly self peeking through. "We need to talk."

"Where the fuck do you get off?" Kathy said, her head snapping left, eyes locking on Harras. "You've been AWOL, doing God knows what."

"And you," she said to Pete. "What in the hell is even going on? We need to get our ducks in a row before you can expect me to sign up for another tour on the Titanic, okay?"

Harras chuckled.

"We're saying the same thing," he said. "We need to be on the same page. But before you tell me your side—here's mine. After I got shot ... well, once they figured out I was going to live but it could be played off as a death, the Bureau took me off the grid. Their agents spun it so I was dead to the world, even before I was out of surgery and in full agreement. When I woke up, they gave me a choice. Go out, risk being in the crosshairs of whoever went after me, or help them. They wanted me for one more case, under deep cover, if I was willing and able. I laid the groundwork here for a while—no one really knew I was alive until I clued Dave in a few nights ago. Part of my time was spent healing, the rest was spent in New York, trying to track Vincent Salerno."

"The goodfella who got shot up a few months back?" Kathy asked. "Wasn't that in Miami?"

"Yes, but his trail wove back up north," Harras said. "I needed to figure out what brought him here, and what brought him into Pete's path in New York—what made him almost kill Pete, and come after him again. If that's what he was doing, or if he was coming down here for something else."

"Well," Pete said, "don't let me slow you down."

"Like I told Pete, Salerno had a line on something big, huge— something that was worth risking his entire life as a made guy. But now I think I know more about what that is," Harras said, gripping the bumper seat in the back of the van as the vehicle made a sharp turn. "Salerno was chasing after Doug Ferris, the father of your stripper friend, Destiny—"

"Jen. Jen Ferris," Pete said, his voice sharp. "Her name was Jennifer."

"Right, sorry," Harras said, realizing his misstep.

Pete ignored Kathy's glare.

Harras cleared his throat and continued. "Turns out Doug Ferris had a line on a Colombian connection unlike any other," he said. "A major pipeline that had gone dry. Can you guess why? Because, believe it or not, you're directly tied to it."

Pete shrugged.

"Los Enfermos. The biggest drug gang Miami's ever known. The giant funnel that takes all that fine Colombian snow and turns it into money? They were gone, or at least severely paralyzed," Harras said, pointing at Pete. "Even before you came back to Miami and eliminated the dregs of the gang—"

"Actually, I believe you did that, by running over that Oliva guy and making his skull splatter," Kathy said. "But who's keeping score?"

"I was saving your life, if I recall," Harras said. "Anyway, the Colombians were looking for a connect, a new gang they could trust and use to get their drugs on the street in Miami and across the Eastern Seaboard. Doug Ferris had a line on that info. Not the info itself, mind you. But he knew someone who could speak to La Madrina herself."

"La Madrina?" Pete asked.

"The godmother, basically," Harras said. "The head of the Colombian drug cartels is a woman—lady by the name of Andrea

Muñoz. Nasty woman, rough character. We've—well, the Bureau's—been trying to take her down for years. Problem is, we can't seem to find her and we can't seem to find anyone that knows her. So, even being two degrees away from her is something, and to Salerno, it meant money. Big money. He corners Ferris and gets nothing. Guy didn't give up his source—because he didn't really have one, just a friend of a friend, basically.

"Salerno kills him. He finds out his daughter, Jen, had been tracking him down using a PI from Miami named Fernandez. So Salerno starts going down the list. Spends so much time trailing you, he even enlists some of his mafia brothers to tag along, thinking it's DeCalvacante business. You, being the imperious prick you are, embarrass him enough that his pal lets slip to the bosses what's going on. So suddenly the heat is on Salerno from inside the house. While you're in Miami dealing with La Iglesia de la Luz, he kills Jen Ferris and then, desperate, he comes after you when you pop up again in New York. He gets nothing, thinks you're dead, and jets."

"Did Salerno think the person with the connection to this Muñoz woman was here?" Pete asked. He felt the car revving up, the sirens starting to blare.

"They are here, Pete," Harras said. "That's the thing. Salerno came down to get them. Someone got to him first. Someone, I think, who might be the same someone your girl took out just now. Someone wanted us to believe it was Salerno's mob bosses trying to clear the decks, but I'm not sure. Now, rogue Mafioso or not, the DeCalvacantes are coming to town, too. They don't like it when one of their top guys gets clipped without their approval. And, while they don't know a lot, they do know one thing: Salerno was coming to Miami to find you."

"So, we're up shit creek again, basically?" Kathy asked. "All because we don't know who might know this Colombian drug kingpin?"

"Oh, we know who knows her," Harras said. "That's part of the problem."

"What?" Pete asked. "Who is it?"

The van they were in hit the brakes suddenly before turning around, the siren's squealing getting louder. The three of them turned to the front of the car to see the two officers in the front seat speaking into the radio frantically. The cop on the passenger side looked back at them, an expression of shock on his face.

"Looks like your lady's gone," he said. "Beatriz de Armas split from the hospital."

Pete turned to Harras, who responded with a quick nod.

"Bingo."

# CHAPTER TWENTY-ONE

Coral Gables Hospital was a blocky, nondescript building that felt out of place next to the bunches of palm trees and greenery propped up around it. The area felt relatively quiet, aside from the bustle forming around the ICU.

As Harras, Kathy, and Pete followed Hudson down the long hospital corridor, they saw Hudson get intercepted—by Rachel Alter.

"I got called over," Alter said. "What's the latest?"

"Weird they'd call you in. But it looks like the bird has flown," Hudson said, motioning toward what Pete guessed was Emily's room. "She snuck out when the guard went to take a leak. They thought she was asleep."

"So what now?" Kathy asked, ignoring Alter. "We were here to try to talk some sense into Emily—try and figure out what the hell is going on."

"Now? Now nothing," Hudson said, a look of disdain smearing across her face. "This is police business. I brought you two along because Robert said you were good, but there's nothing to do if your friend's gone AWOL. We'll take it from here. They're searching around the area. She couldn't have gone far."

Alter looked at Kathy and then Pete, as if to ask what was going on. Pete wasn't sure he had much to add.

Footsteps echoed down the hallway, and Pete turned toward the sound.

Eddie Rosen approached the group, looking sharp in a tan suit, a black briefcase in his hand. "Mr. Fernandez, Ms. Bentley," he said. "I don't know your friends."

Harras shrugged.

"The police asked me to come down here," Rosen said, looking at Alter. "So, here I am."

"You're Eddie Rosen?" Alter said. "The owner of the house?"

"That is correct, Ms.—?"

"Alter," she said. "Miami PD. I'm usually on the Cold Case Unit, but they asked me to come down here—staffing's not as robust as you'd think. Do you have a minute to talk? We need to get a sense of what was happening and why—"

"Am I a suspect of any kind?"

"No, we just—" Alter said.

"Then I'm not sure why I'm here," Rosen said.

Hudson positioned herself in front of Alter, her confusion over the cold case detective's appearance impossible to hide.

"I've got this, Rachel," she told her colleague. "Mr. Rosen, I'm Nisha Hudson. I work in Homicide. As I'm sure you've been informed, there was a shooting on your property and we're going to have to ask you some questions."

"Ms. Hudson, a woman broke into my house, surely followed by some gangland thug who tried to kill her," Rosen said, before motioning toward Pete. "This man—Fernandez—happened to be there in time to stop it. Case closed. Now I hear the woman—de Armas—is missing. She's the one you want to talk to. I don't see how I can add much to this."

"That's for us to decide," Hudson said.

Rosen shrugged. "Ask away, then," he said. "I can't go home, since my house is now a crime scene."

"Why was Emily at your house, Eddie?" Pete asked.

Rosen narrowed his eyes at Pete. "I have no idea," he said, eyebrow raised. "I wasn't there. I don't know the woman. She must have broken in."

"Pete says she opened the door from the inside, pal," Harras said. "Does that make much sense to you? What kind of break-in artist decides to hang out for a while?"

"Who are you, may I ask?' Rosen said, looking at Harras. "What authority do you have here? This doesn't concern you, Fernandez, or his lady-in-waiting over here. I have no idea why Beatriz or Emily or whatever she's called today was in my house. I have even less of an idea why Pete was there, or why a man like Isleño Novo came in, guns blazing. Needless to say, I'm very concerned for my own safety. I merely came to let the police know where I'll be staying until this blows over."

"Again, Mr. Rosen, we need to sit down and talk for a bit," Hudson said, exasperated. "Either here or at the precinct."

Rosen looked at Hudson. "I'll meet you at the precinct, then," he said. "Hospitals make a germophobe like me nervous."

Hudson nodded. "I'll see you there in a bit, then," she said. "I'll talk to my people first. Let me warn you now, Mr. Rosen—do not play games. You are expected. Show up with a lawyer if you like, but I will not be stood up, you hear?"

Rosen responded with a sly, humorless smile. "Wouldn't think of it."

The older detective walked off without responding, shaking her head—clearly displeased with how the evening was shaping up.

"What's Mujica think of all this?" Pete asked Rosen. "Can't be a good look, huh? Gangland killer comes gunning for his number two? Hearing rumblings that things are a little unhinged out there."

Rosen tilted his head slightly, like a predator sizing up slow-moving prey. "I haven't asked him," he said. "Nor will I. Can I speak to you for a moment—privately?"

Pete nodded and followed Rosen as he strode toward the elevator bank down the hall.

"What was that all about?" Rosen said, the words tumbling out like a long, sharp hiss.

"You tell me, Eddie," Pete said. "Seems like the Mujica organization is taking some heat."

"Isleño Novo was a mercenary, a hired assassin who does whatever the highest bidder wants," Rosen said, his voice not rising above a whisper. "And now, the highest bidder wants to take out me and Alvaro."

"For what?" Pete asked. "For Salerno? You think it's the Italians?"

"Could be," Rosen said, reaching the elevator bank and pushing the DOWN button. "That's my guess. They think we took Salerno out, Lord knows why. We gain nothing from luring that fat fuck to Miami just to ice him."

A moment of silence passed between the two men before Pete pressed again.

"Emily Sprague is Beatriz de Armas," Pete said. "When were you going to tell me?"

"You're the detective," Rosen asked. "Aren't you? Oh, wait. You're retired. My mistake. Well, look, you figured it out. Now go find her and maybe you can get back together. I need to look after myself and my boss. It was nice knowing you."

The elevator doors pinged open and Rosen stepped in, turning around to face Pete.

"That's it?" Pete asked. "What about Javier?"

"He's dead," Rosen said. "I mourn him in my own way. But you couldn't figure out who killed him. I'm worried about the living Mujica now. And you should be worried about yourself."

The doors started to close.

"Is that a threat?" Pete asked, reaching out, trying to hold the doors open.

Rosen took a step back, a bemused smile on his face. "Oh, Pete, come on," he said. "That's not a threat. It's a fact. Do you really think Isleño Novo was gunning only for me? I'd be dead ten times by now."

Pete released the doors and watched them close.

"He could have been working for anyone," Harras said, sipping watered-down coffee from a Styrofoam cup. "If Novo was the new Silent Death, he was a freelancer. And a pretty damn good one, from what my intel says, recent slip-ups notwithstanding."

They were seated at a small four-top in the hospital cafeteria—Kathy, Harras, and Pete. Alter had gone home to relieve her babysitter and Hudson was on her way back to the PD. With Emily on the run, their usefulness to the police was nil, Pete mused.

"I think you're right about Emily having some kind of connection," Pete said, laying his hands on the table, palms down. "I traced her movements after I last saw her—around the time of Varela/Posada case, when we first ran into Los Enfermos."

"You've brought stalking your ex to a whole new level there, Pete," Kathy said. The joke was sharp and mean, a sign that they were still on shaky ground.

"When I saw her in that building, I knew right away who she was, even with the new dye job and Rosen trying to avoid saying it outright," Pete said. "Emily made it out of the country with a lot of Los Enfermos's money. But what if that wasn't all she had? What if she had info on Los Enfermos's drug connect?"

"La Madrina," Harras said.

"But where does Ferris come in, then?" Kathy said. "How did a low-level goon like that get the info?"

"Not sure," Pete said. "But my guess is, at some point, you need to start ... well, shopping around, you know? Letting people find out that you have this connect."

"Good logic, good assumption," Harras said, nodding. "So you think Ferris was deputized with the info, or a hint of the info—and that tipped off Salerno?"

"Right," Pete said. "Enough that he knew it involved me and enough to get him back to Miami to hunt me down, or try to."

"Not to burst your ego bubble, but what if he was after someone else down here?" Harras asked.

"Emily?" Pete said.

"Right," Harras said. "And that got him on someone else's radar."

"Then he gets killed," Kathy said. "But who took him out? And why?"

"I've got another question," Harras said, turning to face Pete. "What in the hell were you doing at Eddie Rosen's house at that time of night?"

"Yes, that is an excellent question," Kathy said. "I woke up to—" She hesitated.

Harras noticed and smirked. "You two gonna clue me in on something?" he asked.

"Shush, let's not lose focus," Kathy said. "Pete, go. You're on the spot."

Pete gave his friends a quick recap on Osvaldo Valdez, his mother, her friend Diane Crowther, and Terraza.

"Jesus, hasn't been a quiet time for you," Harras said. "So your mother leaves your dad, starts living the swinging Miami life with her friend, then ends up dead in an Overtown hotel. And you're trying to zone in on this spot where she worked?"

"Right," Pete said. "A bar owned by Alvaro Mujica, Eddie Rosen's boss."

# CHAPTER TWENTY-TWO

**"W**hat's your point?"

Detective Rachel Alter's shoulders were hunched slightly, her posture defensive, as Pete formulated a response. *She probably regrets letting me know where she lives,* he mused. Once he realized she'd exited the hospital, Pete left Kathy and Harras and made for Alter's Kendall townhouse. He had some questions.

"Don't you see?" Pete asked, stepping toward the half-open door, which was being blocked by Alter. "Alvaro Mujica owned the bar where my mom was working before she died. That's a big clue. Mujica is one of the most recognizable crime figures in Miami. Don't you think this is substantial? Enough to at least bring him in for questioning?"

Alter sighed, then looked inside her home before turning back to Pete. She appeared worn down, but her sharp features and dark brown eyes cut through the day-to-day exhaustion.

He reached for the door, stopping as she started to speak. His adrenaline rush had crashed, leaving him feeling spent—emotionally and physically. He was pushing himself too hard. But that didn't matter. This was new evidence. A step toward figuring out who

171

took his mother away before she could become more than a faded photograph for Pete. He had to press. Hard.

"It's late. Ella is asleep. I've had a long day," she said. "And, sorry to be so curt, but your mom's case is not the only thing on my docket. I realize it's important to you—so important. But it's one of hundreds of cases that are freezing cold in Miami, and while it's great you've found new information, I don't think I have the juice to disrupt whatever case the Vice team is putting together on Mujica just to drag him in and ask him about how he maybe knew a woman thirty years ago at a jazz club he owned, okay? It's easy when you're a PI, or whatever you call yourself. You don't have to answer to anyone. But I'm not in the Wild West, Pete."

Pete nodded.

She gave him a sympathetic smile in return as the door closed.

Pete reached out his hand and stopped the door.

Alter's eyes widened.

"Did you talk to Mosher?"

"The cop on the scene?" Alter said. "Yes, of course. Years ago, but yes. Why?"

"Do you have a lead on him?" Pete asked, moving his hand back as Alter's shoulders sagged. She was tired. Tired of him. He got that a lot.

"No, I mean, not right on me, okay?" she said, the door moving now.

"Anything could be helpful, just let me know where—"

"We'll figure it out, don't worry," she said softly. "We'll figure it out."

"I don't want to 'figure it out' later," Pete said. "My mother—her death—feels very real. Very present. It's like she was gunned down today. And finding this information—information that, look, I'm not one to tell you how to do your job, but … information that you should have known. This shouldn't be a surprise to you. Why wouldn't you check to see who owned the bar where she worked? Why didn't Valdez? It's sloppy. And I need to know why. She was my mother. Every bit of info, even the trivial, brings me a little closer to figuring this out. Help me."

"Good night, Pete," she said, her tone flat and emotionless. She was done.

The door clicked shut, followed by two locks sliding into place.

Pete clenched his fists. He felt a mild gust whisk by him as he watched the lights flicker off in Alter's home. He let out a long breath and pulled out his phone. He shot Kathy a quick, two-sentence text.

Rachel Alter was done, certainly. But Pete wasn't. He wasn't done pressing on his mother's case. He never would be. And, now, he was thinking that cold-case detective Rachel Alter might be much more than what Pete first imagined.

"I wasn't expecting to hear from you," she said. "But I'm glad."

"Thanks for picking up," Pete said. "I—well, I needed to talk to someone."

"That's my expertise," Allie Kaplan said. "I've got some time to talk now."

Pete slid into his car and turned it on, but waited before backing out of Alter's driveway.

"It's about my mom."

"You never talked about her much," Kaplan said. Pete could tell she was flying high, giving Pete room to fill in the space.

"I was told as a kid she'd died in childbirth," Pete said. "But now—I've learned ... I'm—well, I'm investigating her death. And now I know that wasn't true. That many people lied to me about it, including my own father."

"Wow."

"It's really unmoored me, I think," Pete said. "My father was my rock. And now, to think that there was this person, my own mother, who I could have known if not for someone else—for some killer. It really eats at me."

"How did she die?"

"Choked out in a hotel room," Pete said, his words gruff and distant but his delivery almost childlike. He was getting close to the pain, and he was trying to be standoffish. But he couldn't keep his defenses up forever. "She was a drunk."

"Was she in recovery?"

"No ... I mean, I don't know, but I don't think so," Pete said, his right hand clutching the car's gear shift. "But I just feel like so much ... potential ... so much help was lost. We could have been there for each other. My dad, I loved him, but he never understood why I drank. He was a 'one glass at dinner' guy. If that. But it explains the way he looked at me. It explains the defeat in his eyes when he'd see me hung over or drunk. It wasn't just worry. He saw my mother all over again."

There was silence on the other line.

Pete pressed on. "I have to close this case," he said. "I have to find out what happened to her. I can't imagine leaving a child to grow up without a parent. I can't do that myself."

"What do you mean?"

Pete relayed the news and updated Kaplan on his situation with Kathy.

"Well, it's been an eventful few months," she said, not joking. "Why don't you come in and see me tomorrow? It's late, but I do want to keep talking, okay? I think it'd help."

"What do I do?" Pete asked, not responding to Kaplan's question, not even asking Kaplan—he was almost talking to himself. To the universe.

"You're the detective, so that's up to you," she said. "But if I see a problem, I try to solve it directly. I think you need to face up to whatever you think that is as it relates to your mother. I don't know what that entails, and I certainly don't condone violence or law-breaking of any kind … but there's some catharsis to be achieved by tackling things head on. And I think you could use a little of that right now."

Pete thanked her and hung up. He pulled the car out of park and headed west, the Oscar Peterson Trio's "I Got It Bad" weaving through the speakers, Peterson's dangling piano lines telling a somber tale of loss and regret.

"Where are you?" the text from Kathy beeped.

Pete tapped out a quick reply: "Be back soon."

Allie Kaplan's words, her peaceful intent aside, hung over Pete like a mission statement, a religious calling. He had to face the problem head on. She was right. And the time for dancing between the raindrops was through.

*Who killed my mother?*

Pete scanned the crowd, which was lurching closer to the makeshift center ring. The barn, at the far end of a large, acres-wide field littered with abandoned farming equipment and a wide sprawl of parked cars—ranging from large, luxury SUVs to rusted, decades-old Buicks—reeked of shit and poultry, like a moldy petting zoo. The air felt heavy and toxic, fat with chemicals and dirt.

Getting in had been easy enough. Pete, dressed in a faded Jenny Lewis shirt and a black, retro Florida Marlins cap and jeans, stuck out from the mid-sixties, guayabera-wearing male majority, though there did seem to be a few FIU or UM frat boys wearing tight black workout gear and sporting Chinese symbol tattoos.

Pete had heard of the cockfights, of course. It was a staple of the Miami underworld. Illegal animal death matches that happened on the edge of the Redlands, closer to the Everglades than to downtown Miami. It was the next-level haven for two-bit *bolita* players okay with watching two animals snipe and claw at each other, until death do they part.

Few people aside from Mujica could risk running such a regular gambling operation. Few people had the funds to grease the locals and the police—convincing neighbors not to call the cops, convincing the cops not to bother coming down if and when someone did call.

For all his play-acting, Mujica was far from a mild-mannered local fruit farmer. He was a criminal, and quite busy for one claiming to be retired. Alvaro Mujica had built his fortune running an illegal gambling—or *bolita*—operation, first in New Jersey, then Miami. He'd maintained control through violence and a no-tolerance policy when it came to potential competitors.

And now, if Pete's guess was right, he was trying to expand—trying to move into the more lucrative drug trade that was in a tailspin after the implosion of Los Enfermos. But those kind of moves required manpower, guns, and—most importantly—a connection to product. Mujica had two out of three, but the piece he was missing was the most important.

"*¿Con quién vas?*"

Pete turned. The older, larger man seemed to be looking in Pete's general direction, his movements slow and dazed. Pete saw the half-empty Corona in his hand and the weeks of stubble on the tanned man's face. It took Pete a minute to realize he was asking him who he was betting on.

"*No sé, todavia,*" Pete said. *Not sure yet.*

"*Bueno, apurate, niño, esta empezando,*" the man said, roughly moving past Pete to get closer to the ring. The fight was about to begin.

But Pete wasn't here to watch two roosters murder each other. He looked over the crowd. The lighting was dim, and Pete could only see figures and shapes moving in unison, screaming as a bell rang and the two birds clattered toward each other, hesitant at first, the pecks and flaps becoming more frequent and violent as time passed.

That's when Pete saw him, standing off toward the rear of the bar, two men at each side as he sat in what looked like an ornate tailgating chair. Even here, in the most casual of environs, Alvaro Mujica was all business—dressed in a tailored navy-blue suit, his thinning hair slicked back. The *bolitero's* rough, grotesque features were exacerbated by the contrast of the flickering lights and the infinite blackness of the Miami night.

Mujica wasn't watching the match, though. No, he was basking in the glow of something bigger. Of the event itself. The fact that he, a king of men, could do as he pleased. Surrounded by guards, watching as friends, strangers, and who knows who threw money in a pot to see this contest of pure animal violence unfurl like some kind of blood-soaked theater. He wasn't here to see who won or lost. He'd already won.

Pete darted through the crowd, trying his best to seem casual— just another guy trying to get a better look at the fight, which was growing in intensity, the roars from the crowd spewing out with more frequency. Bodies jostling and shaking fistfuls of cash in the air, yelling "*Dále!*" or "*Métele, cabrón!*" or any variation that implored the birds to destroy each other.

By the time he was a few feet from Mujica, the man and his bodyguards noticed him, and no amount of playing it cool could get him closer.

The first guard to reach him was bulky and tall, the only hair on his face a thick and triangular soul patch under his bottom lip. Pete recognized him as one of the men guarding Mujica when they'd come to his house. He wore dark shades despite the poorly lit room, and his tone was direct and immediately unfriendly.

"Get back."

"I have to talk to Mr. Mujica," Pete said, but before he could continue, another guard appeared, not as bulky, with a fuller head of light brown hair and a somewhat shaggy beard, no friendlier than his colleague.

"Don Mujica is not taking visitors now," Bodyguard #2 said, grabbing Pete's right arm. "Move along."

If the guy hadn't grabbed his arm, Pete might have stepped back and decided on another tactic to get to Mujica. But the combination of the unwanted touch, his exhaustion, the mix of emotions—fear, anger, confusion—that had been setting up shop in his brain finally created a spark. He felt his training kick in, and before he could think, he'd grabbed the man's wrist—the hand he'd placed on Pete's arm—and pulled him back, executing a near-perfect *irimi nage* throw.

Pete turned to face Bodyguard #1, who was charging at him, gun drawn. Pete gave the thug's gun hand a quick chop, then shot his palm into the man's face, sending him down onto the dirt. *Kote gueshi*, he thought. Both men got to their feet slowly and began to fall back—not beaten, but surprised and annoyed, at least. The crowd didn't react—still focused on the waning fight, one rooster hobbled and bloody, the other circling with a manic bloodlust in its dark bird eyes.

"Don't try again," Pete said, surprised at the calm and clarity of his own voice. He'd been in skirmishes since his training, found himself in challenging situations that required him to call upon not only the physical aspects of aikido, but the spiritual—but never like this. He'd channeled his anger and frustration into something useful, instead of flailing into a rumble with no sense of how to manage it.

Out of the corner of his vision, Pete saw Mujica's other two guards hanging back, unsure whether they should take on this attacker or protect their boss. They were doing the smart thing. No doubt they were armed. If things got out of hand, they could just shoot Pete.

Pete fought the urge to dust off his hands as he walked toward Mujica and his two remaining guards. By now, even the crowd of onlookers had noticed the scrum, and a few had shifted their attention from the cockfight to another, similar duel.

"Stay where you are," Bodyguard #3 said. He was a thin, lanky dude with a well-kept beard and close-cropped hair. "We don't want this to escalate."

"Tell your boss I want to talk," Pete said, his voice husky and spent.

Bodyguard #3 turned to Mujica and whispered into his ear. The old gangster looked over at Pete and nodded. He motioned with his hand for Pete to step closer. Bodyguard #4 nodded and patted Pete down briskly, his hands gliding over him, finding nothing. He stepped back and nodded for Pete to enter their makeshift sanctum.

"*Señor Fernandez, un placer,*" Mujica said, his voice gravelly and low, like a Cuban impression of Marlon Brando's Don Corleone. "*¿Qué me cuentas?* What causes this violence on a night of celebration? Is the cockfight not enough action for you?"

"I'm not here to watch birds," Pete said. "We need to talk. Somewhere else."

Mujica nodded. He shrugged and stood with a speed of a man twenty years his junior.

"Then let's talk," he said. He snapped his fingers at #3. "Chino, tell Cunningham to get the car and pick us up. It's time to go home."

**P**ete followed Mujica's black Lexus NX SUV to the house he'd visited months before. So much had changed since then. The details about his mother. Kathy. Harras. Emily. But this time Pete was in control. He knew what he was doing. And he knew what he wanted to find out.

"*Déjame con él, no te preocupes,*" Mujica said as his bodyguards—minus the injured #1 and #2—watched them take seats in the same dining room they'd shared before. They did so with no hesitation, uninterested in whatever their boss and this other man were going to discuss. Once they were gone and the dining room door had closed with an almost silent *click*, Mujica folded his hands and looked Pete over, a grimace forming on his weathered, pockmarked face.

"I am granting you a great courtesy, Pete Fernandez," Mujica said, the words bubbling to the surface slowly, thoughtfully. "You interrupted a rare moment of relaxation for me. You failed me before. I do not know where this de Armas woman is. My painting is not hanging on my wall. My son's killer remains on the loose. Yet, here you are. Calling upon me like some petty servant. This one time, I will humor you. Tell me what you want. Then you can leave."

"Graciela Fernandez."

Mujica's expression didn't change. He looked at Pete, waiting for more. When he realized the detective was waiting for him, Mujica pursed his lips.

"Do I know this woman?" he asked. "Is she a relative?"

"My mother," Pete said. "She died when I was very young."

Mujica nodded.

"I am sorry for that," he said. "But, again, I don't know what the name should mean to me."

"Did you own a bar—a jazz venue? Terraza?" Pete asked. "She worked there for a short time."

Mujica paused, scanning the wall behind Pete.

"It's possible," Mujica said. "I've owned and sold many properties. The name is familiar, but that was a long time ago. A lifetime ago."

"She was dating the owner, or someone pretending to be the owner," Pete said, leaning forward, trying to get Mujica's full attention. "Still doesn't ring a bell?"

Mujica's mouth morphed into a dark, menacing grin.

"¿Quién me crees, Pete Fernandez? You think I'm some new puppy?" Mujica asked. "I survived Castro's interrogators. I'm sorry your mother is dead. But I didn't know her. You can leave."

Pete stood up. He heard the door open. It would be #3 and #4, eager to escort him out. Despite Mujica's dismissiveness, Pete found himself believing the older man—which only raised even more questions. Questions he would not be able to ask now.

He started to turn when Mujica spoke again.

"I am not without resources," Mujica said. "Help me, and I can help you."

"What?"

"You heard me, hijo," Mujica said, a sly smile on his face. "You're a good detective. Do what I hired you to do, and I can return the favor."

"The painting was bullshit, wasn't it?" Pete asked.

"¿Qué importa?" Mujica said. Does it matter? "I need to find that woman. When I do, I will find out what happened to my son, plus much more. Now I have nothing but questions."

"You want in on the drug trade," Pete said. "That's why you wanted me to find Beatriz. To connect to La Madrina."

For a moment, Pete thought he saw a flicker of rage flash across the gangster's rugged features. He couldn't be sure.

"I did not say that," Mujica said. The aging criminal turned his attention to the door. "Chino, Noe—*entren.*"

Two of his men entered the room and hovered by the door.

"So, what are you telling me?" Pete asked.

"Do the job I hired you to do," Mujica said, standing up. He moved his hand toward Pete in a dismissive gesture—a sign to his bodyguards that it was time for them to escort Pete out. "Then I might be inclined to think back to those days. Maybe then I'll remember why your mother didn't live to see your third birthday."

Carmen Valdez-Mitchell walked out of the main entrance at Flagami Elementary School, in the southwest part of the city. She was a teacher. Pete knew this because he'd done a basic background check before deciding to intercept Osvaldo Valdez's only daughter.

The decision to seek her out had come to Pete as he drove home from Alvaro Mujica's estate, the gangster's offer hanging over him. Mujica was dangerous. Pete knew that. He'd made a mistake working for him before. He also knew that, even if he were successful—even if he thought it would be a good idea to turn Emily over to Mujica—the information he got back in exchange might—at best—only resemble the truth. Information through a filter was no good to Pete, and it was clear Mujica knew more than he let on. No, it was time to dig into his mother's case his own way—and that started with Osvaldo Valdez. In his absence, that meant tracking down his next of kin.

He would have probably figured out Carmen was Osvaldo's daughter just by looking at her. The green paint smeared on her red blouse. The slightly unkempt hair. The look of satisfied exhaustion. Pete knew it well. Had seen it in his father's eyes, on the few nights he'd been awake when his father got home, bone-tired, blood and dirt on his shoes and pants. But on those nights where they got the guy, or closed the case—his father's expression was hard to ignore. Not glowing—there was nothing to celebrate when someone was killed. But a look of acceptance. That, for one moment, the odds had been evened and maybe there was a little bit of justice in the world.

"That her?" Kathy asked.

"Yeah," Pete said as he moved toward the woman, Kathy a few steps behind him.

"Carmen Valdez?" Pete asked.

She turned, surprise on her face, her usual routine disrupted by two strangers. She was in her early thirties: tan skin and straight, dark hair; her brown eyes large and probing.

"Yes?"

"My name's Pete Fernandez. I'm a private investigator," Pete said. He could see her start to distance herself, the half-step back, the dulling of the eyes, but he pressed on. "I knew your father. Osvaldo?"

"Oh?" she said, intrigued for a millisecond, before looking around. "Do we have to talk here? In front of my job?"

"There's a really great Cuban steakhouse nearby," Kathy said.

They both turned to her.

"What?" Kathy said. "I'm pregnant. And hungry."


Palomilla Grill was a tidy, well-kept, no-frills Cuban spot five minutes from Flagami. The food tasted fresh, the vibe was comfortable and casual—not to mention affordable.

"How did you find me?" Carmen asked, unfolding her paper napkin and placing it on her lap. They'd ordered appetizers—no one wanting to commit to a full meal—but Pete took the ceremonial move as a good sign, regardless.

"Despite trying to ignore his calling, Pete is actually a decent detective," Kathy said, taking a long sip from her sparkling water. "And you weren't exactly hiding."

"I don't have anything to hide."

"That's good," Pete said. "I thought you might be able to help us. I talked to your father—a few, well, hours before he ... died."

"Before he was murdered, you mean," Carmen said, her words coming out at a piston-like speed.

"Yes, and I'm sorry for your loss," Pete said.

"Thanks, but you can spare me the condolences," she said. "I loved my father. I know he loved me. But he was a flawed man. Very old-school. We had lots of disagreements. He had issues with how I lived my life. But over the last few months ... of his life ... things had calmed down. He seemed to mellow out in his old age, I guess."

"My father was a detective, too," Pete said. "Pedro Fernandez."

"I know," Carmen said, smiling thinly. "I figured out who you guys are on the way here. It took me a second. I chase six-year-olds around all day, then go home and chase my own toddler. But the names sounded familiar."

"That's us," Kathy said. "Familiar and also mysterious."

Carmen nodded, unsure if it was meant as a joke or insult—probably both.

"I was approached by your dad a while back," Pete said, leaning forward. "He said he had some information on my mother. How she died."

"How did she die?" Carmen asked.

"Up until now, I thought she died during childbirth—I never got a clear answer, but when you're a kid, you just accept those things," Pete said. "I never knew her. Just images and textures. A faded memory."

"That's terrible," Carmen said. "I'm sorry."

"It's okay," Pete said. "You can't miss what you never knew, I guess?"

"But still," Carmen said. "She was your mom. I'm sure she loved you. It's tragic she never got to know you well, or the other way around. My parents drove me nuts—but I got to yell at them. I got to be there for my dad when my mom died. We were a unit."

Pete felt Kathy's hand slide up his back softly, then noticed he was clutching the flimsy restaurant table. He let go and leaned back.

"Yeah, yes, thank you," Pete said. "I would have liked to have known her. But that's part of why I'm—we're here. I never got to talk to your father. And I'm worried that—"

"Whoever killed him did it because of the info he had?" Carmen said.

"Yes," Pete said.

"What did the cops tell you when your father died?" Kathy asked.

Before Carmen could respond, their food arrived—*tostones*, *platanos maduros*, *yuca frita*, and a pile of *croquetas de jamón*. The smell of the food wafted over them, providing a momentary respite.

"Tell me?" Carmen said as she finished a bite of yucca. "Nothing. They have no leads. They have no idea why anyone would want to gun down a retired ex-cop. It's not like he'd just retired, or he had enemies waiting in the wings. My dad was a Homicide detective. His cases dealt with the dead. He was a good detective, too. Worked those cases to the bone. So, yeah, the cops don't have any leads. At least not any they share with me."

"My mother was found dead in an Overtown hotel room on New Year's 1984," Pete said, looking down at his hands. "Your dad was the first Homicide detective. He worked the case. According to the file I got from the Miami Cold Case Squad, he never closed her murder. She'd been strangled and beaten badly."

"I'm sorry," Carmen said, her voice low.

"What I don't get, though, is why he would reach out to me—years later?" Pete asked rhetorically. "He knew, while I was in the dark, about my mom. He kept that under wraps."

"Did you ever think he was asked to keep silent?" Carmen said. "That he didn't want to hide it from you?"

Pete hesitated. The thought was not foreign to him. Osvaldo Valdez was not the only Miami police detective sitting on the truth about Graciela Fernandez. The biggest obfuscator of information was Pete's own father, Pedro—who surely knew what went down, and decided it was best for Pete not to learn the truth. The fact haunted Pete. His father had lied.

"I have my theories on that," Pete said, pushing past the idea. "Did your father ever mention the case? To you? To your mother?"

"No, Papi kept work to himself," she said. "He wanted his time at home to be peaceful, about family—not bloody or gruesome. He was a conflicted man, but a good man. I appreciated that."

"What about his papers? His belongings?" Kathy asked. "Did you get to go through them?"

Carmen nodded.

"Yes, as much as I could," she said. "I'm his only child, and my mom is gone, so it all rested on me. We put the house on the market, but I've got all his papers. I haven't read them all, but I do have them."

"I know we just met," Pete said. "But what are the chances you'd let us go through those papers?"

"Sure, fine," Carmen said. "As long as lunch is on you. What's the worst that could happen?"

"We don't use that phrase anymore," Kathy said with a smile, dropping two twenties on the table. "Let's go."

Carmen Valdez-Mitchell lived with her wife in a medium-sized house in the Hammocks neighborhood of Miami—which was on the far west side, past Kendall and closer to the wide swamp that was the Everglades, and all the reptilian and insect life that came with it.

The house was well-kept but cluttered. A sign of the busy, frantic life the two led. Carmen turned slightly as the three of them walked down the long hall that linked the left side of the house—kitchen, living room, office.

"Sorry for the mess," she said. "I didn't know we'd have people over. Melissa's at work. I usually scramble to tidy up or cook something in the few hours I have before she comes home with Atticus."

Atticus was their three-year-old son, she'd explained on the way back as they rode in her slightly run-down 2013 Taurus.

As they reached the end of the hall, Carmen opened a door, which led into what she called "Melissa's supposed office"—a room stacked with books, papers, pictures, and boxes—which made it far from a functional workroom.

"I have the same kind of space in our—well, my—old apartment," Kathy said, moving toward the door. "Office-slash-storage-slash-storage."

"Yeah, sorry," Carmen said. "This is where we put all my dad's stuff. See those gray filing cabinets in the back? That was all his. I've gotten maybe one or two drawers in."

"Can we stick around until we're done?" Pete asked.

Carmen nodded as she stepped back, allowing Kathy and Pete to move into the small office.

"Yeah, that's fine," she said. "Though, Atticus goes down around eight. If you're still here then—"

"We'll get out of your hair before then," Kathy said with a smile.

Pete closed the door as Carmen's footsteps echoed down the long hall. "You wanna take one cabinet and I'll take the other?" he asked.

"You're the boss."

"What's that supposed to mean?"

"Nothing, believe it or not," Kathy said, moving toward the right cabinet and opening the top drawer. "Did you notice how disorganized this place is?"

"Well, they have a toddler."

"Wasn't a criticism," Kathy said. "Just a detail. It's those little things that hit me as I get further along. How big a change it's going to be."

"We'll be fine," Pete said, his back to Kathy. "We can handle this."

"We will?" Kathy said, turning around. "Let me rattle off some fast facts for you, my dear: I have been kicked out of my apartment.

I am pregnant. You are the father. We are not together. These things are all related and yet we're still going from task to task, working on this case like nothing else matters. And hey, I'm guilty, too—it's nice to be distracted, but—"

Pete stepped toward her, placing his arms gently on her shoulders. She looked up at him.

"We'll figure this out, all right?" Pete said. "I'm not trying to ignore it. I'm not trying to avoid it. I've done that for too long. Tomorrow, I'll go get your stuff from Marco's—"

"I appreciate the sentiment, really, because it's very adult of you, but ..." Kathy said, "I don't want to just hop from Marco to you, all right? I—and, how do I say this?—I also have some concerns about your general 'safety,' you know? People like to shoot at you, Pete."

"Hear me out," Pete said. "I'm not offering my place up as some kind of relationship barter, okay? I just want to make sure you're healthy and rested and this baby gets everything it needs. As for us ... well, we'll figure that out as we go, I guess? Or not. I'm not sure. But I don't want you worrying about where you're going to sleep or basic stuff like that. I'll be there for you and the kid, no matter what. You will be safe."

Kathy nodded slowly, then stepped toward Pete. She pulled him into a stiff hug. "That's good," she whispered into his ear. "That's a good start."

The research moved quickly, with Kathy and Pete taking one of the file cabinets each—sifting through the drawers methodically as the afternoon faded into early evening. The documents they found painted an incomplete picture—of a meticulous cop who diligently recorded every bit of information on every case he worked, but did little to record his life outside of the precinct.

The files were divided into three categories, from what Pete and Kathy could tell: clippings from newspapers that might prove interesting in relation to an existing case, notes or jotted thoughts that might tie into a case Valdez was working on and, finally, handwritten notebooks that paired with specific police reports. Some cases—the more complicated ones that spanned years and remained unsolved—took up stacks of notebooks. The notebooks reminded Pete of the ones that filled his backpacks in middle school, Mead binders with wide lines and perforated edges.

Valdez's career had mirrored Pedro Fernandez's in strange ways, Pete noticed. The cop had graduated to detective a few years before Graciela Fernandez's body was found, and was assigned a number of cold cases, some partnered with Carlos Broche, Pete's dad's old partner and a man Pete had considered like a second father, at least until he'd uncovered the truth about him and his ties to the Silent Death over five years ago, during Pete's first, hesitant case as an investigator. Valdez also seemed, unlike most of the Miami PD at the time, to be untarnished—a straight shooter who worked by the book and tried to keep his head down.

"Anything yet?" Pete asked, not looking up from the piles of notebooks spread around his feet on the floor. "I'm getting lost in these cases, but none seem to connect to my mom."

"Nothing, no," Kathy said, rummaging through the bottom drawer of the last cabinet. Their final shot. "It seems like he was looking into Los Enfermos back then, though, along with your dad and Broche, to a degree. Had some interesting theories."

"Like what?"

"Like, here," she said, shuffling through some pages in a blue notebook. "He connects some of the early Silent Death's murders—all drug killings, mind you, in the early 2000s—to Los Enfermos, which at the time were growing in power, thanks to their secret benefactor-slash-boss, Orlando Posada."

Orlando Posada had been a cop partnered with Gaspar Varela, another Miami officer, who spent years in prison for a murder he hadn't committed. Varela had been framed by Posada in order to push out one of the department's few good cops and minimize the chances of Posada's own conspiracy being uncovered. Pete had managed to exonerate Varela a few years back, but at a steep price—the discovery that Varela's own daughter, Maya, had been involved in the death of his wife. Posada never stood trial, gunned down by Pete in a standoff that almost cost Kathy her life and ended any chance of her unborn child surviving at the time.

"The Silent Death killed for the highest bidder," Pete said, turning to face Kathy. "Javier wasn't affiliated with a particular gang."

The Silent Death case had brought Pete and Kathy together, and opened the door to a career as a private detective that Pete still found himself evading. Maybe it was time to accept what he'd become. What they'd become.

"Maybe, maybe not," Kathy said. "I mean, wasn't that guy Novo pretending to be the Silent Death when he attacked you and Emily?"

"Or maybe he was the Silent Death," Pete said. "The new one."

"Right, but like any good freelancer, I imagine Javier had preferred accounts—people he got steady work from," Kathy said, standing up and stretching. "By the time he put on that freak suit, Los Enfermos were in full swing."

"So, you think Valdez was trying to connect those dots?"

"It looks like it," Kathy said. "But I'm not sure what that means, if true."

"It means it's all tangled up, everything from the beginning," Pete said. "The entire journey here has been tied up by this gang of killers. Every step of the way."

"That's a bit melodramatic."

"But, think about it—the Silent Death was my first case. Los Enfermos were there. Posada framed Varela to hide Los Enfermos from notice. Los Enfermos killed my grandfather. La Iglesia de la Luz hires Los Enfermos to take us out when we get too close to finding out the truth ... and now this? How are they involved now? Are they even alive?"

"You're asking the wrong person, dear," Kathy said. "I don't keep track of who's running what drug gang. I'd rather gouge my eyes out, or look at an electoral map."

"But don't you see?" Pete said, as if seized by some sudden jolt of energy. Kathy inched back. "Los Enfermos have been involved since the beginning. With everything."

"I think we need a bit more proof that a multinational gang of drug dealers has been out to get you since day one," Kathy said. "And, sure, maybe Valdez was onto something—that Los Enfermos have been part of the fabric of this town for decades ... but what does that mean? Didn't we know that?"

"Not to this extent," Pete said, standing up and pacing around the small room. "We thought—each time—that we'd cut off the head of the beast. First Posada. Then Lionel Oliva and La Iglesia de la Luz. But what if that was wrong? What if someone else has been in charge all this time?"

"And ... what? We've just been knocking off his lieutenants and annoying him?" Kathy said. "Or her, to be fair."

"Exactly."

"Well, I would file that under 'very bad,'" Kathy said. "It would also explain a lot. Specifically, as I noted, your continued bad luck when it comes to getting shot at. The whole dying for a while sucked, too."

Pete didn't respond to Kathy's joke, instead turning his attention to the last drawer. He pulled out what looked like a stack of three notebooks, two looking much like the dozens they'd flipped through before. The third, though, looked like something else. Something special.

Pete scanned the first two notebooks before placing them off to the side with the others.

"More case notes from Valdez, dated right before my mom died," Pete said. "Was murdered."

"What's that one?"

"Not sure," Pete said, cracking it open. "It's bound ... looks like some kind of ..."

Pete took in a quick, sharp breath.

"What?" Kathy asked, moving closer. "What is it?"

She moved behind Pete, looking over his shoulder as he flipped through the pages.

It was one of those expensive notebooks with a fancy leather cover that pretentious writer types used to jot down the first drafts of their great American novels. But instead of overwrought similes and watered-down Fitzgerald imitations, these pages were covered in what Kathy could best describe as art—collages, drawings, pastels, paints. Magazine picture cutouts, headlines, and lists and snippets of text in a flowery cursive hand. The drawings were vivid, sharply drawn and filled in with colored pencil, markers, and what had to be crayon, faded with age. The headlines were carefully cut from newspapers and magazines, the former yellowed and faded, the latter wrinkled and bent with age.

Pete's hand lingered on a spread near the middle of the book—a drawing of two people, one of them Pete's father and the other, from what Pete could recall from photos, was supposed to be Graciela. Between them was a toddler. They were seated at a table, with a birthday cake in front of them. The boy had a small balloon in hand, a confused but happy look in his face, dark hair threatening to cover his eyes. The caption, hastily written under the detailed sketch, took Kathy's breath away.

"*Memories from Pete's 2nd birthday—1983.*"

The dream book veered from art project to cathartic diary with alarming speed. On one page, Graciela was listing the various places she and Diane would visit the following night; on the next, she'd spend a half-dozen pages sketching Pete and his father from memory, clearly pining for the normalcy and strength that had come with her home. But even these drawings—meant to evoke a security Graciela no longer had—were peppered with jarring images and jargon.

*You're drinking too much.*

*Don't let Pete see you.*

*Sleep it off.*

*Are you drunk?*

*Where were you last night?*

Pete stopped turning the pages when he reached a hyper-detailed self-portrait that was slashed twice in red marker, the words I CAN'T STOP scrawled in jagged script parallel to one of the lines. He closed the book and stood up. He'd seen enough.

"Are you okay?"

He ignored Kathy. He couldn't deal with the inside of the book yet. He had to look at this as a detective first, a son second, if he had any chance of processing it all.

"It's a dream book," she said.

"A what?" Pete asked. His voice was off, shaken. His eyes were red, his posture wobbly. The dizziness he felt was new to him, unnatural, like he was losing control of himself with no hope of coming back.

"Like, an art project," Kathy said, taking the book from Pete gently and looking through it, spending a few seconds on each page. "You paste things that represent your dreams—snippets of words, images, things that reflect your state of mind. It's something you use to stay creative, or to stay engaged with yourself, I guess. I used to do it a lot in college. I mean, it's more than just that, but that's the crux of what she was doing here, I think."

"But ... why does Osvaldo have this? Why did he have this?" Pete said, staring at the opposite wall, as if it'd open up and answer him. "And where is his notebook on the case?"

"What do you mean?"

"We've been sitting here for hours, flipping through pages and pages of the man's work," Pete said. "He was diligent. Meticulous. He kept journals on every single case he worked. Why didn't he have one for my mom? And why did he have this?"

Kathy nodded. She didn't have an answer.

"Let me see that again," Pete said.

She handed him the book. He started flipping through the pages, not reading, but scanning quickly—almost desperately.

"There ... there are pages missing," Pete said, showing the perforations from the notebook to Kathy. "Someone ripped out the last chunk of this."

"You really are a detective."

"Don't you see, though?" Pete said, holding the book open, staring at the spot where the pages were torn out. "These pages could be the answer."

"Where are they, then?" Kathy asked. "I mean, maybe your mom tore them off herself?"

"Possible, but this book seems so carefully crafted and meticulous," Pete said, running a finger over the book's cover. "It just feels out of place for her to do that." He pulled out his cell phone and started to dial.

"What are you doing?" Kathy asked.

Pete ignored her. A few moments passed and he spoke. "Hey, it's Pete, I'm putting you on speaker." He pushed a button on his phone and placed it on a stack of manila envelopes between himself and Kathy. "Kathy's here."

"What's happening?" Nisha Hudson said, her voice distorted and distant-sounding. "You called me."

"Any leads on where our friend Beatriz de Armas is?" Pete asked.

"Nothing concrete, but it's obvious she fled the country," Hudson said. "Aside from that, I can't really comment. Ongoing investigation and all that."

"Got it, thanks," Pete said. "Keep me posted if you can."

Hudson hung up.

"What are you getting at?" Kathy asked.

"Emily left a business card at the scene of Osvaldo's murder," Pete said. "She was there."

"Or someone wanted you to think she was there," Kathy said.

"True," Pete said. "But that means whoever was there, whoever did leave that clue—could have a clue *we* need ... those pages."

"I give you three stars," Kathy said. "Good hunch, questionable follow-through."

Pete didn't respond.

She could tell her joke hadn't landed right. She pulled him into a quick hug. "We will figure this out, okay?" Kathy said. "You're doing it the right way—step by step. Now we know where to look next. Did you see anything else in that book?"

Pete flipped to the back of the book, but found nothing else—just a few blank pages. He started to respond, but was interrupted by a slight knock on the door.

Pete checked his watch. They'd been there almost four hours. It was close to ten in the evening. Kathy opened the door.

"You guys about done?" Carmen asked expectantly. It was clear she wanted these two strangers out of her house. Pete understood. Her eyes danced around the room. It was mostly intact—anything taken out of the cabinets in neat piles around the space.

"Yeah, yeah," Pete said. "Thanks so much for letting us take over the space. Do, uh, do you mind if I borrow this?" He held up the dream book. He felt sweat on his palm, his fingers hot on the book's leather binding.

"Sure, that's fine," Carmen said. "I dunno what I'd use it for. I guess, um, just give it back? Eventually?"

Pete nodded and followed Kathy out of the cramped space and down the home's main hallway, Carmen behind them. She held the door as they filed out.

"Thanks so much," Kathy said, shaking Carmen's hand.

The woman nodded, her expression kind and genuine. "It's fine, seriously, don't sweat it," she said. "I hope you found what you were looking for."

"Yes and no," Pete said. "But it helped. A lot."

They exchanged a few more pleasantries and then said their goodbyes.

Kathy led Pete to where she'd parked her car. "What now?" she asked as they walked down the front porch steps.

He looked shaken, on edge, and confused. "We find Beatriz de Armas," Pete said. "We find Emily. Then we get answers."

# THE GOOD THAT WON'T COME OUT

*October 5, 1983*

**G**raciela felt that nervous, sinking feeling again. Something wasn't right.

The problem was not with her, though she wasn't exactly succeeding at life these days. No. With her job.

She'd ignored the signs at first. The late-night deliveries. The guys in dark suits coming by every few days to talk to him. Her boyfriend, she thought at first, but even that was complicated and not right.

But something else wasn't right. This wasn't standard operating procedure at a restaurant. She'd been a waitress before.

She'd tried to ignore it tonight. Focus on wiping down the bar and counting the cash. But it was happening again. He went to the door first, a skip in his step. He wanted to be there before anyone else. He opened the door and blocked her line of sight. Graciela could only make out a figure in a dark suit.

*Delivery man, my ass*, she thought.

They two men spoke in hushed whispers for a minute, maybe less. Graciela watched as the man on the other side of the door backed away. Her boyfriend—or whatever he was—lingered for a moment.

He closed the door slowly and turned around. He seemed to just notice she was there, a slight surprise in his expression.

"Hey," he said, trying to keep it casual, Graciela thought.

His smile almost wiped away her concerns. That look in his eyes—lusty and familiar. She knew the only reason she still had the job was because of him. She'd been written up a few times. For coming in late. Coming in drunk. Slacking off. Taking long breaks. But no one was going to fire her. She was the boss's ... something. He wouldn't fire her, either. She knew that. The sex was too good. Great, even. He loved her, Graciela thought. She figured she was only partially deluding herself.

"What's going on in that head of yours?" he said, sitting at the bar, folding his hands like an expectant customer.

*What's in my head?* Graciela thought. Where to begin. Was it the surprised gasp she heard on the other end of the line, when she told Pedro where she was working? Like a scared child, except it came from her husband, a Miami Homicide detective who saw dead bodies with regularity? Was it the look on her young son's face as he heard his father tell her she couldn't see him anymore? Because she "looked bad"? Because she never seemed to show up, and when she did, she was either high or drunk?

The worst part? Pedro was right. Graciela was fading fast. And it wasn't pretty.

She couldn't stop. She didn't know how to stop. If she wasn't high, if she wasn't feeling something else, anything else to numb the world she'd created for herself, then she could barely function. Getting high was the first thing Graciela thought of in the morning—*How am I gonna cop today? How can I get a buzz at work without anyone noticing?*—and the thoughts haunted her throughout the day. It was all-encompassing.

"You're not fun, G," Diane had told her a few nights back. "All you do is get drunk and cry now. It's the worst."

She was right, too. Graciela was spinning out. Days without doing anything. Staying inside the dark, cold apartment. Drinking. Not eating. Sleeping—passed out, really. She was a vampire. If not for her job ... well, her benefactor, really—she'd be broke. If not for Diane, she'd be homeless.

In those rare moments when Graciela could think clearly—those brief flickers of sobriety—when she'd had a full meal, maybe taken a hot shower, and didn't feel like a complete piece of shit, she could envision what she really wanted. What was truly important to her. Her family. Her baby. Her husband. Her house, to lie in her bed, to feel alive. Not like some walking corpse. Not throwing up blood at four in the morning, smelling of cigarettes and cheap liquor. Not in her "boyfriend's" bed in some nondescript hotel, because he refused to take her to his place. Not hung over on the bus because she missed Diane leaving for work. Not making out with a stranger in an alley because he bought her a drink or let her take a toke or shared his coke.

That's what was bouncing around her cloudy, fucked-up head, mixed in with the static and numbing buzz that was now her permanent setting. A hangover that never seemed to go away. That was her life now.

"Oh, nothing," she said, trying to smile. "Just trying to finish up here."

He nodded and she thought about the call she'd gotten that day. Pedro's friend again. The cop from Vice. He wanted to meet.

# CHAPTER TWENTY-THREE

Graciela Fernandez's dream book might hold the answer to her own murder.

One of the last people to have access to the book was Emily. But Emily was long gone. Or was she?

These bits of information swarmed around Pete as he entered The Book Bin, Kathy a few paces behind. Isabel was at the front desk, discussing the pros and cons of a recent fantasy series with one of their regulars. She waved as they headed toward Pete's back office.

"I see this place remains trapped in amber," Kathy said, sliding a finger on a dusty shelf.

"Used bookstores have their charms," Pete said, stepping into the office and closing the door behind Kathy.

He sat behind his desk and opened up his laptop. As it turned on, he swiveled his chair and began rummaging through his desk's main drawer.

"Are you going to tell me why we're here?"

Pete pulled out what looked like a tiny scrap of yellow paper. "Got it," he said to himself.

He placed the paper flat on the desk. The yellow slip was shaded in pencil, revealing some writing Kathy couldn't make out. Pete slid the Post-It note to Kathy.

She grabbed it and glanced at the difficult-to-make-out words. "What is this?" Kathy said, straining to make out the words. "Emily, her other persona and a name I've never heard?"

"Daniela Burgos," Pete said.

"Right. Not ringing a bell."

"It didn't for me, either," Pete said. "But I found the pad when I searched Emily's place—back when I first ran into her. The name came up, but there wasn't much there—an address, DOB. I filed it away. With everything going on, I didn't think to go back to it until now."

"If this is one of Emily's pseudonyms, we should check out that address ASAP," Kathy said. "But I'm not sure what the rest of the list means. Bogota and Havana are crossed out—and 'US? Not viable' is kind of ominous."

"Let's find out," Pete said, getting up. "I shot Harras a text. Maybe he can get one of his friends to do a check on this Burgos person's whereabouts."

Pete closed his computer and walked out of his office. Before he and Kathy reached The Book Bin's front door, Isabel waved them down.

She had one hand on the store phone. "Wait, wait, he's here, actually," Isabel said. She turned to Pete. "It's a friend of yours. Robert? I didn't know if you were taking calls."

Pete nodded thanks and grabbed the phone. "Yeah?"

"Got your text," Harras said. "That address you sent me? There's nothing there. Vacant lot."

Pete let out a disappointed sigh. "Then we're at a dead end," he said, shoulders sagging. "Shit."

"Not really," Harras said. "At least, not yet."

"Oh?"

"Yeah, looks like someone by the name of Daniela Burgos left the country a day after we lost Emily, after her run-in with the Silent Death," Harras said. "Can't be coincidental. You think this is Emily?"

"It's gotta be," Pete said. "Why else would she run?"

"I am only hearing one side of this conversation," Kathy said, jabbing Pete's shoulder.

Isabel looked on with concern.

Pete tapped a button on the phone base and Harras's voice filtered through the machine's speaker system.

"So where'd she go?" Pete asked. "Where'd Emily run off to?"

"Cuba," Harras said. They could hear car sounds and traffic in the background. "Someone named Daniela Burgos flew to Havana, and as far as I can tell, she's still there."

The decision had been made quickly. At least by Pete. He was off to Cuba.

The threads felt tenuous to Pete, but worth the risk. Emily had been in Osvaldo Valdez's house when or soon after he died. Pages from Pete's mother's dream diary were gone—pages that could hint at who killed her. Emily was on the run.

Kathy pushed back. As did Dave. It was too risky, they'd said. They were right. Pete had never visited the island that was home to his parents and grandparents. Never considered it beyond a fleeting thought. Despite the general thaw in relations between the United States and Cuba, the island was still a dictatorship under the thumb of a man named Castro. Just because it wasn't Fidel didn't change that truth.

As curious as Pete was to see the island, this trip would be brief. An opportunity to really explore Cuba—and his family's connections to it—would probably have to wait.

Everything had been painless heading to José Martí International Airport. Everything is usually fine until it isn't. Pete had reached Miami International Airport thinking he was on his own, only to find Robert Harras waiting at his gate. Pete tried to dissuade him at first, but after a while came around to the idea of having a partner on this mission.

"Wasn't gonna let you leave the country and not come back," Harras said as they settled into the gate.

"How kind of you," Pete said. "Feeling guilty?"

"About?"

"Your disappearing act, for one," Pete said. "Then your fade-out. Are you that desperate to be rid of us?"

"Don't take it so personal—Jesus," Harras said, shaking his head. "This was bound to end at some point, don't you think? We can't always be chasing psychopaths and risking our lives, can we? It was my time to step away."

"But you came back," Pete said. "Why?"

"Unfinished business."

Pete let out a terse laugh.

"Your ego's bruised, isn't it?" Pete asked. "You can't face that maybe this case is too tough for you."

"I don't like to lose," Harras said. "It's something we have in common."

Harras hoisted his carry-on and walked past Pete. The flight had begun to board. Pete waited a moment before following.

The flight was brief and uneventful—so short the flight attendants barely had time to dish out drinks and a light snack—which was fine for Pete. Air travel was not his preferred mode of transport. They didn't talk much, beyond basic pleasantries and short-term plans for once they reached the island. They'd deplaned and walked down a winding walkway toward the main airport building, lugging their carry-ons.

They reached baggage claim when Pete felt a tap on his shoulder.

"Pedro Fernandez Jr.?" the uniformed man said. He was mid-fifties, stocky, tan skin. His English was stilted but clear as he uttered Pete's full name. "Come with me."

Pete looked at Harras, who shrugged in response. Harras tried to follow, but two other officers blocked his path, shaking their heads. Pete could hear Harras explaining his credentials as the man led Pete into a room off the main airport traffic path. It was sparse—a table, two seats, and no windows. Pete had been interrogated enough times over the years to know what was coming next.

"*¿Hay un problema, señor?*" Pete asked. *Is there a problem?* Pete's Spanish was technically fluent, but definitely rusty. It was moments like this one where he regretted not keeping up with his first tongue.

The man didn't respond to Pete's question. Instead, he motioned for Pete to take one of the seats as he sat across from him.

"Pete Fernandez, from Miami," he said, matter-of-factly. "Son of Pedro Fernandez. Grandson to Diego. Correct?"

Then Pete understood. His grandfather, Diego, had been an attorney general—one of six—in Cuba before Castro took power. Fidel Castro had been dead for years, but that didn't mean the Castro name failed to carry weight, or that old grudges had been erased completely. If anything, it allowed people like this man to cherry-pick which ones to focus on. Diego Fernandez had escaped Cuba in the early days of Castro's rule, hiding out in the Argentinian embassy while his grandmother and father went to the United States first.

Pete hadn't even considered that this might pose a problem for him. Stupid.

"Yes, yes," Pete said. "I've never been here, to Cuba. I've never visited the island."

"Welcome, then," the man said in stilted English. "My name is Lidio Delgado. I am the head of airport security here. I have received word that you should be questioned."

"For what, though?" Pete said, stumbling over the words, letting them out slowly, hoping he wasn't saying the wrong thing —or in the wrong way. "I've done nothing wrong."

"The sins of the father often affect the son, or grandson, in this instance, Pete Fernandez," Delgado said. "Please hand me your visa and your cell phone."

Pete didn't move. "My visa? Are you insane?"

"Your grandfather was a traitor to this country. That is on the record," Delgado said, his expression placid. "We do not allow spies or seditionists into the country. I see you have an FBI attaché of sorts, Mister—Mr., what—Harras, no? So, we can only do so much, you understand? But we will be watching you closely, and we will be holding onto your visa until it is time for you to leave."

"What does that accomplish?"

"You're a Cuban first, Mr. Fernandez, American second, whether you like it or not," Delgado said. "You will be treated as such. Like a native. Not as a tourist or a special guest. When you decide to head back to Miami, to your capitalism, you will get your little papers and phone back, too. Until then, welcome home."

Delgado extended his hand and waited.

Pete pulled his visa from his pocket and slid it over to the man. He handed his phone over next.

Delgado pocketed them and stood up. "I hope you enjoy your time here in Cuba, Pedrito," he said before walking out. "Be careful."

Just a few moments into the cab ride, Pete was struck by a sense of detachment—of other. They were not home. They were only 220 miles from Miami but, in many ways, on another planet. The streets, buildings, and people had a faded, worn quality that went beyond the actual. Pastel blues and pinks popped out, clashing with the wider strokes of brown, gray, and black.

Pete, of course, had seen photos of the country—many from before Castro's takeover, but also plenty of "today's" Cuba—but they could not match the reality of a country in disrepair and decay, a land clinging to functionality, chugging along because while the infrastructure was rotting, it still managed to putter on for a bit longer. Pete saw tired faces, rusted vintage cars, faded cobblestone streets, all under the same glowing orange sun that pelted Miami with tropical heat and a bright, seemingly endless summer.

This was not some grand return—a chance for Pete to reconnect with the land that birthed his parents, a chance to reclaim some treasured legacy. This was a desperate man visiting a foreign land that was a shell of its former self. This was what it felt like to be on a sinking ship, Pete thought.

"What now?" Pete asked. His shirt was drenched with sweat and his palms felt clammy. The idea of wandering this city—this country—without any documentation wasn't doing wonders for his mood. But he was here to find someone. He'd worry about the rest later.

"We're going to see a book dealer."

"What?"

"I have a contact here, guy named Angel Padura," Harras said. "He's worked this town for a while. Was a cop. Retired now, sells antique books. Does some PI work on the side; thought he might be a good first stop."

Pete nodded.

"Junior, huh?" Harras said.

"I don't use it," Pete said. He had expected some ribbing from his friend over his name. It was just a question of when.

"Maybe I'll just call you Lil' Pedro from now on?"

Pete didn't respond. After a moment, he felt Harras's hand on his shoulder.

"Hey, don't sweat the visa thing," Harras said. "It's an old trick. They do it to anyone with relations dating back to Castro or before. You'll be fine. Focus on why we're here."

"To find Emily."

"To find those pages," Harras said. "To find out who killed your mother."

"Yeah," Pete said, looking down. "Any other leads from your sources on Emily?"

"Nothing concrete, but they're buzzing a lot, which tells me they're keeping secrets," Harras said. "The only nugget they'd share was that something was going down in Havana. She isn't running from so much as running to."

"To what, though?"

"That's the mystery," Harras said. "But I've got some people in here we can talk to. First we'll set up shop with Angel, then we'll fan out."

"A few months ago," Pete said, turning to face Harras. "You mentioned something about hearing rumblings about Los Enfermos. Anything else on that? Because when I was going through—"

"About someone else taking over?" Harras said. "Yeah, Kathy mentioned you going on a riff about Los Enfermos always being around. And, honestly, you're probably right. They have been around for a while, in different forms. It wouldn't surprise me if they were the main customer for the Silent Death, or whoever took over that gig. They didn't go away when Posada died and I'm sure they've come back in some form now. The buzz I'm hearing is there's a new head guy—and he's stepping on the gas. Lots of drugs funneling into Miami lately, and that can only mean one thing: Someone's got a new connect."

"But what does it all mean?" Pete asked. "In terms of Javier Mujica? My mother? Emily? Hell, in terms of me? Salerno came after me, after he killed Ferris and his daughter—looking for info. Looking—"

"For a contact with La Madrina—a way to tap the flow of drugs," Harras said. "And when Salerno came to Miami, we *thought* he was gunning for you. What if he was after someone else?"

"Emily?"

"Possibly," Harras said. "The gang managing the drug flow into Miami has been hobbled. Someone needs to step in and take over."

"Right, in the wake of Los Enfermos," Pete said. "But if you're saying Los Enfermos are still alive…"

"These two things can exist at the same time," Harras said. "Los Enfermos could be regrouping and the Colombians could be open to new business partners. Maybe they're one and the same. But, either way, someone didn't want Salerno to find that info."

"Mujica?"

"It'd make sense," Harras said, "for him to be looking to get a piece of that pie. But he's a *bolitero*. Gambler. Dealt in some drugs, I guess. What does a fading Cuban gangster want with the drug trade, this late in life?"

The car lurched forward, sending Pete and Harras tumbling forward. Pete looked up to see that the driver, a wiry, tan-skinned man of about forty, had wheeled around, the whites of his eyes yellow and glassy. He had a gun pointed at them.

"*Los Enfermos mandan sus saludos, cabrónes!*" he said as he fired two shots into Harras's head.

Pete watched as his friend's skull snapped back, blood and brains splattering the car's dusty back windshield. Before he could move toward his friend, the driver had swiveled, pointing the gun at Pete's head.

Pete gripped the man's arm with one hand, then sent his free palm speeding into his elbow, repeating the motion until he heard a wet crack, followed by a high-pitched shriek. Then he pulled, yanking the driver into the backseat. As the driver screamed, Pete sent a flurry of quick, focused punches into his face and throat—leaving the man's mouth and eye red with blood, a low groan escaping his lips.

Pete felt himself panting. His vision blurred. He looked past the fallen driver, whose head was lolling back and forth on the seat, car horns honking in the background as vehicles wove around their stopped cab. He yanked him up by the collar, pushing everything else—Harras, dead in the backseat, Emily, Cuba, everything—out of his mind. For now. For a minute.

"Who sent you?" Pete said, teeth gritted. "Who do you work for?"

The man, blood gurgling out of his mouth, eyes half-open, grinned. Smiled. His tongue slithered out, as if checking for missing teeth, then he spoke in a slow, curdled voice. "*Tu puta madre, Pete Fernandez,*" he said. *Your bitch mother.* "*¿Listo para morir en Cuba, hijo de puta?*" *Ready to die in Cuba, son of a bitch?*

No. Pete wasn't ready to die. He punched the man again, this time in the middle of his face.

The man responded with a reflexive whimper, then slumped back, unconscious.

Pete felt his body sag forward in response, as his eyes drifted left, toward the fallen, destroyed face and body of his friend. It didn't feel real. Surely this was a trick. Another mirage. Another FBI ploy to get Harras off the grid. But Pete knew that wasn't the case. Harras had gotten out. Managed to close the book on his career. But his own hubris—his refusal to accept defeat—had brought him back. On this trip, on this case that felt more and more complicated the deeper they went. And now, here he was, in a beaten-up old cab on the streets of Havana, his head blown open by an assassin's bullet, with no one around to help or even give a shit.

"Fuck," Pete said. "Fuck."

The adrenaline seemed to will him out of the car, his knees buckling as he stepped out, the blood in his head pounding, screaming to get out. His eyes welled up with stinging, godforsaken tears as he looked into the car, at the broken body of the killer, a man he'd never know, and his friend—a corpse now, a dead man. Murdered in a foreign country for who-knows-fucking-why.

Then, sirens. Different from the ones he was familiar with, but the message was the same. Less than an hour after landing on the streets of Havana, Pete was in the crosshairs of the police. The same police and government that had chased his family off the island.

He ran.

Angel Padura lived a few miles from El Capitolio, Cuba's capitol building—which was modeled after the Capitol Building in Washington, D.C.. But, Cubans being Cubans, they built theirs a few feet taller.

Padura's apartment was near the key Havana plazas, in a cramped one-bedroom that, like most of the country, seemed to have seen better days. The furniture was sturdy but worn out, the small living room anchored by a deflated-looking brown couch, two mismatched rocking chairs on either side. The bulk of the room was taken up by books—stacked on tables, double-stacked on shelves, and almost covering the flimsy table stationed in the living room's far corner. He lived simply. He'd had adventures. Challenges. But now he was tired. He found joy in his books and his routines. When the doorbell rang, he knew something was wrong. He felt himself tense as he walked toward the door.

Padura opened the door slowly. He found a man, his T-shirt covered in blood, eyes wild, shaking on the other side.

"¿Quién eres?" Padura asked, his Spanish slow and thoughtful, before shifting into a terse, but functional English. "How did you come here?"

"Help me," Pete Fernandez said, his voice shallow and strained. "Robert Harras sent me. He's dead. I need your help."

Padura sat Pete down on the tattered couch. He left the space for a moment and returned with a large glass of water, which Pete drank down hungrily. When he finished, he handed the glass back to Padura. His words came out slow and labored.

"¿Qué te pasó, hijo?" Padura asked, sitting in a rickety looking chair across from Pete. *What happened to you?*

"Robert Harras," Pete said, his tongue thick and a cold sweat forming down his back. It was starting to dawn on him. Not just that Harras was dead, but that he was here—in Cuba—alone, with no way back. "*Mi amigo. Es FBI. Te conoce ...* He said he knew you ... he had your address in his pocket. I ... I came here. I didn't know where else to go. They have my papers ..."

"¿Apellido Fernandez? ¿Nieto de Diego, no? They took your visa when you got in?" Padura asked, seemingly unperturbed. He knew, based on Pete's name, exactly why they'd swiped his identification. "You should not have come here."

"What?"

Padura cleared his throat. "I told Robert this," Padura said, standing up and taking Pete's glass. "Los Enfermos are strong here. They were born here. To come into the hornet's nest and think you won't get stung was stupid. Very stupid."

Padura started to walk back to his kitchen.

"I need help," Pete said, his head in his hands. "I need help finding someone. And I need help getting back home."

Padura stopped and wheeled around. "You're far from home, *papo,*" Padura said. "This isn't Miami. I can't really even have you here for long."

"I have nowhere else to go."

"*Yo sé, yo sé,*" Padura said, taking his seat again with a dismissive wave. "*Te están buscando.* They are looking for you—the police.

A former FBI agent, no less—has died on Cuban soil. This is bad. Problematic, to say the least. They will want to keep it quiet, as will your country. They'll also hear from bystanders that another man—perhaps even that another American—left the scene. You'll become a person of interest. Then they'll learn that this dead FBI man came to Cuba with another man, Pete Fernandez. They will put the two pieces together. Then they'll be looking for you. All of this will happen in the next twelve hours. That's how much time you have before you need to turn yourself in."

"Turn myself in?"

"I will accompany you," Padura said, in a low, calming voice. "I can get you in front of the right person. They won't want to deal with you. They'll put you on the first plane back to Miami. That's my guess. But your time is limited. Right now, *mi vecina entremetida* has probably dialed the police to tell them a madman was banging on my door."

"So ... so what do I do?" Pete asked. He'd never felt so helpless. Or he couldn't remember the last time he'd felt this way. Probably years ago, drunk on who knows what, wallowing in an abyss of his own creation. But this felt different, too. He had to right himself. "Look, I need to find this person."

Pete rummaged through his pockets and pulled out the photo—bent and worn. It was an old photo, from New Jersey. Pete and Emily at a party. She was wearing a stylish red dress, Pete in a rumpled brown suit, his eyes glassy and distant. He didn't even remember what the party had been for.

"This is Beatriz de Armas, or Emily Sprague," Pete said passing the photo to Padura. "She has information I need. It ties into Los Enfermos."

"*Eres terco*. If you keep looking for Los Enfermos, Pete, they will find you," *You're stubborn*, Padura said, scanning the photo before handing it back to Pete. "*Y te van a matar*—like they got your friend. What is she doing in Havana?"

"I thought she was running from someone, but she might be meeting people here," Pete said. "Los Enfermos ... or someone like them."

"She ran the wrong way," Padura said. "Why would she come here, to the heart of Los Enfermos? *No tiene sentido*. It does not make sense."

"I just know she came here," Pete said, rubbing his temples. "She has a connection—a drug connection … La Madrina, from Colombia. She also has info—information I want. About how my mother died."

"La Madrina," Padura said, looking at his hands. "Always La Madrina, eh? *¿No te ocupas con problemas pequeños, eh?" You don't deal with small problems, do you?*

"You know her?"

"Know of her," Padura said. "*Muy diferente.*"

Padura stood up and left the room. When he returned, he tossed something at Pete—a rumpled black T-shirt and faded blue jeans.

"If La Madrina is here, you may need to stay a bit longer," Padura said. "You stand out enough as it is. Having blood all over your clothes doesn't help."

"Thanks."

"Get dressed," Padura said. "Then we'll go meet a friend of mine."

El Museo Nacional de Bellas Artes de la Havana was a massive, two-building structure on Trocadero Street. It housed art dating to Cuba's colonial period, with rooms devoted to landscapes, costumbrismo paintings focused on daily Cuban life, and religious pieces.

Pete kept his gaze low as he followed Padura past the entrance and into the museum's ornate and sprawling nerve center. The beauty of the building's classical exterior and winding, awe-inspiring décor briefly distracted him from their purpose. But not for long. Padura wasn't much for browsing, leading Pete quickly through the museum's rooms—past stained-glass skylights, detailed and lush landscapes of Cuban beaches, and a number of different variations of the Virgin Mary—to a large room that was packed with portraits and landscapes that shared the same precise, thoughtful eye for detail.

They were not alone. Someone was standing at the opposite end of the room—la Sala cambio de siglo, the turn of the century gallery.

Padura walked over first, then motioned for Pete. He approached Padura's friend from the other side. All three of them looked at the painting in front of them—*Embarque de Colón por Bobadilla*, by Armando García Menocal.

"Pete Fernandez, *de Miami*," Padura said, looking around the room, as if he were just another museum-goer and talking to himself. "*Meet mi amiga Mariela.*"

Pete glanced at the woman to his right.

"*Qué bien me conoces, Angel*," Mariela said. *You know me so well, Angel.* Mariela batted her long eyelashes at the rumpled Cuban detective.

According to Padura, Mariela previously had been known as Miguel. That changed recently, as Cuba's staunch anti-LGBTQ policies loosened in the wake of Fidel Castro's death. Mariela wore a long, flowing purple dress, which complemented her strong features, lightly touched with makeup. "And, Pete, to what do I owe this pleasure? Angel doesn't call on me that much anymore."

"You always know what's going on," Padura said, switching to his terse English, a wet cough escaping his mouth. "*Mi amigo necesita tu ayuda, Mariela.*" *My friend needs your help.*

"*¿Y no puede hablar tu amigo?* Is he hiding over there?" Mariela said, pretending to peek over an invisible rock at Pete. "I haven't seen this boy around."

"I'm new," Pete said, keeping his voice flat and low.

The gallery they were in was empty, but from what Padura and Pete had seen, the museum was not. Someone was bound to walk in at any moment. They had to keep their conversation brief and innocent-looking. Which meant each word counted. Pete felt naked and raw. Like everyone's eyes were on him, the stranger. The man out of place. How much of it was true, how much was his own anxiety and fear?

Visions of Harras—his head jerking back, the cloud of blood and bone spreading—slashed into his mind's eye when Pete least expected it.

"Bueno, Mr. New," Mariela said, walking to another painting, on Pete's left——"La flor blanca," The White Flower, a colorful, menacing portrait of a lovely young woman, surrounded by intricate and colorful flowers. Behind her looms a solitary hand—clutching a jagged knife. Mariela tapped a finger to her chin, still acting as if she was just a browser on a humid Havana afternoon. "*¿Qué te trae por aquí?*" *What brings you here?*

"I'm looking for a woman," Pete said, handing Emily's photo toward Mariela, the image facedown.

Mariela snatched it discreetly.

"She arrived a few days ago. She probably doesn't want to be found. She has something of mine. Something that belonged to my mother."

Mariela scanned the photo, looking around the still-empty gallery before scanning the photo. Her dark eyes lingered over it for a few moments. Her expression remained placid and unmoved. She handed it back to Pete hastily before responding.

"*La conozco, sí.* I know her. She looks different now," she said. "*Tiene pelo negro.* Shorter. But yes, I've seen her. Here and there. *No habla español muy bien.* She's keeping a—how do you say—low profile. But I know where she's staying. She is here on business."

"What kind?" Pete asked.

Mariela looked at Pete, a sharp smirk on her face. She pulled out her cell phone and pretended to talk into it. She was doing her best, Pete admitted to himself.

"*El tipo de gente que matan como si estuvieran cepillandose los dientes,*" she said, any sign of humor gone from her voice and face. *The kind of people who kill like they're brushing their teeth.*

Pete looked at Padura. His new friend nodded.

"Mariela ... you can trust her," Padura said. "She's a friend. *Ella conoce las partes complicadas de la ciudad.* She can help you." *She knows the complicated parts of the city.*

"Can you take me to her?" Pete asked. "To this woman?"

"*¿Estás loco, papi?*" Mariela asked, shaking her head. "*No, no, eso no lo puedo hacer.* That's not how I operate. I will try to set up a meeting. That I can do. *Pero es muy difícil, entiendes?* I'll call Angel when it's done. Until then, see the sights. *Diviértete.*"

With that, she turned and walked toward another part of the gallery, pulling out a pad from her purse and jotting notes down as she passed the paintings on the wall. Her message was clear: She was done with Padura and Pete.

The call came in around midnight. Padura had gone to sleep, leaving Pete to stew in his own anxiety for hours.

Pete picked up the phone midway through the second ring. He could hear Mariela's low breathing on the line, but nothing else. She was waiting. "It's Pete."

"*Encontré a tu amiga*. She will meet you," she said, a tinge of humor in her voice. "I didn't realize your history was so ... colorful. Imagine my surprise when I heard who your *abuelito* was."

"I'm a complicated guy, I guess."

"*Nos encontramos en La Zorra y el Cuervo, en la avenida 23, entre la N y O,*" Mariela said. "Come by yourself. Padura doesn't need to get into this any deeper. *A veces me preocupo por él.*" *I worry about him sometimes.* Mariela hung up.

By the time Pete put the phone down he saw Padura was standing in the doorway that led to his small bedroom.

"*¿La encontró?*" *She found her?*

"Heading to meet her in a bit," Pete said.

Padura darted back into his room. He came back with something small in his hands, wrapped in a dark towel.

"*Toma*, take this," Padura said, not meeting Pete's eyes. "*Tíralo si no lo necesitas.* I shouldn't have it. But you might need it."

Pete unwrapped the towel slowly, revealing a small, snub-nose revolver. It felt worn to the touch, the metal dull and scratched. This gun had lived, Pete thought as he hooked it on his belt, at his back. He draped his shirt over it, only a slight bulge hinting that he might be carrying something.

"Thank you."

"*De nada,*" Padura said, nodding. "*Nos separamos ahora,* Pete. Don't come back. Take this friend of yours and go home. They'll give you your visa. She probably has hers. *Te matan si te quedas en Cuba. ¿Me entiendes, amigo?*"

Pete nodded. He understood. *Run if you want to live.*

"Before I go," Pete said, his voice choked with emotion. "I need a favor ... another favor."

Padura nodded.

Pete scrounged in his pocket for the scrap of paper.

"I need this information sent to the email address I wrote at the bottom," Pete said. "It's urgent."

Padura took the slip of paper and scanned it. "You are asking a lot of me," Padura said.

"It might be my only shot off this island."

"*Está hecho,*" Padura said. *Consider it done.* He gripped Pete's shoulder. "*Camina con cuidado,*" he said. "*No dejes que la muerte de tu amigo sea en vano.*" *Don't let your friend's death be in vain.*

Pete started to respond, but found that the words wouldn't form. "Go."

Pete stepped out into the sweltering black night.

La Zorra y el Cuervo was a jazz club, the vibe murky and mysterious—red overhead lights fading into the bar's dark, dank decor. Even the front door to the place seemed otherworldly—a refashioned phone booth served as the main entry point, which led visitors down a long flight of stairs to the basement venue.

The band was tight. The quartet running hot, late into the Havana night, the piano coating the backbeat and bass, as the tenor sax player laid it on thick. The crowd—considering the hour—was lively and engaged. Couples dancing. People screaming approval from the bar. The place was pulsing with an energy Pete found comfort in. It reminded him of Miami. He'd only been gone less than a day, but his hometown felt distant and alien.

He felt a tug at his shoulder. He turned to find Mariela leaning on the far end of the rickety-looking bar.

"You come here often?" she said, that smirk on her smooth face.

"Where is she?"

"Ahy, you're no fun," she said, motioning for him to follow.

She pushed open a door near the entrance that led them down a winding, narrow hallway. They were now in the underbelly of the bar. Pete could hear the kitchen—employees screaming orders, the music dulled by the concrete walls that separated the room from the boisterous dance floor.

They reached a door midway through the hall. Mariela rapped on it, then turned the knob.

Pete followed her into a well-lit, small room. The space was empty aside from a small table and Emily. The woman who'd pretended to be Beatriz de Armas and Daniela Burgos sat, arms folded, eyes on Pete.

"You found me."

Pete sat down across from her. He felt Mariela hovering behind him. "Harras is dead."

"I didn't want this," she said, her expression stoic, unaffected by the news. "I didn't want you or Harras to come after me."

"Why did you come here?" Pete asked. "You're right in the heart of Los Enfermos, Em. The people that killed Rick. That tried to kill me. They sent that man—Novo—to kill you—"

"You don't know that," Emily said "I wish you'd just left it all alone—now it's getting more and more difficult for me to—"

"What?"

"You don't know who sent Novo," Emily said. "You have no idea what's going on, Pete. Just go home."

Pete waited a beat. "You were in Osvaldo Valdez's house," he said. "The night he was murdered. Why?"

"I—I was ..." she hesitated. "I needed something. Something he had."

"What?" Pete asked. "What did he have that you needed?"

Emily didn't respond.

"My mother's dream book," Pete said. "You took the last pages, didn't you? What's on them? Where are they?"

"Not here," she said. "But yes, I took them. I have them. I had to—"

"Emily," Pete said, leaning forward. "What the fuck is going on? Who are you trying to protect by stealing those pages? At first I thought you were running—running from the Silent Death, from Los Enfermos ... but I'm not sure anymore. Are you here to meet La Madrina? There's still time to get out of this, Emily. Come with me. Let's go back home. We can figure this out, okay?"

He heard the door click open a second before the realization hit. But by then it was too late. The footsteps stuttered into the room—four, maybe five men. The clicks and clacks of guns being cocked and loaded, certainly pointed at Pete's head. He felt a barrel—it had to be the barrel of a gun—connecting with the back of his skull. His eyes stayed on Emily.

"I'm sorry, Pete, but I can't let you fuck up what's going down tonight," she said, her voice a shattered whisper. "It's out of my hands now."

Then Pete's vision went black.

# CHAPTER TWENTY-FOUR

"*Levántate, mijo.* Get up," the voice, refined and breathy said in a familiar, stop-start English. "Come on. We don't have much time."

Pete felt his eyelids flutter open, but his vision was still coated in darkness. He felt rough hands on his arms, tugging at ropes holding them together. He was on a chair—a small, rickety one—and his head felt foggy and heavy, like he'd been sleeping for years but still not rested. The air was thick with dust and smoke. The last thing he remembered was Emily's face. The expression of resignation that he'd already become familiar with, long before crossing the Florida Straits to find her again. She was gone.

"*Muévete,*" the voice said. "We have to go."

He felt the ropes drop to the floor and arms slide under him, lifting him out of the chair.

"*Tu amiga Beatriz me traicionó,*" the voice said. "I don't like that. Now I have to get my hands dirty. I might break a nail."

*Mariela.*

"Where—where am I?"

"*Cállate,*" she said. "*No tenemos mucho tiempo.*" We don't have much time.

"But, how?" Pete said, his voice slurred. "How am I alive?"

"Your friend, she did this. *Ella te ayudó,*" Mariela said. *Emily helped you.* "She had to—how do you say it—act tough for her people. There is a big meeting happening now. *Todos están ahí.*"

"She told you where I was?"

"*Camina,* Pete," Mariela said, exasperated. "*No tenemos suerte sin limite, niño.*" Our luck isn't unlimited.

She pulled-slash-dragged Pete for a few steps. As they reached the door, he stood more firmly, still not fully balanced, but able to carry most of his weight. She opened a door slowly, and light filtered into the room, which Pete could now see was a shed of some kind—light on carpeting, much less decorations. It was littered with tools and yard equipment. The chair where Pete had been tied was at the center of the cramped space.

"Who brought me here?"

"Los Enfermos, for sure."

"Which ones?"

"*Papo, ya debes saber que Los Enfermos no son pandilleras y nada más.*" she said, pulling her along with him toward the light. *Los Enfermos aren't just a gang.* "Your friend made it seem like you would be killed—had her men stash you in the room."

Pete's limbs felt rubbery, and his steps were hesitant.

Mariela seemed hurried but not panicked. The shed was tucked behind a medium-sized house on a residential street, its windows dark in the morning dusk.

Pete wondered how long he'd been out.

"*Tienes que alejarte de esta isla.* It is time to get you off this island," she said as they reached the rusted, worn-down, off-white Ford Fairmont. She opened the door for Pete before scurrying to the driver's side.

"No, no," Pete said, more to himself, but Mariela heard him. "I need those pages. From my mother's book—"

"Emily's?" Mariela said with a grin. "Check the back seat."

The trip to the airport was quick, Pete and Mariela silent in the rumbling car, the only sound coming from the pages as Pete flipped through the unexpected treasure trove Mariela had scored for him. It was more than he'd imagined—not just the remaining pages of his mother's dream diary, but a small bound notebook that could prove much more valuable—a journal, of sorts, from what Pete could tell. Part scrap paper, part daily rundown. He wanted to immerse himself in the thing, to absorb his mother's thoughts and quirks, but he couldn't now. Not yet. He had to run. Run home.

"Thank you," Pete said. "Thank you for this. How did you get it?"

"It was easy, *mi amor*," Mariela said, her eyes on the road. "Your *novia* isn't a gangster. *Ella no sabe la calle.* When she set you up, she left herself open. So, I acted scared. I cursed her out for double-crossing me—acted very mad. I knew she was heading to her meeting, so I left—headed straight for her place. The pages—were hidden there. Not very well, either. After that, it was just about figuring out where Los Enfermos were hiding you. I knew they had strict orders not to kill you—yet. So I had a little time. It just became a process of elimination."

"You took a big risk," Pete said, clutching the folder loaded with the remaining pages of his mother's book. "Thank you."

"*Mijo*, don't you think I take a big risk here every damn day?" she said, turning to look at him. "*¿Crees que es fácil vivir aquí?* The old hates still exist, and we're only as free as we want to be. Most people don't know what it's like otherwise, so we don't push back. *Estamos adormecido.*" We are asleep.

Pete nodded. He couldn't think of anything to say—anything to soothe the rough edges. Nothing that didn't feel like a platitude or an outright lie. He felt the car lurch forward as the worn brakes creaked to a stop.

"Here we are," Mariela said, as if the last few bits of conversation had never happened. "Don't say my name. If they give you trouble, I don't know if I can help you, but let me know."

Pete leaned over and gave her a hug. A strong, forceful one.

She responded in kind, then pushed him back. "*Adelante.* Mourn your friend. Make his death mean something," she said. "I know Emily is heading back there. She's not made for this kind of thing, and she will have trouble explaining how you got away. She's still running. Maybe you can find her and make some sense of it all."

"Thank you," Pete said. The memory of Harras jumped into his vision, jarring him. "Tell Angel—thank Padura for me. For his help."

"I will," she said. "But he won't care. He just helps whoever is around. Like an old lady collecting stray cats."

Pete tried to smile, then stepped out of the car into the brightening Cuban morning.

"**Y**ou've been making a lot of trouble for us, Señor Fernandez," Lidio Delgado said, shaking his head, a humorless smile on his paunchy face. "Big trouble."

They were seated in the same tiny, stuffy office at José Martí Airport.

Pete hadn't gotten far. A few minutes after reaching the ticket terminal to inquire about departing flights, he was tagged by two uniformed military men and ushered to the back room. Delgado came a few minutes later.

"Your friend is dead, as I am sure you know," Delgado said, flipping through a stack of pages—what looked like printed out memos and records. "This is bad enough. An American dying on Cuban soil. But he is also FBI. Very bad."

Pete didn't respond. His hands clutched the folder Mariela had passed to him. Pages that might contain the truth about his mother's killer.

"Do you have any words in your defense, Pedrito?" Delgado said, eyebrows popping up. "Before we take you into custody? You might be spending more time in Cuba than you had planned, eh?"

"I'm an American citizen," Pete said. "You don't think this'll create problems for you? There's a dead FBI agent in Havana and his family will be asking about his body—not to mention what happened."

Delgado shrugged. "Not my problem, *hermano*," he said. "That is—what's the saying? Above my pay grade."

"I think it's very much your problem," Pete said, his eyes darkening as they locked on the middle-management stooge. "You might want to check the news. My guess is my little message in a bottle got out— and my hometown isn't very happy. You may want to give me my phone and visa back. After that, you might want to get me on the next plane out of here. With my friend Robert Harras's body."

Delgado's expression changed from one of smug victory to confusion. He collected his papers and dashed out of the office.

A few minutes passed. When he returned, he had Pete's visa and cell phone in hand.

"*Te crees genio*, eh?" *You think you're a genius?* Delgado spat. "Well, now you can leave. We don't want your kind of trouble here."

Pete said nothing. He had no quips. No witty retorts. He just wanted to leave.

Delgado handed Pete his visa and phone.

Under different circumstances, Pete would have smiled. He snatched his belongings back and walked through the door toward the ticket terminal. He turned his phone on and saw the expected barrage of notifications—texts, emails, news alerts, missed calls. But one stood out—from Kathy.

The subject line was terse: **URGENT—RE: ALTER**.

The email itself only confirmed a sinking feeling Pete had been denying for longer than he cared to admit.

# CHAPTER TWENTY-FIVE

The plane reached cruising altitude before Pete even considered opening the tattered folder he'd been gripping since leaving Mariela's car. It was creased and crumpled. It was time, though.

Pete unlatched the small tray table in front of him and opened the folder. Inside were four pieces of paper, edges torn carefully. Someone had taken great care removing them from what had once been his mother's dream book. Whatever was inside was dangerous enough for Emily to steal, but not enough for Osvaldo to solve the case. But to Pete it could be just enough to get him onto the next step in his investigation.

The first page was a sketch—rough, in pencil and colored markers—of a long dock, rocks and waves in the foreground. At the far end was a lighthouse. Over the building his mother had cut out letters from magazines to spell something: HOME. Under the cut-out letters, in her shaky scrawl was something else: TOO FAR NOW.

In an open patch of space, to the left of the main image, was a litany of words that cut to Pete's core. It read like a laundry list of regrets—which proved to be exactly what they were.

UNFAITHFUL TO PEDRO
BAD MOM—CALL PETE MORE??
DRUNK
DRUGGIE
GOING TO GET FIRED
TOO EASY TO KEEP GOING …

Next to the top item—"UNFAITHFUL TO PEDRO"—was a long black mark. Someone—Pete's gut didn't think it was his mother's doing—had blacked out some words with a marker. He tried to flip over the page to see if he could find any clue as to what was written originally, but had no luck. He sniffed the page. It smelled faintly of permanent marker. He cursed under his breath. He hadn't expected his mother's own dream book to be redacted.

The next page was another drawing. Two figures—a man and a woman, the woman leaning into the man, her head tilted up toward him. Next to the man's head were a few words, in a loose, sloppy word balloon:

IT'S A BIG ZERO, BABY

The faces were replaced by cutouts from magazines or newspapers—color close-up images of rodent-like creatures, perhaps bats, their mouths open as if screaming. Two rabid mammals in a deadly embrace.

Pete felt his left eye twitch as he looked over the image. His mother's art was visceral and raw. Coupled with the mixed media, it made for a haunting image. Underneath the art was another jagged-looking line of text:

WAS IT WORTH IT???

The final page was barely one—torn in half, with only the top included in the folder. Pete wasn't sure if Emily or someone on her side had kept part of it or his mother had ripped it herself. The page was a mess. Scratchy text, charcoal-fueled drawings of monstrous, demonic creatures surrounded by fire. At the center was a clear, empty circle, with only one word written inside it: PETE.

He felt his temperature rise as he looked over the rest of the page. Two names written in stark, large red letters—followed by two crossed out in the same black marker.

MELTZER
FERNANDEZ

"Meltzer?" Pete asked aloud. The name was new to him. He assumed Fernandez was a reference to his father. He couldn't make out the last name, but he saw just enough of the third one to make a guess. The top points of an "M" combined with the curved bottoms of a "U" and "J" could mean only one person: MUJICA. Alvaro Mujica.

But who was Meltzer? And who was the fourth, final name almost illegibly written on the last page of his mother's dream book?

Pete fell back into his seat. He felt the darkness and despair starting to seep in through the edges, the dam starting to crack.

But he wouldn't let himself be overwhelmed. He'd been through too much to get to this point. And, for once, he had people depending on him. A future. A chance to do right by someone in a way his mother never could.

Pete closed the folder and fell into a brief, fitful sleep.

---

**"W**here the hell is Pete Fernandez?" Kathy said.

The words bounced off the walls of the tiny kitchen nook at Caballero-Rivero Funeral Home on Southwest Eighth Street in Little Havana.

Dave Mendoza leaned back on a vending machine, his expression blank. Kathy's lanky figure loomed over him, hands on her hips. They knew that Pete had been back for a little over a week, but beyond that, they knew little else. She'd been inundated with requests—calls, visits, casual run-ins while out of the house—from an alphabet soup that included the FBI, TSA, and some other acronyms she'd forgotten, and DHS, to name a few. But she had nothing to share with them. Pete Fernandez was in the wind, and even his best friend couldn't tell them when he would surface.

She could easily rattle off a handful of questions the orgs would be jonesing to ask him. Why did Pete leave Cuba? Was he around when Robert Harras was brutally murdered? How had he managed to disappear for a few days while Cuban authorities were left to clean up the mess of his friend's death? How did he avoid being intercepted at Miami International Airport?

She knew Pete had been through this before. Not in the same way, but he was no stranger to being questioned. No stranger to playing defense with authorities. But now he was completely off the grid, not even checking in at home or reaching out to Dave, who had often served as his "in case of emergency" glass case. That small, itchy feeling in the back of her mind—the knowing whisper she often ignored—was getting louder: "He's dead."

"Haven't heard from him," Dave said, shaking his head. "I know he was on the plane that came back with … Harras. With his body. Thought he'd at least be here."

"You'd think, yes. I'm just trying to figure out why he's gone dark on us," Kathy said. "Why not regroup and try to figure out who did this to Harras?"

"It was Los Enfermos," Dave said. "That's the word. At least from what I can tell. The rest, well, we need to figure out."

"We'd better work fast," Kathy said, her eyes red and wet. "I don't know how much more of this we can take." She grasped Dave's shoulder. "How are you holding up?"

"Fine, I guess," Dave said. "Numb. Feels like everything's falling apart in slow motion."

"Any word on where Emily might be?" Kathy asked. "Did she get out of Cuba?"

"Nothing," Dave said. "Tried asking around using all her known identities, but I'm not really talking to—well, most of the people who would have that intel."

Dave was still sober. Working his program. Trying to keep on the right side of the street. However, he still had friends from his days running drugs and dealing with the Miami underworld.

Kathy couldn't bring herself to pressure him. She knew well enough—from just being around Pete and from her own family's demons—the risks that came with revisiting people, places, and things from a past, darker life.

"Nothing, like zero, or maybe a small something?" Kathy asked. "Give me a little hope here, Mendoza."

"Nothing concrete, really," Dave said, fidgeting, rubbing his left wrist. "Mujica's making some moves. Arming up, apparently."

"Maybe he's feeling the heat?" Kathy asked.

"From whom?"

"From us? From Los Enfermos? I dunno," Kathy said. "I can't think straight. I'm exhausted, I'm living out of a suitcase, Pete is gone, and Harras is dead. I'm ready to hop in a car and have this baby in the woods."

"Kathy Bentley?"

Dave and Kathy turned toward the sound of footsteps.

Nisha Hudson, followed by two uniformed Miami officers crowded into the small kitchen area. She scanned the room warily before settling her gaze on Kathy.

"Yes?"

"Nisha Hudson," she said. "I work Homicide. We met briefly when your boyfriend got caught up in that Silent Death business at Eddie Rosen's house. These gentlemen are—"

"Officers Johns and Rucka, ma'am," the younger cop said. He was clean-cut and friendly-looking, his partner in many ways his opposite—older, gruff. "We need to ask you a few questions."

"Okay," she said, stepping toward them. "What about?"

"Were you residing at 8570 Southwest 28th Street?" Rucka said, his voice low and terse.

"I've been staying there, yes," she said. "With a friend."

"Pete Fernandez?" Johns asked.

"Yes."

"What's the nature of the relationship, ma'am?" Rucka asked, his eyes on Kathy's very visible baby bump.

"That's none of your business," Kathy said. "Now, if you'll excuse me and get to the point, I'd really appreciate it."

"We're trying to find your boyfriend," Hudson said. "I'm worried he might be in some serious trouble—probably stemming from whatever happened to him in Cuba a few days ago."

"Well, he is in trouble, but that seems to be his permanent setting of late," Kathy said, growing more impatient. "And he's not my boyfriend, really."

"We're trying to locate Mr. Fernandez," Johns said.

"Join the club," Dave said, the words a low mutter.

"And you are?" Rucka asked.

"Dave's a friend," Kathy said.

"You have a lot of friends," Rucka said, a smirk etched on his face.

"Again, what is this about?" Kathy asked, crossing her arms. "Am I under arrest?"

"No, not at all," Johns said. "We just need to locate Fernandez."

"He's not here," Kathy said, exasperated. "I don't know how else to say that."

"Has he been staying at his house?" Hudson said. "That's what I really need to know."

"Not lately," Kathy said. "He was in Cuba until recently."

"I saw the news," Hudson said. "Boy sure knows how to get himself tangled up in shit, I'll give him that. But I mean, has he stayed there recently—as in, this morning?"

"I have no idea, for the umpteenth time. I haven't seen him there, so if he's been staying there, he's done a great job of sleeping in the utility room."

"We get it, lady," Rucka said. "We just thought he might want to know his house had blown up."

"I was also hoping to make sure he wasn't in the damn house when it happened, either," Hudson said.

"Excuse me?"

"You heard me," Rucka said, his voice flat. "That house is a burning pile of rubble. We've got the fire under control, but everything inside is a loss. Not that a funeral is ever good, but lucky for you there was somewhere you had to be. Otherwise, you'd be dead."

# CHAPTER TWENTY-SIX

Rachel Alter slid the key into the front door lock. She didn't want to let on she knew someone was behind her. She wheeled around, her hand slipping into her small bag and pulling out her police weapon. She clicked the safety on instinct, before her brain could process the man standing before her.

"Pete?"

He looked different. Worn out. His clothes rumpled and dirty, hair out of place. The beard less intentional and more unruly. His eyes wild. He looked like he hadn't slept in a long, long time.

"We need to talk."

Alter motioned for him to come in. He followed.

"The kid's asleep, so please keep your voice down. I was just taking out the trash," Alter said as she sat down on the leather sectional in the townhouse's living room.

"With your police issue?" Pete said. "Nervous about something?"

"What do you want?" She was wearing a black T-shirt and sweats. It was late. She'd been asleep or about to doze.

Pete didn't really care. "It'll only be a minute," he said.

"Does anyone know you're back?"

"I flew back a few days ago," Pete said. "Some people know. Now you know. I'm not hiding."

"You're not out and about, either," Alter said. "Why?"

"Los Enfermos want me dead. They killed Harras. Emily is on the run, too," Pete said. "I thought I was just holding up a tangle of different threads—my mom, Javier Mujica, Emily—but it's all one thing, I think. I'm just not sure how they line up yet."

"Pete, I don't know much about Mujica, you know—"

"Let me finish."

Alter sighed and pulled her legs up to her chest, a defensive posture.

"Mosher is dead."

"Mosher?"

"The first cop on the scene of my mother's murder, remember?" Pete said. "He was retired, too. Living up in Boca. I called his younger brother, trying to find him. He told me Mosher just died. Killed himself. Overdosed on his own meds."

"Well, shit, that's unfortunate."

Pete scoffed.

"What?" Alter asked.

"No one knew about Mosher," Pete said. "Only the people who'd read Valdez's original report, and that has been buried for years. It's also not reflected in the case files you gave me. The only other people who've spent time with Valdez's original notes on the case are me ... and you."

"You have my file. There's nothing else." Alter said, incredulous. "You can't be serious."

"I am dead serious," Pete said, still standing, pacing slowly around the small living room. "And you're wrong. There has to be something else. Something more. These inconsistencies aren't coincidental, Rachel."

Alter started to get up. "I'm going to have to ask you to—"

Pete shook his head. "Now, I'm not great at computers. Not my strong suit. I can search on Google and type in Word, but I'm not a hacker, not by any means," he said. "I was the kind of reporter that was great with quotes and color. I could paint a picture. The in-the-trenches stuff didn't interest me. But my partner is the total package."

"What does Kathy have to do with anything?"

"She did some digging," Pete said, stopping to face Alter. "Found some interesting stuff."

"Cut to the chase, okay? It's late."

"You don't have a sister."

"That's bullshit."

"There's not much history for Rachel Alter before 2000," Pete said. "But there's a lot of backstory for Raquel Altunes. Raquel Gallegos-Altunes."

"Who?" Alter said, her voice cracking.

"Raquel," Pete said, sitting across from Alter, "is you."

"So what?" Alter said. "I changed my name. The PD knew that. I don't get along with my family. When my sister died—"

"You don't have a sister," Pete said, his voice seething now. "But you do have a brother. A half-brother."

Alter remained silent.

"Kathy didn't believe it at first," Pete said. "Gallegos is a common enough name. And you did a nice job of covering your tracks before you became a cop. Going to school out of state. Changing your name. Cutting off contact with your family. So, by the time you came back to Miami, you were a new person. Rachel Alter. Green detective assigned to the cold case squad.

"But something bugged me," Pete continued. "The name stuck in my craw. Kathy's too. See, about five years ago, we knew an Ana Gallegos. We thought she only had one kid—one adult child from her only marriage: Raul Aguilera. Do you remember him?"

"No idea what you're talking about," she said, her response robotic and without feeling. "Please leave."

"Raul Aguilera was FBI. He and his partner, Robert Harras, were working a serial murder case in Miami five years ago," Pete said. "The killer turned out to be a nutjob named Julian Finch. He was paying homage to the earlier killings of Rex Whitehurst. Remember him?"

"Sure," Alter said. "Anyone from here does. I remember Finch, too. But what's your point, Pete? I've asked you to leave, and I'm just about ready to—"

"Call the cops?" Pete asked. "Go for it. I think they'd like to hear what I have to say."

Alter's shoulders slumped.

"Thing is, Julian Finch didn't work alone," Pete said. "He mimicked Whitehurst, but he became his own thing. Killing young girls—girls who were off the grid—by pretending to be a real estate agent looking to help them. He knew I was on his heels. Knew Kathy and I had pieced part of it together. So he came after us. He blew up my father's house. He kidnapped Emily. But we kept coming. One thing we didn't know, though? He had a helper. A protégé. A direct link to Whitehurst. The original killer's own almost-stepson—Raul. Harras's own partner was taking part in the murders, covering up for his guru. The clue that broke the case for us came from Ana Gallegos. Your mother."

"This is absurd," Alter said. "I've heard enough."

"Ella isn't your sister's baby," Pete said. "She's Raul's. No matter how well you covered your tracks, you couldn't erase an actual person. Who found out? Who used the truth against you? I don't think you're a bad person, Rachel. But I do think someone's been threatening you, forcing you to feed me bad intel. And it stops now."

"I never asked for this," Rachel said, her words bubbling up slowly, methodically. "I never wanted to be part of that ... group ... that family."

"Who came to you?" Pete asked. "Who found out?"

"I—I don't know, honestly. It wasn't one man. They all worked for the same person," Alter said. "But they knew. They knew Raul had a daughter. They knew the mother had disappeared. They said they'd tell the world. I just—I couldn't destroy Ella's life like that, but I also had a right to my own, you know? I worked hard to become a cop. I didn't ask my brother—half-brother, someone I knew like a distant cousin—to become a serial killer's sidekick, okay? So why do I need to get saddled with that? Plus, what they asked of me was so minor. It was almost clerical. To just let them know if anyone came digging around certain files. To lose some paperwork in certain cold cases. Graciela Fernandez was one."

"There were others?"

"Yes," Alter said. "One other."

"Javier?" Pete said, stepping toward Alter. "Javier Mujica?"

Alter nodded.

The doorbell rang.

"Are you expecting someone?" Pete asked.

Alter shrugged.

Pete walked toward the door. He peered through the peephole but couldn't make anything out. He stepped back.

"Your porch light is out," Pete said.

That's when he saw the gun in Alter's hands. The police weapon she'd pointed at him earlier.

"He was unhinged, officer, said he couldn't get over seeing his friend killed in Cuba and wasn't sure where to go," Alter said, her eyebrows raised slightly. "He was asking me for help, for some kind of way out of the trouble he was in. Then he attacked me. I had no choice. My niece was sleeping upstairs."

"You don't want to go down that road," Pete said.

Before she could react, he cut loose with the kick, which sent his heel into her midsection. She folded into herself, the gun clattering to the floor. Pete picked it up and slid it into the back of his waistband before standing over Alter, who was curled into herself, clutching her stomach.

"Get out," she said, the words almost inaudible, overpowered by the loud, pained groan that followed. "Go."

"Not yet, Rachel," Pete said. "Not before you tell me who set this up. Who wanted you to bury my mother's murder?"

"It doesn't matter."

Pete wheeled around.

A masked figure stood a few feet away from them, long revolver drawn—a silencer at the end of the weapon's barrel.

Pete pulled Alter's gun from his belt and pointed it at the Silent Death. "Novo's dead. Who're you?" Pete asked. "Is there a Silent Death waiting list? Like Slayer potentials?"

"*Cállate*," the man said. "You know nothing. And that's how it will end."

Pete shot first, sending a bullet into the masked man's left knee. As the figure crumpled to the ground, he sent his heel into the Silent Death's face. The man's gun skittered further into the house. Pete stepped closer, crunching his boot on the Silent Death's outstretched hand. The Death responded with a muffled scream.

Pete leaned forward, his gun pointed at the Death's head as he yanked the dark, wrap-like mask from his face. He wasn't sure who he expected to see—Mujica? Emily? Angel Padura? Someone else? But the eyes and pained expression that looked back at him were those of a stranger.

"Who are you?" Pete said, standing up.

"Don't you remember, bro?" the man said, his teeth coated by a red sheen of blood.

"Stu Lovallo?" Pete said. "The drummer? The creep who followed Emily around? What the fuck are you doing here?"

"It's over, man," Lovallo said, the loony grin still plastered on his face despite the growing pool of blood forming under his knee. He was on another planet. "You've been playing it all wrong. You think you've got it all figured out? They're ten steps ahead of you. Nice house you have, by the way. Well, used to have."

Pete turned around.

Alter was still curled up on the floor, head in her hands, the front door swinging open.

Pete walked toward it, each step picking up speed. As his foot hit the sidewalk, he was in a full-on sprint.

# CHAPTER TWENTY-SEVEN

He knew it was gone before he pulled onto his street. The smell of smoke invaded his lungs from what felt like miles away. By the time he saw the black clouds emanating from where his house, the small three-bedroom he'd bought with his own money—his goddamned house—once stood, he knew it was gone.

Pete Fernandez was not the nostalgic type. The world had pushed him into his role. Murders, explosions, lost homes, and lost friends left little room for scrapbooks, picture walls, or mementos tucked in his wallet. It felt like his life was being destroyed annually, with each year wrecking a different part. He'd gotten used to it. But that didn't soften the sting. At least not this time. It didn't stop the wetness from forming on his cheeks as he pulled his car in front of a pile of debris and burning cinder that had once been a house.

He saw Kathy, huddled next to a nearby police car, the lights flashing as uniforms cordoned off the area. The fire truck was a few feet away, a few Miami firefighters dousing what remained of the flames. Maintenance. This was a full-on loser. Nothing to recover. Pete didn't need a forensic analysis to come up with that conclusion.

He put the car in park and stepped out.

She saw him immediately. In the few days he'd been off the grid, she'd grown—the baby, their baby—had grown. He felt a sharp pang of regret. For doing what he'd done—drunk, sober, always. When he could no longer handle the world, when he needed a minute to reconnect, he'd disappear. It'd been cruel and stupid of Pete to think, Cuba trip or no, that going dark would be a good idea. He expected a punch in the face.

Instead, she pulled him into a tight hug, her breath hot on his neck.

He pulled back. God, he'd missed her. What had he been thinking?

"Pete, Jesus," she said, her voice angry and pleading at the same time, like a cornered fighter with a few more rounds to go—demanding another chance to win. "Where the fuck have you been?"

"Just—looking…trying to figure this out," Pete said, surprised by his own muffled voice, choked by emotion, by the release.

He'd sped over from Alter's place, sure he'd find Kathy dead, their future cut short by a mysterious killer. The relief that the only loss he'd have to deal with was a pile of ash that had once been a house slammed into him like a hurricane wind.

Kathy pushed him away, her hands still clutching his neck. "Trying? Trying what?" she said. "We thought you were dead. Someone destroyed your house. Harras is gone. What is happening?"

"I think we—"

"Pete Fernandez?"

Pete and Kathy both looked toward the street, where an attractive, thirtysomething woman with black hair stood. She wore a stylish blue business suit.

"Yes?" Pete said.

"Hi. Dayna Anderson. I'm a PI based in Los Angeles," she said, a forced smile on her face, as if she were debating whether she should say anything about the dystopian nightmare playing out behind them. "Guess I'm catching you at a bad time, blurg."

"Sort of."

"An attorney I work for wanted me to deliver this in person," she said, handing him a thick package, about the size of a large magazine. "Nice excuse for a mini-Miami vacation. For me, I mean."

Pete took the heavy envelope and had to grip it with both hands. He didn't respond to the investigator's joke.

"Sorry, I keep blocking out the whole 'house on fire' thing," she said.

"Who sent this?" Pete said, looking over the delivery.

"No idea," she said, still smiling. "But they put a ton of requirements. Said to make sure only you got it, in person—" She paused and pulled out a notebook from her back pocket. Nodding, the smile fading. She tried to recover it, but faltered.

"So, my client was working on executing someone's last will and testament," she said. "One of the requirements was this be delivered to Pete Fernandez ... upon the death of Robert Harras."

# CHAPTER TWENTY-EIGHT

**D**ave Mendoza lived in a nondescript, barely furnished townhouse in Kendall, off 130th Street and 92nd Avenue. It didn't feel like a home because it wasn't one—at least not to Dave. It was one of his parents' myriad real estate holdings, and one of the few that wasn't yet gobbled up in legal wrangling. Now, it was serving as temporary housing for Pete and Kathy as well.

"He knew he was going to die."

Pete's words echoed through the small dining room, as Kathy sifted through a stack of pages across from Pete. Dave had left to pick up dinner. It promised to be a long night.

"What?" Kathy asked.

"He knew he was going to die," Pete said. "Maybe wasn't sure it'd happen in Cuba, but it was going to happen soon. Los Enfermos were probably trailing him. He saw it coming. Damn."

Pete let his head drop into his hands. The sprint that had followed Harras's death had been exhausting and full of danger, but it'd also served as a pleasant distraction from the underlying truth: that his dear friend was gone—really gone. There was no subterfuge here. No mysterious smoke and mirrors to fool their enemies. Pete had seen it happen.

But here was Robert Harras. From beyond the grave. Providing Pete with the intel he thought he'd already had. Could this file, in tandem with the missing dream book pages—be enough?

"These papers," Pete said, spreading them out in front of him, as if he were trying to soak up all the information they held at once. "This is Graciela Fernandez's file—the murder book. The police file."

"But you had that already, no?"

"I had what Alter wanted me to see," Pete said. "Which was a lot lighter than this. Like this, look—" Pete reached over and grabbed one of the pages. "This is Valdez's preliminary report, which is nowhere in Alter's file. It talks about Mosher, the first cop on the scene."

"The guy who killed himself?" Kathy asked.

Pete looked at her. "I haven't seen the crime scene photos, but I'd bet what's left of my house that there's something fuzzy about the details," he said. "Either way, Mosher wasn't in Alter's file. When I mentioned his name to her, she seemed confused. Next thing I know, he's dead, suicide."

Kathy stood up. She rubbed her hands over her growing belly. She looked tired. "That's good, but we need to figure out what else those extra pages hold. What new information there is," she said, her hands on Pete's shoulders. "And what they mean—it all means—not just for you and your mom, but for everything else."

"It's gonna be a long night."

The evening gave way to dawn, which gave way to early morning. By the time Dave had gotten out of bed and started revving up the coffeemaker, Pete had some answers. Not all the ones he needed, but some. Which was a lot more than he started with.

"Please tell me you just woke up and wanted to get an early start?" Dave asked, popping his head into the small dining room. "And just happen to be wearing the same clothes? And enjoy being surrounded by empty takeout containers?"

Pete ran a hand over his face. "No dice," he said.

Dave stepped in and took a seat across from Pete. "Okay," he said. "Then tell me you got something."

"Two things," Pete said, his voice sounding weary and worn-out. He slid a short stack of papers at Dave. "Check this out."

Dave scanned the top sheet. "It's a C.I. form," he said. "A criminal informant report. So?"

"I'm a cop's son, so a lot of this paperwork wasn't new to me. These are forms cops—detectives, usually—fill out after talking to C.I.s. Or when they want to file something," Pete said. "Pretty standard. But the name of the detective filling out the form jumped out at me."

Pete shuffled some pages and pulled out a battered folder. He opened it and pulled out what looked like half a piece of scrap paper—crumpled and old. There were dark, horror-tinged images drawn in dark pencil, with a few words written underneath.

"See that first name?" Pete asked.

"Meltzer?" Dave said.

"Yup," Pete said, dropping the page and grabbing the printout of the C.I. report. "Same name as the guy writing this report."

"Okay, definitely a clue, but—help me out here," Dave said. "What is a C.I. report doing in your mom's murder book?"

"Read it," Pete said, handing the sheet to Dave.

Dave cleared his throat. "C.I. #61183 continues to meet with subject on a regular basis," Dave said. "Relationship has become romantic but C.I. emphasizes that it remains under control. Subject is key player in criminal org and has begun divulging low-level information to C.I. during their meetings. Still early days but optimistic about progress—C.I. is aware of risks. Despite my own personal concerns, I'm willing to continue undercover operation for at least a few more months based on value and insight C.I. might be able to provide on illegal activities being perpetrated by ..."

"Keep reading," Pete said. "Don't stop."

"I know, but—"

"Say it, Dave."

"Perpetrated by the ... by the Mujica criminal organization."

Kathy yanked the black Marlins cap down low as Pete pulled onto the street.

"Ever heard of this Dan Meltzer guy before?" she asked. "Did he know your dad? I feel like every cop knew your dad."

"I never met him," Pete said. "But he's still alive. At least according to Hudson. She seemed confused about why I was asking."

"Did you tell her about Alter?" Kathy asked. "Because I'd want to know if I was her."

"I didn't. She was more interested in the Cuba stuff and why my house might have gone boom," Pete said, looking out the driver's side window. "I just couldn't do it. I don't know. I felt … bad for her?"

"Alter lied to you, not to mention pulling a gun and threatening to kill you," Kathy said. "Her getting fired is a mild punishment, I think. I vote 'bye, bitch.'"

"I'll keep that info close for now. We may need it at some point."

Pete rubbed his eyes. He felt the exhaustion wash over him. Not because of anything happening now, in the moment, but because his body was starting to wear down. The lack of sleep. The moving around. The anxiety. All his AA prayers and meditations, all his new age-y aikido spiritualism was wearing thin. He needed a meeting. He needed to slow down. But he couldn't. He wasn't sure he'd ever be able to.

"Talk to me," Kathy said.

"I keep thinking about my mom," Pete said. "About how we're slowly getting this picture of her—this idea of a person—that never existed for me. And, on some level, it's great. I'm getting to know her. On another, it feels so … sad."

"It *is* sad, Pete," she said, gripping his wrist. "It's tragic. You never knew your mother. Your father lied to you about it to protect you. She was murdered. That's a lot of shit to process all at once and, honestly, I'm surprised you're still functional. You have to breathe. You have to give yourself room to be sad, not just running to the next thing, or to the end, okay? We will get there. We will figure this out."

"To think, she was battling back these demons—this addiction— that I had," Pete said. "I feel like we could have talked about it all. I would have learned so much. And she was informing on the mob. She was so brave. It just hurts, I guess … that I'll never really know her."

"I know," Kathy said, pulling him into a tight embrace. "I know."

"How're you feeling?" Pete asked, pulling back and looking at Kathy.

"Tired, bloated, and eager to get this creature out of me," she said, not meeting his gaze. "But we're still a few months out. Assuming all goes according to plan and we, ahem, live."

"We need to figure out what we're going to do."

"In general, or between you and me?" she asked, turning to look at him. "Or what?"

"I want to make sure this kid is taken care of," Pete said. "The same way I was. Sort of. I want to make sure they have a home they can feel safe in. Parents they care about."

"Pete Fernandez, are you trying to guilt me into being your girlfriend? Because that's not high on the romance scale, I have to say," Kathy said. "Even if I am, technically, single and ready to mingle now that Marco refuses to answer my calls."

Pete winced at the joke, but pressed on. "No, this is aside from us as ... as a whatever, couple," he said. "We just need to figure out how we're going to raise this ... person."

"Really?" Kathy said with a sigh. "And here I thought I just spit it out and move on."

They smiled at each other.

She placed her hand on his. "Can we figure this case out?" Kathy said. "First? Then let's figure out how not to screw up this kid's life. Deal?"

"Deal."


Casino Miami wasn't the first place Pete would have named if asked where he'd end up meeting an ex-cop. But he'd also learned not to assume things, especially when on a case. The spacious arena was a hub for gambling, jai alai, and concerts.

As Pete entered, a jai alai game was in progress, with a sparse, disinterested crowd in the stands. Though Pete had spent most of his life in Miami, the game—which involved bouncing balls off a shared wall for players to catch in hand-held baskets—had never caught his attention. Probably because gambling was something he never took much of a shine to. He'd experienced enough risk and chaos in his day-to-day. He didn't need to wager what little he still had in his pocket.

As Pete and Kathy made their way toward a smattering of tables at the center of the venue's rainbow of slot machines and ATMs, they caught a glimpse of an older man in a light gray polo and knee-length khaki shorts. His socks were stretched well past his ankles. All of these details screamed one thing to Pete: this guy was a cop, or had been not long ago.

"Dan?" Pete said as they approached the older man.

"You rang?" Meltzer said, wheeling the rickety chair around. "Assuming you're Fernandez?"

"I am."

They shook.

"Your father was good police," Meltzer said. "Think I have an idea what this is about."

"This is my partner, Kathy Bentley," Pete said.

"Yeah, yeah, I've read your stuff—good writer," Meltzer said. "Even that newsletter thingie you write, the *New Tropical*?"

"*New Tropic*," Kathy said, with a tone that suggested she'd had to explain what *New Tropic* was more than a few times. "It's a news and culture email news—"

"Yeah, whatever," Meltzer said, waving his hand. "Look, I got some time between games. Shit, I got all the time in the world, but I do what I want, and what I want to do is drink, gamble, and watch jai alai. Hudson said you were worth talking to. That gets you in the door. The fact that you're Pedro's kid gets you at least ten minutes. The rest, my friend, is up to you."

Pete and Kathy sat down across from Meltzer.

Pete pulled out a folded piece of paper from his back pocket. "This ring any bells for you?"

Meltzer scanned the paper, then slipped on a shoddy pair of reading glasses that had been hanging from his neck. His eyes darted over the information with more speed. He nodded to himself.

"How'd you get this?" Meltzer said, looking up.

"Long story," Kathy said.

"Cute, but you're asking for my help, right?" Meltzer said. "And I'm retired, but I'm a retired cop. This is confidential stuff. I'll ask again—how'd you get this?"

"I'm not going to lie to you," Pete said. "We didn't get this by request. I honestly don't know how we got it. Our friend—Robert Harras—got it. He was ex-FBI. We just put him in the ground. Died in action. Something tells me he could pull strings we don't even know exist."

Meltzer made a grunting sound. "Non-answer, but fine," he said. "So, you want to know about this C.I.? Why?"

"Stop playing so coy," Kathy said, her eyes hot and focused. "You know who she was. We know who she was. He wants to find out about this case because it was his mom. His mother died working this angle and the only person alive who can shed some light on it is you."

Meltzer smiled slightly, taken aback by Kathy's assault.

"Please, whatever you do," Kathy said. "Do not say anything about my hormones being out of control because of this baby, okay? It just won't end well."

"Wouldn't think of it."

"Great."

"Okay, fine," Meltzer said. "Chalk it up to a cop that was raised on keeping secrets having trouble shaking his upbringing, okay? Your mom—shit, I knew her. I'd had dinner at your house, my wife, your dad, his wife. Hell, maybe I met you when you were a sprout. So, it hit close. She'd left your dad—or he'd asked her to leave. The drinking had gotten too bad. Drugs creeped into the picture. Your dad wasn't having it. Didn't want anything like that in the house."

Pete felt his throat close up. He closed his eyes for a moment.

"So she goes out on her own, parties hard, living with her friend," Meltzer said. "Next thing I know, she's working at this jazz club, Terraza, which was a pretty hot venue at the time—but was mainly a Mujica front. Now, that's my beat—I work Vice—gangs and narcotics. Well, worked. Which, look, I don't need to tell you that being a straight cop in Miami in the '80s was basically like being a unicorn, you know? A rare gem. Few others, that I knew about. Your dad. Varela, that cop that got fucked over. Broche, for a little while. But that was it.

"Anyway, I'm working my beat, trying to keep my nose clean, and shit, I see Gracie Fernandez getting down with the wrong crowd. I should have just raised the flag to Pedro and called it a day. Let him handle it. But instead, I reach out. I talk to her. She promises me—I remember it so well, sitting in my car, parked outside of that bar, she's wearing this tight dress, eye shadow smudged, drunk—she promises me 'Dan, Dan, don't sweat it, this is a phase. Let me shake it off and I'll be home to my husband and boy in a month, tops. Let me go.' So, I fell for it. She was my friend, too. Then it became, well, lemme check in on her. Let me make sure she's okay because Pedro has no idea what's going on—"

"What do you mean?" Pete asked.

"Exactly that. Pedro was in the dark. Was always in the dark."

"About what she was doing?" Kathy said. "He must have had some idea."

"Gracie was smart, too smart," Meltzer said. "She put up a good front. He knew something was hinky, but nothing deeper. Didn't know she was sleeping around, the drugs ... he just thought she was still knocking it back. Plus, he was busy. What, were you—a toddler? Guy's plate was pretty damn full."

Pete stood up suddenly, his body lurching over the table as he gripped the old man's shirt tightly.

"What do you mean?" Pete said. He felt his throat freeze up. He couldn't get his question out.

"Pete, calm down," Kathy said. Pete could feel her hands trying to pull him back, but he ignored the tug. His eyes locked on Meltzer's fading gray irises, his eyebrows widening in panic. A few people around them started to take notice.

"Who told my father how my mother died?" Pete said, each word short and loud, like a bass drum beat signaling the beginning of a march.

"Kid, are you really that out of the loop?" Meltzer said, fixing his collar, a sad smile on his face. "Your dad—one of the best cops I'd ever met. One of the best goddamned people I ever had the pleasure of knowing ... he had no fucking clue, man. He thought your mom died alone in some fleabag hotel, drunk off her ass and zonked to the gills on every kind of drug. He didn't know she was killed. Didn't know someone choked her out. If he lied to you, kid, it wasn't to hide that. It was to hide the fact she was a fall-down drunk and a junkie.

"Broche spearheaded it," Meltzer continued, after Pete had had a chance to pace around the table for a few moments, staring at the walls and shaking his head.

"Pedro's partner?" Kathy said. "Why?"

"Sometimes the truth is worse than fiction," Meltzer said with a shrug as Pete returned to his seat. "Valdez gets to the scene and realizes what the hell is going on, so he calls Broche. Couldn't bring himself to tell Pedro his wife was dead. Broche came down to the scene and pulled rank on Valdez. Said there was no way on Earth

Pedro Fernandez could find out about this. Valdez pushed back—it wasn't his intent to keep Pedro in the dark forever. It was admirable. He was another good cop. Some of the uniforms balked, too, like that guy Mosher."

"Mosher—he died recently," Kathy said, thinking back. "Overdose."

"Yeah, that smelled like shit to me," Meltzer said. "Guy had no vices when I knew him. Except coffee and seltzer."

"I thought …" Pete said, ignoring the conversation, his mouth a tight line. "I just thought he'd lied to me."

Kathy put a hand on his arm, gripping it.

"Think about that," Meltzer said. "It's a question I used to ask myself all the time, whenever I was on a case—be it narcotics, patrol, murder, whatever: Who benefits? Who gets a few steps ahead if you're spending your nights tossing and turning, wondering why your dad kept the deepest, darkest secret from you for decades?"

"You think it was a trap?" Kathy asked.

"Yeah," Pete said, looking down at his hands. "I should have known. I should have seen it coming. My father would never do that. Not if he'd known the truth."

Pete slammed his open palm on the table, the slapping sound echoing across the room.

"Fuck," he said.

"For what it's worth, you mom was a helluva C.I.," Meltzer said, looking at his watch. "She was getting close. She was feeding me good stuff. It's what got her killed, I think. I'd bet money on it. I kept her name out of it, of course. But it just takes one bad cop to figure it out and sell the info to the highest bidder."

"Who was she talking to?" Pete asked, his voice hitting a desperate, frantic pitch Kathy had never heard before. "Who was she seeing? Mujica?"

"Wish I knew for sure. That's the rub, kid," Meltzer said. "It was all deep cover. Maybe it was Mujica. I know the guy was no angel. But she was scared. So scared that if she revealed the name, even before she was through, she'd get killed."

"You let her die," Pete said, his eyes slits, his jaw clenched.

"Pete, come on," Kathy said.

"No, no," Meltzer said, nodding. "He's not wrong. I should have been … better at it. I just took it for granted. She was, well, she was a cop's wife. She knew the risks. She was feeding me such good intel, I ..." Meltzer's head hung down. The old man looked spent.

"I thought she had a handle on it, is all," Meltzer said, glancing up at Pete and Kathy.

That's when Pete noticed the man. Tall, muscular and wearing a dark jacket and skullcap. In Miami. His skin was pale from what little Pete could see under the large, reflective shades. At first Pete thought he was just wandering past, but he lingered by the entrance, shooting furtive glances at them. Now he was heading their way.

"You expecting someone?" Pete asked.

"What? Me? Who would want—"

"Gun!" Kathy yelled, her eyes catching the same figure, except she'd seen the glint of metal before Pete did.

Kathy ducked as Meltzer awkwardly tried to crouch under the table.

The man stopped, raised the weapon and sent two bullets in the retired cop's direction. The soft *schtoop-schtoop* sound of the silencer was followed by Meltzer's low, surprised groan as Pete yanked him from the line of fire. They both landed, hard on the grimy jai alai floor.

"You okay?" Pete asked, out of breath.

"Get that sonovabitch," Meltzer said, his voice a wheeze. He tried to get up and fell back instead. But he was alive.

Pete stood up and followed the man, who was entering a dumbfounded crowd, still trying to react to what had happened.

Pete thought he heard something—Kathy?—behind him. A warning. But he didn't have time to go back. And he was tired. Tired of the guns. Tired of the surprises. Tired of the blood. The man was trying to walk through the crowd casually, but at a good clip. He hadn't noticed Pete behind him, not yet—probably thinking he'd stay and care for Meltzer, or wait until the cops arrived.

But the time for waiting was long past. Pete could feel the strands weaving together, around him, pulling at his limbs, tightening around his chest and throat. If he waited—if he took another minute to ponder and plan—he'd be lost. Whoever this man was, he was a small step closer to the truth.

He caught another glimpse of the man, pushing the door that would lead him out onto Northwest 37th Avenue.

Pete started into a sprint. People moved out of his way, looks of surprise and annoyance and fear as he closed the gap. The door began to close and that's when the man—who'd shed his glasses and hat—saw him. His face was an enigma to Pete—another thug, another killer, another problem—but that didn't matter.

Before the man could react, Pete had sent a kick into his midsection, knocking the man out into the street.

He rolled back up fast, but Pete expected that. Expected the gun pointed at his face. He swatted it away, his hand hitting the middle of the man's arm and sending the gun into the nearby grass.

"You should run," the man said, panting.

"Not anymore," Pete said as he sent another kick into the man's stomach. The man folded into himself and Pete sent his knee on a one-way trip to the man's face. His head snapped back with the contact, his body twisting to one side and hitting the concrete, a throaty groan capped off by a loud crunch as he landed.

Pete leaned down and gripped the man's shirt, pulling him up so their faces were close together. "Who sent you?" he said.

"Fuck you, man," the thug spat back, his head lolling back, barely conscious.

"You think Mujica's gonna let you live when he finds out you've failed?"

The man's eyes flickered.

Pete heard footsteps behind him. Kathy's voice in the background.

"Surprised I know what's going on?" Pete said.

"You don't know shit, motherfucker," the man said, but his words lacked conviction. He was bloodied and beaten. He'd be going to jail. Suddenly whatever loyalty he had was in question.

"Tell me," Pete said. "Who sent you? You're dead either way."

The man shook his head again. His entire posture was pathetic. Sagging into Pete now. He was broken. "It was a Mujica guy, I know that," the man said.

"What did he want? Why are they after me?"

"After you?" the man said, a crooked smile on his bloodied and bruised face. "Boy, they're playing with you now. If they wanted to get you, you'd be long dead."

"**T**his is the part where you tell me what the fuck is going on," Nisha Hudson said, leaning over the interview room table, palms down. "Because I am a tired woman a few months from retirement and you are not making it easy for me, my friend."

Pete gave her a "what can I do?"-style shrug. Not the best idea.

She stepped back and crossed her arms. "Listen, I'm not some old-school Cubano cop with lots of nostalgia for your dad, okay?" she said. "I will not turn a blind eye to the shit you're pulling just because I used to knock back cervezas with Pedro. You've been shot at, your house exploded, you almost created an international incident … I am getting a lot of heat to lock you up for *something*, just to make things calm down."

"Do I need to get a lawyer?" Pete asked, his voice tired and irritated. "Am I a suspect in something?"

Hudson clicked her tongue in frustration. "Listen, let me help you, all right? I've got a retired cop in another interview room refusing to talk. Your girlfriend's even worse—girl has some bite," she said. "Plus, I have a suspect who's suddenly lawyered up with someone Marco Rubio couldn't afford. I have witnesses screaming at me about an active shooter at the fucking jai alai. I have news crews all over the place. Give me something to work with here."

"It's Mujica," Pete said. "It seems like he's making a play for the drug trade in Miami."

"Mujica?" Hudson said with a frown. "I'm not in Vice, I'm Homicide, but that sounds wrong to me. Thought the guy was just a numbers runner."

"When Los Enfermos went down, for what I thought was the last time, with all the cult stuff last year—"

"There was a void, right," Hudson said. "But, again—Mujica trying to fill it doesn't track."

"Why not?"

"You went to Cuba to find your girl, Beatriz or Emily, right?" Hudson said. "Why was she there?"

"She was taking a meeting—with La Madrina, I think," Pete said. "To, I dunno, get her foot in the door with the flow of drugs."

"Right, well, first off—I don't think Emily Blanco is ready for prime time when it comes to being a gangster," Hudson said. "Do you?"

"I don't know."

"Okay, so—if she's trying to horn in on the drug trade, is she working with Mujica? Doesn't seem like it, right?"

"She's working with the leftovers of Los Enfermos," Pete said. "They're reforming, somehow. Cuba is home turf for them."

Hudson paced around the room, hands behind her back. "Okay, let's leave that on the imaginary chalkboard for now," she said. "Now, tell me—why would Mujica care if you're talking to a retired cop?"

"Because Meltzer was running a C.I.—my mother—before she died," Pete said, the words echoing in his head. "It's what got her killed. If I get closer to that, I get closer to pinning a body on Mujica."

"Huh, well, you're not bad," Hudson said, finally cracking a slight smile. "But humor me for a second. Are you invincible?"

"What?"

"Answer me—are you an escape artist? Are you impossible to kill?"

"No, well—"

"Right, okay, so do you think that Alvaro Mujica, a badass, ex–Bay of Pigs motherfucker who probably has more bodies on his résumé than I have pounds to lose, would have trouble putting you in the ground if he felt like it?"

Pete didn't respond.

"Didn't think so."

"If it's not Mujica, then who?" Pete asked.

"Not saying it's not," she said. "I just don't think whoever it is wants to kill you."

She sat down across from Pete, her voice now hushed and conspiratorial.

"You know what I do in situations like this? When it feels like I'm tangled up in wires and string and I'm never gonna find the source?" she said. "I simplify. I take a step back and go bit by bit, even if I have to start over. If I'm listening right, you were brought into this by Mujica, right? He asked you to find this Beatriz woman. You found her, but you didn't find what he wanted, right?"

"He didn't say what it was," Pete said.

"You're smarter than that," Hudson said. "I'm sure there were things he wanted. Information. Whatever. But Alvaro Mujica is an old man. His son was just murdered. You don't think the question he wants answered before he flops over is the truth about his son? Who killed his boy? So he can kill them?"

Pete got up.

"Was there something or someone you missed?" Hudson said, looking up at him. "That might make a difference."

"Thanks, yeah, I think I know what's next," Pete said. "Can I go?"

Hudson responded with a quick nod. "I'd say 'Keep out of trouble,' but I don't think that's in your playbook."

# SPIRIT IN THE DARK

*November 15, 1983*

"They're running drugs out of the bar."

The words hung in the front seat after Graciela spoke them to Dan Meltzer.

The car, a rusty Pontiac, reeked of cigarettes and takeout. They'd parked a few blocks down from Terraza, the Miami streetlights barely illuminating the desolate sidewalks and storefronts around them. If you were walking around downtown Miami this late at night, you were either looking to cop or up to no good.

"You sure?" Meltzer asked before taking a long sip from his coffee. "That's a big thing, Gracie. Real big."

"I'm sure," she said. "It's a front. Fuck. I don't know how I missed this. I've been so far up my own ass I didn't even realize the mess I'd gotten myself into."

"Does Pedro know?"

"No, no, no way," Graciela said. "I mean, he knows where I work, but—"

"Then he has an idea," Meltzer said. "What about that woman, Diane? Your roommate?"

"I can't even talk to her about it," Graciela said, rubbing her palms on her work slacks. "She's so caught up in her own life and work … she wouldn't even know what to make of it, if she believed me. This is bad. I'm tangled up."

"Take a deep breath, okay?" Meltzer said, turning toward her.

He looked exhausted. His face gaunt, dark bags under his eyes. This was weighing on him, too. He was putting his colleague's wife on the line to crack a case. A career-making case, but still.

"I don't know what to do," she said.

"Tell me who the boyfriend is and we pull you out tonight," Meltzer said, his tone halfhearted. He knew what Graciela's response would be.

"I can't," she said. "Not yet."

"Gracie, whoever this guy is—he's not a good person, all right? He's mixed up with some bad people. He doesn't love you. He doesn't want to help you," Meltzer said. "At least let me put some guys on you, take some surveillance pictures … anything."

"I don't know."

She thought back to him. Her boyfriend. This man she thought she might be starting to love. But that was fading. She just couldn't hold onto it anymore. He seemed aware, too. Graciela was pretty sure he was married. Maybe had a kid. He'd been coming to Terraza less and less. The meetings—not dates anymore, who was she kidding?—had become perfunctory and scheduled. The passion whittled away slowly. The routine was locked in: he'd invite her to a hotel, they'd fuck, he'd leave some money for her and walk out while she slept off whatever high or low had dragged her into the room … like she was some kind of whore. The money helped, sure. She could always use it for … something. But the lingering feeling—the sense of constant, ever-present dread—was always there. She just wanted it to end. She just wanted to black out. To go to sleep and not wake up.

"I can't get out now," Graciela said. "I don't even know where I'd go—what I'd do. I'm a fucking mess, Dan. Can you take me home, please?"

He started the car and they were on their way, the radio silent, everything quiet except the sounds of the streets.

*I'm a fucking mess.*

She was sick. She was more than a mess. She'd thrown up blood again last night. She wasn't sure why. She just hoped it'd get better on its own. She wasn't sure it would.

She didn't even feel like drinking anymore. When she put the bottle to her mouth, she felt it pulling her in, taking something out of her, out of her insides. It was taking part of her. She wasn't Gracie anymore. She didn't even do the basics, anymore. She barely showed up at work. When she did, she ended up in trouble for screwing up an order or breaking a glass—on a good day.

She wasn't dumb. She knew the problem. But she couldn't stop. She couldn't stop using. The sex. This life. She would tell herself, hunched over the toilet or crying on the street, that it's for a greater good—that she'll help the cops take down this … whatever it is. But that was a lie. She couldn't stop because she didn't want to. It was getting harder and harder to even get a slight buzz. The thrill of it was dead. So she was left to chase down the numbness, and a few inches from that numbness was the void.

Who would love her now? Who would want to share a home with her? What kind of mother could she even try to be for Pete? She felt like nothing. She didn't deserve anything.

*I want to die.*

She must have dozed off. The next thing she remembered, Meltzer was shaking her gently.

"We're here," he said. "Keep your eyes open, Gracie."

She nodded, patted his hand and found her way into the apartment. She didn't remember getting inside.

She woke up on the floor. She hadn't made it to the couch. Her head throbbed—like a truck was backing up into her face repeatedly. She could see sunlight sneaking through the blinds, each slit of light stabbing her eyes.

"Gracie, Graciela—"

It was Diane. She was shaking her, patting her face gently, holding something in her hand.

"Who—what?"

"It's Pedro," she said, her voice clipped and annoyed. She handed Graciela the phone and walked off. She was still in her bathrobe.

Graciela had no idea what time it was. "Hello?" Even she could hear how rough and sluggish her voice sounded. "Yeah?"

"It's me," Pedro said, sounding distant and formal. He knew she was drunk. Had to know. Always knew. "I wanted to ... ah ... It's Pete."

"Is, ohmygod is he —"

"Graciela, he's fine, he's fine." Pedro said. "He's been making gurgling noises, sounds—I thought it was nothing, but they're starting to—"

He stopped. A muffled sound on the other end.

*Was he crying?*

"What is it, Pedrito?" she said, almost pleading. "What is it?"

"He's talking, *mi amor,*" Pedro said, the last two words slicing into her. "Not just words but full sentences—almost, I don't know, conversations, and..."

She couldn't form a response. The tears starting to flow, the choking sobs bubbling up inside her.

"He said he, well," Pedro said. "He said 'I want to see my mama.'"

# CHAPTER TWENTY-NINE

"**W**e have to start at zero."

The words lingered over Pete and Kathy as they drove toward Miami Beach on the expressway.

"Well, I have to start at zero," Pete continued. "Hudson was right."

"Pete Fernandez, you are not putting me on the sideline," Kathy said. "That's not your call to make."

Pete took A1A down to Alton Road without responding.

He pulled into the parking lot and left the car idling. Pete stepped out of the car and opened the passenger side door for Kathy.

Slower, weighed down, Kathy struggled a bit to get out of the seat. She gave Pete a sharp glance as she straightened up. "Not a word," she said. "And where the hell are we? Why aren't we back at Dave's?"

"We are at Dave's," Pete said. "One of many spots he has. I told him to pack a bag for you."

Kathy started to respond, but Pete raised a hand in defeat.

"Please, don't argue with me on this," he said. "We're in trouble. Bad. Someone is out to get me, maybe both of us, and I can't think of what I'd do if something happened to you. To our baby. I'll stay in touch. We'll be linked up. But I need to figure this out on my own, and the only way I can do that is if I know you're safe."

Kathy crossed her arms. "You tricked me into this, whatever, safe house situation," she said.

"I did."

"Where are you going next?" she asked. "What can I do from here?"

"I have to go back to where this all started," Pete said. "Retrace our steps. Make sure we didn't miss anything."

"Oh, we missed something," Kathy said. "Something big, if these guys are gunning for us—or trying to make it seem like they are."

They both turned in response to the light footsteps behind them. Dave.

"That shootout at the Jai Alai is all over the news," Dave said. "They didn't name you, but the cops are looking for two 'persons of interest.'"

"I'm not that interesting," Kathy said.

Pete let out a dry laugh. "Guess talking to Hudson wasn't enough," Pete said.

"Dave, can you give us a minute?" Kathy said.

Their friend nodded and headed toward the elevators near the far end of the garage.

"Is this where you kill me?"

"I should," Kathy said pacing around the parked car. "But you're right. Which, trust me, pains me to vocalize."

"Wait, can you say that again?" Pete said, cupping a hand around his ear. "I'm 'bright'? Or, wait, did you say—"

"Shut up," she said, stepping toward him. She pulled him in fast, her mouth on his. The kiss was quiet at first—subtle, almost chaste. But soon they were locked in each other, a release as much as an embrace, finally accepting what they'd been dancing around for what seemed like an endless season.

"Well," Pete said, pulling back for a moment, before kissing her again. "I—I wasn't expecting—"

"Be quiet," she said, her voice soft, as she peppered him with quick, staccato kisses on the mouth, as if she were unsure when they'd be together like this again. "Just let this be, okay?"

"Okay," he said, wrapping his arms around her, squeezing her into him. "We're okay."

251

"I think so," she said, sniffling slightly as she ran a hand through Pete's close-cropped hair. "I hope so."

They kissed again, then blended into one another. They held on, whispering between moments of affection, the tears coming now, like they were waking from a nightmare that felt all too real.

# CHAPTER THIRTY

The facts scrolled through Pete's brain like a fast-moving stock ticker.

His mother had been murdered. He'd known that. Potentially by someone she'd been dating while living apart from his father. That man was somehow part of the Mujica organization. Possibly Mujica himself.

Her murder had been covered up almost immediately—thanks to the efforts of Carlos Broche, partner to Pete's dad, and Osvaldo Valdez, the Homicide cop on the scene. For years, Pete's father believed his wife had died from her own vices, and he had softened the truth to their son, making Pete believe his mother had died from complications in childbirth.

But she'd been an addict. A drunk. A mess. Like Pete.

Pete didn't resent his father. He understood the man. His intentions were good. As were those of the elder cop, Valdez.

Carlos Broche? Not so much.

The man had been like an uncle to Pete—he'd known him as far back as he could remember. Burly, quick with a curse or jab, a bit unkempt, but always around to lend a hand and support Pedro Fernandez and his small family.

But Carlos Broche had secrets. Like many officers and detectives on the Miami force who lived complex, double lives.

Broche paid the ultimate price—his face blown off as Pete faced off against the original Silent Death at the *Miami Times* printing press. Pete had thought that was the end. Tragic, unfortunate, but over.

*Or was it?*

As the case grew more complex, one thing Pete and Kathy realized was the tenuous, perhaps fuzzy line connecting the case that brought them together—that of the mob gun-for-hire known as the Silent Death—with the gang that seemed to haunt their every waking moment: Los Enfermos, an evolving, deadly, and regenerating drug cartel.

Could the new Silent Death be part of Los Enfermos? Were they tied to Mujica somehow? And why did Pete feel like it all pointed back to his own past? To his own mother?

It was time to find out. But as Hudson had advised, Pete was starting from the beginning. He was starting with Javier Mujica. Or at least someone that knew him well.

He parked his car behind a black Hyundai and walked to the front door. The lights were on.

Devon Owens was home.

arras's packet of information—the complete Graciela murder book—came with a note. A hasty printout that only featured a few lines:

*Feeling some heat. Not sure why. But can't risk you not getting this if I can't hand them to you. Call me a paranoid old man. Use your brain, kid.*

Pete's eyes had glassed over reading the note. Hearing Harras's husky voice chiding Pete from the great beyond. But the former FBI man had been right—the heat was on both of them, and it stretched into the streets of Havana, where Harras died. Pete knew he had to retrace his own steps if there was any chance for him to shake the gunmen after him and find out who killed his mother.

That meant finding out who killed Javier Mujica. And finding Emily Sprague-Blanco.

It all started with Javier Mujica. But Mujica was dead and Emily was in the wind. However, there was one piece of the puzzle Pete hadn't looked over. Javier Mujica's old manager, Devon Owens.

Pete rang the doorbell and waited. He heard footsteps approaching seconds before the door opened. A thin, reedy man, well over fifty, stood across the threshold. He gave Pete a slow, lazy once-over.

"Yes?"

"Devon Owens?"

"Son, you came here," the man said. "To my house. That means you tell me who you are first."

"Pete Fernandez. I'm a private—"

"Say no more," he said. "Come in. Was wondering when your ass would show up."

Pete followed the man into the stuffy, dark house. The smell of dust and paper flooded Pete's nostrils, and from what little he could make out, the cramped home was loaded with piles of books, records, and errant papers, with seemingly little order to why things landed where.

Owens motioned for a seat on a gray, grimy couch after restacking a few of the piles, making room for a tiny seat. He took a spot across from Pete.

"Get you anything?"

"No," Pete said, sitting down. "I don't think this will take too long."

"Angel Menendez sent you, right?"

"How'd you know?"

"Only guy that seems to cover the scene, or give enough of a shit to know who manages who," Owens said. "And, well, he called me."

Pete let out a sharp laugh. "Warned you about his former colleague?"

"In a way," Owens said with a smile. "Said you were sharp. Looking for background on Javi. I said I would share what I could, but I also wasn't going to stick my neck out all that far, if you know what I mean."

"Care to enlighten me?"

"You know Javi's last name," Owens said, his face blank. "You know his daddy didn't like his only son spending his time on the piano instead of the family business. You think he's going to take kindly to the man teaching his boy how to make a living on the keys? No sir. But I also know talent, I know the scene. I know my way around the piano, too. We were a good match, Javi and me. He had the spark, just needed the direction. We did well for a while there."

"What happened?"

"Slow down, son, slow down," Owens said. He got up and walked toward the back of the house. When he returned he had two bottles of Heineken. He offered one to Pete, who shook his head no.

"Not a drinker? Smart man."

"Doesn't agree with me."

"Heh, yeah, been there myself," Owens said. "Should've listened ten, maybe twenty years ago. Now, well, now it just feels too late, right?"

"Never too late," Pete said. "It's never too late to change your life for the better."

Owens's eyes widened slightly.

"You a twelve-stepper, huh? That's admirable. Maybe down the line. Maybe if the headaches get worse and the money gets tighter."

"It'll happen," Pete said, not wanting to press too hard. "Just a question of when."

Owens raised his bottle. "Well, here's to when, then."

He took a long pull of the liquid before continuing.

"Javi was my protégé, like a son to me," Owens said, his voice going soft, his eyes scanning the quickly emptying bottle of beer as if he was looking for some secret message. "I found him playing open mic nights, slapping out mediocre covers. But I saw something in there. A spark. Talent. Something I had once. An energy, even through the inexperience and the hesitation. I'd managed people before. I'd been all around the world, myself. In groups, solo, whatever. I was a touring musician. Not a big name, not a headliner—there was no Devon Owens Quartet. But I got by.

"So I got into managing, mentoring at first," Owens said. "But Javi was something else. We clicked right away. We were the same person. He hated his dad. Wanted to be his own man. Now, I never knew my father—he ran off long before my memory kicked in. But I knew that fire. I knew that hate. And it could drive you, man. It could make you do amazing things if you let it. Next thing I know, Javi'd moved into my house, we were jamming, drinking, making music every damn night—and I was working the phones. Getting him some real bookings. Some real fans. He was sparkin.' People started to buzz about him. Then he formed the first group—that group was tight. You could warm your hands on that stage, they were so hot."

"You set him up with a tour, right? A package?"

"Yeah, yeah, a few of them," Owens said. "But that last one, that was a special tour. We burned through Europe, man. It felt so good, watching him and his crew. Was almost like I was up there, too. And well, Europe! London, Paris, Madrid ... can't get better than that. The drink, the women, the music ... I felt like I was in my twenties again. Felt like I could take on the world."

"Then he met Emily."

"She came on strong, man, let me tell you," Owens said, leaning back. "But it never struck me as odd, you know? It felt genuine. It wasn't a play. She had no idea who he was, not at first. She was just living there, in Spain. We were making our way through and we saw her in—let me remember—Barcelona, yeah. They hit it off immediately. But it was a bad mix, too strong. Got sour fast."

"They argued?"

"No, she just took over," Owens said, shaking his head, as if trying to forget a bad dream. "Before I could get a handle on anything, the tour was cancelled, the band had broken up, and Javi wanted to come back here to Miami. He didn't even explain way. Just said it was time for a change and he wanted Emily to manage him. That was that."

"What happened to Javi after that?"

"I only know what I heard, okay? And some rings true, some doesn't," Owens said. "But he fell back into bad habits. Now, I wasn't any kind of teetotaler, but I knew when to stop. Knew when it was time to fall into bed if I was gonna make a gig the next night. Once I was gone, once his bandmates were gone? Javi went wild. Not just drinking, either. Drugging, benders that would last for weeks."

"What was Emily doing?"

"No idea," Owens said with a shrug. "She got him a residency, some gigs. Was talking about building a new band around him—but by then, it seemed like things had gone cold between them."

"What do you mean?"

"I came by their place—that bar where Javi was playing—a few nights before ... before the accident, before they got to him," Owens said, his voice cracking slightly. "It was all nice, diplomatic, and friendly. They needed some information from me, wanted to, y'know, 'pick my brain,' and I said sure, bygones, and figured I'd get a free meal, fix whatever drama there was and move on with my life. But it was all business with them. No affection. They basically sat at different ends of the table."

"What did Javi want?"

"Javi? He didn't want nothing," Owens said. "It was his girl who was doing all the talking. You know, dancing around—'How are you?' 'Been busy?' 'How is your family?'—before cutting to what she wanted, like a shark, circling around, making it seem calm and peaceful, until it wasn't."

Pete waited. He inched forward in his seat.

"See, when I was managing Javi, I knew he was a junkie and a drunk," Owens said, licking his lips. "Never let him touch a cent I didn't see coming out of my pocket, okay? Shady? Maybe. I don't care. But it kept that kid correct, kept him tipsy but not falling over. High but not comatose. And all his earnings, all that touring money, was still resting in an account, collecting interest. Now, when Javi said, 'Devon, it's time we part ways,' I was ready to just hand over the account number and call it a day. But he never asked, and I was kind of pissed, I admit. Why should I bend over backwards to give this kid this money? He can come to me. Hell, send your daddy to come shake me down. And I needed to live, you hear? I needed to eat. So I dipped into that. Fed myself. Clothed myself. Took care of myself while I waited for the next thing."

"But they found out."

"She found out," Owens said. "And she was mad, boy. She needed that money, she said. Right now. Life or death. Didn't I care about Javi and all that."

"What did she need it for, though?"

"She wouldn't say, not right away, at least. But I'm a slippery snake, man. I don't just hand over the keys to my car and hope you'll bring it back. And, eventually, she let me know. She was that desperate for that money. As if her life depended on it."

Pete leaned forward. "What was it for, Devon?" he asked. "Was she involved in something bad?"

Owens scoffed. "She was a paper gangster," he said, a bit of fire in his words. "Amateur. She wasn't bad. Good-looking girl, smart, college educated. Kind of woman who has a career, drives a new car every year, gets a mani-pedi whenever the fuck. Has a family. Or had one. But here she was, she was playing with the big boys, trying to act all hard and slick. But I could see her coming from a mile away."

Pete started to repeat the question, but was interrupted by Owens.

"She told me, eyes wide as two twin moons, 'Devon, we are in serious trouble. I need that money. I need to make this deal or Javi and I are as good as dead. Do you want to see this man—who you love like a son—dead? Do you?'"

# CHAPTER THIRTY-ONE

**M**ujica.

It all pointed back to him. But could the old gangster murder his own son? What would drive a father to do such a thing?

*Nothing. Unless you're a mobster. And your son has betrayed you.*

Pete dialed the number as he sped down Le Jeune Road toward Miracle Mile. This couldn't wait.

"We're good, okay," Dave said, his voice sleepy. It was late. "You can skip the hourly check-ins, she is totally—"

"Dave, I'm not calling about that," Pete said. "I need a favor. A tough one."

"Shoot."

"What are you hearing about the cartels? About drugs coming into Miami?"

Pete hated himself for asking. Hated that he was forcing his friend, an addict suffering from some form of PTSD, to relive the pain of the last year. But he needed to know. Dave would understand.

"What do you mean? You gotta be more specific—"

"I'm hearing there was a deal of some kind going down, something big, around the time Mujica's son was killed," Pete said. "Trying to line these things up."

The other end of the line was quiet for a beat.

"There was a lag of time, after the stuff with the—with the cult last year. I was hearing Los Enfermos were gone, dead," Dave said, the words halted and pained. "There was a void. Lots of people vying to be the funnel—the contact for the Colombian cartels, for La Madrina. No idea who—but I heard rumors even the New York families were sniffing around. But you knew this."

"I did," Pete said. "But talking to Javier's old manager added a piece I didn't see. We knew Emily had some kind of information from her dead husband, Rick. We assume it was a connect with the Colombians. Then it turns out she needs money to close some kind of deal. Maybe with someone else? The Colombians? She's worried they're gonna get killed. Then Javi does get killed—Emily is on the run, and Salerno ends up dead, too, while some guy looking like the Silent Death is back, gunning for me and Emily. I'm trying to wrap my head around this before ... well—"

"Before you end up dead, I get it," Dave said, his voice lowered. *Trying to hide the conversation from Kathy.*

"And someone in the Mujica organization, maybe Mujica himself, knows something about my mother's murder," Pete said, seeing the disparate pieces drift toward each other, slowly forming something clearer—some taking longer to fit, others snapping into place with little resistance. "I have to go to the source. There's no time—no chance—for anything else."

"Wait, what? To Mujica—again?" Dave asked. "No, you can't—"

"No, not Mujica," Pete said. "But close enough."

He tapped his phone display and slid it back into his pocket. He punched the radio switch and let the opening chords of Sharon Van Etten churn out of the car's tinny speakers. Her voice crooning about a comeback kid.

It was time to circle back. Time to close the loop.

**I** was surprised when you called," Eddie Rosen said, stepping into the light. They were standing on the fringes of Morningside Park, a large multipurpose waterfront park northeast of the city's Design

District. Rosen had picked the location. Pete wasn't clear on why—and he didn't care.

"Seems like you've been very busy," Rosen said, trying to fill the silence.

"I need answers," Pete said. "And your boss doesn't seem inclined to share what he knows with me unless I come back with answers on Javier's death."

"Well?" Rosen asked. "Do you have anything? Or did you just feel like wasting my time tonight? You know this is a busy time for me."

"Basel season?" Pete asked. "Get to put your art dealer hat on?"

"Yes, but not just that," Rosen said. "This is tiresome. I don't think we're finding any closure on Javi's death, and you constantly picking at the scab doesn't help me. I need my boss to move on. We have business to attend to."

"I'm not going away."

"I can see that," Rosen said, frowning. "Believe me. So, again—what do you want?"

"Mujica," Pete said. "He lied to me. I'm not sure how, or the specifics, but I need to talk to him. Face to face. About my mother."

"Your mother?" Rosen said, a scoff escaping his mouth. "What?"

"He owned the bar where she worked," Pete said. "Her murder was covered up, too. Miami PD didn't want my father to find out the—"

Rosen shook his head.

"Pete, Pete, listen to yourself," Rosen said. "You, of all people should know better. This is a big zero, okay? Do you really think the Miami police were altruistic in their efforts to hide those details? Who did you talk to?"

Pete didn't respond.

"How many good cops do you know that worked on the force back then?" Rosen said, stepping closer. "Three? Four? Your dad, Gaspar Varela, Valdez ... that's it. Your dad's partner was taking a payout. Orlando Posada was running Los Enfermos. Do you think they wanted your dad to go hot and heavy, trying to find who killed his wife, if it put their livelihoods at risk?"

Pete shook his head.

"Yes," Rosen said. "Look, you're the detective here, not me. Who'd you talk to, Meltzer?"

Rosen didn't wait for Pete to respond.

"Dan Meltzer was a good cop," Rosen said. "But that ended long before your mother was killed. Hell, it was long before you were even born. Context is important, Pete."

"You don't know what you're talking about."

"Then why did you call me?" Rosen asked. "Just to hear me pontificate? Just to ignore me? I don't think so. Look at the pieces, Pete. Think. This isn't about finding a person with a painting. My boss, he can buy a museum's worth of old Cuban paintings. But what can't he buy? What can't he get? Knowledge. Your friend, Emily, she has that. And he wants it."

"What does Emily know?"

"The truth," Rosen said. "All of it."

A sharp breeze cut through the humid Miami night, and the park felt much less desolate to Pete.

Rosen looked around, his cool demeanor wiped away by nerves.

"You came alone, right?"

"Yes, why?"

"I shouldn't be here," Rosen said, pacing around, hands in his pockets. "You've put me in a really bad spot. Again."

"Wait," Pete said, grabbing Rosen's arm as he started to walk away. "You can't just leave."

"Oh?"

"I need to know, Eddie," Pete said, trying to keep his voice from pleading but failing. "Who did this? Who killed my mother? Why are they after me now?"

"You're the detective, Pete," Rosen said. "Shouldn't be hard for you to figure out."

Rosen pulled his arm free and walked toward his car. He didn't look back.

Diane Crowther closed her Cadillac's driver's side door and walked toward her front porch. Her footsteps *clack-clacking* on the concrete walkway. It was well past midnight. Crowther clutched her bag as she scanned the dark, empty front lawn. She stopped a few feet from the front steps when she heard the voice, low, menacing, but familiar.

"You lied to me."

She turned around, a short gasp escaping her mouth. She could barely make the figure out, but she knew who it was. Had been expecting him for some time.

"I had to," she said, her voice breathy and hesitant, as if waiting on her brain to send the right signal. "I'm—look, of course I'm sorry."

Pete stepped forward. Crowther gasped. He knew why. He looked bad. Ragged. Sleep had become a side gig, something he did between movements. He couldn't remember the last full, sit-down meal he'd had. The bloodshot eyes more red than white.

He'd kept moving after his run-in with Rosen. Moving and searching. Digging. Retracing the steps he'd taken before—the ones he could. It all went back to Graciela. Graciela and Diane—her best friend.

"Crowther isn't your married name," Pete said. "Is it?"

"Of course it is," she said. "I met my husband—started over. Got away from that life."

"How is he?" Pete asked. "Or, better said—where is he?"

Crowther hesitated. Pete kept going.

"He doesn't exist," Pete said. "You never married. You changed your name. It's the kind of thing most people wouldn't check. But when a nosy private eye—the son of the woman you knew decades ago—comes sniffing around, you had to think fast, right? Give him just enough so he'd leave you alone and not put this whole, cozy life in jeopardy. How am I doing?"

"How dare you—"

"You hid your tracks as well as someone with your means could," Pete said. "But I've been doing this a while. Maybe five or six years ago, this would have slipped by. But not today. Back in the day, you were struggling to get by—barely paying rent on your tiny place, sharing it with a roommate. Spending the rest of your money on booze and coke. Then suddenly your last name's Crowther—very fancy, by the way, a nice touch—and you can buy all the things you wanted. Nice place—too rich for your career, lawyer or not. When people asked, if they asked, I'm sure you had a good story. You married an older businessman. He took care of you. Then he died. Was that the way you chose to play it?"

"Fuck you."

Pete ignored the insult.

"Who's paying you?"

Crowther turned away.

"I don't have to listen to this."

"You don't, I guess," Pete said. "But the police might be interested."

Crowther stopped, her head snapping back to look at Pete.

"I haven't broken any laws."

"The people who wired you the money—that nice salary—for years have, though," Pete said. "My partner got your bank records. Pretty fun reading. Gallant Enterprises, right? Sounds so vague it has to be innocuous, huh? The company's fairly under-the-radar, and if anyone got that deep, they'd see a Rob Crowther listed as the CEO. Dots connected, nothing to see here."

"Exactly."

"But there is no Rob Crowther," Pete said, shrugging his shoulders. "There is no rich husband. Just you and the money, which started appearing in your bank account after my mother died. After you changed your name."

Crowther sagged. She ran a hand over her eyes. "What do you want?"

"The truth," Pete said. "All of it."

She looked around before returning her gaze to Pete. "Follow me."

Crowther's place was sparsely decorated, sprawling, and Pete felt lost despite having been in her house once before. The woman who'd been his mother's best friend led him across a wide living room and through a short hallway that ended in another loft space, this one more packed: bookshelves, photos, older furniture clustered in corners. More lived-in.

"Have a seat," she said, pointing to a large sofa that was positioned next to a few large bay windows. "Anything to drink?"

"No."

She nodded to herself and sat across from Pete in a small desk chair.

"I thought I'd gotten past you," she said, a wistful smile on her face. "Thought I'd given you just enough to keep moving."

"You had," Pete said. "But I came back to it. It made me wonder what wasn't fitting. You didn't fit."

"Why not?"

"It was too light, too easy," Pete said. "I believed you were my mother's—Gracie's—friend, but there was no follow-up. You didn't pester the cops about her death. You didn't have a life in mourning."

"I mourned for her," Crowther said, her tone hard and defensive. "I lost my friend."

"But the checks softened the blow, right?"

Crowther dropped her head into her hands. "I had no choice," she said, her voice muffled. "I had nothing else."

"Who came to you?"

She looked up at Pete. "It was never one man," she said, pleading, her tone begging for some kind of forgiveness. "Some days it was one guy, then another. Eventually, it just showed up in my account—like a direct deposit."

"What did they ask of you?"

"Just ... just to be quiet," Crowther said, her voice cracking. "Even then, I told you more than I should have. About her boyfriend. About our life."

"Who was he?" Pete asked. "Who was she seeing?"

"I don't know."

"You're lying."

Crowther shook her head. "I wish I knew," she said. "It was more the—uh—the after they were interested in."

"The after?"

"Her death," she said, pausing to catch her breath. "They needed it to go away—to cover it up. I know they had people ... cops that would work for them. To cover it up."

Pete stood up. "But why?" he asked, his volume rising. "Why go to such lengths—go as far as paying you a healthy salary for decades—to hide what happened?"

"Your mother knew a lot, learned a lot," Crowther said. "She was in a dark place, a mess—but she was smart. She knew what to look for."

Pete turned to face the large windows, which provided him with an expansive view of the Miami skyline.

"You're dying, aren't you?"

Crowther didn't respond.

"Kathy and I could piece together a bit—frequent medical visits, that sort of thing," Pete said. "But this seals it. Why would you reveal anything, even what you told me before, if you had no fear of the end?"

"You're right," she said, staring off toward the far wall, as if she were looking for a missing item. "It's cancer. Pancreatic. I don't have a lot of time."

Pete said nothing.

"I don't expect your sympathy," she said. "I cashed in my friendship with your mother for security. I regret that. But I also wonder what would have happened if I hadn't? Dead at thirty? No way those people would let me live, and it's not like the Miami police weren't rife with their own problems."

"My father," Pete said. "You knew him."

"It was too much," she said, waving him off. "It'd sign his death certificate, too. These people—they don't play nice. They would've killed us all."

She got up and turned toward the hall. "I don't need your forgiveness," she said. "I didn't expect it. But I have something else that might be of use to you."

Pete followed her into a large bedroom, waiting in the doorway.

She walked into an adjacent closet. He heard rustling noises, a few drawers opening and slamming. A moment later, she'd returned, a small slip of paper in her hand. The paper had once been glossy, but now it was faded and torn. The text across the top was blocky, neon: ART PARTY. Below, just above the tear was a subheadline—*START 1984 IN STYLE!*

"A party flyer?"

Crowther nodded slowly. "It's where your mother went," she said. "Before she was killed."

"Why do you have it?"

"She wanted me to come with her," she said, shaking her head. "I don't know why I didn't. I just didn't. The festivities started at Terraza, and I was having fun there. I didn't want to get in a car and go somewhere else. I told her I would, and then ... it was too late."

"That's not everything," Pete said. "You're still hiding the truth. The whole thing."

"No, that's it—what do you mean?"

"You knew what was going to happen," Pete said. He was guessing, but took a shot. "You knew she was going to die that night, didn't you?"

The shot landed.

She crumpled to the bed then, her head in her hands. The sobs came fast and loud, guttural and painful, like someone trying to exorcise something from deep inside, something she hadn't even known was there until right now. By the time Pete walked away, she'd curled into herself, her cries muffled by her soaked sleeve as she rocked herself back and forth.

# CHAPTER THIRTY-TWO

**"I**t's me."

Pete knew the voice on the phone immediately. The familiar lilt. The breathy delivery. A voice that had once enchanted him now sent a shock through his system.

*Emily.*

He slid into his car and started to back out of his space in Crowther's parking garage. He waited for more.

"We need to talk."

"Where are you, Em?"

"Don't call me that," she said, her voice flat, emotionless. "I need to see you. I need to clear everything up before I go away."

"Are you in trouble?"

"Of course," she said, her veneer cracking a bit, panic creeping into her voice. "I will be for the rest of my life. But ... I don't know. I need help, Pete. I need some help."

"Where are you?"

She told him. His tires screeched as he pulled his car into a sudden U-turn.

"This is not syncing up with the whole 'I promise to stay alive' idea," Kathy said a few minutes later, through the car's Bluetooth speaker.

"It'll be fine," Pete said as he pulled off the expressway and toward the Mujica compound.

"It is not 'fine,' Pete," Kathy said. "You're heading into the belly of the beast with no idea what you're doing. Haven't you learned any—"

He didn't realize he'd pushed the button until after he'd hung up on her. Pete felt a burst of shame, but knew it was the right thing to do. He could mend that fence later—if later was a thing that happened. For now, he needed to focus. Clear his mind and figure out what the hell was going on.

All the evidence pointed to Mujica as the man behind it all—but Pete was unsure. Why did the aging gangster hire him to investigate the murder of his son if Mujica was behind it? Was it a power play to take over Los Enfermos and get into the drug trade? Or something more complicated? Did Mujica know his mother? Did he kill her? And Harras, too? Was Emily on the other side? Had he captured her? Was she using her connection to Pete as a last-ditch effort to save herself?

Pete couldn't answer any of those questions definitely. Not yet. But he at least knew the questions. He had to find Emily. He had to talk to Mujica.

The large, ranch-style house was dark aside from a few exterior lights. Pete saw a figure standing near the winding driveway. He pulled the car up to the front door. The figure approached—hesitant at first, then moving with more purpose.

Pete lowered the passenger side window.

"You don't quit, do you?" Rosen said.

"It's not in my nature."

Rosen let out a quick sigh. "Why are you here?"

"Where is she, Eddie?"

"She?"

"Emily," Pete said. "She said she was here. I need to talk to her."

"Pete, what are you talking about?" Rosen said.

"She called," Pete said. "Sounded desperate. Is he holding her, Eddie?"

Rosen shook his head. He motioned for Pete to park the car. "Come inside. This is absurd."

"**W**here is she, Eddie?" Pete asked as he followed Rosen further into the sprawling house. Rosen shook his head.

"Not here," he said. "Do you get that you've been played? Why would she be here?"

Emily had lied; that was obvious. He hadn't fully believed her when she called—but his curiosity pushed him to pull the thread a bit more, to see where it lead. Was she just sending him one way so she could escape, or was there more to why she'd told him to come here? Pete's unease grew. He didn't expect Emily to have his best interests at heart, but he also held out hope that a piece of the Emily he once knew—once loved—was still there.

"Take me to Alvaro, Eddie," Pete said. "He and I need to talk."

Rosen nodded and Pete followed him back down the familiar hall to the dining room.

"He doesn't like surprises," Rosen said under his breath as he opened the door. He peeked his head in and Pete could hear him mumbling something to his boss. Rosen turned back to Pete.

"He'll see you," Rosen said. "But he isn't happy."

"I'm past caring," Pete said, sliding past Rosen.

The dining room table was loaded with empty plates and glasses, in the wake of what Pete assumed must have been an epic feast. Yet, Mujica was alone—sitting and staring into his hands, a confused—almost sad—look on his face. He nodded as Pete stepped into the room. Pete heard Rosen closing the door behind him.

"Pete Fernandez," Mujica said. He sounded weaker, defeated—his once strong voice a hoarse whisper "You have the *cojónes* to come back here with no news?"

"News of what?

"My son," Mujica said, as if scolding a young child. "What else?"

"I figured you knew the answer," Pete said, taking a seat to Mujica's left.

Mujica straightened, his eyes narrowing as he sized Pete up. He wasn't used to be defied in this way, in his own home. He picked up a small silver bell next to his now-empty dinner plate and rang it. In a moment, an older, well-dressed gentleman—Eugenio, the butler—entered the room, a tray in his hand.

"*¿Sí, señor?*"

"*¿Dónde está mi cafecito, Eugenio?*" Mujica said.

"*Ahora mismo, Don Mujica, con perdón,*" the butler said apologetically as he backed out of the room.

Mujica turned back to Pete. "So, come again?"

Pete wove his hands together. "I kept banging my head on this case. First Javier, the painting, just—well, everything," he said. "Then the mess got bigger. My father. Harras. My mom. Emily. But every step of the way, it kept coming back to one person. You pushed me off before, but not again."

Mujica eyes remained locked on Pete's. Calm. Patient. Like a predator waiting for his prey to move before pouncing.

"You're that person, Alvaro," Pete said. "It all ties back to you. And I'm tired of spinning around in circles. I need some answers."

Mujica let out a coarse, bemused laugh. "*¿Estás loco, mijo?* Have you lost your godforsaken mind?" he said, leaning forward, a shocked smile on his face. "You come to my house to accuse me of what? Murdering my own son? Killing your mother? Being a criminal?"

Mujica shook the bell again and yelled. "*Y tráeme un juguito, Eugenio, okay?*" *Bring me a juice, too.* He returned his attention to Pete. "Are we done?"

"We're just getting started," Pete said, his expression flat. "You hired me to find out who killed your son—albeit indirectly. You said it was because his wife—Emily Blanco, who I happen to know well—stole something that belonged to you. That was a lie."

Mujica sighed. "Your point?" he said. "I wanted to find this woman. She has something of mine. I hired you. You failed. We're done."

"Vincent Salerno died soon after you put me on the case."

"Who?"

"I'll humor the playing dumb, because we're not getting anywhere otherwise," Pete said. "Salerno was a top lieutenant in the DeCalvacante family in New York. He was also the man that almost killed me a year ago."

"I'm sorry he failed."

Pete ignored the jab. "He was also looking for something, information that I think you were looking for, too, in the wake of Los Enfermos falling apart."

"You're an expert now? A gangster scholar?" Mujica said, leaning back slightly, as if to get a better look at Pete. "You know how we all operate now?"

He laughed—a brief, empty sound—before straightening up in his seat.

"*No es tan bravo el león como lo pintan,*" Mujica said. *Your bark is worse than your bite.* "*Habla con urgencia si quieres vivir.*"

The threat was clear in his eyes, to even those who couldn't understand his smooth, luxurious Spanish.

Pete cleared his throat. A slight shock of fear hit his system. He was poking a bear here—a man who ran a criminal empire that Pete only understood in the abstract. But this was his one chance to find out the truth, he thought. There were worse ways to go down.

"I know Emily has a contact with the Colombians, and I know you know that. So did Salerno—eventually, after a few bodies dropped," Pete said, keeping his voice calm and patient, like an operator guiding you toward which button to press. "You wanted that info, too—and the easiest way was to get it directly from her. Salerno came to town after Emily. Somehow he died. I don't think you'd be dumb enough to take out a made guy, but someone did, and pinned it on you. All of this happened after your son was killed—gunned down outside his club.

"Why would anyone kill a random jazz musician? One who was just married, dealing with a drug and booze problem? Someone who wanted to get to Emily—to get that info she had and use it for themselves. The *bolitero* trade is dying, Alvaro. We all know that. But when Los Enfermos went down—when they sputtered after last year—there was a void. The Colombians *needed* a funnel into Miami. Without it, there'd be money burning on the table. Seems like a good place for you to step in, no? It'd revive your business, modernize your operation, and ensure your place in history. Only downside? You had to murder your own junkie son to get it."

The slap came quickly, Mujica's open palm slamming across Pete's face and sending him back, almost knocking him off his chair. Pete rubbed his cheek. The blow was meant to shock more than hurt, but it accomplished both.

"*Eres un gran cabrón,*" Mujica said. "*Tu no me conoces. Tu no sabes como me comporto.*"

*You don't know me.*

Pete shook his head, his hand still rubbing the spot where Mujica struck him. He knew it would be suicide—well, more suicidal than what he was doing now—to return the favor.

Before Pete could respond, Eugenio entered carrying a silver tray. He placed a small glass of orange juice and a *cafecito* near Mujica. He didn't show any signs of having heard the scuffle. He nodded and backed way.

Mujica looked at the beverages and then returned his attention to Pete, his nostrils flaring. "*Sale de mi casa.*"

"I have one more thing we need to discuss," Pete said, as if they'd just been having a friendly chat about the census. "And then you'll never see me again."

Mujica glared but did not speak.

"Graciela Fernandez," Pete said.

"*Tu madre,*" Mujica said, almost spitting the words out.

"She worked at a club you owned—Terraza," Pete said. "She was also informing to the cops—on you, or on someone in your organization."

"Was she? *Interesante,*" Mujica said, tilting his head at Pete. Feigning ignorance? "Yes, I knew her. I visited the club often. I was young. It was a safe space—to drink, cut loose, have fun, tu sabes. There were women all over. It was a different time. Drugs, drinking, sex. She was a lovely woman. Funny, sexy, smart. Quick with a joke. She worked there. I paid her salary. I knew her friend—Dina? Dana?"

"Diane," Pete said. "Crowther."

"She wasn't Crowther then," Mujica said. "Something else. I forget. *El tiempo pasa.*" He took a long sip from his orange juice glass, pausing for a split second to look at the contents before putting the cup back down.

"Were you sleeping with her?" Pete said. His tone was without emotion, but his insides were churning—he could feel the beads of sweat forming on his face, the anger bubbling, about to boil over. This was it. "Were you having an affair with her?"

Mujica coughed, a wet, sickly sound. He shook his head, as if trying to rid himself of something intangible.

"No, no, listen, I don't like you," Mujica said, his eyes looking glassy and distant now. "But I'm not lying to you now. I was never with that woman. I barely knew her. I slept around, fucked a lot of women, but one rule I had was to never shit where I ate, you know?"

Pete clenched his fists under the table, the nauseating expression threatening to send him over the edge.

"I—I never ..." Mujica said, his voice faltering. "Never touched ... her ..."

Mujica stood up with a jolt, his hands at his throat, a wispy, chime-like sound escaping his mouth as his face went from pale to red to a purplish blue. Pete stood up—reaching out, trying to help in some way, but Mujica was gone, his body spasming sharply before falling over, his face slamming onto the table with a loud, flat *thump*—followed by more shakes, a wet, gurgling sound spewing from his mouth, red with blood and bile.

"Gkkk ... gk ... gah ... no ... gk," he mumbled, sounds more than words. Pete got close.

"Help! We need help!" Pete said, hoping Eugenio hadn't gone far.

"Done ... it's done ... se *acabó* ..." Mujica said, his eyelids fluttering.

"Who did this?" Pete asked, leaning in. "Who did this to you, Alvaro?"

Mujica let out the scream then—low, animalistic, like a large animal struck down in the wild—as he rolled over, his eyes no longer alive, just white and gone. Then there was quiet, and Pete's only chance at knowing the truth had flickered into darkness.

"**A**rsenic," Alter said. "That's what killed him."

The cold case detective was seated across from Pete. The interview room in the Miami Police Department branch was dim and cramped. It looked identical to the room he'd shared with Hudson a few nights back, but Pete was certain it was different. He was grateful the Miami PD didn't collect rent from frequent guests.

Pete looked up at her.

"Why are you here?" Pete said. "This seems like the opposite of a cold case."

"Hudson called me in," she said. "Guess she's tired of questioning you every time someone ends up dead in your presence."

"Like someone called you into the hospital when the Silent Death got killed at Eddie Rosen's house?"

Alter froze in place. "That was the truth," she said, her voice halting and low. "I told you what they asked me to do."

"I don't think you can blame me for not believing you," Pete said. "Arsenic, huh? Isn't that a little ... Agatha Christie?"

"It worked, didn't it?"

Pete shrugged.

"Am I free to leave?"

Alter placed her hands on the table, palms down.

"Yes, but I hoped we could talk for a minute," she said. "About the last time we saw each other."

Pete shook his head. "Unreal," he said. "Look—what is there to say? You're corrupt. You pointed a gun at me. Your motivations are your cross to bear, not mine. You lied to me, and lied about my mother's case to protect yourself. And now this? Someone is looking to clear certain pieces off the board—and if I've learned anything over the last few years, it's to trust my gut. And my gut says you're crooked."

"You're right," she said, frowning slightly. "I made some bad decisions. But I have responsibilities. I am a parent. I needed to make tough choices to keep my child. She's more than my niece. And while I regret what happened, I can't take it back. So, yes—I'm sorry."

Pete started to get up, but Alter took his arm.

"Please, Pete," she said, a tremor in her voice. "I know you don't owe me anything. I've already raised a few eyebrows asking to speak with you—like this, as they investigate Mujica's murder. Just hear me out."

Pete sat down, crossing his arms.

"I can't lose this job, okay? I can't have them find out what you know, or what you allege," she said.

"Alleged? Okay. Great way to motivate me—question my skills."

"That's not what I meant. I just—I just can't. What can I do?"

"Nothing," Pete said. "I don't want to destroy your life, Rachel, all right? It's not on my to-do list. That's loaded up with stuff like 'stay alive' and 'find a home.' This case has derailed everything, but it's taught me some things, too. One of them is that I don't have to see every little bit through. So, you can rest easy—as well as someone who's done the things you've done can—that your cop bosses won't be hearing from me."

"Thank you," she said, her chin trembling slightly. "Thank you. I'm a good cop. I just made—"

"Spare me," Pete said, standing up and walking toward the door.

"Wait, one more thing," Alter said. "About Mujica."

"What about him?"

"He did it."

"What?"

"He's responsible—he had your mother killed," she said. Her hands were shaking. She couldn't meet Pete's eyes. "He covered it up. Had me cover it up from the inside. First to stop your father from coming after him. Then to stop ... you."

Pete shook his head. "Why are you telling me this now? Why should I believe you?"

"You have no reason to, I guess," she said. "But it's the truth. And now that he's gone ... well, I guess I feel like I need to clear that off, you know? Get it out of my head."

"It's easy to confess when the threat is neutralized, huh?" Pete said. "Easy to say someone did whatever you want. Whatever makes your story fit."

"It's true, though," she said. "One of Mujica's men approached me—years ago. They knew the truth. About me. Said that if I didn't help them—help them conceal the file, or alert them to anyone tampering with it, that I'd be outed. My life would be ruined."

"So now you're telling me this to avoid the same fate?"

"That's part of it, I guess," she hesitated. "But it's also because I regret ... how things went, with us. I felt like we could have been more. Been friends. If we'd been honest."

"Well, that's a shame," Pete said, standing up, avoiding Alter's grasp. He turned back to her as he opened the door. "Don't worry. I don't plan on ruining any more lives tonight."

He walked out. He heard the beginnings of a muffled sob as the door clicked shut.

# CHAPTER THIRTY-THREE

"**A**nnie Clarke?"

Annie wheeled around, a few cans of beans falling from her overloaded grocery bag. She recognized Pete and Kathy as she stooped down to gather her scattered belongings. Pete stepped forward and started to help.

"Scared the shit out of me," she said, trying to get herself organized.

"Sorry," Pete said, offering to hold one of her bags as she fished around in her purse for her keys.

"How do you know where I live?"

"We're private detectives," Kathy said. "It's what we do. Plus, you didn't give us your card after we shared a few drinks at Le Chat Noir, so we had to do some digging."

Annie forced a smile. "Do you, uh, want to come in?"

Pete nodded. They followed Annie into her small but well-lit apartment. The studio was sparsely—but tastefully—decorated, with a few thoughtfully placed posters and minimal furniture aside from a love seat and TV set. The kitchen didn't look like it'd been used.

"Can I get you a water or something?" Annie said, her voice quavering. "I have some whiskey—but I guess you can't have that?"

"Right," Kathy said, looking down at her visible baby bump. "But now my mouth is watering, so thanks."

"You know why we're here?" Pete asked.

"What? No, I mean, I figure you're just—y'know, detecting—following up on stuff."

"That's part of it," Kathy said, sitting down on the love seat. "But there's a reason we need to talk to you, specifically."

Annie pulled out a small chair and plopped down, resigned.

"You knew more about Beatriz than you let on," Pete said.

"What do you—"

"Don't insult our intelligence," Kathy said. "Like I said, we don't have a lot of time."

"You said you'd only met her that one time, but that's not exactly true," Pete said. "In fact, it looks like someone with the name Beatriz de Armas had a restraining order against you."

Annie wove her hands together and took in a long breath.

"That was bullshit," she said, her voice hushed.

"Please enlighten us," Kathy said.

"She was mad, she was jealous," Annie said. "Because Javi loved me. He wanted to be with me, but he couldn't get out of his marriage."

"Oh, sweetie," Kathy said. "If I had a car for every time I heard that."

"So, you stalked her?" Pete asked.

"I didn't ... stalk her," Annie said, looking away, as if trying to find some guidance in the wall moldings. "I just showed up at her house or where she was sometimes. To talk. To try to reason with her."

"But something happened?" Pete asked.

"Yeah, I caught her," Annie said. "In the act."

"In the act?" Kathy asked. "In a meeting?"

"No, well, yes, but not a business meeting," Annie said. "I caught her fucking around on Javi. Cheating on him."

"I can't really suggest you have the moral high ground here," Kathy said. "But continue."

"It was a while ago ... Javi had told me we had to stop, well, whatever we were doing," Annie said, her eyes watering. "Said that there was no chance she was going to end the marriage. There were bigger things at play, and he was boxed in, especially if he wanted to keep living the way he had been. His father had cut him off, and Beatriz was supporting him—managing his career and keeping him afloat. So he said we could keep messing around at the club, as long as she didn't notice, but any chance of it becoming ... real ... was gone. And I—I lost it. I was crying, screaming ... I just got in my car and headed to his place.

"I mean, I'd had all these fantasies, you know? That it would be our home. That one day, he'd come in the bar and tell me she was gone, that he was finally free, and then he'd get help to deal with his shit and we could just be out in the open. And now all that was gone. And I wanted to talk to her. To scream at her. To make her realize what she'd done."

Kathy reached over to Annie and placed a hand on hers.

Annie nodded at the gesture before continuing. "But when I get there, I see her—I see her pulling out of the garage in her car, and I just ... followed her," she said. "I try to keep a low profile, or so I think. And she pulls up to this restaurant, Peruvian place, 1111. They valet her car, and I'm in my own car, hands shaking. And I think, fuck it. So I valet my car and go inside, and that's where I see it."

"What did you see?" Pete asked.

"She's walking in, and this guy is greeting her, pulling her in close," Annie said.

"Like a hug?" Kathy asked.

"A hug, but more, this wasn't just a friendly hello," Annie said. "They were kissing, passionately. This was intimate. They were in love. And I was ... so upset. Because why can she have her cake and eat it too, you know? She can fuck around on Javi, but he can't be in love? Just because she has the money? I lost it."

"What do you mean?" Pete asked.

"I screamed, I started yelling, cursing at her," Annie said. "Calling her a fucking bitch, a whore. I think I threw my bag at her—"

"What happened?" Kathy asked.

"The staff took me aside. They called the cops and I got arrested," Annie said, hanging her head down, ashamed at reliving the story. "I'm not proud of what happened. I've been over it so many times—in my own head, in therapy. I could have handled it so much better."

"The man ... who was he?" Pete asked. "Did you recognize him?"

"No idea," Annie said. "He was handsome, older. But I didn't get a great look at him. That place is dark and all I could tell was it wasn't

Javi, and then I flipped. He moved out of the way fast—which makes sense now, in retrospect. He didn't want me to see him."

Pete cursed under his breath. Mujica? Who else could it be? Was the dead gangster sleeping with his own son's wife?

"Was it Alvaro?" Pete asked. "Did you consider that?"

"I mean, I thought about it, but ... I just couldn't get a good look at him," Annie said. "It was impossible, and I was losing my mind."

Pete sagged in his chair. He felt like they were chasing down shadows.

"What happened after that?" Kathy asked, her hand still on Annie's.

"It was a blur, most of it," Annie said. "Hard to remember. I was held until morning."

"Did you talk to Beatriz after?" Pete asked.

"No, I couldn't," Annie said. "I never saw her again."

"Why not?"

"Because Javi was murdered the next night."

"It's going down tonight."

Pete stepped on the gas as he and Kathy sped down Biscayne Boulevard, Dave's voice coming in loud through the car's Bluetooth.

"What are the details?" Kathy asked.

"Sketchy, but my contact says someone from the cartel is meeting with a new, prospective client tonight downtown—and they're pulling out all the stops ... security, passwords, you name it," Dave said. "It's high-stakes."

"Is La Madrina here?" Pete asked.

"No," Dave said, almost laughing. "Second she steps foot in the U.S. she's in jail, dude. If we are even in the same zip code as her, something's gone horribly wrong. No, one of her lieutenants is running point. But my guess is our girl will be there. Wait—okay, I've got the details. I'll text you the address. Happening in a few hours."

"Any leads on where Emily might be before the meet?" Pete asked.

"If she was smart, she'd be scoping out the area first," Dave said.

"Got it," Pete said. "Let's hope we snag her first."

Dave hung up.

Kathy turned to Pete. "This is the part where you say 'Wow, this really sounds like a job for the cops—so glad that we have an honorable and smart police force here in sunny Miami,' right?" she said.

Pete shook his head. "No," he said. "I need to find Emily. She's the key to this whole thing."

"Wrong," Kathy said. "*We* need to find Emily."

"Kathy," Pete started to say, before Kathy interrupted.

"No, I'm helping," she said. "Even if it's just to drive you and serve as a lookout, okay? No arguments. There's no time."

Pete shook his head. He knew when she got this focused, this direct, there was little he could do to dissuade her from anything.

The meeting spot was the venue formerly known as Picadilly Garden, off North Miami Avenue. The club had once served as a home to theme music nights like Pop Life or Revolver—an excuse for millennial kids to dance around to songs that came out when they were toddlers or barely embryos, like the Smiths, New Order, and Talking Heads. Pete had plenty of blurry memories of swaying to the Cure a half-dozen drinks in, the blinking lights and thumping bass keeping him upright—for a while. But now the venue had been converted into a party rental space—making it a perfect meet. The older neighbors were used to seeing people coming in and out, random cars parked around and, sometimes, loud music. They wouldn't bat a lash at what would be happening in a few hours.

He caught her a few blocks away, as he was circling the perimeter. She was wearing a long black overcoat—which stood out awkwardly in the Miami heat—and a light scarf around her face. She was sipping a glass of wine at a bar named Foggy Notion. Pete had visited the spot, a few locations back, when he did that sort of thing. She didn't react until the car pulled up close to her seat. She grabbed her purse and seemed ready to leap out of her chair—until Kathy lowered her window. Recognition flickered on Emily's face—cautious but familiar.

"Get in," Kathy said. "We have a lot to talk about."

**"Y**ou're pregnant," Emily said as she slid into the back seat. She closed the door and Pete got back on the road.

"Observant as ever, Emily," Kathy said, looking at their old friend in the car's main rearview mirror. "Nice to see you, too."

"Don't you have somewhere to be?" Emily said, her tone sharp. "I figured Pete would try to find me before the meet, but didn't expect you to show, too."

"No, alas," Kathy said, giving little. "My freelance career has fizzled a bit since I made it onto Los Enfermos's most wanted list—again. I do have to do some Art Basel coverage I need to work on, but I can do that in my sleep."

Emily squirmed in her seat.

"Where are we going?" she asked.

"Nowhere," Pete said, turning down a one-way street. "We need to talk."

The street was industrial, factories and warehouses coated in graffiti and promotional posters. There was no one around. Pete pulled up to the curb and flicked the car's blinkers on before parking. He turned around to face Emily. She looked frazzled. Shaken. She was still Emily, of course, even with the black hair and half-baked disguise. He'd never look at her and fail to find beauty or feel that nostalgic pull, but she seemed different now. On edge. Her eyes darted around the car and her hands fidgeted in her lap. She was trying to play it off, but some things can't be hidden—especially from someone she had almost shared a life with.

"Who's the—um, is it that guy? What's his name?" Emily said, avoiding Pete's stare. "Marco? I'd heard you were engaged—"

"No, uh, Marco ... Marco and I split," Kathy said, refusing to turn around.

"Oh," Emily said, looking from Pete to Kathy and then back to Kathy. "Oh."

"Yeah," Pete said. "It's complicated."

"That's nice. I'm—ah—I'm happy for you."

"Oh, cut the bullshit," Kathy said, letting out an exasperated breath and turning around. "You're why we're here, okay? This isn't three out-of-touch friends running into each other at Soyka, Emily. You're in major trouble. You've created major trouble. People have died. You may have tried to get Pete killed, whether he wants to believe it or not."

"What are you talking about?" she said. "I've tried my best to keep Pete from getting killed, actually."

"Oh really?" Kathy said with a short, dry laugh. "Could have fooled me."

"That thing with Mujica?" Pete said. "You told me you were there, at his house—I went, to help you. Then the guy drops dead."

"I didn't know that was going to happen," she said, defensively. "I wasn't setting you up."

"Emily, for the millionth time—what the fuck is going on?" Pete said. "What are you thinking? Running drugs? You think that was going to be easy, something you could do on the side to keep up with your lavish lifestyle?"

Her shoulders sagged. She looked out the rear passenger side window, out toward the empty lots and block-like buildings that populated the desolate street. It looked like it was all catching up with her at once—the globe-trotting, the changed identities, the drugs, the money—or so it seemed to Pete. He wasn't sure what he could believe about Emily anymore.

"You've got it wrong," she said, looking up at Pete. "I never wanted it to be this way. I'm not in control. I'm not running the show."

"Who is, then?" Kathy asked.

"I'll get to that," Emily said. "Pete, the last time I saw you in Miami—I was never coming back. Rick had left me enough money—whether it was his or not—to go anywhere and live comfortably for a long, long time. Miami had ruined me. Hurt me. You had hurt me. I didn't want to be reminded, every time I pulled into a gas station or went grocery shopping, of some terrible, haunting memory. Getting kidnapped, shot at, us ... it was bad. I needed out. Everyone else was moving on, so why not me?"

"So you left—then what?" Pete asked. "Why not just fade into the sunset, then? Why are you here?"

"Rick's papers were garbage to me. I just wanted the money," she said. "I didn't know what kind of information he had. I didn't care. The money was there, and if Los Enfermos wanted to chase me to Europe to get a few million, then fine. But I didn't think they would, and I was right. But someone else did. Not for my money, but for my contacts. My information."

"La Madrina," Pete said. "Rick had that in his notes. You knew how to reach her."

"I did, I do," she said. "Rick was the gatekeeper for Los Enfermos—he crunched their numbers in Miami, he made sure the Colombians got paid, and he made sure bad people on this side shut the fuck up and stayed in line. I learned that after the fact. Part of his job was dealing with the money people in the cartels. But I didn't know that. I didn't know half the shit he was doing until you found it all out—until you brought it into the light during that whole Varela thing a few years ago. And then I was done. I just wanted to be gone. So I left."

"Who reached out to you?" Kathy asked.

"I'll get to that," Emily said, shaking her head. She didn't want to be rushed. This was her story to tell. "I went to Europe. I'd always wanted to live in Spain, so I settled in Barcelona for a while. I lived well, ate well, explored—I had money. Why the fuck not? It was nice. I learned Spanish. I relaxed. It all seemed okay for a little while. I wasn't even dating, I was just—living. Reading. Walking. Listening to live music."

"That's when you met Javi," Pete said.

She caught wind of his tone. Her response was sharp. "I loved him," she said. "Don't let anyone ever convince you otherwise, okay? We were in love. From the minute we met. I knew it was going to be something."

"Spare us the Taylor Swift lyrics," Kathy said. "What happened?"

"Fuck you," Emily said, the words hissing out of her mouth. "If you want to hear this, let me tell it."

Kathy lifted her hands up in mock surrender. "So you fell for Javi, then came back here?"

"Yes, that's the big picture, but he needed help," Emily said. "He was drinking a lot, doing a lot of drugs—his playing was suffering, and his manager—"

"Owens?" Pete asked.

"Yes," Emily said, slight surprise creeping into her words. "I guess you have been chasing this down."

"He's gotten better at this," Kathy said.

Emily shrugged. "His manager was a mess," she said. "As bad as Javi was. Amphetamines in the morning, shooting up and drinking to even out, treating the whole thing like it was some kind of rock band. Javi was too talented for that. So, after we got together, he asked me to take over—gave me the keys to the whole operation. So I fired Owens, disbanded his group, and got Javi a residency in Miami—I wanted him to play every night, to get better and to get clean. I'd dealt with ... men like him before. You can't fix their addictions, but you can try and distract them, as long as it works for you. Once it doesn't, you have to move on."

Pete remained silent. He didn't need to ask who she was referring to.

"Then you came back?" Kathy said. "Back to Miami?"

"I fell in love and ended up coming back to the place I hated most," she said, looking at her hands, as if searching for a sign as to how things had gotten to be such a mess. "But it had to be different. I lied to him, which was bad. It never works to base a relationship on lies. I told him I had enemies in Miami—which, I guess, isn't a complete fabrication. Told him the only way I could come back would be if I had a new identity. He said he knew people that could do that, but it wouldn't be easy. That's when I learned who Javi really was. Where he was from."

"The Mujica factor," Pete said.

"His family, yes," Emily said, leaning back. She was loosening up. The familiarity—even if loaded with unresolved issues and anger— was smoothing things over for her. "He was vague about it when we first got together, and I didn't put the pieces together. I'm not a follower of the Miami underworld, despite what happened to you— and with us. The name 'Mujica' didn't ring a bell. But then he got me a set of papers—"

"Beatriz de Armas—it had a nice ring to it," Kathy said with a smirk.

"Right, once that came together so fast, from the other side of the world," she said, "I knew something was off. He told me—he was high off his ass, but he told me. And I almost left him right there. I didn't need that. I didn't need to be entangled with more drugs and crime. But I did love him. I should have left right then."

"But you stayed," Pete said.

Emily nodded. "I did, yeah, because I felt like this was something, I dunno, special. Not like Rick ... I mean, Javi was a good guy, or so I thought, but he was also safe ... reliable, different from you, Pete, and that was important. I'm sorry," she said, looking at him, her eyes watering. "We never talked about it. We never resolved it. Even if we fell into bed with each other at the worst times, we never sat and aired it out, you know? By the time you'd started to get your life together, it was too late. We'd missed our chance. But now look at you—you're alive, healthy, doing what you're meant to do, and you've found someone. You're going to be a father. That's good. I'm happy for you, I guess. And a little jealous we couldn't line things up the right way for us. But that's life, huh? Not black and white, loaded with grays and missed opportunities."

"This is all very sweet," Kathy said. "But there is some level of urgency here. Whoever has been orchestrating all this has blood on their hands—Harras's blood, and maybe even the blood of Pete's own mother. Not to mention the fact that they're after us—they blew up Pete's house. They're gunning for us. They've been gunning for Pete— or trying to make it seem like they were—for a while now."

"I wouldn't let them kill you. I drew the line there. They could get what they wanted without killing you. But I wish you'd taken the hint and backed off earlier."

"Well … thanks, I guess?" Kathy said. "Who's 'they'?"

"I'll get to that, I promise. What about Pete's mom, though?" Emily said, genuine surprise in her voice. "I thought she died giving birth to you?"

"You know that's not true," Pete said, frustration seeping into his tone for the first time. "You were in Osvaldo Valdez apartment when he died. You took the pages from my mom's dream book. You had them when I saw you in Cuba. Why? Why were those pages edited before I got them?"

"It's complicated," Emily said. "I'm under pressure from all sides. From people I thought were helping me. From people out to get what I had. I didn't want to take those pages, Pete. You have to believe me. I didn't want to disrupt your ability to solve your own mother's murder."

"But you…did?" Kathy said. "A whole fucking lot."

"What names were blacked out?" Pete said. "Who are we not looking at? My mom's death was a lie—at least how she died. A secret kept from me and my father. She was murdered—and I think it had ties to the Mujica organization. Why would you protect the people responsible for this?"

Emily didn't respond.

"Anything you'd like to add to this?" Kathy asked.

"What do you mean?" Emily said, shaking her head slightly, feigning confusion.

"I just find this whole conversation, well, super-convenient for you, and I'm not really in the mood for that," Kathy said. "I get we're all old pals, you have this deep, afterschool special history with Pete, the father of my baby, and it's nice to sit here by this abandoned lot and think back on the good ol' days, but you're not some innocent, Emily—you're complicit in this. You're somehow tied into what's going on—and I think you need to tell us that part of it, before we can even think to kick back and sign each other's yearbooks, okay?"

"Who's your partner, Em?" Pete asked, pressing. "Was it Mujica?"

"I don't have a partner. Not anymore. It's more complicated than that. They got me involved in things I never wanted to be a part of."

"What?" Kathy asked. "Complicated enough that you need our help?"

"Yes. I'm at the end of my rope. I can't figure this out by myself. Before you guys picked me up, I was trying to figure out how to handle this meeting tonight, how to find a clean way out of this mess," Emily said, her eyes red and pleading. "I need an exit strategy. I needed to get clear. I can't do that by myself."

"You said that before, Em—when you called me," Pete said. "When you said you were at Mujica's house. You hinted pretty strongly that you were in trouble. Why'd you want me there?"

"I didn't want to do that. You have to believe me. That was the last straw," Emily said. "I was done after that. I was done lying. Done putting people in danger. I kept telling you, Pete, to keep away—that I could only protect you so much. That was the end. It was a trap, and I knew it. I'm so sorry."

She wiped a few tears away from her face, trying to avoid Kathy and Pete's stare.

"But something went wrong?" Kathy asked.

"No, it went right," Emily said, shaking her head. "Alvaro was killed—and the hope was, your case would die there, too."

"But I spoke to him," Pete said. "Before he took the poison. I learned he had nothing to do with my mother. Or at least that's what he said."

Emily nodded, but said no more.

"They wanted to shake me off the trail," Pete said, nodding to himself. "That's why Alter tried to be so definitive—she had no idea I'd spoken to Mujica, that I knew he wasn't the man who killed my mother."

"I need to get out," Emily said, shaking her head. "I'm in way over my head. Please. I know I don't deserve this, but I don't know what else to do."

"But you haven't answered my question," Pete said. "Mujica's dead—so who's behind this? Who's trying to take over the drug trade?"

"Alvaro's death definitely created a problem," Emily said, wringing her hands. "Not just for his organization, but for the other power players in Miami. That's part of what I need to resolve tonight—"

"Wait a goddamn minute, will you?" Kathy said, turning to Pete, her voice exasperated and sharp. "You were working with someone— probably Mujica's organization—and part of that involved shooting at us. Why is that not a bigger deal?"

Pete nodded. "She's right," he said. "Los Enfermos killed Harras. The Silent Death went after me, Harras, you—why? Gunmen almost killed a retired cop we were interviewing."

"I swear to you, on my life, that I used whatever sway I had to make sure you weren't killed," Emily said, refusing to meet Pete's eyes. "I tried not to disrupt what you were investigating with your mom. But the stuff involving drugs and Mujica ... I was trying, in my own way, to warn you off. This isn't your fight, Pete."

"Not until you need us, right?" Kathy said.

"A lot of people wanted the information I had, the connect with La Madrina," Emily said. "It created major problems—not just for Mujica, but for other organizations. I was the doorway to a lot of money. Like, billions. If they could get to me, get to that info and make a deal, it'd change the entire landscape of organized crime. The Italians, other Miami gangs, Mujica—everyone wanted a piece of it. Everyone. I needed to protect myself. I had to find a way to not only stay safe, but maximize what I had."

"No pressure," Kathy said.

"I never wanted this," Emily said, her voice rising. "I wanted to escape. To get away from here, from you, from this world—to just enjoy this money that had fallen into my lap. The only mistake I made was to fall in love with Javier Mujica."

"Emily," Pete said, his voice calm. "You almost got me killed. You almost got Kathy killed. People have died. Maybe you haven't made the call, but you're involved. If you want our help, you need to come clean. To us, to the cops—to everyone."

"I will," she said, nodding vigorously. "Believe me, I will. But I need to get through this meeting. I need to let these people think I'm still doing what I promised. Otherwise, they will burn down everything to get to me—I'll be as good as dead if I don't walk into that meeting tonight. And so will you."

Pete and Kathy remained silent.

"Help me," she said, reaching out her hand to Pete. He took it. "Please. Come with me. Scope out the meeting. Call the cops. Let them run a sting. Let them shut it down. That way I'm arrested like anyone else, so it doesn't seem like I've double-crossed anyone. Then I go out, clean. Into the program. Once that's done, I'll tell the police—you, anyone—everything. I just can't have a bounty on my head. I can't run now."

"Let's go," Pete said, gripping her hand. She leaned forward, the hug awkward and stiff at first, but soon melting into a genuine embrace.

"Oh, God," she said, whispering, her face wet with tears, the words choked off by sobs. "I feel almost hopeful now. I feel like this weight is being taken away."

# CHAPTER THIRTY-FOUR

Pete parked a block away and nodded to Kathy.

"Do not wait for me," he said, trying to be stern, but also certain she wouldn't listen. "If someone comes close to the car, bail, okay?"

"Understood, *mon capitaine*," Kathy said. "Is Dave coming? Again, reminder, that place is probably swarming with armed drug dealers and, sorry to break it to you, I doubt your ex is going to do much to save you if things go to shit, okay?"

"Dave's on his way," Pete said. They'd dropped Emily off back at her car, so she could come to the meet on her own. Pete leaned in and kissed Kathy. As he pulled back, he snapped the glove compartment open and fetched his gun. He slid it behind his back, resting on the waistband of his jeans, as he straightened up. It felt reassuring to have it back in place, he realized. Kathy exited and stepped into the driver's side seat.

"Don't be a hero," she said, lowering her window. "I can't barge in there, pregnant, like some Kool-Aid Man, all right? Watch the meet, wait for Emily's signal, then call the cops. That's it. Whatever protection spell she's cast on you is gone, okay?"

Pete nodded, the sound of the window whirring back into place the only noise he could hear as he walked toward the abandoned building.

"**M**y boss is not happy," the man said, his voice booming through the empty event space.

The place was dark, the only light coming from a weak bulb in the middle of the room. There were no usable chairs, either—all the furniture was covered by cloths and nothing was on display or ready for use. It felt like a room in transition, which made it ideal for this kind of meet.

The man speaking was tall, well-built, his dark, leathery skin covered with intricate tattoos. His head was clean-shaven and he wore a dark blue muscle shirt to showcase his thick, contoured shoulders and arms. His eyes were black—the irises almost eliminating the white that surrounded them. He was flanked by four men, each one carrying a large submachine gun. Across from them was Emily— looking thin, shaken, and very afraid.

Pete had come in through a side entrance—a door left open, which he then locked from inside, to thwart any curious thugs looking to secure the perimeter. He'd found his way up to the second level balcony via an unguarded stairwell, giving him a clear view of the proceedings. But he wasn't guaranteed a passage back—eventually one of the men would open the door, do a walk-through, and Pete might have to blast his way to freedom. If that was even an option. But, for now, he had a good view, a loaded gun, and time to think— and listen, his phone at the ready.

"You promised us a connect," the man said. "A reliable one, too. Like we had with Los Enfermos. Instead, we get a dead FBI agent, the Italians breathing down our neck because one of their made guys is dead and no money. She is not happy, and when La Madrina is not happy, she throws a tantrum."

Even from his perch, Pete heard the sound of hands and fingers tightening around weapons, the clearing of throats that implied something dire. He didn't have a lot of time.

"We're working out some ... problems," Emily said, her voice raspy. She was out of her depth. The nerves she'd shown in the back seat of the car seemed amplified, even from a distance. She wasn't a gangster. How had it come to this? Pete wondered.

"Not our problem," the man said.

"Listen, Ordell, you—"

"Call me Mr. Robbie, lady. This is business. We are in business together. We respect each other, okay?" he said. "I'm the messenger, all right? I work the connect. La Madrina tells me 'get my product to Emily Sprague-Blanco, I trust her,' I do it. If La Madrina tells me, 'Give it to the guys dressed as Elmo on Biscayne,' I do it. And I did it. But then I hear that the money ain't funneling back, and that's a big fucking problem. Because that's my money, too, you see? Part of your payout is mine, and the big money goes back to Co-lom-bi-a," Robbie said, letting the last few syllables stretch out as he took a step toward Emily.

He grabbed her face, pulling her close to his. She didn't flinch, but Pete could see her eyes narrow at the invasion of her personal space.

"Now, the boss lady says you two go way back, to Los Enfermos days," Robbie said, moving in closer to Emily, as if pulling her in for a kiss. "Your dead hubby and her had some dealings. He tipped her off to some bad moves by the crew. Cost him his life. But you were a smart girl. Saved all your dead man's files. Knew it'd be worth something. And here we are. Lookit you, standing tall, like some kind of Donatella Corleone bitch."

He shoved her back.

Emily flailed, but regained her balance in time, avoiding a fall. She straightened out her blouse and met Robbie's eyes as if nothing had transpired.

"My partner and I are fixing the problem," she said, her tone flat, as if reciting a few lines from a recipe. "You and La Madrina will get what's owed, plus interest, very soon. We're sorry for the delay. We had to ... recalibrate our operation."

"'Recalibrate our operation,' I like that, all businesslike," Robbie said smiling, his big white teeth shining like beacons of light in the darkness of the club. "Real nice. You some serious shit. You may fool a long-distance bitch in Bogota, but you ain't fooling ol' Ordell, baby. I know who the partner is, you see. And he's trying some ballsy shit. No guarantee it's gonna work. Still early days, yeah? Too soon to tell. I hear some of his contacts are starting to figure out just what the fuck is going on and who they signed up with. His enemies are, too. Mr. Pretty Picture Man gonna step into the light real soon, honey, and let me tell you—sometimes the light stings your eyes. Sometimes you go blind."

Without another word, Robbie backtracked a few paces, motioned to his men, and stepped to the side. Pete watched Emily—her moves suddenly jerky and confused as the men raised their weapons and opened fire, the staccato sounds of submachine guns cutting loose overwhelming the cramped space.

Emily fell fast, her body twisting and bending at odd angles as they riddled her with bullets.

"Don't fuck with La Madrina, my dear," Robbie said, his voice fading as he snapped his fingers, his armed henchmen falling in line behind him like well-behaved school children at the end of recess. "Because then you're fucking with me. And Ordell doesn't like to get fucked like that."

The heavy front door slammed shut, the clang of metal on concrete echoing through the event space, joining the guttural scream bursting from Pete's second-story perch.

The space felt toxic, poisoned—gunpowder and smoke mixing together to form a noxious scent. He'd remember Emily's face—bloody and ripped apart by the bullets, her face tilted toward Pete, her mouth half-open, as if asking Pete a question, surrounded by anguish and fear and hate.

*"How did you let this happen?"*

# PART IV
# SERPENTS

# CHAPTER THIRTY-FIVE

There'd been a time when Pete couldn't imagine a world without Emily Sprague. Before she became Emily Sprague-Blanco.

She would be Pete's wife. She was his better half. They shared romance, arguments, and laughter and pain. They'd been in the trenches together. But time has a funny way of widening gaps and dulling emotions. Emily Sprague got into a cab loaded with her stuff, leaving a hung over Pete on the curb. She became Emily Blanco. For a brief period, despite the wedding ring on her finger, they came together again. But that ended in hoarse screams and pain and blood. Then ... nothing. Two people who'd battled and struggled for what felt like an eternity just ... stopped. They became two pieces of flotsam drifting in different directions.

And now she was dead. Four days dead.

The police had found nothing. The funeral was over.

But the secrets remained.

Her apartment was barren, much like "Beatriz's" place a while back. A small two-bedroom on South Beach near Alton Road had served as Emily's temporary base of operations. Pete had sweet-talked the landlord, an elderly woman named Fran who'd probably been born when Miami Beach was incorporated. She'd let him into Emily's faded digs, but Pete had come up mostly empty. A few boxes of books, a closet full of clothes, and a filing cabinet loaded with newspapers and press clippings from Javier Mujica's final performances and European tour. Pete had been over the place at least three times, and he was starting to push his luck. Fran would be back—it was close to sunset, presumably her bedtime—and he'd have nothing to show for it. The same questions lingered.

*"I don't have a partner. Not anymore."*

Emily had been playing both sides. She'd brought someone in to help her manage the relationship with La Madrina, and she was trying to extricate herself from it. But she'd been too late, and had paid with her life.

He went back to the file cabinet. He pulled out the stack of clippings and started to flip through them—more slowly now, spending time on each. Concert reviews, a profile in *Tropical Life* spotlighting Javi, tour coverage from different locales in Europe— Paris, Barcelona, Berlin, London. Pete had seen this all before.

He was tired. His body ached. He had a pregnant woman waiting for him at their makeshift home in Dave's condo. A voice in his head reminded him it was okay to rest, okay to stop. But something pushed him on. He unfolded a tabloid sheet and caught it midair. Another clipping. From the *Miami Times*. A short spread on Art Basel, the annual art festival that had become an international destination for the art community elites. The story seemed out of place until Pete took a closer look at the piece's main photo—a nondescript shot of a small art space participating in the event, hosting a gallery of notable works. One painting, in particular, stood out—and sent every piece of the puzzle sliding into place.

# DON'T EXPLAIN

*December 27, 1983*

Gracie was going home.

Well, soon. She just needed to tidy a few things up.

The realization—the final, damning one—had come in a mundane way. Not while curled up in the fetal position on the bathroom floor, not while getting dumped into a patrol car. It came one morning, after Diane had once again left for work without her. She'd dragged herself out of bed, head hammering, mouth dry, lips cracked. She stumbled to the kitchen, poured herself a cup of lukewarm coffee, and looked outside, onto Diane's small balcony. The sun was shining—a typical Miami day, but the kind of day residents take for granted. A radiant, bright and, well, beautiful morning. The sunlight felt new—like a knife slicing through the haze and grayness that was the apartment ... her life. How had she not noticed it before?

"Do I want to always live like this?" she said out loud.

And she realized she didn't.

She needed to fix herself.

And she wasn't going to get anywhere like this—with drugs and drink and every vice imaginable a few inches away from her. She needed to go home. She wasn't sure if Pedro wanted her back. If their marriage could be saved. But she needed to be with her son. She needed time to heal.

"That's all I know," she'd said to Meltzer, later that same day.

"You can get out now, Gracie," he'd said, worry in his voice. "You don't have to press."

But she did. She had one more thing to do. One more thing for her own peace of mind before she gave up the man she'd been sleeping with for months. Then she could go dark. Then any belief that this man loved her, had any plans to be with her—that he was anything more than a twisted sugar daddy—would disappear, like ash in a breeze. He just wanted to fuck her. He didn't love her. He didn't know Graciela's dreams or hopes. She was just someone he had sex with and roughed up and left alone, to sleep off the drugs and drink and whatever else he helped put inside her.

"I heard him last night, talking on the phone," Graciela had told Meltzer. "He thought I was passed out on the bed, but I wasn't. I always listen."

"Dangerous," Meltzer said. "But smart."

"There's something—some kind of deal going down on New Year's," she said, voice hushed, even though the apartment was empty. "He's meeting some people at a hotel—same one we meet at usually. There'll be a party there, some kind of art-themed event. They're going to start some kind of arrangement—a new business relationship. He called it 'something different, but important to benefit both organizations.'"

"They're just meeting him at the hotel?"

"There's gonna be a party at the bar first," Graciela said. "I invited D as my date. She seemed hesitant. New Year's is a big deal for her, so, I dunno. But she's coming. I won't be alone and she'll have fun once the liquor starts to flow and the salsa kicks in. We'll party together one last time, you know?"

"Just be careful, okay?"

Graciela thought back to the moment the man had gotten off the phone and gently shaken her awake. He invited her to the party. Asked her to be his date. For a moment, her plan seemed to wobble. Did he love her, she wondered? Was she misjudging him? Part of her wanted that to be true. Part of her really wanted his affection. His love. Something.

"I'll get you as much info as I can at the party, see if I can scope anything out from the meeting itself," Graciela told Meltzer.

"I don't think that's a good idea," Meltzer said. "Too dangerous. It's time to pull the pin, okay? Let us know who this guy is, the details on the meet, and we'll take it from there."

"No, look, it'll be fine—he trusts me," she said, brushing him off. "If I bail now, there's no evidence of anything. The meeting could go south and we've got nothing, and then I'm in his sights."

"I repeat—leave now," Meltzer said. She could feel his tone change from police contact to friend. He was genuinely concerned, and that worried Graciela. It was the first time he'd broken character. "If we don't know who this guy is, we can't protect you. It's too big a risk. What if he knew you were listening in?"

"Dan, I've been doing this with you a long time," Graciela said. "Let me close this out the right way. Leave you guys in a good spot."

"Your call," Meltzer said and hung up.

She called Pedro the next day, the bright sun and Florida morning as lovely as the last. She had a plan now. He seemed surprised to hear her voice.

"I want to come home," she said. "I want to get help. I'll go to a doctor, rehab, AA—whatever. I want to fix this. Fix myself. I want to be there for Pete, okay?"

Silence on the other end.

"I want to see him grow up," she said. "Ride a bike, learn to swim, everything. I want to be his mother. I want to tuck him in and be there in the morning when he wakes up. I don't want him to know that his mother was…a mess. Like this."

"What about us?" Pedro said. "Are you coming back to all of us?"

"Maybe," she said. "I don't know yet. Maybe I can be a good wife, too. I need to clear out this mess I made, Pedrito. I need to figure things out. Find a way back. I feel like I'm dying."

"When?"

"Soon," she said. "Soon."

She hung up. She felt a lightness around her, like she was floating, or being pulled by a strong wind.

"I want to live," she said to herself softly.

# CHAPTER THIRTY-SIX

**K**athy let out a long sigh as she reached the door to the Cernuda Arte Gallery on Ponce de Leon Boulevard in Coral Gables. Though the main hub of Art Basel was in South Beach, the city of Miami took the event as a chance to show off anything even mildly artsy, giving free rein to galleries from SoBe to Broward to spotlight local artists and visiting ones looking for any kind of buzz.

Kathy loved the idea, but loathed covering the event. It was sprawling, overwhelming, and, most annoying, she couldn't drink. Being pregnant was not something she planned on doing again. At least in the past, she could knock back a few glasses of free wine, grab some vapid quotes from whomever looked like they knew the difference between Pollack and Basquiat, and call it a day. But now she was stone cold sober. This was hell.

She texted Pete again. She hadn't heard from him since the early afternoon, when he'd mumbled something and left Dave's apartment. She knew that tone. He was onto something.

Normally she'd want to tag along. Experience the rush that came with figuring out just what the hell was going on. It was one of the reasons she loved their dynamic and, she had come to realize, loved

Pete. They played off each other well. They helped each other get to the answer. Even now, homeless, on the run from a gang of unknown killers, and desperate to figure out who had taken out two of their friends, she felt a warm comfort, a coating of faith that she couldn't shake.

But she wasn't up for the chase tonight. Her back ached. She had to pee every five minutes and she felt winded just walking across a room. No. Let Pete run around the city. When he found something, she'd know. Then she'd help. For now, she was fine with working up a few Basel sidebars for the *New Tropic* and calling it a night. She wouldn't even be here if she didn't need the money. Funds were close to nil, and the private-eye game wasn't very lucrative when you were running for your life without a paying client. And, well, maybe she needed some fresh air. Some time outside and not looking over her shoulder.

She'd finish this story on Cernuda, which specialized in Cuban art; shoot off a quick, apologetic email to her editor for the hasty piece; and call it a night. Pete would slide into bed when he felt the time was right. She'd chide him in the morning. And, maybe—just maybe—they'd eke out a few more days to figure out what the hell was going on.

Emily's death had rattled her, in ways she hadn't fully realized until now. She'd known Emily before Pete had. They'd been friends—not close, but the kind of colleague you'd get drinks with after work, compare notes on who the office creeps were, and stuff like that. She was beautiful, seemed to have it all together—but Kathy had learned that perceptions could be way off. She didn't know Emily was engaged to a raging alcoholic at the time, that she'd been forced to move back to Miami because her father-in-law had died, and was resigned to taking a design desk job at the local paper because she had bills to pay and little choice in the matter.

Emily would never truly be her friend, Kathy had realized early on. She was too sharp, too cunning, and took things too personally. But Kathy cared about her because Pete did, and she still remembered the glint of love in his eyes when he and Emily had a brief reunion while Emily was avoiding her marriage to a presumably clean-cut Cuban boy named Rick Blanco. A clean-cut guy who had been laundering money for an international drug gang. A clean-cut Cuban boy who inadvertently left enough bread crumbs for his wife to follow into the lap of not only the Colombian cartels, but the Mujica organization. Rick Blanco had signed his wife's death warrant—and Pete had gotten a front-row seat to her execution.

It all felt so sudden, so intense, especially so soon after Harras, a man Kathy had thought she'd loved, once—at least for a few fleeting weeks. His death seemed almost surreal, like a bad joke that leaves you waiting for the punchline that's already been delivered. Emily and Harras. Two losses that added up to an overwhelming sense of vertigo and confusion, at the worst possible time.

She entered the gallery, which was packed with the entire spectrum of people that came to Art Basel events: the art insiders, looking to add to their collections; the art dealers trying to con their way to the next sale; gawkers desperate for something to do on a Saturday night; the locals desperate to create a sense of community or familiarity in the sprawling, sweltering tapestry of streets and neighborhoods that called itself a city. Some were dressed to the nines. Others in chanks and shorts. Many in-between. The art was your standard, early twentieth-century realistic fare—seascapes, landscapes, still lifes, paintings of older Cuban government officials and—

Kathy stopped. Her eyes landed on a large painting across the room. It was a battle scene of some sort. But that was standard. Cubans loved their war stories, right? Loved their memories of *la madre patria*. No, what struck her wasn't the art itself—which, look, was fine. Kathy wasn't an artist. She'd dropped out of college. But she could fake it enough to write some copy for a website that no longer clocked content in inches. No, what struck her was a frightening sense of familiarity, a sense that she should know something about this piece of art, and the fact that she didn't—the fact that the bit of info she needed to pop into her slow, pregnant brain—could very well prove dangerous.

She shook her head. She needed to eat. That's it. *Low blood sugar.*

"Get a grip," she muttered to herself, as she reached into her bag, hoping a sweep of the large purse would come up with a granola bar or some kind of stopgap food that could tide her over—at least until she could leave this space—*was it hot in here?*—and have a meal. Maybe sushi. Jesus, she would kill someone for a glass of Chardonnay and a spicy tuna roll right about now.

A tap on her shoulder.

She turned to face the tall man behind her, his face not registering until she noticed the small gun in his hand, pointed at her but hidden from the people around her.

"See something you like?" he said, a sly grin on his face, his eyes saying what he couldn't vocalize: *Don't scream. Don't make a sound if you want to live.*

She nodded, as if being clued in on something she should have picked up on earlier.

"Fuck."

# CHAPTER THIRTY-SEVEN

He was too late. The Cernuda Arte Gallery was packed—brimming with the Basel fringe you'd expect to see at an off-brand event like this. But he was too late. Pete knew it. He'd seen the painting immediately. He'd sped across the room. Armando Garcia's Menocal's "Segunda Muerte de Maceo" hung in the gallery as if nothing, as if the months of searching and bloodshed and misery had just been a way to pass the time. The painting—fake or not, Pete now realized—had never been lost. Had never been stolen by Emily, or lost by Javier Mujica. It'd rested in the hands of someone else. Someone Javi had trusted. Someone his father had trusted, too.

He picked up his phone and tapped the display a few times. It began to ring.

"Where is she?" Pete asked.

"Hello to you, too, I guess," Dave said. He sounded groggy.

"Kathy—put her on."

"She's … not here. She had to cover some Basel event. She said she'd left you a—"

A sharp pain in his neck. A tingling. The prickling pokes of a thousand needles.

"Where ... where was she supposed to be?"

"A gallery in the Gables," Dave said. "She seemed annoyed, but I guess the gallery requested her specifically. They're debuting some kind of long-lost Cuban art and wanted her there. Which is weird, because it's not like—"

"It's Rosen," Pete said. "It was Rosen all along."

"Excuse me?"

Pete hung up. He grabbed a man walking by him who seemed to work at the gallery. He pulled back, a slight hissing sound escaping his lips.

"The man, the guy who owns this painting," Pete said, motioning toward the Menocal. "Where is he?"

"Mr. Rosen?" the slim, disgruntled twentysomething said with a sneer. "He's gone. Like, an hour ago. Seemed distracted. Left with some lady who was, like, pregnant—"

"Where did they go?" Pete said, not letting go of the man's arm, his grip tightening.

"Um, fucking excuse me?" the man said, pulling away. "Who died and made you Captain Grabby?"

"Where did they go?"

The man shrugged. Pete read the flimsy nametag on his blazer. Rex Nagorski.

"Listen, Rex, I need your help," Pete said, dusting off the man's sleeve. "I need to find Mr. Rosen. I want to make a bid on this painting."

"Well, you can just do that through me—"

"I can't," Pete said, trying to keep his cool. "I can only do it in person. It's how I do business. I need to look the other guy in the eye, you know?"

Nagorski seemed to understand, nodding slowly. "Well, I know he went to South Beach," he said. "He wanted to swing by one of the big events before heading home—I think he mentioned the Hyde Beach thing, on Collins?"

"Hyde Beach, the club?" Pete asked.

"I mean, yeah, like where else?" Nagorski responded. "I think DJ Tiesto is spinning and—"

Before he finished, Pete was halfway to the door.

A life-or-death situation was probably the only way Pete would consider coming to Hyde Beach. A massive, high-end, club-slash-pool-slash-restaurant, Hyde Beach was where the rich and cool intersected and luxuriated. On a normal night, it'd be packed with celebrities, the nu-wealthy, and those on the fringe trying to join either group. Bottle service, VIP areas, and bars in general weren't Pete's scene, and this was not a normal night for Hyde Beach. Art Basel had taken over the city, with streets rerouted, police everywhere, and foot traffic at a maximum. Even putting the pedal to the floor, it'd taken Pete almost an hour to get to the front door of the club. An hour he couldn't afford to lose.

Pete pulled out his phone and dialed Dave as he approached the Hyde Beach entrance. The burly, tattooed security guard manning the velvet rope already giving Pete a healthy dose of side-eye.

"Any luck?"

"Yeah," Dave said. "Guy at the door's name is Tisdale. Tell him you know me. Let him know I remember that thing we did with Creeden. That should help."

"Got it," Pete said before hanging up.

He could feel the security guy's palm on his chest a few seconds before contact was made. The blonde, well-built guy had a look that mixed beach bum charm with gym rat grit. His expression was blank.

"See the line?" the man said, his voice booming over the thumping music escaping the door each time it swung open.

"I need to get inside," Pete said. "Can you help me out?"

Tisdale scoffed. "Dude, are you high? You look like you just got barfed up by an Eddie Bauer catalogue and you're probably closer to forty than twenty. Why are you even here? Isn't there a Pearl Jam concert you can go to?" Tisdale said with a tinny laugh. "Hit the back of the line. Maybe I'll feel bad for you by the time you get here, around two in the morning."

"Dave Mendoza says hello."

"What?"

"He says hi," Pete said. "And he wants to let you know he remembers what you guys did with Creeden."

Tisdale's face blanched. An almost imperceptible nod came next, followed by a swift move that pulled back the velvet barrier. He motioned for Pete to enter.

"Just do me a favor," Tisdale said, his expression strained. "Tell Dave we're even. And if anyone asks, you snuck in, all right? I don't want to lose my job over this."

Pete nodded.

"I don't plan on being here very long."

# CHAPTER THIRTY-EIGHT

The club was a dark pit of noise, bodies, and sweat—people grinding on each other, waiters swerving around groups of dancers, swimsuit-clad drunks splayed out on lounge chairs—all in pitch black, with speckles of red, green, and blue lights flickering through from the main stage, where the bottom-heavy beats were emanating via DJ Tiesto's massive, multi-turntable platform. The crowd—at least the members sober enough to listen to the music—had gathered around the giant, sky-blue pool that made up the centerpiece of the venue's exterior. The drone of conversation, screams of adulation directed at the stage, and the pulsing music shut down Pete to everything else, and forced him to rely just on the muddy visuals of the dark club.

Then he saw him.

Eddie Rosen.

He was seated alone, almost immune to the din of the club and the claustrophobic crowd, sipping a glass of what looked like champagne. He'd noticed Pete, too, and motioned for him—a casual wave that was almost friendly. *C'mon, let's talk, pal. We can figure this out.*

Pete wove his way through the crowd, eyes locked on Rosen, whose expression remained relaxed and unchanged. This unnerved Pete more than he wanted to think about.

By the time he sat down across from Rosen, Tiesto had stepped away on a break, shifting the eardrum-busting volume level from 20 to around 15.

"You found me," Rosen said, leaning back, eyes on Pete.

"Where is she?"

"No banter for you, huh?" Rosen asked. "All business?"

"Where is she, Rosen?"

"Oh, relax, will you?" Rosen said. "Brooding vigilante doesn't suit you. She's alive. She's fine. But we do need to talk. I just didn't want you coming at me, guns blazing, so I came here."

Rosen stood up and straightened his jacket. He looked down at Pete.

"Well, come on," Rosen said, the smile still plastered on his clean-shaven, smug face. "I don't have all day."

# CHAPTER THIRTY-NINE

"**S**hit, it looks like a party up in here," a familiar voice said as Pete was led into a room. The melodic street patter came from a well-built man wearing sunglasses and sporting a large .44 Magnum in his hand, as casually as one would hold a pencil while putting together a grocery list. He nodded as Pete followed Rosen inside.

Ordell Robbie.

"This him? This the man himself, Mr. Pete Fucking Fernandez?" he said, taking a step toward Pete. "Thought he'd be bigger, you know? Tougher looking, on account of all that bullshit he put us all through. Oh well. What do they say? Never meet your heroes or some shit like that?"

"Ordell Robbie, this is Pete Fernandez," Rosen said.

"I know Mr. Robbie," Pete said, fighting the urge to lunge at the man who'd ordered Emily's death. Knowing he had to hold on if there was any chance of getting Kathy out alive. "Too well."

"You do?" Robbie said with a hesitant smirk. "Damn, guess I missed that historic moment."

311

"You killed Emily Blanco," Pete said, tilting his head to catch any shred of reaction on the gangster's face. "Or does your buddy Rosen not know that yet?"

Robbie backed up slightly. He hadn't thought anyone was in the rental space when Emily was murdered. He was shaken. But it was only a momentary misstep.

"You one crazy dickhead, you know that?" Robbie said. "Coming in, throwing accusations around like some two-bit district attorney. You better relax, my man. Ordell Robbie does not take kindly to bullshit."

Pete looked at Rosen, whose expression had remained stoic. That's when it made sense.

"You had her killed," Pete said, as much to himself as to Rosen and Robbie. "She wasn't of any use to you anymore, so you—"

"Shut the fuck up," Rosen said, losing his cool, his usually well-placed hair suddenly mussed. "You're not in charge here."

The space was on the large side, resembling a hotel ballroom minus the chairs, with a conference table at the far end, which was surrounded with places to sit. Robbie, Rosen, and Pete were the only people inside. Pete could still hear the thumping music, but it felt much further away, as if they were listening underwater.

"Where is she, Rosen?" Pete asked.

"Pete, really, let's not get cute, all right?" he said, no longer even trying to remain calm. "You are not getting out of this alive. Kathy might not either, so quit acting like there's a negotiating window here, all right?"

Rosen nodded at Robbie and the larger man headed out via an exit across the room. Rosen returned his attention to Pete.

"I guess this is when you expect me to tell you everything?" Rosen said, unable to hide his smug expression. "Where I tie your little clues together and you have a 'Oh, wow, how did I miss that?' moment before you die? I guess I can give you that much…"

"Not exactly," Pete said. "It's a big zero, anyway."

Rosen's expression faltered—flickered. He hadn't expected Pete to be defiant. Not this late in the game.

"What?" Rosen asked, trying to regain a bit of his composure.

"The line was in my mom's dream book," Pete said. "You used it when I saw you recently."

"That's your big clue?" Rosen said, his words coming out like a sneer. "A saying? Wow, I underestimated how bad you are—"

"No, it just sealed it for me. Your boss was an old-school *bolitero*," Pete said. "Not into the drug trade. Not that much, anyway. So when Los Enfermos went down—even though he was the most obvious person to step in and fill the void, he probably didn't want to. Maybe he was considering it because someone was pushing him, but his instinct said something else."

"Alvaro was past his prime," Rosen spat, teeth gritted. "So what?"

"You're a businessman, Eddie," Pete said. "You saw an opportunity and took it. How could you say no, when it fell into your lap like that?"

Rosen didn't respond, instead looking at his watch.

Pete decided to press. "When you found Emily, probably when Javi introduced you, you saw an opportunity there. You knew who she was. Knew what kind of connections she had," Pete said, stepping closer to Rosen. "What did you offer her, Eddie? To get in touch with La Madrina? To try and take over what was left of Los Enfermos?"

"Javi was a fool," Eddie said. "I loved him like a son, mentored him, guided him—but all he wanted to do was play his stupid music and get high. He could have ruled the city—been better, smarter than his father. Instead he wanted to fuck women, drink, pass out, play music, and do it again. When he showed up with her—she was stunning. Smart. Fearless. And connected. I knew who her husband had been. I knew who she was right away. I didn't believe that 'Beatriz de Armas' bullshit."

"So you went after her," Pete said. "And then had her killed."

"You make it sound like it was hard," Rosen said, clicking his tongue. "She was ready to bail herself, was starting to realize the mess she'd gotten herself into with Javi. She didn't want to nursemaid another drunk. She wanted a real man."

Rosen's eyes met Pete's and he smiled. "Yeah, she told me everything about you," he said. "About what a sad little sack you were—and are. When Mujica said he wanted to hire someone to find out who killed Javi, well, who better than you? Someone I knew would never solve it. Someone who I knew was a failure of a man."

Pete didn't take the bait. Had this been five years ago, he'd have already swung at Rosen. But these kind of jabs fluttered past him now.

"Where is Kathy, Rosen?"

"She's coming. Don't worry," Rosen said. "Ordell went to get her. And your baby-to-be. I'm not big on murdering women or children, but I guess I'll have to do both today."

"What do you want?"

"From you? Nothing," Rosen said. "This isn't a final transaction where you save your life, Pete. No. We're done. I need everything nice and tidy, and you're not tidy. You're a stain. I need my decks to be clear."

"For La Madrina," Pete said.

"Heh. So you do know more than I gave you credit for. Okay," Rosen said. "Yes, for her. To ensure she's comfortable entrusting me with her drugs. Comfortable with me running her product into Miami and beyond. I have the manpower. The firepower. But you— you and your stupid FBI agent friend, Emily, everyone—you're all buzzing around like disease-riddled flies, and it's fucking obnoxious.

"If it wasn't for Emily, I'd have killed you the second you interfered, or seemed like a real threat. She begged. She pleaded. Said we'd only need to scare you away, that you weren't smart enough to become a problem. I should've never listened to her, but you know how seductive she can be, right? By the time I took charge, by the time I realized *she* was the one that needed to go, so I could deal with you, it was too late. Too fucking late."

Rosen's voice had grown louder, more desperate. He took a few paces away from Pete. "Where the hell is he?"

"Trouble in paradise?" Pete asked. Now he was the one smiling.

Rosen wheeled around. "What did you do?" he said, pulling out his gun and pointing it squarely at Pete. "Where is Ordell?"

Pete returned the favor, pulling out his gun—his father's gun. The weapon Pedro Fernandez carried for decades as a police detective in Miami. The weapon Pete had used to kill too many men. The gun that had saved Pete's life more times than he wanted to think about. The gun Pete swore he'd never use again.

"I made a promise to myself," Pete said. "After what happened with Salerno ... almost dying ... I promised myself I'd be better. Smarter. Rely on things like this less. Think more. Not just stumble around and hope I could figure it out."

"That's sweet, but—"

The bullet cut through the air and slammed into Rosen's shoulder. He fell back, clutching the wound as his gun clattered to the floor, a surprised yelp of pain followed by a low, moaning groan as he landed on his ass.

"Fucking asshole," Rosen said, wincing. "You're dead. I can kill you with a word."

Pete ignored him. "But I decided to make an exception today," he said, gun still trained on Rosen, "for the man who murdered my mother."

Rosen's eyes widened. He slid his body back, as if he could outrun Pete's slow and steady pace.

"Huh … wasn't expecting that old chestnut. What gave it away?" Rosen said, genuine surprise in his voice. "Was it Alter? That cunt."

"No, she tried her best to protect you—or at least throw me off the trail," Pete said. "It was the flyer, of all things. For the party on the night my mother was murdered. That was the spark."

"A flyer?" Rosen said with a scoff. "I don't even know—"

"I thought Mujica had done it at first, but why would he hire me if he killed my mother? It didn't make sense," Pete said, shaking his head. "Then I did some digging, just to cross the name off my list—and discovered Alvaro had spent some time in the clink, including the night my mother was murdered."

"Her fucking diary …" Rosen said, the words speeding out of his mouth like the hiss of a venomous snake. "That stupid dream book …"

"Guess you hadn't covered all your bases, huh? Hadn't figured Osvaldo Valdez did some digging beyond what was expected of him. Alter could only edit the file so much," Pete said. "No matter how hard you tried to cover up what you did, the truth bubbled up. I got to know my mother in a way we never expected. As a strong, independent woman who—even dying—clawed her way to the light. To be seen. You can't bury her anymore."

"You're a dead man," Rosen said as he reached into his pocket. Pete's gun remained trained on the roving hand, waiting. Rosen pulled out his phone—dialing feverishly, still sliding away from the slowly approaching Pete, his footsteps almost matching the dull beat of the music coating the walls.

"He won't pick up, Eddie," Pete said, as they reached the far wall of the ballroom, Rosen's back against it and Pete standing over him, gun a foot away from his head. "We need some time to chat."

"H-how ... what ..." Rosen said, shaking his head. "I don't know what you're talking about."

"Ordell Robbie is a staple of the Miami underworld. He likes things to remain copacetic and calm. When Emily connected with La Madrina, she hired Robbie to be her eyes and ears down here. He's a known quantity. Could play both sides. You're the opposite of that. You're a wild card. You think he wants to be running interference for you with the Colombians? When I saw him talking to Emily, I knew I needed to find out how to get to him," Pete said, crouching down, his face close to Rosen's, the gun barrel pressed into the man's cheek. "And, well, what do you know? I have a Miami underworld staple of my own. Remember Dave Mendoza, Eddie? Guy used to run drugs with the best of them, with people like Ordell. Long before you dipped your toe in the water. Before you tried to be a big fish in a dirty, toxic pond. So all Dave had to do was ring up his friend Ordell and, well, here we are."

"Fuck you," Rosen said, his voice a sputter as he folded into himself. "You piece of shit. Fuck you, fuck your slut mother and fuck Emily, too. I hope you all rot in—"

Pete swung the gun across Rosen's face, the soft, wet crack of bone and cartilage not enough—so he swung back, the handle hitting teeth and slicing his lip wide open, gushing blood over the bottom of his once-smug face.

Rosen folded into himself, a pile of bruises, blood, and pain. A broken man.

"It's over, Eddie," Pete said, standing up, sliding his gun behind his back.

Pete noticed a change in Rosen's expression. From utter defeat to something else. Something more sinister and knowing, his face perking up.

"What is it?" Pete asked.

"*Apenas estamos empezando, señor Fernandez,*" a woman's voice—strong and confident—said from the doorway that had led Pete into the ballroom. *We're just getting started, Mr. Fernandez.*

Pete turned around to see a small entourage of armed men enter the room, scanning the space before stepping aside, like courtiers preparing a space for royalty. Pete moved for his gun, but was soon dissuaded by the armed men and their semiautomatic weapons.

A woman walked in. About Pete's age, perhaps a few years older, her dark black hair flowing around a hard, stoic face. She was dressed in a sharp, black suit—her eyes looking Pete over methodically, as if analyzing a new purchase. She made a quick motion with her hand and a new set of guards walked in, leading Kathy and Dave into the ballroom, more guns pointed at them. They looked glassy-eyed and resigned.

*Ready to die.*

"Who the hell are you?" Pete said. He felt exhaustion wash over him. This was not the plan. "What do you want?"

"*Me llamo Andrea Muñoz,*" the woman said. "*Tu amigo tiene algo que me pertenece. Y lo quiero—ahora mismo.*" Your friend has something of mine—and I want it. Now.

Pete's creeping sense of defeat had exploded into an aching, desperate, and growing panic.

Andrea Muñoz.

*La Madrina.*

# CHAPTER FORTY

"**W**here are the drugs?"

La Madrina was speaking English now, no accent—her voice was clear and calm, like a patient parent explaining to their child why screaming at the dinner table was not appropriate. Her guards flanked her as she stepped closer to the fallen Rosen.

"You'll get your money," Rosen said, struggling to get up, a red smear of blood on his face. The front of his shirt was soaked with more blood, making it look like he'd dunked his head in a vat of dark red paint. His eyes had a crazed, desperate glint to them. "It's just ... it's just taking a minute."

"Your friend, Mr. Robbie, he didn't seem to think so," La Madrina said. "Said you were unreliable. That my drugs were gone."

Rosen started to respond, but La Madrina raised her left hand.

"My patience ran out long ago, Mr. Rosen," she said. "I do not come here lightly. There is a jet waiting for me that I intend to be on within the hour. I also intend to have either my money or my drugs on that plane, too. If not, I will have your head. Which one will it be, Edward?"

*The fucking nerve of this guy*, Pete thought. Not only had Rosen stabbed his boss, Alvaro Mujica, in the back—to get a chance to run his own Miami drug gang, but he'd tried to double-cross the head of the Colombian cartels. Pete would almost be impressed at Rosen's audacity if it wasn't overshadowed by sheer novice stupidity.

"Robbie is lying to you," Rosen said, but Pete could tell his heart wasn't in it. Rosen was broken. Even the cornered cat knows when his ninth life is ending. "I will have your money … I just got … distracted."

La Madrina nodded to her men, the move so subtle Pete almost missed it. Then they were on him, pushing past Pete and hoisting Rosen to his feet, dragging the man toward the room's far exit. He did not go quietly.

"No! No, please—listen, Madrina, please — this is a major mistake … I can help you … please!"

The wailing continued, whatever drop of respect Pete had for the man dissolving within seconds. Eddie Rosen had been a cool, collected, and precise businessman when Pete met him. Now he was a shattered shell of a person, desperately clawing for purchase as gravity pulled him into the abyss.

Pete shifted his attention to Kathy and Dave, who were seated on the other side of the room, quiet and despondent. He met Kathy's stare—empty, defeated. What did they know that he didn't?

"It's a shame about this," La Madrina said.

"I can't say I'm sad to see Eddie go," Pete said.

La Madrina let out a brief chuckle. "He's a little shit."

"Then what do you mean, a shame?"

"About you and your friends," she said, motioning toward Kathy and Dave with her chin. "If I ever apologized, I would here."

Then it snapped into place and Pete felt like he'd been kicked in the gut. There was no way they were getting out of this alive. No way the head of the Colombian cartel was going to fly into Miami illegally, take out an underling in front of a handful of witnesses, and leave any that were not in her direct employ alive. It didn't matter if Pete, Kathy, and Dave cared little for Rosen. They'd seen her order his murder. They'd been in the same room with one of the most wanted women—hell, people—on the planet. She couldn't let them live to tell about it.

"I promise you it will be quick," she said, starting to turn around.

"It'd better be," Pete said. He caught Kathy and Dave perking up out of the corner of his eye.

"Excuse me?"

"It'd better be quick, I mean," Pete said. "Because the cops will be here any minute."

Her demeanor shifted slightly—a tiny, almost nonexistent crack appeared on her tough, crime-boss veneer. A fleeting, tiny shadow of a doubt. Pete felt so wired—so on edge—that he could almost read her mind. Feel her deepest thoughts come into focus: *Could this punk have cornered me? La Madrina?*

"A desperate ploy. Admirable, I think. But it's only serving to annoy—"

"I don't care if you believe me," Pete said with a shrug. "But do you really think I'd come in here with no backup, to face off against the guy who killed my mother? Who killed one of my best friends? Who had my pregnant girlfriend held prisoner?"

The crack got a little bigger. La Madrina's calm face was now fighting to hold back a seething anger.

"You're lying," she said, stepping toward Pete—a few paces away from her guards. "You're going to end up making your friends' suffering worse. Now I'll have my men enjoy—"

Pete grabbed La Madrina roughly, yanking the fit, strong woman toward him with one hand as he pulled his gun out with the other. In less than a second, the end of the barrel was resting comfortably on La Madrina's temple, as Pete's forearm pulled her neck back, her hands gripping for release. He could smell her perfume. Feel the sweat on her face. This was not what she had planned for, either.

"I'll be totally clear with you," Pete said, eyes on the three closest guards, who'd yet to drop their weapons. The three on the far end of the room, guarding Kathy and Dave, were inching closer now—guns drawn and raised as well. "Don't make me kill your boss."

"Shoot him! ¿Qué estás esperando?" La Madrina said, her voice more like a growl.

But her men hesitated as she writhed in Pete's grip. He wasn't sure how long he could hold her. She was powerful, her nails digging into his arm. Like a wild animal being pulled into a cage.

"Drop your guns," Pete said. A few of the guards listened, some still held on—unsure what was worse, risking their boss's life or risking her potential future rage by losing their arms advantage. "Drop your guns, I said."

The two stragglers were moving toward dropping their guns when Dave moved. It hadn't been planned—at least not by Pete. His friend leapt on the closest guard, one of the early adaptors to Pete's request, pulling him to the ground. *Shit, no—no, no, nonononononono …*

One of the armed guards turned around, aimed, and fired—a few quick rounds sending Dave to the ground, his hands clutching his midsection, a dark pool of blood already forming. Kathy lunged to the ground, trying to take cover.

"No!" Pete said, screaming as he clutched La Madrina closer, feeling his arm press on her windpipe as he pressed the gun barrel on her head. "Drop your guns! Drop your fucking guns!"

Both men did. But the odds had changed. Kathy was on the ground, her arms covering her stomach—fearful of another spray of gunfire. Dave was on the floor, dying. Time was not on Pete's side. His breathing was ragged. La Madrina had noticed. Her grip slackened. She was waiting.

"Get out," Pete yelled at the guards. "Leave. Now. Go outside."

The men hesitated—looking toward their leader. She nodded and they began to file out, slowly, each one looking back as they exited—as if trying to ensure that she was safe. A few stepped over Dave, avoiding him like one would sidestep a passed out homeless man on the streets of Calle Ocho. Just another body to ignore.

When the door shut, Pete let La Madrina go, stepping back—his gun still trained on her as she tried to compose herself.

"You will live tonight, and die tomorrow," she said, a smile creeping onto her face. "I promise you that."

"Fuck you," Pete said.

"Your friend is dying," she said. "You don't have time to argue with me."

Kathy got up—slowly, trying to maintain her balance—and walked toward Dave, crouching next to their friend.

"He's losing a lot of blood," Kathy said to Pete. "We need to get him to a hospital … Pete …"

Her voice had become a choked sob. La Madrina was right. They had no time.

"To think, you could have gotten out of this with a quick, painless death," La Madrina said, almost to herself. "And now, this."

"I still have a gun on you," Pete said, a tinge of fear in his voice. Her sudden confidence threw him off. Something was up. "Don't forget that."

"And he," she said, as the main door swung open. "Has a gun on your girlfriend."

The Silent Death walked in, his demeanor relaxed but alert, gun arm raised and pointed at Kathy's head. Dave made a soft gurgling sound at his feet as the Death stepped over him.

"Hola, Pete," the Death said, his voice coated in gravel. "Qué gusto verte de nuevo."

*So nice to see you again.*

# CHAPTER FORTY-ONE

"I guess this is how it ends," Kathy said as she took a seat next to Pete.

She was shaking. They both were. Dave Mendoza—their friend, someone they'd come to love like a brother was bleeding out on the floor, erratic gurgling sounds the only sign that he might still be alive. The Death had ushered them toward two empty chairs near the exit. The same droning, insufferable music pounded the conference room's flimsy walls. La Madrina was pacing around on her cell phone, trying to negotiate some kind of covert exit back to Colombia. Eddie Rosen was probably dead, too. Pete knew he and Kathy were likely not far behind.

The Silent Death—even after the demise of his last incarnation, Isleño Novo—was back to torment them one last time, it seemed. He hovered near the entrance, walking around the room slowly, looking back to check on Pete and Kathy every few moments.

"It's not over," Pete said, trying to keep his voice to a whisper.

"Do you have anything that might provide at least a glimmer of hope to support that?" Kathy said, her sharp humor replaced by a longing desperation for any kind of chance. "What are they even doing? What's taking so long?"

"Muñoz is one of the most wanted people in the world," Pete said. "She can't just walk outside and wait at the airport. She needs to know her transition from here to the plane and into the air is going to be seamless."

"Glad we've gained a few minutes of life because of hashtag travel delays."

"It's not going to end this way," Pete said, his eyes trained on Kathy's. He felt them glass over. Felt the tears start to well up. "Not for you. Not for me. Not for her."

He placed a hand on Kathy's pregnant belly.

"It can't," he said.

Pete felt a tug at his shoulder. Felt himself being yanked up by the Death. The masked man shoved Pete around, so that they were now facing each other.

"Enough talking," he said, gun pointed at Pete's face.

"Wait, not yet," La Madrina said from across the room, still on the phone—she started to make her way toward the commotion. "Paciencia, por favor." *Be patient, please.*

Pete moved. That brief moment—with the Death's attention split between him and La Madrina would not come again, and time was ticking away. Dave might be close to gone, but he still had a chance to save Kathy. His child. His world.

Pete sent his palm hurtling at the Death's masked face and felt it give as his hand made contact with the man's chin. The Death stumbled back, but retained his footing—and his gun. Pete didn't hesitate—and sent a kick up to his throat…He watched as the man's head snapped back. This time, he fell. Pete ran toward him, stomping his wrist and taking the assassin's gun. He felt around his pockets and found his own gun, sliding the Death's silencer-equipped one into his back pocket. He yanked the Silent Death's mask off, expecting to see someone—anyone—that echoed back to the last few months. But what he saw staring back at him was a nonentity—the bland Latin features could have belonged to any man Pete had passed on the streets over the last few days, even years. Just another hired gun wearing a mask. The Silent Death wasn't a person—he was a tool. Someone else gunning for them.

Pete stood up. *Time to end this.*

He heard the words first. Muñoz's voice laced with hate and vengeance.

"You son of a bitch."

Even with the music, the gunshot cut through the room. It took Pete a second to realize he'd been hit, the burning in his back getting stronger, the ache turning into screaming pain. He looked down at the Death—out cold. He felt his body fold, his knee hitting the ground first. The heaviness in his shoulders and back. He thought he heard a scream behind him. Then he was on his side. He couldn't feel his hands. The room was spiraling around, losing focus. He felt his mouth filling with liquid—*water? No, blood*—as a shadow draped over him. *La Madrina.*

His eyes took longer to focus now. Everything in slow motion. Every sound dulled and distant. He'd been here before. On the brink. He'd tried so hard to avoid this. To live a life. To become the son his parents—his father *and* mother—had deserved. A good man. A good detective. A good father. He'd done his best. He knew that now, at least.

"Of course, I need to clean up Isleño's mess. What a fool I was to think a man could do a woman's job," she said, her words sounding distant and distorted to Pete, his vision blurring every few seconds. "Goodbye, Pete Fernandez."

Pete opened his mouth as if to say something—felt his lips forming the words—but no sound escaped his mouth.

"What?" La Madrina said, leaning forward. "What did you say?"

"I said," Pete croaked, his voice sounding more like a croak. "It's not over."

La Madrina stood up and shook her head dismissively. "He's already gone," she said, more to herself than anyone else.

Then her head snapped to one side in a jerky, abnormal way—a byproduct of the chair Kathy swung at her head. La Madrina's face contorted into a grimace of shock and pain before she tumbled to the ground, clutching the side of her skull, a long, wide gash down her cheek. She was screaming. Even Pete could hear her, though he felt the edges start to darken—his vision flickering out. Then he heard noises. Doors swinging open. Yelling. A crowd storming into the tiny room. Kathy now. Close to him. Her hand holding his head up. Her voice—soft, soothing, coated in sobs but trying to focus. He wanted to sleep.

"Hold on, Pete," she said. "Hold on, goddammit."
He tried. He wanted to meet his girl.
But the blackness came again.
"Don't go," he heard a voice say. "Pete, don't leave us."

# CHAPTER
# FORTY-TWO

The beeps and pings and sighs of the hospital room had burned themselves into his brain by now.

Everything hurt. Blinking felt like a chore. He wasn't sure how long he'd been awake.

But he was awake.

He was alive.

Pete Fernandez tried to smile, but even that seemed uncomfortable. He felt someone leaning over him, Kathy

"Good morning, Mr. Man," she said, kissing him on the forehead. "You were in and out most of yesterday. Glad to see you're back."

"Barcly," he said, his voice hoarse. "What'd I miss?"

Kathy slid a chair to Pete's bedside. The room was sparse in terms of furniture, but loaded with flowers from Allie Kaplan, Dave—who was recovering down the hall—and Pete's Book Bin employee Isabel Levitz, plus the usual get-well-soon paraphernalia one could easily find in the gift shop on the ground floor. He hadn't seen many people—couldn't remember if he had, anyway—since being admitted. The ambulance, overhead hospital lights, panicked doctors and nurses ... then darkness. He'd only started to piece things together a few days ago—or so it seemed. Kathy had told him it'd been a week. It felt like a lifetime.

"Not much," she said, trying to put a smile on her face. "Just me sitting here and watching you snore."

"Sounds like a relaxing alternative to our last few weeks," Pete said, his throat dry. "How's Dave?"

"Surprisingly well, all things considered," Kathy said. "The wound was messy, but the bullet didn't hit any essential organs. Lots of blood, though. Had he stayed passed out for much longer, it could've been a lot worse."

"Dave's a survivor," Pete said. "What's on tap for today? Maury Povich and local news?"

"Someone here to see you, actually," Kathy said, wiping at her eyes and standing up. "You think you're up for a visitor?"

"Sure," Pete said, half-heartedly. "As long as they're here with two medianoches from La Carreta."

"You've never been the lucky type," Kathy said. "It's Detective Hudson. You want me to ask her to come back? She seemed pushy. Shocking for a cop, right?"

"It's why I survived—so I could get interrogated by a cop one more time."

"Then your wish has come true," Hudson said, rapping her fingers on the door to Pete's room. "Clear to come in?"

"Detective," Pete said.

"Mr. Fernandez," she said, walking toward his bed and placing a hand on his good shoulder. "You have a habit of almost dying. Let's try to stop that, all right?"

"I'm 0-2 in the dying department," Pete said. "How can I help you, detective?"

"I wish I could say I just came by to check on you, but that would be a lie. That's just part of it. The other part was to say thanks. You tipping off Alter made for a huge bust," Hudson said, taking the seat Kathy had vacated. "And Alter did the right thing, letting me know so we could get some firepower to pull you out of there."

"And, in the process, you got La Madrina."

"For now."

"What do you mean?" Kathy asked.

"Well, the lady has to go to trial, that's how it works in our slowly fading democracy. At least for now," Hudson said, not turning to face

Kathy. "And, not surprisingly, the lady's got money. And money buys lawyers. Good ones."

"Well, that's where Rosen comes in, right?" Pete asked. "You got him to flip?"

"We did," Hudson said.

"But …?"

"Rosen hung himself in his cell this morning," Hudson said, her mouth a flat grimace. "Guard found him dangling after a shift change."

"What?" Kathy said. "How does that fucking happen?"

"It does fucking happen, unfortunately," Hudson said, running a hand through her short, close-cropped hair. "We are not perfect. As you and your partner have been fond of pointing out with regularity."

"What does this have to do with me?" Pete asked. He was getting tired. This conversation was the most activity he'd had in days and it was starting to wear him down.

"We need someone to testify," Hudson said. "Someone who saw La Madrina order a murder, or comment on her business. As you can imagine, there aren't a lot of people alive who can do that, present company excluded. I'm gonna take a wild guess that you don't want your wife—"

"Girlfriend, sort of," Kathy said. "Let's not get ahead of ourselves."

"Your girlfriend," Hudson said. "Let's say you don't want her in the line of fire for this one."

"Shit," Pete said. "What happened to Rosen? He seemed ready to tear down everyone in his Rolodex if it meant a few years shaved off his sentence."

"Buyer's remorse, I guess," Hudson said. "Eddie Rosen was an echo of a man when we found him—physically and mentally. He'd cashed in every chip, every relationship he had, for a shot at becoming a drug kingpin, a chance to one-up his old boss. He had Mujica murdered; he set up his protégé, Javi Mujica; murdered Emily Sprague, a woman he'd manipulated and fooled; and that's just off the top of my head."

"And my mother," Pete said.

"Right," Hudson said. "It caught up with him, I guess. What's a few years to a pariah? Who does he have to come home to? His life was over, I guess."

Pete shook his head. He'd only just learned Rosen survived La Madrina's assault, and had hoped to get a chance to talk to the man. To learn what had driven him to murder Graciela Fernandez. Emily. Harras. Eddie Rosen had torn out a huge part of Pete's life and past, and now he'd never get to look him in the eye.

"I'll testify," Pete said with a shrug.

"You will do no such thing," Kathy said, stepping closer to Pete's bedside, her glare focused solely on Hudson. "Or have you forgotten you're going to be the father of Currently Unnamed Fetus here?"

"She has a point," Hudson said. "I can't argue that."

"What happens if I don't?"

"Can't be certain," Hudson said, shrugging. "But there's a chance she walks."

"Let me think on it," Pete said. "I'm tired."

"I'll get out of your hair, then," Hudson said, standing up. "Seems like you've got plenty going on."

"Can I ask you a question?"

"Shoot," Hudson said.

"Why did he do it?" Pete asked. "Why did Rosen do it?"

Hudson's expression softened. She knew what he meant. She knew Pete wasn't asking about Javier Mujica, or Vincent Salerno. He wasn't asking about Osvaldo Valdez or Alvaro Mujica. He was asking about his mother. A woman he never got to know. A woman who could have taught him so much—who could have helped him navigate the landmines and pitfalls that had left him bruised and battered as he crawled toward his own stint as a parent. Why was his mother dead?

Hudson sat down again with a sigh.

"Eddie Rosen was a sick man. But not insane. He was conniving. A snake. He killed because he thought he had to—each time. He killed Osvaldo Valdez because he found out the retired cop was digging around your mom's file. He killed Javier Mujica because Javi's side piece found out he was banging Javi's wife, and that put his entire plan—to con Emily into connecting him to La Madrina— at risk. He killed Alvaro because his cover was almost blown. Once Eddie found out your girl Emily had intel on how to connect with La Madrina, nothing else mattered. Even when that rogue Mafioso, Salerno, came barreling into town, desperate to find Ms. Emily, he didn't bat an eye. Took the guy right out, made the Italians believe it was Mujica and made Mujica believe the Italians were hungry for blood. You know what was sick, though? He loved Mujica's boy like his own. Javi Mujica wasn't close to his father—hated him a lot of the time. But he was close to Rosen. He learned a lot from the guy: how to run a business, how to be a self-made man. Imagine how cold and calculating a son of a bitch you have to be to murder someone you love like a son because you want something his wife has. That's some cold shit," Hudson said. "So why did he kill your mother? A woman he was having an affair with? A man your mother—if I'm reading that dream book right—thought might love her? Because he was a rat, pure and simple. Your mom was smart. She had her problems. Demons. But she knew it was time to get out. Time for the adventure to end. She came back to what she knew—police. You know she called your dad? Asked to come home?"

Pete shook his head. He had no idea.

"Yeah, he told her to come home. They were going to try again," Hudson said, choosing her words wisely, knowing the impact they'd have on Pete. "She'd already told Meltzer she was out, after she set up Rosen once and for all. Meltzer tried to talk her out of it, but she didn't want to leave things unresolved. But it was too late. She didn't have enough time. Rosen was too powerful. He had the entire Mujica organization at his fingertips."

Pete sagged further into his bed. Kathy rested a hand on his head for a moment.

"What about the Death?" Pete said, trying to change the topic. "Who was it under the mask this time?"

"Guy by the name of Andres Barrera," Hudson said. "Formerly of the Sinaloa cartel. Went freelance. Once Novo was dead, he took over."

"Not for long."

"It's a high-risk gig, it seems," Hudson said.

Pete couldn't tell if she was making a joke.

"Thanks for coming by," Pete said, looking away from the detective and toward his hospital room's large window. They overlooked Kendall Drive.

"Rachel Alter resigned, by the way," Hudson said. "She's moving. Somewhere up north. Vermont, I think."

"Oh?"

"Don't play dumb," Hudson said. "It's not a good look. We found out about her background—which, to be frank, would not have been a deal-killer in terms of joining the force. It's never the crime, as you know, it's the cover-up. But the tampering with evidence, the informing to Rosen whenever anyone accessed the file—she has a cop's blood on her hands. She kept a cold case cold, and she sent you down few wrong turns. When she tried to pin it all on Mujica to you, she knew there was no going back. That it'd only be a matter of time before you figured it out and turned on her. Maybe that's why she helped you in the end—for some kind of redemption."

"I hoped she would," Pete said, rubbing his eyes. "I hoped there was some good in there."

"There was, lucky for you," Hudson said. "Maybe that's why she quit before we could fire her. Either way, she's broken the law more than a half-dozen ways."

"Will she go down for it?" Kathy asked.

"She should, she really should," Hudson said. "Honestly, if she didn't have a kid, if I didn't know she acted under extreme duress, I dunno ... I guess I could press it harder. For now, she's not a cop. She's out of my hair. That's the best I can hope for."

Hudson got up again, this time more definitively.

"What's next for you?" she asked, looking at both of them. "I mean, beside creating a little person."

Pete's eyebrows popped up, as if he'd been thinking about the answer to that question for years.

"A new life."

# CHAPTER FORTY-THREE

*Nine months later*

Pete Fernandez's eyes fluttered open, and for a moment, he had no idea where he was.

Then the image came into focus. The morning light sneaking in through the blinds. Kathy's arm draped over him, her face buried in a pillow. Their breathing in sync as he craned his neck to see the small bassinet on her side of the bed. Grace, three months old, had begun making the gurgling sounds that precede a cry—of hunger, usually. But Pete knew for a few seconds there'd be quiet.

Their apartment was large, but in flux. Located in the loft-like space above The Book Bin, the space had been remodeled by Pete and Kathy to accommodate them, reworking it into a spacious three-bedroom that led directly to the bookstore below. At least that had been the plan. But like any large-scale remodeling, stuff took longer than expected and stuff came out different than they expected. That left Pete, Kathy, and little Grace living in a much smaller space, as the rest of the apartment morphed into something else. It didn't help with a sleeping baby, to say the least. The Book Bin, for all intents and purposes, wasn't really a bookstore anymore—the sign out front read Bentley & Fernandez Investigations. Underneath, in a clear font it also read Used Books for Sale, Too. Dave, who'd passed the lease on the store to Pete months back, put the rest of the building in Pete and Kathy's name shortly after he and Pete were released from the hospital.

"Time for you two to settle down," he'd said, as he wheeled himself to their waiting car. "Let me help."

The unexpected gift was the backbone of their day-to-day. The used books were still sold, but that side of the business was secondary, and mainly run by Isabel, who was now full-time—splitting her work between managing the book sales and organizing Pete's chaotic schedule, when required.

It'd taken years. Fits and starts. But Pete finally felt settled. Part of something. The pieces had always been there—the work, Kathy, Miami. But he'd pushed back. Dulled his senses. Evaded. Run. He could spend years bemoaning the time lost, but that'd be counterproductive.

The thump on the door surprised him—for a second. But the now-familiar sound, like an open palm slapping something solid, didn't scare him. It was another source of comfort. It was Neko and Polly Jean, their two rescue kittens, alerting Pete and Kathy that they, like their human sibling Grace, needed to eat.

Pete slid out from under Kathy's arm, trying his best to let her enjoy these last few minutes of rest before she'd have to nurse their daughter. He caught a glimpse of his phone. The screen lit up a nanosecond before the vibrations hit. Hudson.

"What's up?" Pete asked, before the police detective could speak.

"Are you awake, Fernandez?" Hudson asked. "Because I might have some work for you."

"Nisha, we have a newborn. We're always awake."

"How's that family of yours, then?" she asked.

"Good, I think," Pete said, his voice low. "They're sleeping at least, thank God. Grace wakes up a few times a night, so we've been alternating."

"Kid likes to eat," Hudson said. "Good sign."

Kathy stirred behind Pete, wrapping her arms around his midsection as she pulled herself into a half-sitting position.

"Who is it?" she asked.

Pete gave her a quick kiss. "Hudson. Not sure what she wants."

"I'm still on the line, you know," Hudson said. "You could just ask me."

"And I'm still on leave," Pete said.

"You can't take leave from being a private eye," she said. "You know that. Plus, this is good. Don't you like making money?"

After La Madrina and Rosen were taken into custody, and once the remnants of Los Enfermos, the Silent Death, and his mother's case were swept together, Pete and Kathy decided the time was right for a break. To bring their child into the world. To see if this thing they'd been dancing around—them, as a couple, not just friends— was viable and, well, to breathe. That had been months ago, when Pete got discharged from Baptist Hospital.

"Leave us alone, Miami PD," Kathy said, rolling over, grasping at a few more moments of rest. Grace rustled more. She was up. It'd be a minute, tops, before she started crying for food, or something. Pete stood up and walked toward the door of the bedroom. As he opened it, a black and a gray kitten skittered into the room, mewling for food. Pete stepped out of the bedroom and toward the kitchen, closing the door behind him, Neko and PJ in hot pursuit.

"Cut to it, detective," Pete said as he reached for a can of wet cat food from the stack on the kitchen counter. He pulled open a drawer and found the can opener.

"The name Raul Alvarez mean anything to you?"

"The University of Southern Florida quarterback? From the '80s?" Pete asked. He'd stopped opening the can. Hudson had hooked him.

"Not anymore," Hudson said. "He's dead."

"Dead? What happened?"

"Boating accident," Hudson said. "His toxicology report was a rainbow of drugs and alcohol."

"Shit," Pete said. "That's terrible. No offense, but is that why you called? I mean, it's tragic, but—"

"His wife doesn't think it was an accident."

"How is that even possible?"

"She needs help, Pete—help that I can't give her when the case is closed from our POV—you follow?" Hudson said. "Coincidentally, I know a half-decent private dick who's been spending time tickling babies and living off his savings. She needs someone to look into his death. Someone with a little more freedom to move ... and act."

"Nisha ... I can't, I'm basically on dad duty," Pete said. He was conflicted. He knew Hudson could hear it in his voice. "I mean, I wish—"

"Are we taking the case?"

He hadn't heard Kathy come in, Grace slung over her shoulder, milk-drunk.

"Do you want to know what it's about first?"

"Not really," Kathy said, gently rocking the baby. "I want to work. It's time."

"Tell the wife to come by," Pete said. "We'll see her."

"She's downstairs, outside your front door," Hudson said. "Her name is Theresa Alvarez."

Pete touched the screen, ending the call. He turned to face Kathy, ignoring the cats' cries for food.

"Are we doing this?"

She stepped toward Pete and gave him a quick kiss on the lips.

"Two fools and a little baby," she said. "Maybe that can be our motto? Hop in the shower while I put on my bathrobe and wow this lady with our beautiful offspring and my amazing bed hair."

Pete watched as Kathy and Grace headed toward the stairs. He reached for the counter, trying to balance himself, the wave of gratitude and excitement almost knocking him over.

He used to hate it when he talked to himself. It was something he did when he was drunk. On his knees, broken, battered. "Come on, Pete." "Get up." "You idiot." Desperate, half-baked attempts at moving limbs and a brain dulled and soured by drink. As he got older, as the gap of time between his last drink and today grew and stretched, Pete became more forgiving of the quirk. He was in touch with himself in a way he'd never imagined. He felt alive.

*Finally.*

He finished feeding the kittens and stretched his arms as he walked toward the bathroom, the case of Raul Alvarez already bouncing around his mind. Murder? Maybe. They'd figure it out. They always did.

He muttered the two words to himself fifteen minutes later, as he opened the door that would lead him down into the offices of Bentley & Fernandez Investigations. On to the next thing. The next case.

"Let's go."

## THE END

# ACKNOWLEDGMENTS

I could not have written this book without my editor and Polis Books founder Jason Pinter and agent Dara Hyde. Full stop. Both were generous with their time, understanding, quick to offer advice and support, and ever-present. They rode along with me and moved mountains to make sure I had as much time and space to write the book I wanted, even when I didn't think I could. Dara's been an advocate and friend to the Pete books since the beginning, and Jason's done everything in his power to get these stories out into the world in a thoughtful, meaningful way. I'm not sure I could've finished this book without their help, and I'm grateful to them for their guidance and friendship.

I was lucky enough to be part of a very smart, diverse and vocal writers' group when I was first chipping away at *Silent City*, and it's something I've continued to find invaluable: feedback from other writers. It's also one of the first bits of advice I give new writers: join a group, or find great beta readers. Fatherhood prevents me from having the time to meet with other writers regularly, but I'm lucky to still have a core group of first readers who keep me in line, call me on my excesses and catch mistakes before they reach the wider world. Huge thanks to Elizabeth Keenan-Penagos, Justin Aclin, Kellye Garrett, Erica Wright, Amanda di Bartolomeo, Meg Wilhoite, Paul Steinfeld, Jennifer Rice Epstein, Alan Gomez, Hatzel Vela, Andrea Vigil, Rebekah Monson, and Phoebe Flowers. Asking someone to read your novel is no small favor—it takes hours of time to read, even more to boil down your thoughts in a concise and effective way. I'm lucky to have so many great writers and friends in my life.

I'd also like to thank the amazing, established authors who took time out of their busy schedules to say a nice thing or two about this book—Alafair Burke, Michael Harvey, and Lisa Lutz. I know all too well how tough it is to balance work, life, and writing. Add an entire novel to that pile and it might tip over. Thank you.

A big thank you to Erin Mitchell for her continued marketing savvy, to my mother-in-law Isabel Stein for her editing prowess and general support, to Ellen Clair Lamb for her proofreading skills, to

Sophie Appel for her design help, to my staff and bosses at Archie Comics for their support of this second career, and to my friends and family—who were always willing to lend a hand or give a much-needed pat on the back.

As Pete's trip pumps the brakes, I'm given to brief, nostalgic trips back to the beginning—to the days when *Silent City* was just a growing Word file on my desktop and something I didn't talk to many people about. It shouldn't come as a surprise that a special place in this story is reserved for those who were there at the start—who didn't scoff when, about a decade ago, I said I wanted to write a P.I. series about a messed up Cuban-American journalist in Miami, to honor the novels that got me hooked on the genre. Books like George Pelecanos's Nick Stefanos books, or Dennis Lehane's Pat and Angie novels, or Laura Lippman's Tess Monaghan series. Instead of shrugging or rolling their eyes, these people simply said some version of "I believe in you, and I will do whatever I can to help you." So, here we are—five books in—and the trip that seemed so unimaginable then is entering its first wide turn. Thanks to those friends, who are too many to list. Your support meant the world to me.

To the readers—whether you've been riding alongside Pete from the beginning or just joining the party—thank you. Nothing beats the rush of an unexpected note or email from a fan letting an author know someone's enjoyed their book. Nothing surprises us more. Knowing these stories have brought entertainment to anyone means the world to me, and I'm grateful for your time and passion.

Most importantly, I'd like to thank my smart, honest, and amazing wife Eva, for her loyalty, friendship, and candor. For always pushing me to do better, to not settle. For being a loving, thoughtful, and present mother to our two children and for propping me up when I'm losing steam. I love you.

To those bemoaning the end—if it's any solace, I always feel like whatever Pete book I finish is going to be the last. Who knows what the future will bring?

Alex Segura
Queens, New York
May 18, 2019

# ABOUT THE AUTHOR

Alex Segura is the author of five novels in his acclaimed Pete Fernandez series: *Silent City*, *Down The Darkest Street*, *Dangerous Ends*, *Blackout*, and *Miami Midnight*. Both *Dangerous Ends* and *Blackout* were nominated for the Anthony Award.

He has also written a number of comic books, including the best-selling and critically acclaimed *Archie Meets Kiss* and *Archie Meets Ramones* storylines. He co-writes the Lethal Lit podcast, which eas named one of the Best Five Podcasts of 2018 by the *New York Times*. He lives in New York with his wife and children. He is a Miami native. Follow him at @alex_segura.